THE FOX

IN HIS HENHOUSE

DUBIOUS MATES SERIES
BOOK ONE

CONSTANCE REMILLARD

HEADY PRESS

Cover design by Black Dash Studio. Public domain image: *Female Nude, Back View* by Alexandre-Jean Dubois-Drahonet, 1831.

Copy edit by Kathleen Haley.

ISBN: 979-8-9898865-3-1

Library of Congress Control Number: 2024921899

Printed by Heady Press. Philipstown, NY, USA.

Deepest gratitude to all my incredibly generous beta readers, with special thanks to Bev for her assistance in fine-tuning Cumbrian dialogue, and to Elizabeth for verifying the French.

PREFACE

This novel uses two types of symbols to indicate breaks. The first denotes a lapse in time or location known as a scene break.

༺༻

The second indicates a change in character point of view within the same scene.

***

This work also contains material which may be unsettling to some. If you wish to be forewarned, read on for a list of content warnings. If you prefer to read without spoilers, stop now and skip ahead.

The Fox in his Henhouse is a romance set in three acts. Its characters do not always act honorably towards one another, but as a work of historical fiction, their actions speak to norms held in the past. These actions also serve as plot devices.

This book contains: cursing, thieving, sex, dubious consent, coercion, corporal punishment, alcohol, pipe smoking, dementia, and prostitution. To the best of my ability, these topics have been handled in a respectful manner true to the time period in which the story takes place. A few artistic liberties were taken, which I point out in my note to readers at the end. A glossary of regional and foreign words used in the story can also be found here.

~ *Constance*

ACT I

LUST

It was with a good end in mind—that of acquiring the knowledge of good and evil—that Eve allowed herself to be carried away and eat the forbidden fruit. But Adam was not moved by this desire for knowledge, but simply by greed: he ate it because he heard Eve say it tasted good.

Moderata Fonte, from *The Worth of Women*, 1600

CHAPTER ONE

CUMBERLAND, 1835

"Charles, please, you can't! What if you are caught?" Eleanor pleaded in an anxious, insistent whisper. She didn't want Father to wake. It was late and the house was cold. It was always cold.

It was also dark. They'd not dared light a precious candle.

"There's barely a soul about, sister," her sibling hissed back. "A mostly empty Abbey still, no one will notice. They'll think it was a fox. Same blasted fox that took our hens, crafty beast."

Eleanor knew Charles had almost wept that morning to find the henhouse emptied of their last two birds, for they had nothing left to trade, nothing at all, and any chicks begged off neighbors now wouldn't lay till springtime.

"But if you are caught, Charles, the fine . . . We'd never be able to pay!"

"I won't get caught, hush. Besides, the Abbey's new lord brought a veritable flock with him; two will hardly be missed. Now go back to bed, and if I've not returned by daybreak simply tell Father I've gone into town."

Eleanor was only more alarmed by this. "But if you're not here come morning—"

"I'll return, sister. Go back to bed."

"Only, Charles, I wish you wouldn't!"

"Yes, well, I wish I needn't," her sibling bit back. "I wish a lot of things, Ellie, but right now I wish simply to keep us alive come winter."

Eleanor watched Charles wrap tight their father's heavy cloak and slip out into the chill, black night. She stood a moment longer in the kitchen, Father's rattling snores from the next room reminding her that she ought to be grateful for a sibling as unreasonable as the one she had. For without Charles to so stubbornly look after them, she and Papa would be in far worse straits.

She stared at the kitchen's dim, bare shelves, praying for Charles's safe return. She sat there some while before she crawled back into bed.

Lord Wellesley had just sat down to a glass of whiskey before a roaring hearth in the one room of his crumbling new home that was reasonably comfortable. There were other rooms serviceable, but the work needed to bring this old castle back to life was formidable. He'd not bargained on Almsdale Abbey being in quite such disrepair. Nor had he counted on Cumberland being quite so bloody rustic. It was just what he needed, but it was also damnably bleak. The village hadn't a bookshop, barely a decent tavern, and no whorehouse he could unearth.

Amusements there were not.

Yet the barren landscape was spectacular and suited his craggy mood perfectly. The work might last years and suited him just as much. He knew he'd need skilled tradesmen come spring, but in all he was glad he'd come. Anything to escape the hell London had become.

He was sipping his whiskey, contemplating lighting a pipe, feet propped on a stool before the blazing fire, when he heard a ruckus in the hall right before his steward, John Cuthbert, wrenched open the parlor door, dragging a mess of skirts behind him.

Wellesley, or Wells as his crew called him, glared at his man for the interruption. "This had better be worth my time, John," he grumbled.

Cuthbert shoved what looked to be a filthy human before his lordship, declaring, "Caught her stealin' chickens, Yer Grace."

"Chickens?" Wells almost laughed but instead frowned at the dirt-streaked face scowling back at him. "Why the hell bring her here and not before the magistrate?" He sensed not an ounce of contrition from the sharp green eyes shooting daggers at him.

"Because y'*are* the magistrate here, Yer Grace," Cuthbert ground out.

"Bloody hell," Wells muttered, sighing deeply as he rose from his seat. He was as annoyed by the interruption as he was by Cuthbert's continued, deliberate misuse of what was rightfully his father, the Duke of Allendale's, title.

"Bring her in," he ordered, and Cuthbert pushed the skirt forward till she stumbled to her knees.

"Get up," Wells snapped.

The girl stood and squared off, looking as if she wished to punch him, and this despite the fact he was as tall as his steward and just as broadly built.

"You stink." Wells registered his disgust.

"Chicken shit, my lord." Her eyes flitted to his steward. "Your man made me wallow in it."

Wells held his breath even as he held up his hand to stay

Cuthbert from cuffing her one. "Impertinence only adds to your guilt, girl." He kept his tone terse. "You've one chance to explain yourself now before I give my sentence. Be quick."

"How kind of you, my lord." Her voice dripped disdain. "Only however should I defend myself? I sought to relieve you of two of your chickens, thinking you might indeed have more than your small household need keep."

Cuthbert did cuff her then, sending her reeling backwards and showing Wells a pair of well-formed legs beneath her skirts, making his thoughts abruptly shift.

"John, a bath; I can stand the stench no more. And whatever's left of dinner, bring that as well."

The girl had gotten up, wiping blood from her freshly split lip as Cuthbert slipped from the room. Wells sank his bulk back into his chair.

"I'd hoped for a quiet evening this night but you've gone and ruined that." He frowned, taking her in more closely. "Step here, into the light, that I might see you better."

She did as bid but hated him for it, he could tell—yet another proud Cumberland native, as fierce and unyielding as the landscape itself.

"Let down your hair," he ordered.

"I beg your pardon!" she burst out.

"And take off your cloak. I wish to look at you."

Her eyes seethed—if eyes could seethe. Wells found the idea amusing. "Or would you rather I remove it?" He smirked.

"I'd like to see you try," she growled back.

He gave her a slow, salacious grin. "Very well." He rose, moving towards her even as she backed away, looking cornered. "Not so fierce now, are we?" Wells laughed, to which she spat at his feet.

In an instant he'd grabbed her, ripping off her cloak and tearing her bodice in two before he yanked her hair loose and quickly stepped back to appraise.

She looked shocked by the speed of his actions, her breaths ragged and pupils dilated, but the effect was not lost on Wells, who saw in her potential, and decided in that moment she'd do.

"Not bad." He surveyed her more critically. Her proportions were pleasing, even if she was too thin. "How old are you, girl?"

She glared at him, tight-lipped.

"I said—"

"I heard what you said," she snarled, coming back to life. "And as I am not in a court of law I don't have to answer you that."

His lips twitched. "Ah, but it appears I *am* the law here and therefore you will do exactly as I say unless you wish to make things even worse for yourself." His eyes stole over her once more, making her visibly shiver. "I believe there is a steep fine for stealing, if not time in the gaol. Or is it still tradition here in Cumberland to lop off a thieving limb?"

That drew her ire; her entire face pinched.

"Why yes, sir, we are so backwards here it is a wonder you grace us with your presence at all." Her tone was barely civil. "Pray, how long do you plan to remain in Cumberland, my lord? More importantly, how long will your chickens here reside?"

He laughed, full-throated and deep, which seemed to surprise her only more, her eyes growing wider still and her ample bosom heaving nicely where he'd just exposed her stays.

"I imagine I and my chickens will be here for some time, miss, making us neighbors. So you will tell me your name and age forthwith," he sharpened his tone, "and you will address me with less impudence."

"You are not the Duke of Allendale," she jabbed.

"Not yet." He held her gaze. "But I am his heir apparent, so you will afford me the respect I am due."

She swallowed before she curtsied inordinately low, allowing him an even better glimpse of bosom. "Charles Merrinan, *Your Grace*, five and twenty."

Wells winced. The curtsy impressed, but her abuse of title went too far; bad enough he suffered Cuthbert that liberty.

"Charles?" He chose to ignore her insult, for now. "You appear undeniably female to me."

"My parents wished for a boy."

Wells was about to respond to this newest revelation when his steward returned with an ample tub plus six additional men carrying steaming buckets of water they proceeded to pour in. A seventh man unloaded a bar of soap and Wellesley's banyan, then plunked down a tray of hot stew.

Wells was unsurprised by the look of hunger he saw mar the girl's face. "Leave us," he ordered but stopped Cuthbert at the door. "I'll ring when I am done."

His man merely nodded before he left.

Wells flicked his gaze to the bath. "I refuse to carry out my sentencing while you still reek. Bathe, and the meal is yours."

Her jaw dropped.

"Do you not understand me?"

"You . . . cannot . . ." she stammered.

"Order you to strip and bathe before my sentencing? Yes, I believe I can, and just did, so hop to it." He stared back at her, unflinching.

***

Charles Merrinan wanted nothing more that instant than to weep. Instead, she swallowed her pride and willed herself to remain unaffected by this unbearable, pompous *prick*. She allowed her mind to shout the word, anger churning deep within her breast, and for a brief moment that anger drowned out her fear. Though to bathe before this man meant . . .

A shudder wracked her body as she silently cursed herself for not heeding her sister's pleas. She inhaled a shaky breath and forced herself to speak.

"I should expect, as a gentleman, my lord, you will turn the other way while I disrobe."

"I am no gentleman, Charles, and very much intend to have a look at you."

Her face flushed with heat.

"*Now,*" he intoned.

She bit her tongue, lifted her chin, and with trembling hands worked to undo the hooks on her tattered dress. It was bad enough she'd been caught thieving chickens, but this latest insult to her person was worse than expected. She'd abased herself before to keep her family fed, but to strip before some lustful lord was without doubt the lowest she'd ever sunk.

Yet her stomach grumbled loudly at the stew.

Charles dropped her dress, struggled a moment with her stays, then in naught but her shift stepped quick as could be into the tub, sinking below the steaming water with a hot hiss of air. She hid from him for as long as she could, glad he'd caught but a brief glimpse of her form.

When she came up for air, he tossed her the soap, which she deftly caught.

Charles scrubbed herself in the tub as Lord Wellesley sipped his whiskey and watched, his eyes on her intense. She did her utmost to ignore his searing gaze, sneaking furtive glances at him as she soaped one leg. He was an imposing lord, thickly built with a dark thatch of hair and a chiseled, angular face—quite unlike the typical London fop. She peeked at the frayed brocade drapes and worn velvet cushions of the room; his lordship's parlor had seen better days. When she perched a second leg on the edge of the tub for soaping, she heard Lord Wellesley inhale sharply, down his drink with a clink, and firmly set it aside.

"The stew grows cold, Charles. It's time you stepped out."

She promptly sank back under, praying she might disappear into the water forever. Instead, she felt a hand grab her arm and haul her, sputtering, to her feet. From there his lordship took a long, hard look at her body, his burning eyes letting her know he liked what he saw beneath her flimsy, clinging shift.

Charles shuddered again.

Lord Wellesley handed her his banyan and stepped away to pour himself another drink. He told her, "Eat."

She wrapped the robe about her before she perched upon his footstool, bowl in hand, to begin to savor each bite of blessed meat stew. Heaven. She was so engrossed in eating she barely noticed how he watched her from his chair. Yet when she licked the bowl clean without even thinking, she heard his body rustle.

"Now that you no longer offend my olfactories, miss, I am ready to discuss your sentence."

Charles put down the bowl, stood to attention, and kept her gaze lowered in penance. "My lord."

"For the two chickens you attempted to steal from me I wager the fine for thieving is likely twenty pounds. Add to this the cost of a hot meal and bath, not to mention my wasted evening, and I'd say the debt you owe me comes to thirty."

She gasped, but he proceeded, not the least bit rattled.

"Now I am going to assume, as you were thieving chickens, that you haven't the thirty pounds I am owed, nor does your family. Am I correct?"

She nicked her head yes.

"And as we haven't a functioning gaol in this crumbling old Abbey I can't very well lock you in a cell either."

Charles hung her head lower.

"Therefore, I propose you work off your debt, over time, in service to me."

She expelled a quick breath of relief. "My lord, you are most generous. I shall happily—"

Wellesley stopped her with a wave of his hand, then stood up, walked over to her garments, and promptly dropped these into the bath. "It still reeks in here," he grumbled, leaving her agape at his audacity.

He continued on, oblivious. "And, as I am in need of a mistress for the foreseeable future, I daresay you'll do well enough."

Charles nearly choked, her mouth opening and closing as each attempt to speak was overcome by a fresh wave of terror, shame, and sheer outrage. She could scarcely breathe for such tumult as now overwhelmed her, refusing to believe this man had just uttered that word. Her mind panicked, her heart raced, all while Lord Wellesley calmly watched her work to form a coherent response.

It took some time.

At last, her turmoil tamed, Charles steadied herself, drawing all the dignity her battered soul could muster. "I am not a whore, my lord," she told him, "and so with all due respect I must decline your offer."

"I realize you are not a whore, girl, else I would not have proposed you become my mistress. They are obviously not one and the same."

"I am sorry, my lord, but I do not see the difference." She willed herself to remain calm, to answer him rationally, without emotion.

He let out a sigh. "A mistress, Charles, is not paid outright, but is housed and cared for, given allowances and gifts, and in return, serves my bed how and when I should desire it."

She bit her lip, wholly unconvinced.

"She beds only me, Charles, not other men. *That* is the difference."

Charles desperately tried to overcome the panic she felt

overtake her in earnest. "My lord, I am not . . ." She swallowed. "I fear you mistake the kind of woman I am, for I am not—"

He cut her off, his irritation mounting. "You are not a lady, miss, for a lady does not climb into coops at night stealing chickens. Furthermore, no respectable young lady bathes naked before a man who's not her . . ." He peered more closely at her. "You're not married, are you?"

She dropped her head.

"I didn't think so," he scoffed.

"Lord Wellesley," she attempted again to be meek, "I would beg you, please, consider my reputation."

"Your reputation?" He nearly snorted. "Good God, woman, what tattered reputation would that be, pray, here in Cumberland?"

"My reputation in this community, my lord, remains more than intact, it is untarnished!"

"So you are intact." His look made her blush all over again. "It appears you will need some educating in your duties then."

"I have not agreed to your proposition!" she shouted, incensed.

With a flick of his eyes he tore her down. "It was never a proposition, miss, it is your *sentence*."

***

The fear that had been lurking beneath the girl's pride burst upon her face, making Wells flinch a little at his own behavior, for she'd stood up to him admirably; he liked her mettle.

"Come now, don't look so dismal," he told her. "I daresay there are plenty of women in London who'd trade places with you in a heartbeat."

"You flatter yourself, sir." Her voice was cold. "Besides, if London women are so pleasing, why not return posthaste?"

He suppressed a smirk; she had both pluck and wit.

"Let us say I prefer the challenge of Cumberland's decidedly more bracing climate." His eyes locked onto hers, equally cool. "I do not wish to send to London for a mistress, and as you have conveniently presented yourself to me this night I see no reason why I shouldn't sample more *local* flavors instead."

Her fists clenched. "I am not a dish, my lord." She gritted her teeth. "I am a free human being with the right to—"

"You lost your freedom the moment you were caught," he snapped. "And I will brook no more argument from a thief." He glared at her then, tired of talk and distracted by the curling of her flaxen hair, which was drying nicely by the fire and giving her a decidedly softer look. He strode to the door, pulled the bell, and went to fill his glass, pouring her one as well. "Drink up, Charles," he told her, "as it will only help improve your mood."

Yet the moment he handed her the glass she threw its contents in his face and bolted for the door, only to run smack into Cuthbert, who nimbly hauled her back.

Wells pulled out a handkerchief to wipe his dripping brow and equally damp mop of hair. "As always, Cuthbert, your timing is impeccable," he muttered.

His steward shoved the girl back inside. "Y' rang, Yer Grace?"

"Yes." Wells was still drying his face while refusing to meet the girl's eyes. "I have decided yon thief here will serve her sentence in service to me for the foreseeable future, so I would ask that you deliver her family two chickens tomorrow first thing, informing them of her new employment here at the Abbey and returning with whatever clothing she owns that does not *stink*. I expect the villagers will know where to find her people. And get rid of this offending water forthwith." Wells made another face.

"O' course, Yer Grace." Cuthbert let out a loud whistle between his fingers to summon the same men who'd delivered the tub. Within seconds the horde arrived to dismantle the contents, in no time emptying the room. And then Wellesley's steward closed the door behind him, locking it with a click.

Wells watched the girl sink into such despair she looked like she might crumple, like she longed to dissolve into the worn Persian carpet till she was one with the rug's mottled fibers. He imagined it took every bit of strength she had not to shed a tear before him.

She was made of sterner stuff.

Wells watched her struggle with herself before he poured her another glass, feeling an annoying twinge of conscience. "Now is not the time for self-pity, miss." He handed it to her. "Drink up."

This time, she downed it.

CHAPTER TWO

Charles Merrinan wished to God this arrogant lord would pour her another drink, for she could hope only for complete stupor now to survive Wellesley's next move. That she should be forced so low—all for but attempting to feed her family—was a thought her muddled mind could not shake. Yet she'd no one to blame but herself. Herself and that damned thieving fox.

"Tell me what you are thinking, Charles." His lordship interrupted her thoughts, patting his large lap with his thick, large hands. "That I may assuage your fears."

His hulking shape was a blur as she stumbled over, having downed enough whiskey to stop putting up a fight. She allowed him to settle her across his thighs, leaning into him a little even, propped against his broad chest. She mumbled drunkenly, "Bloody fox caused my bloody ruin."

"A fox, eh?" He began to pull back her hair, tracing a rough fingertip along her jawline. "What fox, pray tell?"

She sighed, shifting in his lap, the motion causing her robe to reveal more than she liked as she tried to draw it closed. "The fox that stole our chickens, my lord. Took the last two last night, and without eggs we shall never manage another winter."

"I see," he murmured into her neck, softly kissing her there and running his tongue to the hollow of her throat, making her shiver. "Which makes *you*, my dear, the fox in *my* henhouse."

"Our father's in poor health, my lord, and my sister's not strong enough to—"

"Wrestle chickens?" He interrupted her again, leaning her back to part her robe and reveal more flesh, dipping his dark head of curls to kiss her there between her breasts, and there across the tops, his fingers pulling open her damp shift.

Charles felt her heart beat faster. "I'd no choice, my lord. Surely you must see we have but fallen on hard times. It is not my nature to thieve, sir, truly it is not."

"Of course not," his deep voice rumbled into her bosom, opening the banyan to her waist now to palm one orb through her shift, his lips seeking the other's pert point.

"My lord!" She gasped as he sucked the pink tip through the cloth into a tight knot of pleasure.

"You are not a whore, Charles, you are my mistress now. No shame in that. I will ensure your family is cared for this winter; they shall not want for food. Nor shall you."

She let out another gasp as he sucked her other bud into a similar taut peak.

"And despite what you may think of me, Charles, you shall not lack for enjoyment from our pursuits, I promise."

"But my lord I know nothing of—"

"You'll be a quick study, girl, I can tell."

"But what if—?"

"We shall make sure that does not happen."

"But how—?"

"Hush now, woman, I do not wish to speak." And his whiskey-flavored breath stole over her mouth to part her lips with his tongue, until he'd entered and silenced her completely.

14

Lord Wellesley had poured the girl a second and third drink, just to loosen her up, but had stopped at a fourth, lest she be no fun at all. He'd put up with enough this evening to deserve something in return, bloody hell. Besides, he may not be a gentleman but he was also no cad.

He had given Charles Merrinan one glass too many, however, for she'd fallen asleep while still on his lap, despite all attempts to rouse her. He'd simply carried her to his bed then and crawled in beside her, none too sure she wouldn't sneak off come morning just as soon as she was sober.

Yet where the devil would she run? he mused. *London?* Wells grinned at the thought. He could easily haul her back from whatever hovel her family inhabited here, for it would be simple enough to find a woman with her rare features in a village as small as this. He gazed at the mass of red-gold hair strewn across his pillow and longed to knot it in his fist, grasping the thick, smooth strands. She was quite the specimen, this Charles, with her strikingly symmetrical features and alabaster skin. She'd be a feast once he fattened her up, because he could count the poor girl's ribs she was so slim. Still, laid out on his bed she was shaped like Venus, like a statue of the goddess—and a far cry from any other female he'd encountered here in Cumberland.

Before he drifted into slumber Wells decided Charles Merrinan would make a dull winter at Almsdale a damn sight more delightful. If nothing else, she'd keep his wits sharp for when he'd be forced to return to London, to suffer that godawful circus again.

Charles awoke to the sound of snores, only they were not her sister Eleanor's breathy little snorts, nor were they her father's disjointed honks. They were light and rhythmic, confusing the dream-like images that threatened to upend her: a fox, two chickens, a warm bath, bare skin . . .

She startled awake, stifling the urge to shriek as she discovered a robust, naked man beside her. Everything returned in a rush. She took precisely two seconds to steady herself as she felt his weight shift, tensing before she made to bolt.

An arm snaked out to check her. "Not so fast, Fox."

She froze—

"Can't fly the coop now."

—before she groaned at his terrible pun.

"I think I shall enjoy irritating you," Lord Wellesley's low voice chuckled.

"You do it well, my lord," she grumbled back.

His hand began to stroke her flank, making her involuntarily quiver as she realized with fresh horror that she was naked too.

"It pleases me to get a rise out of you." He pushed himself against her, something hard pressing into her backside, making her suck in her breath. "Literally and figuratively, my dear."

Charles stilled, the pounding in her head the throb of her own frantic heartbeat. He pushed his body deeper against her own, his hand at her waist creeping up to fondle one breast while she remained paralyzed by his touch.

"Shall we continue what we started last night, Charles?"

She swallowed hard, desperate to dissuade him. "My lord, I beg you: By light of day now please reconsider my sentence."

"I could not be more pleased with my sentencing, miss." He planted his lips to the back of her neck, beginning to nibble flesh. "And have no intention of changing my mind, none." He nipped skin with his teeth. "In fact, I am more than pleased. I

am"—she gasped to feel his hand slide between her legs—
"utterly delighted."

Charles came alive, breathing short gulps of air as his
fingers began to ply her most intimate parts in earnest. She
didn't know what to do. She was frozen by fear and more
horrifying yet, the stirrings of growing arousal.

"Tell me you have touched yourself before, Charles," he
taunted as she inhaled another hiss of air. "That you know
how to pleasure yourself." His hand continued its maddening
strokes while she grew only warmer and weaker, furious at how
thoroughly her body betrayed her.

"Ah," his tone teased, "I see you do, Fox. You welcome me
already." And he suddenly slipped a finger inside her, coaxing
an involuntary gasp from her lips even as she reflexively arched
her hips to accept him, his sex still hard at her backside, eager.

"I should like to see you enjoy yourself, I think." He quickly
rolled her onto her back, making her eyes flash up at him in
panic. "Ladies first, my dear." He slipped another finger inside,
making her mouth fall open with surprise, his face grinning
down at her before he fell to feasting on her breasts, all while
his maddening, stroking touch made Charles feel as if she
would burst. She hated herself for reacting as she did yet was
wholly unable to stop her response.

"Please," she begged. "My lord!"

"Please what?" His mouth left her bosom long enough
to say.

"I . . ."

"You shall have to be more explicit than that to get what
you want, girl." His hand teased deeper as he lifted his head
from her breasts, his eyes liquid with heat.

But she was beyond words, beyond all rational thought it
seemed. Raw bodily instinct overwhelmed self-control as she
rashly, shockingly pulled his head down to kiss him fast and

fierce. Charles did not know herself in that moment, her mind having fled its normally sane self.

Lord Wellesley, tongue down her throat and hand at her core, merely pushed her over the edge in response, making Charles shatter exquisitely beneath him.

***

Yet before Wells could further his own pleasure, Cuthbert walked in without so much as a knock. Cursing the man with his next intake of breath, Wells rolled off the girl while she yanked up the covers to hide herself.

"Damn blast it, John, announce yourself!"

"Beg pardon, Yer Grace." His man worked to suppress a smile. "But the stonemason's here, says he's not got all day." His steward's gaze barely registered the girl in Wellesley's bed. "And her family's been told." He nodded towards Charles. "Pleased as punch t' get the chickens."

At this she peeked above the covers.

"There's a letter from the Duchess as well," Cuthbert stated before tromping back out, making Wells expel a loud sigh, all desire having shriveled at the mention of his mother. He sat up in bed and stretched his arms wide before he poked the girl beneath his covers.

"Ow!" she got out, muffled.

"We shall continue your instruction later, Charles. I've business to attend to." He swung his legs over the side of the bed, flexing his torso once more.

Her head emerged from the covers to stare as he strolled across the room to piss the pot. "Looking your fill, are you?" he taunted above the stream, back still turned to her. Wells knew he had an admirable backside.

"I am not," she said stiffly.

"Are too." He turned to grin at her even as her mouth fell

open the moment he stepped forward to retrieve his clothes from the chair. Wells took pride in the fact he looked like no ordinary blueblood, his body more that of a common laborer than lord. God knew he'd worked it to the bone his many years at sea.

He pulled on his trousers over his muscled thighs while the girl appeared as flustered by his nudity as she was flummoxed by her plight.

"Given your behavior last night," he declared, "I don't trust you not to bolt the moment I leave this room." He eyed her close. "Meaning you are to remain naked in my bed till I return, understood?"

She bit her lip, defiant.

"Ah." He met her look. "I see you do not." He strode to a tall chest of drawers to begin pulling out an assortment of silk neckties. "We shall resort to other methods then." He grabbed her arm in a sudden move to tie her to the bedpost, overpowering her enough to secure the other arm just as fast.

"You cannot bind me to this bed as if I were your—!"

"Prisoner?" he cut in. "How apt, considering your sentence. We shall simply make my bedroom Almsdale Abbey's new gaol."

She looked aghast at his suggestion.

"You are most attractive when angry, Fox." And she was, inordinately so. It wasn't her fiery-gold hair alone, but the fire in those emerald eyes and the round contours of her rich curves.

His finger traced her cheek to land upon her lip, still fat from Cuthbert's slap last night, pulling it down a little before he leaned in for a kiss. "I look forward to exploring your foxlike, predatory foxlike nature when I return," he murmured before he grabbed his waistcoat and shut the door firmly behind him.

Wells smiled to think he'd left his new mistress both tongue-tied and tied-up: quite the sight.

***

Charles Merrinan was not dumbstruck for long, for within seconds of Lord Wellesley's departure she began to work free of her restraints. Silk ties made for slippery knots, though those knots had been shockingly well made, requiring no small degree of effort. Once released from her binds she searched in vain for his lordship's banyan, or her clothes from last night, anything to don, before she remembered with sinking heart what had been tossed into a tub of bathwater.

With a snort of frustration she grabbed the first item of clothing she spotted, one of his lordship's long shirts, and slipped this over her head as she stole a chair's throw for shawl. Then Charles snuck out of the room and down the Abbey's dark hall in search of food first, clothes next, and after . . . some way out of this mess.

CHAPTER THREE

Lord Wellesley's morning was not going to plan. He'd been denied the satisfaction of debauching his new mistress in order to meet with a stonemason he'd then managed to offend—*stubborn Cumberland fool*—which would only delay repairs further if he had to send to London for tradesmen. Not to mention the fact he'd missed his shave and breakfast so now found himself both irritable and hungry.

Also, he'd still not looked at the letter from his mother.

As he made his way to the kitchen, mood darkening and stomach grumbling, his sole consolation was the knowledge a certain fetching female remained bound to his bed, awaiting his return. Yet even this, it seemed, he'd be denied, for upon entering said kitchen, who should he spy but the girl herself, rolling out dough, sleeves pushed up and hair escaping its loose knot. He thought again what raucous hair she had—strawberry blond now came to mind. But how the devil had she escaped his bed?

He snuck up on her softly, stepping from behind to quickly encircle her waist, eliciting a shriek and a struggle, which he quashed with his voice. "I thought I gave you strict orders to remain in my chamber," he grumbled into her ear, hands reaching up to cup her breasts beneath what he could only surmise was one of his own damn shirts.

"You left me to languish," the girl ground through her teeth, "with nothing to eat or drink, not even clothes to wear. What did you think I'd do, Lord Wellesley?"

"Remain tied to my bed." He gently bit her ear, making her yelp with surprise.

"Then tie better knots!"

He laughed, once again enjoying this girl's pluck while he loosened his hold and reached for a biscuit beside her. Only she slapped his hand so fast he was shocked, but no more than she. She recoiled from his grasp, immediately sucking in her breath.

"My lord, I did not mean to—"

"Swat at me as if I were a child?" His mood swiftly darkened as he twisted her arm behind her and pressed her body flush against the table. "I'll grant a mistress some allowances, Charles, but cross me too far and you'll be punished for it."

"Truly, my lord, I did not mean to—"

"I've a mind to take you right now," he hissed, "whether you want me or not." He slid his free hand up her thigh, there between her legs, as her body trembled with what he could only assume was rage and fear and . . . Wells clucked low in his throat. "Or maybe you won't mind at all, goodness you're slick."

***

Charles scowled at him, furious yet again at the awful effect this man had on her disastrously disloyal body. "The pan was hot, sir, and I did not wish your fingers burnt." She slowed her breathing to try to calm her racing pulse. "But by all means, please, *scald* yourself."

He relaxed his grip but did not release her, his hand still plying her slippery folds until she had to bite her sore lip to keep from moaning.

"Go on then," he breathed in her ear. "Don't let me stop your biscuit making." She could hear the mirth in his voice. "I shall simply wait until the pan's cooled and you've grown warmer still for me."

She let out a growl of pure frustration then, for his hand was now working her in earnest, even as he bid her finish the dough, teasing her in a low tone that he was hungry, and wasn't she hungry too? He'd like to feed her, he whispered lower still, feed her and fill her till she was fit to—

And she burst, legs shaking from the waves of pleasure that crashed over her as he kept her upright, then turned her about to read her face, beaded with sweat and rife with what Charles hoped was abundantly clear: unadulterated fury.

Wells removed his hand from her legs and before her very eyes licked his fingers clean, making her blush to the roots of her hair.

"You are one delicious fox," he told her, smiling wickedly. "Let us see if your biscuits taste just as good." He reached for the pan, this time with care. "I see they are indeed quite hot still. You were right to warn me off."

His words only infuriated her more.

"Perhaps I will believe you next time," he taunted.

And that did it. She grabbed the rolling pin from the table and wriggled out from under him, inching towards the door, clutching it tight.

"Now don't do anything rash, Charles." Lord Wellesley bit into her biscuit. "These are quite good, you know. I assume you bake bread too?"

She stared him down, attempting to gauge his next move, and her own. "My lord," she leveled at him, "any woman worth her salt can bake."

"Then it is indeed good we have a woman now at Almsdale. I shall expect a fresh loaf daily from you, miss."

She studied him from a distance as she continued her slow creep towards the door, testing the rolling pin's heft as if weighing her fate. She considered again her options, reconsidered why she'd made biscuits at all, and in a flash she had decided. "May I ask, sir, how long you intend to remain in Cumberland without a cook?"

"I intend to bring a chef from London eventually." He grabbed another biscuit before he moved to fetch a kettle and set this upon the stove. "Or send for one from France."

She was amazed he knew how to boil water, further amazed to see this lofty lord open a sack of beans, grind them in a mill, and retrieve two mugs from a kitchen cupboard. It struck her again how he did not behave like a duke's heir. And the smell of fresh ground coffee began to make her mouth water.

"We've some fine cooks here, my lord," she carefully chose her words, "who'd suit your kitchen well, should you look to hire sooner."

"Do you now?" he asked over his shoulder. "I suppose I might sample their cuisine." He smiled at her. "I am beginning to think there are some hidden treasures here in Cumberland." His eyes met hers. "Unexpected, but most pleasing."

"Not all that glitters is gold, Lord Wellesley." Charles inched closer to the room's threshold.

"Yet still you stand in my kitchen, miss, not made off with my rolling pin and halfway out the Abbey."

She narrowed her gaze. "You took my clothes, sir, so I am hardly in a position to flee—for now." She halted her step.

"You *do* seem to care an awful lot about your reputation."

She watched him remove the boiling kettle to pour hot liquid over the beans, the smell hitting her nose so deliciously she could not help but inhale. The scent brought back such bittersweet, long-buried memories that she involuntarily stepped forward.

"Would you like a cup before you attempt escape?" He half-grinned. "I'm afraid Cuthbert burned your offending garments last night, though he traded your family two chickens for fresh clothes this morning."

She felt all the blood drain from her face even as he approached her with a mug.

"Sit, girl, you look faint. Drink this and eat a biscuit; for God's sake put some meat on your bones."

Charles let him guide her to a chair and push her into the seat, feeling numb to his touch, numb to all but a deep sense of despair. She let the rolling pin drop to table in order to curl her hands around the mug. And then she stared into its dark, steaming center, feeling utterly and completely lost.

***

Wells watched her, perplexed. "Do you not drink it black? I'm afraid we're out of milk again, need a more reliable source here. So many bloody details to consider." He grabbed another biscuit to stuff into his mouth, placing one beside her.

She continued to gaze into her mug, unresponsive.

"Charles," he raised his voice, "you were not without words but a minute ago yet appear now catatonic, woman. *Eat.*"

"You burned my clothes." Her head whipped around to face him. "You had the audacity to simply . . . without asking, without considering . . ." She shook her head at him, the hurt on her face undeniable. "How could you be so cruel?"

"Cruel?" He was taken aback. "They were ruined, what else should Cuthbert have done with them?"

"What else should he have *done* with them?" She was aghast. "Men," she spat the word with disgust. "Worthless, utterly, every damned one of—"

"Now look here." His hackles rose. "I'm certain there's a seamstress or two about your village and I dress my mistresses in far better clothes than the rags you sported last night. So there's no need to twist yourself in—"

"You *donnat!*" she shouted, incensed.

Wells could only guess at the meaning of her vernacular.

"I cannot simply walk into Timmon's Dress Shop to order myself a frock, courtesy of Lord Wellesley," she fumed. "What do you think people will say? They will know at once I am being kept here, a fallen woman. And what do you think they will say of my sister then, eh? That she is an equal disgrace, equally ruined. And then the men in town will all come sniffing about after her, thinking to sample her wares just as you have sampled mine."

Wells was shocked but impressed by the passion vibrating through her, which made her even more attractive to him than she doubtless knew.

He watched her take a deep, steadying breath. "You had no right to burn my clothes, my lord; they were the only clothes I had. Your man brought no other dress back with him this morning, no valise of finery from my father's home, because we've had to sell everything we own to keep from starving. And now you've gone and destroyed the only—"

He put down his mug to take her hand in his. "Charles, I am sorry I—"

She yanked it from his grasp. "You are sorry for nothing! You don't give a fig about anyone but yourself. And I could have salvaged my dress. Are all titled Londoners so removed from reality they do not understand filth washes out? Bloody hell, it is almost winter and you burned my father's sole cloak!"

Her voice had risen to such a fine pitch he thought she might implode, making Wells do something he rarely did: apologize twice. "Charles, I repeat, I am sorry I . . ."

She put her face in her hands to breathe.

He was for once rendered speechless, staring at this woman who'd landed in his house last night and was proving to be quite the arousing handful.

She finally looked up at him, those sharp green eyes boring into his own. "You will not dress me like a tart," she bit off, "and I will not suffer the humiliation of visiting the village seamstress. You will provide me with needle and thread and simple, functional cloth that I may sew myself a new dress and new cloak for my father. And I am going to pray your man had the sense not to burn my stays last night, for if he—"

"If he did," Wells interrupted, taking her hand again in his, more gently this time, "I will send to London for new small-clothes. We will measure you here so you are not subjected to a village fitting." He did not point out the fact her words had sounded suspiciously close to an order, for one did not command a duke's son. Ever.

This time she did not pull from his touch, but merely breathed, nostrils flaring as she inhaled the steaming coffee.

**

Charles felt suddenly drained of anger. She was still amazed by Lord Wellesley's words, shocked a man of his position even knew *how* to apologize. Although too much had happened in too short a time for her to know quite what to do with this revelation.

"I am sorry if my tone overstepped, my lord," she added for good measure, recognizing she had likely offended his lordship and was still wholly at this man's mercy.

It was a sobering thought.

He patted her hand before he let it go, getting up to pour himself another cup. "Then let us say the matter is settled and you will give me a list of items to purchase. It appears my morning is going decidedly poorly for me to offend first the stonemason and now you." He sat down across from her, asking himself almost, "Is everyone in bloody Cumberland so easily riled?"

"Only when London comes to visit," she muttered under her breath, then asked him point blank, "You met with Mr. Adams, I presume?" Charles finally took a sip of the delicious black liquid, followed by a small bite of biscuit.

Her taste buds bloomed with delight.

"Yes, stonemason Adams refused the work." Wellesley grimaced. "Said he wasn't interested, which is only going to set me back a good—"

"Oh, he needs the work, my lord. He'll not refuse you twice." She chewed more biscuit and immediately felt better for it.

"He was quite clear he didn't want it, miss. *Quite*."

She pursed her lips. "Lord Wellesley, might I offer your lordship some advice?"

He arched a brow at her.

"Rather than command the people of Cumberland, you may wish to cajole them a bit instead, flatter them some. I am sure it is a foreign concept to your lordship, but men here like to feel valued, competent. Mr. Adams is the best stonemason these parts. You'd be wise to hire him and he'd be wise to take the job. Offer fair compensation and he'll do excellent work for you."

Wellesley looked at her. "And what would *you* know of masonry, woman?"

She stuck out her chin. "I've managed my father's house these ten years past, my lord, and seen firsthand Adams's work. He is skilled and efficient, and takes pride enough in his craft not to cut corners."

He merely stared at her.

"Or don't take my word for it, my lord, it is nothing to me."

He grinned outright. "You are a gem, Charles, truly. Thank God you fell into my lap last night."

She glowered at him for that.

"I think we shall get along well here this winter, don't you?"

She took another bite of biscuit. "I have no intention of spending the winter trapped in your Abbey, Lord Wellesley, and intend to settle my fine as soon as possible." She allowed a faint smile to play at her mouth. "If you wish for daily bread, sir, I expect such labor to pay down my debt. And I should like to see a running tally of services rendered towards the thirty pounds I owe."

He laughed out loud. "A running tally, eh? And would your pretty head even know how to read my accounting, Charles?"

"Try me, *Your Grace*." She dared to insult him again.

"Oh I will, Charles." His eyes glittered savagely. "I will try you in every conceivable position, in every room of this house, upon every surface and in every manner most wicked."

His words made her cheeks flame and her insides flip, even as her resolve to survive him hardened. "Then I imagine my debt will be paid quickly, *Your Grace*." She abused the title again, just like she'd heard his steward do. If Wellesley's man could get away with it, she'd push too. She'd insult this overbearing lord as often as he insulted her.

"Pray tell me what I earn for each loaf baked, my lord— and for each manner of pleasure your appetite demands."

He met her gaze with a look of equal determination. "That shall depend entirely on how well you bake, girl, and how well you bed me."

CHAPTER FOUR

His lordship had left Charles in the kitchen with orders to bake him and his men several more loaves—along with the promise he'd be back for his other pleasure too. She simply sat and sipped the exquisite, aromatic coffee, suddenly less afraid of Lord Wellesley and more content to savor the cup. It had been years since she'd tasted coffee. A veritable lifetime.

Charles looked about the kitchen once more, noting its wear but also its ample hearth. The room was well stocked with stoneware, cutlery, and pots, and her eyes briefly landed on a bread knife, fast dismissing the thought.

Escape felt futile—and a bread knife paltry defense.

Besides, if Lord Wellesley truly meant to restore Almsdale Abbey, wages for Cumberland would follow with well-paying, lasting positions in service. She continued to linger over her brew while mulling over options she knew she didn't have, for if she fled his lordship he'd fine her family the thirty pounds, and when they couldn't pay, Father would be sent to debtor's prison in London. Which would leave her sister, Eleanor, destitute or—God forbid—leave Ellie to become Wellesley's mistress instead.

Charles shuddered at the thought. No, she'd gotten herself into this mess and would somehow have to get herself out. She stared again at the kitchen cupboards, the giant slop sink, the worn stone floor and narrow, slatted windows. She was as good as ruined already, but so long as no one found out, so long as she *appeared* honorably employed here at Almsdale, perhaps Eleanor might even benefit. Perhaps she could eventually earn enough to put aside a small dowry for her sister, anything to spare Ellie the humiliation she herself must now endure, already *had* endured. Perhaps, if she were clever enough, she might use Lord Wellesley much as he planned to use her. She briefly felt more hopeful.

Until his band of men descended.

"She still 'ere?" shouted one, grabbing a biscuit.

"Stayin' on, looks like." Another elbowed his way in, more biscuits gone.

"He's an eye for 'em, he does," laughed a different, burly fellow, pinching Charles's thigh.

"Leave be," she snarled, scooting back in her chair and snatching up the last biscuit.

"Oi, that were mine!" cried another.

She stuck her tongue at him and popped the biscuit into her mouth, only to have her arms grabbed from behind, a familiar voice grating, "What're *you* doin' here?"

The steward.

"Foraging for food, you brute." Charles spoke around the biscuit in her mouth, trying to shake Cuthbert off as she finished chewing, but he only tightened his grip.

"Wells said t' keep you in his bedroom." His words elicited hoots and whistles from the men.

"Lord Wells gave instruction I was to bake bread for him," she harrumphed, having finally swallowed the last bite. She decided she'd take orders from but one man in this house, and it would not be that man's lackey.

"Did he now?" Cuthbert breathed down her neck, keeping her arms pinned behind her. "Then why don't I see no loaf, but biscuit crumbs instead?

"Because I haven't started in yet! Now let go, oaf!"

He did, roughly pushing her from him as she barely caught herself at the table's edge. Suddenly a sea of men's faces all leered at Charles, eyeing her state of dress, or lack thereof, and she blushed, furious at being subjected to their scrutiny.

"And why in God's name did you burn my clothes?" she threw in Cuthbert's face. "As if I had a wardrobe waiting for me." She scowled at him, trying her best to look fierce, but his eyes merely crinkled with mirth.

"Because y' reeked, gel." His eyes continued to laugh at her. "Goddamn chicken thief."

They all erupted in loud guffaws, making her blush only more. She wished she could crawl into a hole and die right then and there, the way these awful, blasted Londoners made her feel small and dirty and . . .

"There, there." Cuthbert patted her shoulder. "We're only havin' a bit o' fun, miss. Ain't much o' that in this bloody old Abbey."

The men muttered agreement amongst themselves.

"'Sides, I spared yer corset, only piece not covered in shite." He eyed her shape beneath the cover of her clenched shawl. "And good thing I did, as it looks like y' need it."

The horde howled and jeered again until she yelled, "Out, get out! The lot of you! Let me bake in peace!"

And to Charles's great relief, they eventually did leave, but not before Cuthbert had returned with her stays, tossing them over a chair and eliciting only more lewd laughter.

❧

Wells set aside his mother's letter in disgust, deciding he would not give her the satisfaction of a response. He'd done as she'd asked this season, yet here she was again, needling him. He'd found a perfectly appropriate bride; it was hardly his fault the lady had run off with a better man.

He poured himself another drink from the parlor's sideboard, further contemplating his mother's words and his own fate, for he only ever drank at such an early hour when confronted by the Duchess. At least today's encounter had been by post rather than in person, though he knew she'd visit sooner or later. His mother was never dissuaded, the sort of woman who showed up on one's doorstep at the most inopportune of moments. The mere fact that she was hounding him again to marry after the humiliation he'd just endured in London spoke volumes. She was a force of nature, *Maman*, and he hated crossing her path.

Which reminded him of another force of nature currently in his kitchen who should by now be done baking him those loaves. He ought to make sure his new mistress had not run off, though without clothes there was slim chance of that. He imagined Cuthbert burning them for that very reason, good man that he was, and determined right then he'd take his time procuring her the sewing supplies she'd requested. Keeping her *un*dressed was, after all, his goal.

Wells smiled to himself, picturing the girl naked in his bed. A mistress was ever so much better than a wife.

What was more, as a Cumberland native, she knew the townsfolk. He might use her to his advantage, for she'd already told him the stonemason needed work. If he asked the man again, albeit more politely, he might yet get him to agree, at perhaps even more reasonable a price. God knew things had to cost less out here. And if she knew the mason she likely knew a carpenter as well. And hadn't she mentioned a cook? He was tired of Tom's dull repertoire of daily rabbit or venison stew.

Perhaps Charles would prove as useful as she'd prove pleasurable, for she was a quick one, he could tell. Though a woman could be too clever sometimes; he'd have to watch her. She might steal from him again, items more valuable than chickens next. Not that there was much of value currently at Almsdale.

He stole a glance about the parlor as his finger disturbed a layer of dust so thick it coated his skin like custard. And *this* was the best room here . . . Still, he'd vowed to restore the Abbey to its former glory and so keep it his escape for the day he'd be forced to become the next Duke. A day not far off, else his mother would not be hounding him to marry as his father lay ailing.

Wells quickly buried the thought. He did not wish to dwell upon his fate. He wished only to hide here in Cumberland, enjoying its rough terrain, rough inhabitants, and even rougher winters. That and its strangely named women, for why the devil anyone would give such gorgeous girl as Charles a boy's name he could not fathom, especially a chit as lusty as she. He'd been pleasantly surprised at how readily she'd responded to him, given her fierce protestations otherwise. But perhaps fierce here meant fierce in other ways. Perhaps she'd even come to enjoy him.

He grinned to himself, imagining his Cumberland mistress rivaling the fairest of London's courtesans. And she would, he thought, because he'd damn well train her himself.

Charles pulled out the loaf and went in search of butter and jam. It was a decidedly sparse kitchen, devoid of finer dishware and hardly any herbs or spice, yet the stew last night had filled her belly nicely; she'd long lost all culinary refinement. The days of living like a lady had regrettably vanished upon her mother's death.

As for *behaving* like a lady . . . She cringed at the thought of her dear Mama gazing down at her firstborn daughter's deplorable state: indecently dressed in some depraved lord's castle, awaking naked this morning in said lord's bed. Charles flushed to think she'd cravenly kissed the very man hell bent on debauching her. How could she have been so brazen? More importantly, *why* had she done it?

It had surely been a mere physical response to a virile male body, akin to an animal's urge to mate. And she'd make damn sure it did not happen again.

She was still rummaging about as she pondered her own carnal urges, opening one empty cupboard after another, when she froze, sensing a presence in the room.

"Hello, Charles," his lordship greeted, making her quickly spin about. "I've arrived for a taste, timed it perfectly I see."

"My lord." She curtsied, aware of the effect this had on his lordship, for she was now cinched into shape below the loose fabric of his shirt, her stays pushing her breasts up and out. "I cannot find butter, sir." She returned to her rummaging, bending to search lower. "Nor do I spy any jam. May I ask what you and your men have been living on?"

"Stew," he spat the word with distaste. "Meat stew, night after night. But if it's the price to pay to escape London's *Ton* by God I'll pay it."

"And what, pray, is so terrible about London that has you fleeing to Cumberland, my lord?" She glanced up at him.

"None of your blasted business, woman."

Charles was reminded to watch her tongue. "Forgive me, my lord, I shan't mention London again."

"Don't," he said forcefully, then took up a knife to begin slicing into her loaf. "The butter's up high, by the way, far left cupboard. Have to hide it from Cuthbert, who eats it by the block, the brute. You are not to tell him or any man here where it's kept, else I won't share with you, either."

She was surprised by his shift in tone and even more surprised when he winked, making her smile shyly in response before she climbed atop a chair, found the hidden stash, and brought it to him.

Lord Wells buttered them each a slice before he took his first bite, his handsome face at once suffused with pleasure. A sigh escaped Charles's lips as butter hit her tongue too. She closed her eyes in deep satisfaction while she chewed, and when she opened them, she caught him watching her, their eyes connecting for a second before she wrenched her gaze away.

"Heaven, is it not, Charles?" he told her softly. "After weeks of stew, to indulge in a loaf of bread is nothing short of bliss, I admit." He stared at her again. "I may not miss London, but I do miss her food."

"Cumberland is a far cry from London I'm sure, my lord, but nothing beats fresh bread and butter. To taste butter again is divine."

"Have you gone long without?" He frowned. "I shall send some to your family."

"Thank you, my lord. My father and sister would be grateful for any provisions you can spare."

"Have you other family nearby they may depend on?"

"None, sir. But a neighbor, Mrs. Saunders, lives not far. My sister will manage if there is food this winter. She might trade for peat then; the Saunders' son will deliver it, ensuring she and our father don't freeze."

His brow furrowed deeper. "Should we not simply move them to the Abbey instead?"

"What?" Charles was horrified. "No. No, of course not!"

He remained puzzled. "But you say they will freeze, and as

I told you I'd ensure your family is cared for, it seems easier to keep them here than to—"

"They must never know why I am here, my lord," Charles implored. "I don't know what your man told them this morning when he . . ." She took a breath to slow her racing heart. "It would kill them to discover how low I have fallen."

***

"You have not fallen low," Wells snapped, irritated by this recurring theme of hers and its annoying ability to engender guilt. "There is no shame in being a man's mistress. If anything it is a coveted position for a woman who—"

"Of course, *Your Grace*." She insulted him again. "For a woman who works for a living it is no doubt a coveted position. But not for a lady of class." Her nostrils flared. "I know what you think of me, Lord Wellesley, but my father and sister do not share your estimation; I'd prefer they continue to esteem my virtue."

He peered more closely at her, realizing he'd need to rein in his new mistress's continued abuse of title, lest she follow his own men's conduct and become equally insufferable. Only how to convince Cuthbert and crew to give up the joke? He would work that out later. Not now.

"You're not like the other villagers, are you?" he asked instead, his words more statement than question.

She remained silent.

"Yet you consider yourself a native."

"I am, sir. Cumberland born and raised."

"But you were educated."

"My father was the village headmaster, my lord."

"Hmm," he pondered, then took another bite of bread, deciding to change the conversation entirely. "I've a mind to eat this whole delicious loaf, what say you?"

She timidly smiled back. "First coffee and now butter, my lord . . . It is *I* who am in heaven, sir."

"Good," he stated. "Then I am content, despite this morning's upsets." He peered at her more closely before he reached his hand to trace the bridge of her nose, landing at its tip. "You are very pretty, Charles, and will be prettier still, once we fatten you up."

Yet she did not warm to his praise, saying only, "I am neither fair nor foul, my lord. But if it pleases you to think me pretty, so be it. Looks matter little here in Cumberland, Lord Wellesley. The land treats all the same."

※

After devouring the better half of a loaf, his lordship left Charles in the kitchen with orders to bake him three more. To which she'd replied she would see that tally towards her fine started and wished to write a letter to her sister, to assure her she was well.

Lord Wellesley had simply looked at her a little strangely and nodded yes before he'd left her blessedly alone to contemplate both bread and recent events—in other words, to contemplate her sentence. But first Charles needed to take stock of kitchen staples: oats and flour aplenty yet only plain leavening in sight. She'd have to beg starter off a villager if his lordship wanted sourdough. She imagined the look of pleasure on his face once he'd tasted *that*.

As she mixed and kneaded more dough her thoughts turned to the future, a future now inextricably linked to Lord Wellesley, or Wells, as his men called him. She'd met his father, the Duke of Allendale, once long ago when she was quite small, for she remembered the day he'd paid her father a visit, taking tea even with Mama. He'd been a large, grand man, she recalled, but not unkind, letting her sit upon his knee to play with his gold cufflinks. She remembered how pleased he'd been when she'd told him her name.

Wellesley was not so large as his father, or perhaps only seemed less large now that she was grown herself. He had his father's aristocratic carriage—*no, his arrogance,* she amended in her head—yet his appearance lacked style. The fact he'd served her coffee and was holed up in the Abbey with but a rowdy band of Londoners to wait on him hinted at how removed he was from polite society, from acting like the Duke's son. Not to mention those same Londoners also inexplicably insulted the Dukedom by addressing Wellesley as 'His Grace.'

Wells did not dress in terribly fine clothing either. He struck her as unkempt for a lord, having not even shaved this morning. Had he no valet? She was not sure what to make of him, nor why he'd disparaged London with such vehemence. She was not so foolish as to press him more, but she suspected Lord Wellesley was fleeing something, and she could only wonder what.

Charles wondered a great many things while her hands rolled and punched dough, wishing most of all that her new master were less handsome. She blushed to picture him naked as the dawn this morning: mischievous slate eyes above square, carved cheekbones. Proud patrician nose below curls too unruly for a man. Broad shoulders over corded torso with legs sculpted like the Greek statues she'd seen in museums Father had taken her to in London. Those images reminded her how unlike the limpid gentry Lord Wells truly looked. He was coarse by comparison, and she was shocked to discover her body tingling with renewed arousal, despite the threat of imminent ruin.

Oh God, had she just imagined her ruination?

Charles upbraided herself. It would do no good, she thought, for Lord Wells to know she found him attractive; the man was full of himself enough. Besides, she was wicked for even thinking such thoughts.

She mentally shook herself, focusing on shaping the loaves. She must think strategically now and not fall for his lordship's physical charms. Rather, she must fall into his favor and use him to improve Eleanor's chances at a proper match. She held no hope of marriage for herself, nor did she wish to be forever under some man's thumb. Bad enough she was now under *this* man's thumb. The day Eleanor was securely settled and Papa at rest beside Mama was the day she would begin to see about pleasing herself.

Until that day Charles would concentrate on the here and now. As she turned the loaves out into the hot brick oven she let her thoughts wander more. Perhaps someday she'd own a little cottage all her own. Or dress as a man and travel the world. Perhaps she'd even teach in a village school somewhere as Papa had. Whatever she did it would be hers to decide and hers to own, and if she had to give her body to Lord Wellesley to achieve her freedom so be it. She'd be neither the first, nor last, woman on earth forced to resort to such means.

She only wished she'd been given a choice in the matter, rather than fall into this lord's all-too-handsome lap.

Wellesley did indeed pay a call to stonemason Adams, surprising the man with his visit. The outcome had been favorable this time, for the mason had agreed to the work after Wells had let slip both Miss Merrinan's name and estimation of the tradesman's skill. His mistress was going to prove more useful than he'd hoped.

"She did, did she?"

Wells replayed the mason's words once more in his mind.

"*Yes,*" he'd answered the fellow. "*Told me I'd be a fool to hire anyone else.*"

The Cumberland native had laughed outright. "*Aye, she's a spitfire, milord, tells it like it is, always has. I'll have to thank her next I'm by.*"

Wells had had to remedy that thought fast "*You'll find her at the Abbey now, Adams, as I've employed her in my house.*"

"*You lookin' for servants then, sir?*" He'd eyed Wells closely. "*You'll not do better than t' hire Charles—a wise choice as she knows who to trust and who t' steer clear of.*"

He'd told the man he might hire more staff in future, but not at present, as there was enough to deal with structurally at the Abbey. Which had set both men to talking masonry again.

Wells rode his mount back slowly, rehashing his conversation with the mason even as he took in the rocky landscape around him. Cumberland was as rugged as he remembered, the views of mountains breathtaking in their expanse. His horse ambled along, in no rush it seemed, and Wells let his thoughts amble in similar fashion. He'd acquired needle and thread in town, but he hadn't known where to start when it came to purchasing bolts of cloth for his mistress, nor was he eager to have her clothed. He would send Cuthbert on that errand in a day or two, for the looks he'd received both in the small shop and on the main street . . . No wonder the girl had blenched at him hauling her into town for a fitting. Cumberland was decidedly not London. He'd need to learn local ways if he were to make the Abbey his home.

He'd also need to give Miss Merrinan a title of sorts in his household now that word would get out he'd employed her. Housemaid? Scullery? Could she cook as well as she baked? He didn't want her sweating in a hot kitchen burning tender flesh and smelling like onions in his bed. Chambermaid was better suited to her duties as she'd be spending plenty of time in his chamber.

Yes, he smiled to himself. Chambermaid would do.

CHAPTER FIVE

Eleanor Merrinan was worried. The man who'd appeared at their doorstep that morning had politely informed both her and Papa that Charles was now employed at the Abbey. Not only would they be given food this winter in payment, but were there belongings he might take back for her sister? No? Then good day to you, miss. That's all he'd said before he'd left her agape, a chicken under each arm and a basket of provisions at her feet.

Her father, Sir Benedict, had stood slightly behind her in the course of this conversation, yet he'd not uttered a word to the man, making Eleanor worry as much about Papa now as she did Charles. She'd need to spin Father a fine tale regarding this change in events, for his muddled mind would find no peace with Charles gone. He'd awake each day no doubt demanding to see his eldest daughter, just as he still asked daily for poor Mama.

A struggling chicken jarred Eleanor from her thoughts as she tightened her grip on the bird and continued the short walk up to the coop. The air was brisk and she hadn't her shawl, both of which made her shiver. Nor had she expected to receive chickens instead of her sister at so early an hour. She wondered what could possibly have happened for Charles to go from thieving to employment in the span of one night. Already she missed her sister as she dumped both birds into the ramshackle run. Eleanor was irritated by her emotion, feeling somehow abandoned, for she and Charles had never been parted before. She wondered what work her sister could possibly be doing for the new Lord of Almsdale Abbey. And then she imagined how miserable the coming long winter would be without her, with only Papa for company in their cold stone house.

Eleanor glanced up at the sky—a brilliant blue horizon over the rock-strewn grey fells, no other cottage for miles. She hurried back to fetch the man's basket at their doorstep, where it sat like a dog, waiting to be let in. She picked it up, walked inside, and set it on the table where Papa sat staring into space, an empty cup and plate before him. She put the kettle on to boil, then unpacked the basket's contents, discomfited almost by the abundance of riches she discovered inside.

Father, at least, would dine well this day. Eleanor had lost all appetite.

❧

Wellesley's men had made quick work of Charles's loaves, not even bothering to slice pieces but tearing off great hunks with their greedy paws. She'd watched in horror as they'd devoured her hard work, having not witnessed such a rough group of men as these before. Even in Cumberland, where lads were raised on moor and heath, the men had better manners. These Londoners were uncouth in comparison, chewing with open mouths and spitting on the floor. She could scarce imagine where—or why—Lord Wellesley had acquired such lowlifes and merely backed her way out the kitchen door in slow, steady steps, hoping to escape more notice.

Cuthbert, alas, caught her.

"Oi!" he shouted above the din, holding fast to her arm. "You'll thank Miss Merrinan for the loaves, boys, as she'll be bakin' for us now."

"Bakin' for his grace, y' mean," piped up one, the others erupting into laughter.

"More like a bun in 'er own oven soon enough," offered another.

"Tell his grace more'n one woman's needed in this musty ol' abbey."

"Aye!" chorused more as Cuthbert pulled her into the hallway.

"Let go!" Charles chafed under his grasp.

"They don't mean no harm." His voice sounded less harsh. "Lonely's all. 'Aven't seen a woman in months out 'ere."

"They're louts, all of them," she muttered.

"And you're that much better?" He threw her a look. "Thinkin' t' ply yer charms on his grace t' gain more'n his chickens."

She opened her mouth in shock, then thought better and closed it.

"I know what you're about." His gaze narrowed. "And I'll make damned sure his grace ain't tricked by yer fair face."

Charles stuck out her chin. "Why, aren't you clever, Mr. Cuthbert, for seeing through my oh-so-devious plan to seduce the future Duke of Allendale. No doubt my body covered in chicken shit makes him wish to marry me tomorrow. If you haven't thrown me out before, that is."

Cuthbert's grip tightened so that Charles's wrist ached. "You're a might clever, miss," he warned, "but I'm no fool and you're no typical Cumberland gel. I've me eye on you—you're not t' harm Lord Wells."

She shook her head in disbelief. "Harm *him*? How the devil am I to harm a man such as his lordship when he's harmed me, by God! Do you think I wish to be his mistress, sir? Want to be imprisoned here, baking bread for you ruffians? Please, discard me! By all means, toss me out and I shall happily take leave of you all."

He let her go, but his parting words stung. "Hurt him and I'll hurt you, miss."

Charles kept walking even as he tossed another barb at her. "And put some bloody clothes on afore y' drive them yobs mad!"

Charles was still fuming, having finally found her way back to his lordship's bedroom to ransack his wardrobe. She barely noticed the room's rough condition: a wine-stained rug and dirt-streaked windows, the thick layer of dust that coated the mantlepiece and picture frames. If the steward wished her better dressed she'd don trousers like a man and tell his 'yobs' to go to perdition next time they addressed her in such uncouth manner.

She did not like Lord Wellesley's man, Cuthbert.

In fact, he was just as crass and overbearing as his master, but she did, at last, find a pair of velvet breeches that sat her better than his lordship's other trousers. She stole a cord of rope from the room's moth-eaten drapes to hold these up, then found a belt, or leather holster of sorts, to cinch his large shirt at her waist. She even found a short waistcoat to hide her bosom better.

Charles stared at herself in the cloudy mirror of his lordship's room. A boy in men's clothes stared back, but she was decent at last, which was all that truly mattered. Hair she twisted into a bun to hide beneath a kerchief tied tight across her scalp. And as for shoes . . . She silently prayed Cuthbert had spared her boots. Stockings Lord Wellesley had in abundance, though they were all much too large. Everything was overly large; even the room seemed largely empty to her, with fewer furnishings than one would expect for a duke's son.

Still, the less female she looked, the better.

"Where's the girl?" Wellesley surprised from the door.

Charles froze a moment, her back turned to him, before she dropped her voice. "Dunno, Yer Grace."

"And what, exactly, are *you* doing in my room?"

"I . . ." She kept her voice low. "Makin' the bed, Yer Grace." Her affected accent rang false.

"Making my bed, eh?" Heavy steps entered the room. "Now that's a first."

He approached while she kept her head turned, busying herself by tucking sheets and fluffing pillows.

"Sam, is it?" he asked with suspicion. "Or are you Jack?"

She froze.

"Or is it Charles, perhaps?" He caught her tight about the waist, swinging her around to face him, the look on his face pure delight. "Oh you are priceless, Miss Merrinan, dressed as a boy, my, my."

She felt her face stain red.

"This *is* an interesting twist on things, one I rather like. Let me look at you." He turned her around. "Is this how you were planning to escape me?" Wellesley grinned. "Not a bad plan, my dear. Trouble is, you are decidedly too shapely for a boy, and your hair altogether too resplendent." He yanked off her kerchief and unspooled her bun with a tug, his eyes approving her cascading locks.

"Decidedly too loose on you, my clothes"—his hands began to appraise—"but I picked up needle and thread for you this morning, so you may take them in a bit." He cupped her backside. "Especially my old breeches. I think the tighter the better for your figure, Charles. You should turn them more into pantaloons."

She glared at him for making light of her garb and her situation. "I asked you to bring me bolts of cloth, my lord, not just needle and thread."

"You did." He pushed her onto the bed to begin undoing the belt she'd only just notched at her waist, then swiftly unbuttoned her waistcoat—*his* coat, rather. "Only I was quite unable to choose fabric. I'd no idea where to start. Cuthbert will fetch what you need when next he's in town."

She lay there stunned as he continued to talk while undressing her, slipping off the coat and unknotting the rope at her—his—breeches next.

"And I must thank you for the advice regarding Mr. Adams, Charles. After mentioning your name he agreed to start in straight away." The back of his hand gently traced her cheek as he looked down at her, tenderly almost. "Did you bake more bread as I instructed?" His hand dipped to her neckline.

"Yes, my lord," she barely got out.

"Good." His finger fell to the top of her stays through her shirt. "I think I like you best *un*dressed, Charles, though you may beg to differ." His other hand slipped inside her breeches. "Or perhaps you won't."

She was mortified he'd found her again responsive.

"Tell me what you'd like me to do next, miss," he whispered at her ear, his hand beginning to caress her sex. "I promise to accommodate your wishes."

She let out a small gasp, her body arching as he increased pressure, his tongue tracing a line down her bared throat.

"Tell me or I'll stop."

"Don't . . ." she tried.

"Don't stop?"

"Don't *torture* me so." Her breath came in short little gulps.

"Is that what this is, Charles?" His hand teased further. "Torture?"

"Yes," she breathed.

"My dear," he chuckled, "you've no idea what torture is." And he kissed her so that a moan escaped her throat, his body pressed so hard atop her own she felt his sex through his clothes, wanting her, and she him.

Only she hated herself for it.

***

A loud knock at the door made Wellesley's body tense. "If I am interrupted one more time . . ." He gritted his teeth, calling loudly, "*What?*" as his hands upon his mistress stilled.

"Dinner, Yer Grace," Cuthbert hollered from hallway.

"Go away!" Wells thundered.

"I did knock this time, sir."

"You'll pay for this, Cuthbert!"

"Yes, Yer Grace."

Wells could 'hear' his steward's smile clear through the closed door.

"Shall I have a tray brought up, or would you and the gel prefer t' dine downstairs?"

Wells swore beneath his breath. "A tray, damn you, and drink."

"O' course, Yer Grace."

Disappearing footsteps let him know his man had left.

His mistress, meanwhile, had frozen beneath him. Wells removed his body from her, grumbling to himself the day had been ruined by one too many fools and telling her she may as well get dressed. "Wouldn't want you looking indecent once dinner arrives," he muttered.

She quickly slipped back into his waistcoat and began

rebuttoning the front while he let out a loud sigh, watching her. "Am I never to have the pleasure of debauching you, Charles?"

Her mouth pinched. "I daresay you are trying, my lord."

"And I daresay you appear now almost willing."

"I have little choice, my lord."

"There is no shame in becoming my mistress, woman."

"So you repeatedly tell me, *Your Grace*."

"Then why do you not accept it?" he lashed out. It was one thing when Cuthbert abused the title, but her blatant disrespect crossed a very clear line.

"Why must I accept anything you tell me?" she fired back. "Am I not free in mind, if no longer free in body? You may command my obedience, Lord Wellesley, but you cannot command my thoughts, or my soul."

He stared at her a moment. "What are you, a revolutionary?"

"No, I am well read."

"Rousseau, eh?"

"And Locke and Hume and—"

"Damn it, woman, I don't want a clever mistress, I want a warm body is all!"

"Then you've the wrong woman, my lord, and I suggest you find another!"

He pushed her back to the bed so fast he loomed above her, bearing down. "There isn't another woman here now but you, Charles, and as I've bedded no woman since leaving London, you will do my bidding, and you will keep your mouth shut."

She glared at him in silence, eyes fierce, provoking in him only greater lust this time, for he wanted her right then and there, dinner be damned, and shockingly, he wanted her to want him just as much.

"Cat got your tongue at last?" he taunted.

For answer, she spat directly in his face.

Wells was stunned a beat to feel wet spittle slide down his

face but quickly came to his senses as he gripped her throat. "Do that again and I'll whip you myself," he hissed before releasing her.

She gasped for air as he rose from the bed to wipe his face on his sleeve, enraged. "You forget who I am, miss." His teasing mood was suddenly dry tinder. "You have offended one too many times."

He remained impervious to the alarm writ large on her face. "Forgive me, my lord." She bowed her head, the words barely a whisper.

"I can't hear you," he goaded, his temple beginning to throb.

"My apologies, my lord."

"Louder," he demanded.

He watched her rage bubble right below her fear, igniting his temper even more. Wells admired this girl's spirit, but if he did not command her obedience she would try him again. He had to end it, because the sheer impudence of her action—

She bowed her head lower. "I apologize, Lord Wellesley, for my impertinence. It will not happen again, sir, you've my word."

"Better," he bit back, "but not enough, I think." He collected his wits. "I think you incapable of obedience without punishment."

***

In a move that upended her thoroughly, Lord Wellesley dragged Charles to the edge of the bed and roughly bent her over. He yanked down her trousers to bare her buttocks, then fumbled to release the leather holster she'd cinched about her waist.

She knew at once what he intended and gave a silent prayer that he be merciful and quick, but already she heard a whoosh of air precede the harsh sting to flesh, biting her lip not to cry out.

He laid three strokes across her bottom, before his arm abruptly ceased. She thought she felt him shake.

"*Fuck,*" he expelled, flinging the belt aside. She could hear his heavy breathing behind her, then felt his hand haltingly trace the welts he'd just made, his calloused finger on her skin oddly gentle.

Charles flinched at his touch, though it soothed, rather than increased, the burn from the belt.

"*This* is what you do to me." Hurt seeped from his voice. "I've cobbed men at sea for infractions less egregious than yours, but not once," his voice caught, "not once did I ever beat a woman, God damn you."

He promptly stepped away and roughly told her to dress, which she did, pulling up his breeches with trembling hands. She kept her face down, awaiting more, while he sank into an armchair. When she snuck a peek, his expression looked sullen, even pained.

"I trust we've established an understanding now, Charles." Wellesley's tone remained terse.

"Yes, my lord," she whispered.

"Come here," he ordered.

She stepped towards him, only to have him push her to her knees, forcing her chin up so that she looked him in the eye, her tears still wet.

He ran his thumb across her cheek. "I am sorry I hurt you." He stared straight into her. "But you pushed me too far. I cannot command your soul, miss, but nor will I tolerate disrespect from those who serve me."

She blinked back more tears, refusing to break before him.

"Now tell me, honestly, that you will heed me in future."

"I will, my lord." Charles averted her gaze.

"I don't believe you."

"My lord I . . ." Charles almost shook in her struggle to answer this man.

"You have leave, this once, to speak your mind, woman." His voice remained flat. "Pray, take it."

She hesitated, unsure what he was offering, but in a rush burst out, "Lord Wellesley, forgive me, sir, but respect is earned, it cannot be forced." Her eyes dared to meet his, surprised by the look of sorrow therein. "I shall obey your lordship with honest intent, truly, but I cannot always control my response. It is not for lack of respect, my lord, it is a visceral refusal to be," her voice cracked, "*owned*."

Charles awaited his wrath the way a rabbit awaits the wolf: tense and terrified.

He looked at her a little queerly then, body shifting slightly before he drew her onto his lap to embrace her. He shocked her utterly by folding her into his chest and beginning to stroke her hair. She felt his heart beat wildly in his breast, as fast as her own.

"Yes, Charles, a refusal to be owned is something I know well indeed. I shall endeavor to command you with respect, woman, provided you obey. We shall not lack for disagreement, I fear, but if neither wholly owns the other"—he paused to catch his breath—"we may just get along."

He kissed the top of her head then, surprising her even more. She felt the faintest, strangest pull towards Lord Wellesley, despite what he'd just done. Instinctively almost, she pressed her palm to the hollow of his chest as heat flooded her hand, then arm, traveling straight into her soul. It felt as if an invisible thread had just unspooled between them, thin enough it might at any moment snap.

When John Cuthbert delivered his lordship's dinner he set the tray down with a clank, alarmed to see yon chicken thief curled into Wellesley's lap rather than flat on her back. Already she was proving more meddlesome than he liked, not when his grace could ill afford more drama with the fairer sex. John had just suffered a brutal London season with Wells and witnessed firsthand the kind of pummeling the *Ton's* blood-thirsty toffs could issue.

He exited the room as fast as he'd entered, thinking he'd need to find his lordship a different village lass—one a good deal simpler than this miss. He might also find himself a pretty face, he thought as he caught sight of his grace nudging Charles to eat.

Though the lady's sister, Miss Eleanor, had been a sight for sore eyes this morning. More than pretty, that one. She'd nearly knocked him flat when she'd opened the door with those thick, chestnut locks framing warm brown eyes: the eyes of a docile doe. He'd felt like a proper fool, standing with basket and chickens in hand, looking no doubt sloppy to a young lady like she.

Then again, he'd not expected an honest to God *angel* to answer his knock.

John shook off the image, wending his way back to the kitchen to eat with the men. He'd be wise to forget Miss Eleanor Merrinan and focus instead on getting rid of her pesky sister. What the devil Wells saw in that gel he'd never understand.

***

Wellesley roused his mistress the moment dinner arrived, pushing her from his lap with an order to bring him his bowl. She did, walking stiffly, and he felt a fresh stab of remorse for having hurt her, as well as a more selfish stab of regret: She'd be too sore now to enjoy his attentions.

He sighed again, still irked by his behavior. What the devil had gotten into him? He'd acted like a brute, *reacted* to her without thinking, as if she'd been one of his men in need of discipline, rather than his mistress. Had London done this to him? He cursed himself again, though he knew she wasn't going anywhere; his cock could wait another night.

They ate in relative silence, and he saw again how hungry she was, deciding to hand her the rest of his bowl. He'd not only tired of Tom's stews but lost his appetite this night. Contrary to what she likely thought of him, Wells did not enjoy meting out punishment.

Charles did not refuse his offer, cleaning his bowl quickly before she placed it back upon the tray to stand and await his pleasure. He liked that she seemed more cowed, but suspected she smarted more for pride than for actual beating.

At least, he hoped he hadn't hurt her too much.

Fuck.

"Don't just stand there, girl, fetch me a drink," he ordered, "and stoke the fire. Pour yourself a drink too, it'll dull the ache." He leaned back in his chair, staring into the flames and feeling suddenly worn from the day, smarting inside. Wells did not like to be in charge, did not enjoy having to make decisions and correct his staff when they failed to heed his orders. He knew it was his job and he'd do the job he must, but right then he'd have preferred to be anybody in the world but a bloody duke's son.

Anybody at all.

***

Charles did as Lord Wellesley bid, wondering at his lordship's sudden change in mood. Having just learned her lesson, however, she kept her mouth shut and head down. She'd not been whipped since she was a child, and even then only once with a switch, never a leather strap.

His lordship's lashing still burned.

When she brought him his glass he commanded her to sit again, only she hesitated.

"Well?" he prodded.

"My lord, if I may, sir, I would rather stand."

"Of course you would." He huffed a sigh and motioned her over. "Come, kneel before me instead, that I might at least play with your red-gold locks, as the rest of you is too sore for anything more," he grumbled. "It appears your virtue lives to see another day, miss. I should have fucked you first and only then taken you to task." He winced at his own words.

Charles was shocked by such coarse language, though his hand at her head was gentle enough. She did not understand how this lord could be both tender and cruel, thinking an unpredictable master was the worst kind there was.

Her heart sank to imagine herself at Wellesley's every beck and call.

"You must tell me what you are thinking, Fox, amuse me with your mind if not your body."

She sucked in a breath, fearing anything she now said might be misconstrued. She remembered Cuthbert's warning that she not be too clever, that she not 'hurt' his grace. *Hurt!* she thought. As if she could.

"If it pleases my lord to converse, we might discuss the cuisine I have sampled here, as I suspect your lordship prefers finer fare than the stew that continues to disappoint?"

His lips curled. "And just where might I sample such culinary delights?" His hand continued to twine her hair between his fingers.

"Mrs. Jenkins, sir, a widow in town, prides herself on her dishes. She's an excellent cook and even better baker who may be persuaded to work for your lordship." Charles deliberated. "I had thought to fetch starter from her, sir, to bake you and your men a proper sourdough."

"Hmm." His hand now kneaded the back of her neck as she noticed his gaze assess the curve of her bottom, angled as it was up and out.

"And if I paid this widow a visit, how easily might she be persuaded?" he asked. "Your advice with the stonemason proved useful this morning, Charles; I should appreciate your advice with other locals as well."

She began, at last, to relax. "Disparage London's stews, my lord. Appeal to her pride and palate, how you've yet to sample true Cumberland cuisine. Tell her you mean to restore the Abbey, and with it, our region."

His hand gripped her neck possessively. "And that will suffice, you think, to lure her here?"

"She is proud of her heritage sir, as are we all. Just because people are poor in wealth does not mean they are poor in spirit."

"Yes," he spoke softly, "I'm beginning to see that, Charles." His hand massaged her neck more. "I will pay her a visit tomorrow, at midday, in hope she's a dish to share. And I will tell her you ask for starter. She will know your name, yes?"

"Yes, my lord, only I would beg you, please—"

"I will tell her you are employed here as chambermaid, Charles."

"Chambermaid?" She lifted her head in shock.

"Yes." He frowned. "And a perfectly respectable position, I'm sure. I am aware you wish no one to know you are my mistress."

"Lord Wellesley," she began, feeling utterly flustered, "I am not being disrespectful when I tell you she will not . . . She will not believe you if you say I've consented to be but chambermaid here. She will think—"

"Why the devil would anyone *not* believe something I say?" His voice had risen in pitch, making Charles again fear him.

"My lord, I beg you understand it is not your *word* that will be disbelieved, sir, it is the *meaning* of such words as will be misconstrued."

"Just how damned educated are you, woman?" His brow darkened.

Charles swallowed. "She knows me to be educated, my lord, knows me as my father's daughter, and knows that he would never agree to such a position."

"And just who exactly is your father, that he would forbid his daughter such honorable position in service?"

"It matters not who he is, my lord, it matters only Mrs. Jenkins's *perception*." She took another breath. "I do not mean to offend, sir, as there is no offense in being a chambermaid, no offense to any position, in fact, be the work done well and with integrity."

"Save the position of mistress." His eyes flashed.

"That is . . . That is a different sort of position, Lord Wellesley. I am speaking of skilled trades, of—"

"You do not think a mistress skilled to ply her trade in pleasure to her master?" His lips twitched.

"I cannot claim to understand those skills, sir." Charles met his gaze with resolve. "But in Cumberland, people know their place. My family fell on hard times, my lord, else I should be otherwise engaged."

"I see." He was clearly amused. "So chambermaid is beneath your neighbor's esteem of you and mistress out of the question, hmm." He was quiet a moment. "If you wish Mrs. Jenkins to be my cook and bake my bread, then what position here do you propose for yourself, miss? As I am decidedly too old to need a governess." He grinned at his own joke.

Charles decided it was now or never to present her plan. "Housekeeper, my lord." She steadied herself. "Let me oversee your household, help you hire and manage your staff. I know whom to avoid, know where to gain provisions and supplies. I can manage a budget and run house accounts." She began to fear the look she watched spread across his face. "I'd remain properly dressed in uniform by day sir, a respectable position to any, including my father, yet at night remain your mistress, fulfilling those duties required to pay down my debt."

Charles awaited his lordship's response, nervous as a colt and heart racing with hope.

***

Wells stroked her cheek, absently almost smiling. "Oh you are clever, aren't you." His smile deepened. "Clever enough to make the best of any situation, I see." He leaned in to kiss her, savoring her mouth, pulling at her lips a little with his teeth, and leaving her a little breathless once he'd finished. Then he leaned back in his chair, aroused by the taste of her and the thought of her: proper by day and wanton by night. He liked that thought.

"Very well, Miss Merrinan, I shall consider you for house-keeper—on a trial basis, mind—for I see the merit in your proposal, as it behooves me to fill two positions for the price of one."

"Price of one, sir? But that is—!"

"Hush." He placed a finger to her lips. "I am not so foolish as to let you earn towards your fine in double the time, oh no." He shook his head, eyes twinkling. "Your thieving is paid with your body only, my dear, and as you have yet to give me what I want that debt remains in full."

"But—!"

"Shh." He stopped her with another satisfying kiss. "How-ever, I will pay an honest wage for housekeeper, so you may set those funds aside, funds no doubt your family sorely needs."

His eyes flashed a warning. "I am fair, Charles, but no fool. Your family shall still be looked after this winter provided you serve me well as mistress. And as your employer, by right I may interrupt your household duties at any time and place to demand gratification of my body, understood?"

She swallowed. "Yes, my lord."

"And . . . ?" he prompted.

"Thank you, Lord Wellesley."

"Better." He smirked. "You are learning."

She let out a huff of air.

"Was there anything else you wished to say upon the matter?"

She hesitated. "The three loaves I baked today, my lord, surely those—"

"Ah yes," he laughed outright, "paid towards your fine. Let's see now, how much does flatbread go for at market these days here in Cumberland? I'll guess five pence? Multiplied by three, Charles. Do the math for me now if you're to manage my household."

She sank her head. "Fifteen pence, sir, or one shilling and three."

"Precisely. You've a long way yet towards thirty pounds, my dear." He once again laid her head upon his lap to massage her scalp, tangling his fingers deeper into her soft, shining hair.

He felt her body relax into the sensation, though he knew she was disheartened by the math.

"Lord Wellesley, may I ask how much I shall earn as house-keeper of Almsdale Abbey?"

Wells laughed out loud, his hand suddenly gripping her neck. "We shall discuss the details tomorrow, Charles. Right now I wish for silence."

He was going to enjoy this woman. Thoroughly.

CHAPTER SIX

His lordship had not tortured Charles more that night, though he'd made her strip before him to survey the damage he'd done, inspecting her body a little too closely for her comfort. Wellesley had told her she was to share his bed each night unclothed, unless ordered otherwise, for until more rooms were readied there were no other beds for her. She was to begin airing said rooms forthwith in her new position at Almsdale.

Charles was relieved he'd agreed to make her his house-keeper, even if she'd be enslaved to his bed at night. The arrangement meant she could salvage her reputation and so spare her sister, earning funds she might even set aside.

It was an idea previously unthinkable.

When there's a will, there's a way, she quietly told herself—God and Lord Wells willing. She was surprised she felt as calm as she now did, considering how harshly he'd punished her. It was as if her muddled mind had been reset by his egregious beating, the fear and confusion she'd felt since being caught in his coop somehow toppled.

Though she'd not let *him* know this.

When she'd finally been allowed to crawl into his bed, his lordship had not joined her but remained a while longer in his chair by the fire, looking contemplative. She'd watched him from beneath the covers, then pretended to be asleep when he eventually lay down beside her, polite enough not to spoon her raw backside but instead merely stroke her flank, as if he savored such touch.

Despite herself, she found she savored it too.

༄

"Good morning, Charles," Lord Wellesley whispered at her ear, pulling her hair aside to nibble the lobe. "Sleep well?"

His tongue tickled, making her startle and roll onto her back. Groaning in pain, she quickly flipped to her side. He rolled her towards him once more, so that she faced him in the bed.

"You snore," he stated.

"I do not." She kept her eyes shut tight against him.

"You snore like a fox kit," he teased. "Tiny little wheezes."

"My sister snores." She finally opened one eye, adding, "I do not."

"And I say you do." His hand traced the slope of her breast, landing at its tip, lingering there.

She felt a spark run from nipple to gut, hating how readily her body warmed to his touch as he continued to roll the tip between his fingers, as if enjoying how it pebbled.

"You must not hate me that much, Charles." His hand moved to her other breast.

"I never said I hated you, Lord Wellesley."

"Then you like me just a little?" He continued to tease the tip of her breast.

Charles squirmed at the sensation. "There is rather a great difference between like and hate, my lord."

"Yes, there is." He'd brought her other nipple to a similar peak, admiring his handiwork while she bit back a moan. "Kiss me, Charles, like you mean it."

Her eyes widened.

"Go on," he pressed, and when she still hesitated, he added, "You did before," making her blush to remember her response to him but yesterday. She wished she'd controlled herself better.

"Kiss me," he insisted.

So she did, timidly at first, lips touching his own softly, yet when he brought her hand to the back of his head, urging her to take charge, she pulled him to her with both hands, eliciting an agreeable rumble from his chest. She explored him more daringly, entering his mouth to twine her tongue about his own, until she felt desire slick her core. Appalled by her reaction, Charles broke off.

"Well done, my dear," he praised. "Only why stop?" Wellesley's eyes were half-lidded with lust.

"I thought . . ." She was furious at herself for still blushing.

"You have no idea how arousing you are right now, Charles."

"I am not trying to arouse, my lord, I am simply obeying your—"

"Stop hampering your response, girl." His hand suddenly placed her own upon his erect sex, making her gasp. "I am not"—he pressed her hand more firmly to him—"interested in control right now. I am interested in us enjoying one another, in you letting go your inhibitions and allowing your body to simply *feel*."

"Oh," she breathed, air escaping her lips as he curled her hand around his manhood, forcing her to grasp the full, hard length of him. He guided her hand in strokes though she dared not look at what he was having her do.

"There are many ways a mistress may please her master,

Charles, and this is but one. Take me in hand now and coax me to pleasure. I've pleasured you enough, girl. It is your turn to please me."

He lay back, throwing off the covers to expose her hand on his sex, as she gazed in disbelief to see her fingers curled about his massive member.

"Do not disappoint me, Charles." His hand guided her anew. "Feel my response, bring me to release." His voice caught on the word, jarring her into action.

Charles knew it was her job to bring Lord Wellesley pleasure, but until now her position as mistress had not fully sunk in.

She must learn to please.

He let her practice, a groan escaping his lips as he urged her to stroke him faster. She did, shocked by both her own awkward actions and his body's quick reaction, before he suddenly tensed, spilling over her hand, his sex throbbing in her fist. She froze, startled by his response—and oddly proud of herself.

His eyes closed in satisfaction, a smile hovering at his lips, before his gaze flicked to her own.

"Well done, mistress." His smile deepened. "Now wipe me clean and kiss me again, like you mean it."

Charles used the sheet to mop his seed, amazed to find he'd shrunk substantially in size. Then she timidly traced the line of hair that led from his gut to his chest, kissing him there before she ran her tongue along the length. He growled low in his throat, his hand grabbing the nape of her neck to pull her to his mouth as his lips hungrily took her own. His tongue thrust with a renewed need she felt echo in her own loins, making her shiver in response to his demanding, searing kiss.

When he broke off he looked at her sharply, his hand still possessive at her neck before he pushed her to his waist, to where his sex showed fresh interest. "Take me in your mouth now," he ordered, "like your hand, but use lips and tongue, no teeth. Swallow."

In shock she did as bid, his sex filling her mouth to swell in size until it pressed against her throat, his grip on her neck urging her to take him deeper still, until she thought she might gag.

Charles struggled to breathe even as she struggled to please, having no idea what to do or how the devil to do it. She fast gave up trying, letting him simply use her mouth until he finished in her throat, sated.

He pulled her off, panting almost, as she wiped her lips with the back of her hand in disgust at what he'd just done—had just *made* her do. She hid her face in abject humiliation, imagining what her mother would think from her grave, to see her daughter reduced to such rank, sick depravity.

***

Wells lay in a warm stupor, suffused with lingering waves of pleasure. "You are a quick study, Charles." He sighed, content. "And have pleased me well this morning." He placed a hand at her waist. "Shall I please you in return?"

"Don't," she nearly choked, "*touch* me." She turned her entire body from him.

"Charles?" He frowned, reaching for her. "Charles, look at me."

She hid from him.

"Look at me, girl, what is wrong?" He was confused by her reaction but sensed something was amiss. He pried her head loose from her arms, distraught by what he saw.

"You have made me a whore, sir!" she burst in anguish, her beautiful face stricken. "You have made me a whore and I can no longer stand myself!" Bitter, unchecked tears began to spill in streams down her cheeks.

"Oh, lass," Wells took her into his arms, the endearment unexpected on his lips. It was a word from his childhood, from nursemaids, perhaps. He held her tight, not letting her go but letting her tears fall wet upon his chest.

"You are no whore, you are but shocked, Fox, by what you have done. But you are not the first to perform such act. Married women please their husbands thus, husbands please their wives thus—it is an act a mistress learns well. There is no shame in what you've done, none. So do not weep, Charles, do not weep." He was suddenly made miserable by her distress. "I should not have . . ." Wells flinched. "I should have waited; it was too soon. I did not mean to demean you."

She slowly ceased her weeping, clinging to him when but a moment before she'd recoiled from his very being. She suddenly cried, "I do not understand you, sir. I do not understand how you can be both so tender and cruel!"

Wells held her tighter, pressing her naked body more fiercely to his own so that he might absorb her grief. "I am a man, Fox, with base needs, human needs. A brute at times, but never a beast, so you must forgive my actions, Charles. I will go slower moving forward. I see you are more timid than I thought. I should have known better than to rush you, but your body," he sighed, "your body whispered you were ready, though I see now that your mind is not."

She brusquely wiped her eyes. "I am not timid, sir." She sniffed.

He could tell she was trying very hard to be brave.

"I am merely unschooled in such ways, shocked that such acts . . ." She broke off, embarrassed.

Wells thought her tear-streaked face only more lovely in that moment. "I know that now." He gently stroked her cheek, leaning in to kiss her softly on her forehead, her nose, then tenderly on her lips. "Forgive me," he murmured, proceeding to kiss her all about her face, neck, hands, and arms. His lips landed like butterflies everywhere upon her in soft attacks, even across her breasts. He coaxed a smile upon her face and vowed right then he'd win her over. Come hell or high water, he'd make this woman beg for him before he took her again.

When he felt at last assured of her improvement, Wellesley got up to dress, thinking the sooner he distanced himself from his mistress this day the better—though it remained a wonder he had a woman in his bed whom he had yet to . . . bed.

He handed her a sheaf of paper and a well of ink from his makeshift desk: his dressing table. "Take note of all I say, Charles, while I shave. Make a list. There is much to do, now that housekeeper joins my staff." He tossed her a smile before he walked to the room's corner washbasin to pour water into the bowl, then picked up his straight razor and soap.

"My lord." She demurely rolled onto her stomach to prop herself up on one elbow.

Wells peeked at her, admiring how her strawberry locks spilled loose about her curves, beckoning yet again. He strolled back to ever so lightly trace the welts still there upon her bottom, planting a kiss on each cheek, declaring, "Even marred you are lovely, woman, perhaps more so."

To which she inhaled a breath, remaining silent.

He took that as rebuke. "Yet I shall entertain no more thoughts of wickedness, not now at least." He met her eyes. "If you are to be my housekeeper then a uniform is only proper, is it not? And as such might be procured from said village seamstress?"

She nodded, chewing her lip.

"Then I will measure you now as you jot down numbers." He jostled the bed as he stretched himself out beside her. "Height you come to my chin, five foot five I imagine. Hips not quite four hand spans, and we will give them another inch as you need fattening, my dear. Waist"—his hands crept around to squeeze her—"barely three, again with room to grow, and chest"—he chuckled as his hands cupped her bosom below her half recumbent position—"ample handfuls here and were you to spill out of your bodice I'd not mind that in the least."

"My lord!" she protested with a small smile. He was pleased she was in better spirits.

"Solid, sturdy house shoes—you've boots still, do you not? Will the cobbler have your size?"

She nodded.

"Good." He leapt off the bed to return to the washbasin to lather his face.

"And a cloak, sir. I must sew a new one for my father but need fabric." She scribbled something he could just discern through the mirror's reflection: *6 yards tweed, 5 skeins yarn.*

"Won't you need one too?" he asked, reaching for his cut-throat.

She crossed out the *6* to write *12.*

"And what is the yarn for, woman?"

"Gloves and shawl, my lord." She frowned. "Do you not know how cold it gets here? Have you and your men enough warm garments yourselves?"

He pondered that a moment, realizing perhaps they did not, even as he took up the blade to begin shaving his face.

She huffed, adding a 1 to the 5 to make it 15 skeins instead.

"Are you planning to knit us all wool caps?" He laughed.

"You'll be glad if I do, my lord." Wells watched her add another line: *needles, 6 and 8 size.* It gave him a thought.

"With your permission I shall send to London for new underclothes, having now your measurements. Though I daresay you'll not need many as I intend to keep you mostly underdressed." He slid the blade neatly down his cheek as he watched her ears pink. "However, a few choice items"—he paused his cut-throat midair—"are always a nice addition to a woman's wardrobe." He added to himself almost, "I know just the London shop."

He saw her leave *underclothes* off the list, though he insisted she write *Madame LeBrecht's* at the top of the page.

"Let me see." He put down his blade to sit on the bed and review what she'd just written, one hand lazily trailing the length of her bare back. "If you would like another shilling and three towards your debt, I advise you now dress and bake me another three loaves, Charles. No, make it four."

"That will be one and eight pence, my lord."

He smirked and rose to wash his face. "I'm glad you've a good head on your shoulders. I will visit this Mrs. Jenkins today for your sourdough starter and send Cuthbert into town with your list. But right now I've a stonemason to start in on repairs, so have a loaf ready for me when I return." He reached to pinch her thigh.

"Ow!" she yelped, to which he grabbed the list from her hands before he grabbed her face, bending down to give her a firm, commanding kiss.

Wells whispered in her ear, "Once you are healed, Fox, we will finish what we started. And I promise you will like it, Charles, if only you will let yourself."

CHAPTER SEVEN

That morning, Charles baked four more loaves for Lord
Wellesley and scrambled herself two eggs. For the first
time in forever she was not hungry. Dressed in his lordship's
clothes, she'd also held her head high when his men had
entered the kitchen and commented on her appearance. And
she would continue to hold her head high, for if she were to be
housekeeper here at Almsdale she'd need to command these
brutes—unless Wells shipped them back to London and hired
himself some competent Cumbrians instead. Charles would
see about recommending *that* to his lordship forthwith.

She left out three loaves for the horde and hid the fourth
high upon the butter shelf for Lord Wellesley. And then she
decided to use some of that butter to bake his lordship scones.
She needed to remain in his good graces, especially after
yesterday's rough punishment and this morning's fresh embar-
rassment. She was still mortified by her own behavior—and his
—yet made herself focus on baking, not sexual congress.

In no time she'd pulled out a hot pan, letting it cool before
she hid the scones with his lordship's loaf. And then it was time
to explore.

Charles wished to determine the lay of the house, to discover what she'd be up against as housekeeper, and she could tell straightaway the work would be monumental. The Abbey had lain empty far too long—for as long as its fields had lain fallow. Room after room she entered had things amiss: shattered panes of glass with birds' nests in the rafters, or else a colony of roosting bats. The drapery was mildewed and musty while layers of dust and cobwebs covered furniture, the pieces half buried under sheets. Even the walls were grimy; anything and everything she touched felt unclean. Like the mouse prints she found scattered across tables and floors, she, too, left tracks in each dust-riddled room she entered.

Yet the Abbey remained glorious despite its disrepair, its environs spacious and grand, the woodwork of finest quality and each mantelpiece in every room astoundingly unique. She roamed from space to space, amazed. She imagined the house as it had been long ago, ancestral home to Allendale Duchy. No wonder his lordship wished to rebuild and renovate; underneath the years of neglect the Abbey remained a jewel.

One room in particular left her breathless with awe—a room of sea and light, the wall of south facing windows allowing in more sky than imaginable, letting in all of Cumberland itself. The walls were covered with seashells of every art and dimension carefully fit into whorls and patterns to form cresting, rolling waves unlike anything she'd ever seen. Who had commissioned this magical room and why? She walked its four corners, fingers tracing the bumpy shells along the walls, then looked up at the ceiling's dark blue sky to discern constellations painted in proportion to their locations, bits of sparkling quartz embedded in the center of each star. She imagined she stood on a ship, navigating the ocean. She imagined herself an explorer, a sea captain, spyglass in hand.

Charles closed her eyes and breathed.

She lay down in the center of the room—gingerly as her

bottom still smarted—in order to stare better at the magnificent ceiling. The sun streaked in and caught the air she'd disturbed, making the room shimmer with stardust. A breeze from outside rattled the windows, as if sails on a ship, and she smiled to herself, stretching her arms wide in delight, laughing out loud. It was magical this room, and she did not want to leave it. She'd start here as housekeeper and wipe every shell, shine every pane of glass and mirror, until every surface sparkled. She would polish the room's brass sconces, filling each with tallow candles, then return some night to lie here again, in an ocean of moonlight.

For the first time in a long time, Charles felt possibility within reach. She could do this. She could be both housekeeper and mistress to a man she barely knew and trusted even less. She would serve Lord Wellesley that he might serve her, too. This—*he*—was her life now, however unlikely and unexpected, however unwelcome even. She gazed at the room about her once more, closed her eyes, and inhaled another breath.

***

From a corner of the doorway Wells stood in hiding, watching his mistress. When he'd not found her in the kitchen he'd simply followed her footprints on their dusty path about the Abbey. Yet he'd stopped short of announcing himself, loath to interrupt, because he'd not seen Charles so happy and relaxed as this, not even under his competent male touch. *That* was but a physical release, while this . . . This was unadulterated joy. She was radiant. He watched her caress the shell walls and grab at sunbeams filtered through dust clouds. It made him smile to see his Fox so enchanted with a room he'd adored since childhood.

He backed away from the door and quietly made his way

downstairs. He didn't want her to know he'd seen her. It had been a private moment, and he knew how precious such moments were. He'd not take that from her. There would be other moments to enjoy her. Plenty, he hoped, as he smiled to himself, feeling more content with his choice to come to Cumberland.

He'd been wise to leave London. He could feel it in his bones.

❦

Charles eventually left the sea room, having decided that was what she'd call it, and continued her tour about the Abbey, finding huge oil paintings that would also need cleaning—careful cleaning at that. She got lost at one point and arrived at a dead end, following short stairs to a heavy oak door she struggled to push open wide enough to slip inside. It was a turret of sorts, the round room affording wonderful views of the fells, with circular walls hugged by benches of deep red upholstery—in need of airing and repairing, of course. It had an oriental feel to it, this room, the brocade wall tapestries sumptuous in their patterns. She brushed off sections, finding birds and fruit and flowers embroidered into twisting, twining vines. She marveled yet again at the craftsmanship of such work, wondering who had stitched these long ago, when with a WHOOSH and a BANG the thick door suddenly slammed shut, making her breath catch and her heart pound.

She quickly realized the wind had pulled the door shut and went to push it open but could not. She pushed again. She pulled this time. Charles rattled and jiggled and worked at the latch until she beat the door with her fist in frustration, yelping with pain as the skin of her knuckles cracked. She panicked to imagine herself trapped. How could this door now *be* so stuck?

Charles attempted to clear her mind. She would sit and

think a moment. A door did not lock itself, a person locked it, or in this case, the wind had. She began to work at the mechanism, jiggling whatever lay inside in hopes the latch might spring free. It did not. She pushed again at the door, throwing all her weight at it, groaning for effort, yet still it would not budge. And no one knew where she was.

Bloody hell, she swore to herself, thinking Lord Wellesley would be furious if she did not return. He'd assume she'd run off and then stop sending her family food, leaving them to starve and her to slowly decay in this tower, withering away.

No, she exhaled. She was being ridiculous. She was not going to die in this turret. And if he were as stubborn as she thought him, Lord Wellesley would go looking for her if only to drag her back for punishment. Charles began pounding on the door, shouting at the top of her lungs, "Help! Someone! Anyone! *Help!*"

She pounded and shouted for what felt like an eternity, yet still no one came. She slumped against the dusty red upholstery, wanting to weep. To have gone from such highs to such lows again in this place . . . Could she not for once enjoy a moment's peace before life turned on her again? *Bloody, blasted hell!* She jumped up again to pound at the door and shout at the top of her—

The door miraculously opened, Cuthbert's red face peering in at her in shock. He managed to slide the door halfway open as he nearly tumbled inside, straight into Charles, for she'd thrown herself into his arms, hugging him in such relief he had to gruffly extricate himself from her grasp.

"There now, save yer ardor for his grace, woman, enough already," he grumbled.

Charles roughly wiped her eyes and stepped back to apologize. "Forgive me, Cuthbert, I was overcome is all. The door shut behind me and I could not . . . It would not . . ."

He frowned. "And just what were you doin' in this part o' the house, miss?"

"I was exploring the Abbey as I am to be—"

He grabbed her roughly to haul her from the turret and propel her firmly down the hall before him. "More like tryin' t' run off again, I'm sure. His grace'll hear o' this. I told him you were more trouble'n you're worth, and he'll hear it again from me straightaways."

"Mr. Cuthbert," Charles protested, "I am to be house-keeper here at Almsdale Abbey and as such I must insist you—"

"You insist on *nothin'*," he growled, dragging her behind him till she was nearly tripping over her steps. "Damn Cumberland woman," he muttered. "Why can't you be as accommodatin' as yer sister? She's got more sense in her pinky than you've got in yer—"

"You've spoken with my sister?" Charles dug in her heels, resisting his grasp, though he was stronger and continued to drag her forward. "What does she say? How does she fare?"

He was still muttering to himself. "She's a sight better'n you, dressed in men's clothes. What the devil his grace sees in you I—"

"Cuthbert, tell me at once of my sister," Charles demanded.

He stopped to glare at her, his hold on her still tight. "Miss Eleanor is well, and thanked me kindly for the basket o' food and invited me to tea like a proper lady. And she neither spits nor shouts nor swears like the hellion *you* is, miss."

Charles scowled at him. "You have taken tea with my sister, Cuthbert?" She arched a brow. "How she can stand five minutes in your company amazes *me* sir, for yes, Eleanor is a lady, unlike myself—because I have done everything in my power to ensure she remains one."

She saw him wince.

"I take it you've met our father too? And see how we live? Do you think he'd be alive still if I'd the luxury of behaving as Eleanor does?" Her eyes bored into him. "I do what I must, sir, even if it means stealing chickens, so as to ensure my sister remains the honorable woman she was born. So don't you dare compare us further."

Charles heard clapping as Lord Wellesley came into view. "Well said, Miss Merrinan. Well said."

Both she and Cuthbert scowled in equal turn at his lordship.

"Found her locked in the turret, Yer Grace, sneakin' about. No doubt lookin' t' escape."

"My lord, inform your man I was but surveying the rooms I am to oversee as housekeeper here, and that I appreciate neither his tone nor his rough handling of my person." Charles again tried unsuccessfully to free herself from Cuthbert's grip.

Lord Wells looked at the two, a shine in his eye. "I see staff proves difficult yet again . . . And here I was pleased with myself for convincing Mrs. Jenkins to come cook for us."

"You did, my lord?" Charles's thoughts immediately shifted. "Oh, that is wonderful news! You won't regret it, I assure you. Did you try her rum nicky? It's her best dish."

Only Cuthbert yanked her back into line. "Don't you interrupt his grace when he's talkin', gel."

"John," Wells admonished, "you are to treat Miss Merrinan with the respect she is due as housekeeper here."

Cuthbert's eyes widened, at last letting go her arm.

Wellesley's brow darkened. "As my steward and my housekeeper I shall depend upon you both to keep the rest of Almsdale's staff in line, and childish disagreements, such as the one displayed just now, shall not be tolerated. Do I make myself clear?" He eyed them both sharply.

"Yes, sir," they mumbled, heads down.

"Good. Now I'd like a word with Cuthbert first, before I

deal with you, miss, so I advise you to head to my room where you will find paper and ink still, that you begin a list of household supplies needed. As I am sure you have seen, there is a mountain of work to be done here, and I'd like you to start forthwith."

"Of course, my lord." Charles curtsied in Lord Wellesley's breeches, a ridiculous sight she was sure.

His lordship smirked before adding, "And you may wish to *stand*, rather than sit, while your write your list, Miss Merrinan," making her ears burn as she walked away.

***

John Cuthbert launched straight in the moment she was gone, livid that Lord Wells had made this woman housekeeper of Almsdale. The last thing he needed was a hot-tempered miss ordering him about.

"Yer Grace, beggin' yer pardon, sir, but that gel's not fit to—"

"She is quite fit, John, deliciously so, and I daresay perfectly fit to run a household too. It suits my purpose twofold: She remains respectable by day and agreeable in my bed at night. I see no reason to change my mind so don't even try." Wells shot him a look. "I know you don't like her, John, but I insist you learn to work with her. She's got a good head on her shoulders and has proven useful with the locals already."

"But sir, she's usin' you to—"

"Of course she's using me, John. As I am using her. I'd think less of her if she didn't. You've met her family. I imagine they're poor as dirt but come from some class somewhere back, else she wouldn't be so educated, nor nearly so conceited. So you do your job and she'll do hers, and with luck by spring this place will be halfway hospitable."

Cuthbert sighed. It was a losing battle, he knew, but he

looked Wells in the eye anyway and tried once more. "That gel's trouble, sir, and I've me eye on a different miss for you in town, a prettier one who's neither so clever nor so—"

But Wells stopped him short. "John, I don't need another girl, this one suits. You leave Miss Merrinan to me. Besides, I've more pressing business for you to attend to anyway." And his lordship launched into a list of tasks he wanted done yesterday.

John shook his head, thinking his master was as stubborn as his pig-headed new mistress; the two deserved each other.

Wells snuck up on Charles bent over his chest of drawers, writing. His old breeches hugged her buttocks so delightfully he placed both hands at either cheek, making her jump enough to ruin her line, ink trailing across the page. He heard her snort in irritation.

"And how is your bottom today, miss, better, I hope?" His hands slid to her waist as he gently pressed himself against her, sliding them further up her torso to cup her fulsome breasts.

She sucked in her breath, as if unused to a man's wanton touch, and drily answered, "Sore, my lord."

"Pity," he said. "I had hoped to ruin you before dinner, but I see I'll have to wait." He did not intend to ruin her today, or even tomorrow, not after this morning's fiasco. He was going to take his time with her, but he didn't want her to know that. Anticipation, after all, bred desire, and he wanted her good and ready for him when he finally did claim her.

"Have you finished your list of supplies? And what do you make of the Abbey, Charles? I am curious to hear my new housekeeper's thoughts."

She turned about only to find herself trapped in his arms, for Wells had no intention of letting her go. He merely petted her as one would a cat, letting down her hair again and swiftly undoing her shirt. He could feel her pulse begin to race, her breaths quicken, while his hands explored her freely.

"As your lordship already knows," she began with shaky voice, "the Abbey is in great disrepair. The rooms are . . . That is, exterior work must be done first in some places before . . . interior restoration can . . ." She was struggling to speak. "My lord, I beg you I cannot . . . I cannot concentrate when you . . . When . . ."

His lips met the hollow of her throat, his tongue lapping circles there, teasing her relentlessly, till she cried, "My lord, if you do not stop I shan't be able to—"

"What, Charles?" His tongue dipped lower.

"I shan't be able to complete my duties as housekeeper, sir!" She gasped as he freed one ripe orb from her stays to pop into his mouth.

"Lord Wellesley, I beg you . . ."

"Beg me what, Charles?"

"I beg you, stop!"

So he did, pulling away to stare his fill. She looked deliciously bothered and delectably bewitching, her chest heaving with one breast exposed.

He smiled wickedly. "Very well then, continue." He lowered himself into a chair across the room.

"Continue? Now? After you've just . . ." She seemed appalled.

"You bid me stop so you might continue with your assessment of the Abbey. I have done so, therefore, pray proceed." He kept his face blank, though his lips twitched.

She stared back, speechless, as if torn between fury and desire, her body caught. He knew that feeling well.

"I'm waiting." He arched one brow.

And in an instant she'd thrown herself upon him, her lips locking onto his as her hands fisted his hair, demanding he finish what he'd begun. Wells was instantly aroused yet taken aback by her attack, though he returned her kiss with equal ardor. She straddled his lap, despite her bottom's welts, and he pushed off her shirt, pulling at cords to loosen her stays. He strained to fill her and was shocked when she freed him from his trousers, taking him in her hand as he'd only just shown her how to do.

"Christ, woman, you want me, don't you." He broke from her lips, breathing hard as his eyes met hers.

"Yes." She stared back, repeating simply, "Yes."

"You're not ready," he growled, slipping his hand between her legs.

"I am, my lord." She barely hesitated. "I am now."

"No." He took her mouth again, his hand simply working her through her breeches, though he made her shatter too quickly, wound so tight he hadn't even needed to stroke bare flesh.

God, she was too much.

She broke from him then, her eyes meeting his with a look he'd not seen before as she dropped from his lap to her knees and surprised him utterly, parting his legs to slip in between, lips willing to kiss and caress what only that morning she'd been terrified to do.

He struggled for control, her hot mouth on his member suddenly too much for his senses, his all-too-fast release embarrassing. As if he were powerless to resist her.

Wells leaned back in his chair, breathing hard, and watched his mistress lick her lips, a hint of triumph in her eyes. Was Cuthbert right? Would she now use him too well? He searched his mind for an answer. Or was she simply awakened to him, as he'd hoped she might become? He didn't know and almost didn't care. He exhaled, tangling his hand in her hair as she tucked him back into his trousers and laid her head upon his lap, breathing hard yet herself. They remained that way a moment longer in silence.

"Why am I not ready, my lord?" Charles broke their quiet.

He was again surprised by her. "Because of this morning, Fox. I do not wish to scare you more."

"But I am no longer frightened." She lifted her head from his lap.

"I would rather not test that theory." He grimaced.

"Then how will you know when I—?"

"I'll know."

"But that is not an answer that is—"

"Hush, girl, trust me to know."

"Trust is earned, my lord." Her brow creased.

"Like respect, yes, we've established this already." He pulled her onto his lap again, though she winced to sit on his knee. He adjusted her slightly, till she was made more comfortable.

"You have pleased me greatly thus far, let us leave it at that, and let us endeavor to please one another further, yes?" He turned her chin to look at him.

"Yes, my lord."

"You enjoy me a little now, I take it?" His look tested as his finger traced her lower lip, the swell of her bosom rousing him anew.

She blushed. "I am not immune to your charms, it seems, sir."

"I see." He smirked. "Not immune, good, though I shall have to try harder to get you to actually *like* me, no doubt."

And it was her turn to smile, a spark in her eye. "I like that you intend to try, my lord." Her smile became a veritable grin. "As if you wished to court me, rather than command me."

Wells laughed before he kissed her again hard, savoring her awhile, leaning her back to demand her full surrender. "A fox is wooed before it is tamed, yes. And I've a feeling that to command you, Charles, a degree of taming need happen first." He fondled her more, pinching a nipple almost roughly as he added, "Though it would be wise, Miss Merrinan, you not forget your place in the natural order of things."

"I've no illusions as to my position here, Lord Wellesley." She stiffened slightly upon his lap. "My allegiance to your lordship is no longer in question."

"Good." He continued to pet her. "Then let us speak now as to your other duties to me here, for it is not all play we will engage in, miss, but work, too."

She leaned in to tickle his ear with a low, heated breath, breasts falling dangerously close to his lips. "It is my pleasure to obey you, Lord Wellesley," she whispered in a seductive, sultry tone.

And with a groan Wells fell to feasting on her anew, all thought of work having utterly fled his mind.

CHAPTER EIGHT

Eleanor Merrinan carefully poached two eggs for her father, the way he liked them, then sighed deeply, wishing Charles were home to enjoy this rich breakfast too. Why had she not come to see them, and what was she up to at the Abbey? In what position had she found work? Eleanor shook her head, worried.

She had just set a plate before Papa, who'd asked three times already where Charles was, when a knock surprised, too early still for callers.

"Mr. Cuthbert, sir," she exclaimed upon opening the door. She pulled her shawl closer about her, blushing that he should see her in her nightdress, hair unbound.

The man turned a shade red himself. "Ma'am, er, miss." He held out a basket while staring at his feet.

"We did not . . ." she stammered. "We did not expect you so early I'm afraid." Her blush deepened. "But come in for a bite, sir. Have you broken fast yet this morning?"

Mr. Cuthbert merely stared at her, which she took to mean yes, and shooting him a little smile, she bid him enter, which he finally did.

She sat him across from Papa, who looked up from his eggs and began to speak to the man as if the fellow were *his* steward rather than Lord Wellesley's.

Eleanor was mortified.

She quickly placed a hand on her father's shoulder. "Papa," she chided, "you mustn't order our visitor about when he is our guest. Eat your eggs and give the man some peace." She smiled warmly at Mr. Cuthbert, doing her best to smooth any slight made by Papa.

***

John felt his insides melt.

"It is very kind of you to bring us more provisions again so soon, sir. We are overcome by his lordship's generosity, truly."

She placed two eggs and a hunk of bread with butter before him, then proceeded to pour him tea. *Butter!* John thought. *How'd that bloody get in the basket?*

"Yet I must ask you, sir, have you news of my sister? Is she well?" Her face registered concern. "It is unlike Charles not to send word."

He rummaged in his pocket and brought out a letter, which she eagerly unfolded, her relief upon reading it palpable.

"Oh thank goodness!" she exclaimed. "Housekeeper is indeed an excellent position, one she will no doubt . . ." She broke off, skimming the letter. "Yet my sister writes she may not visit for some time. Why?" Her bold, brown eyes met Cuthbert's with nothing short of dismay. "How is she not allowed time off, sir? I do not understand. Surely one day a fortnight, even a month, household staff is allowed a day's rest?"

John cleared his throat. "There were the matter o' the chickens, miss," he mumbled into his plate to spare the young lady more humiliation.

"I see." She looked away. "Well, we shall make do then, and I will write her back, of course."

"Happy t' deliver yer correspondence, miss," he told her.

"Would you?" She beamed at him. "Thank you, sir. I should be most grateful, only . . ." Her face promptly fell.

"Is aught the matter, miss?"

She continued looking down. "It is only . . . I wonder, sir, if when you come next you might spare paper and ink for me?"

He immediately relaxed. "O' course, miss."

She visibly brightened. "I am much obliged, sir. More tea?"

He merely nodded, feeling tongue-tied before this lovely lady, especially as she was in her night-rail yet, and with her dark hair cascading down her back he wanted nothing more than to bury his face into those rich brown waves and inhale her.

She poured him another cup and, noting his plate already empty, delivered him another slice of bread, but not before she'd heaped butter on it again. Their eyes met over the table and she smiled, making John look away a little fast, his cheeks blazing as she chatted on.

"Does his lordship plan to stay long at Almsdale, sir? Does he wish to make a home here for himself? The village must be aflutter with the news, I imagine. And is Lord Wellesley a good man, sir? Is he . . ." She hesitated. "Is he a fair master, now that my sister is employed at the Abbey? She is outspoken, you see, and I should hope he does not count the matter of her"— she struggled—"*indiscretion* all too much against her, Mr. Cuthbert. Charles has not a bad bone in her body, truly. She acts only out of—"

"She's his housekeeper now, miss." He gruffly cut her off. "And he's a good and fair master, one I'd give me life for. She could do worse'n work for Lord Wells."

"I see. Thank you, Mr. Cuthbert. You have eased my conscience much."

"*Yer* conscience?"

"Yes." Her face turned grave. "Charles does everything to ensure our wellbeing, you see, so I feel responsible for her behavior as she acts solely out of concern for us." She made for the stove, clearly trying to hide tears.

John fell a pang of guilt towards Wellesley's new mistress, then pushed aside the thought, ornery woman that she was. He watched Charles's sister, all sweetness and grace, hastily wipe her eyes and fry him another egg. He thought again how different the two were.

"Hungry still, sir?" she called out.

"Don't mind if I do, miss," he answered, watching her. He could watch this girl all day, he thought. And then he berated himself. He'd more errands to run. He couldn't just sit here staring at her.

She served him again then joined him at the table, her father having nodded off at his plate, his soft snores making his chin wobble a little. John looked from her father to her and crinkled his eyes.

The small smile she flashed him was pure sunshine.

❧

Charles sat in the parlor, knitting, while Lord Wellesley and his steward sat across a chessboard, deep in thought. She'd been at Almsdale for over a week now and had managed to send Eleanor a letter and receive one in return, relieved to hear both her sister and father were well, having been visited not a few times already by John Cuthbert and his baskets. They were provided for, as promised, and she had slept the better for it, though she wished to God she might lay eyes on them again herself. That would depend entirely on his lordship's whim, of course, something Charles was as yet unwilling to test.

He'd still not debauched her, letting her bottom heal and

letting her settle in as housekeeper too. Which is not to say he hadn't taken advantage of her otherwise, for she'd been manhandled plenty in his bed, here in his sitting room, in the kitchen, even in the Abbey's halls. That he could sneak up on her so stealthily still took her aback, but he'd not been more cruel; she counted herself lucky, though she recalled his warning well enough. She also recalled how she'd taken matters into her own hands, or mouth, as it were, that day she'd learned on her knees how she might control *him*. Lord Wellesley may have made her his mistress, but that's all he would get from her, and not a bit more.

Charles had also taken in his lordship's breeches and shirt, fitting these to her person better and feeling more comfortable in male garb. She found she liked men's clothes; Lord Wells told her he liked her in trousers too. But this would change as soon as her new uniform arrived from the dress shop.

She almost wished it wouldn't.

She'd begun airing two bedrooms already, layers of neglect nearly overwhelming at the outset, but she'd told herself she had a job to do and would do it doggedly. Her family would have food and heat this winter—that's all that mattered. She'd taken stock of several of the Abbey's rooms with his lordship, the two deciding together which should be scrubbed and which would require more structural repairs first.

In secret she'd also begun work on the sea room, though she'd not told Lord Wellesley this, wishing to keep it to herself. Every morning she went first thing, after she'd finished baking and while the men were still noisily at breakfast. She gave herself an hour only in the magical space, but already she'd made progress.

***

Wells stole a peek at his mistress across the chessboard and thought of all he now knew about her, and just how little that truly was. He had used his ability at stealth—a skill he'd perfected at sea of all places—to secretly follow his house-keeper about on her first day of work. Unsurprisingly, he'd found her in the shell room, busily scrubbing. Yet he was grati-fied she found pleasure in her new position, because a happy mistress was, after all, a pleasing mistress. Wells might like his women spirited, but Charles Merrinan had pushed his limits before; he had no desire to cob her again. Ever.

He watched Cuthbert frown at the board, searching for a move with which to deflect.

"Take your time, John." Wells got up to fetch himself a drink. "More whiskey?" he called over his shoulder.

"Don't mind if I do," Cuthbert answered even as Welles-ley's ears pricked.

"*Rook to castle*," he thought he heard Charles mutter to his steward. From the corner of his eye Wells watched her casually walk over to whisper something else into John's ear, then continue to the hearth to stoke the fire, cool as a cucumber.

Wells returned to the board and handed Cuthbert his glass.

"Interesting move, John." He neatly countered with his own. "Where to now?" He looked his steward in the eye as he settled back into his seat.

Cuthbert swigged his drink and grimaced.

"Or should I ask Miss Merrinan's opinion instead?"

She stiffened but remained focused on her task, stitches moving fast about her four needles in click, wrap, clack.

"I should think I have no opinion, my lord," she answered calmly.

"Oh I should think you do," Wells said, just as calm.

***

Charles sucked in her breath.

"Sit with us, miss," Lord Wellesley ordered, and she knew at once she'd been found out.

Cuthbert downed the rest of his whiskey and set his glass aside with a clink. "I'm out, sir, let her play t' end. I've an early start tomorrow as 'tis."

"Very well," his lordship replied. "Good night, John."

"Yer Grace." Cuthbert left them.

Alone.

Charles remained frozen in her seat, though her needles knit and purled with even speed. She feared Lord Wellesley was displeased.

"Well, don't just sit there, girl, come finish the game," he grumbled. "How long have you been staring at Cuthbert's attempts and biting your tongue, I wonder?"

She gulped but put down her knitting to take the steward's still-warm seat. "Forgive me, my lord. It is easy to let one's mind wander when one's hands are otherwise engaged."

"Hmph." He motioned to the board. "Your move."

She executed it with ease.

Wells countered.

Yet her next move left him visibly agape, and she could not bring herself to speak the words expected, fearing reprisal if she should.

"My, my." He shook his head, leaning back to stare at her. "You *do* surprise."

Charles lowered her head. "My lord, I wished only to help Cuthbert save face, as you have beaten him roundly these past three nights and I thought it a little much for him to bear more—"

He let out a choked laugh, shaking his head. "*You* wished spare *Cuthbert's* pride? You, who deride the man near daily?" He bit his lip against more laughter. "Oh you must hate to see me win. I should think this is less about Cuthbert than it is about me, miss."

"Not everything is about you, sir." She instantly regretted her words.

His eyes bored into her. "No, it isn't, is it?"

She refused to meet his gaze. "I'll not interfere again, my lord, you've my word."

"Your word, eh?" When she dared a glance those same eyes narrowed at her. "And just what is your word worth, Charles? Worth more than Cuthbert's? A man I'd trust with my life, *have* entrusted?"

"My word is as good as any man's, my lord."

"As good as John's I think not."

"And why should a woman's word hold less weight than a man's?"

For a moment their eyes locked on one another, his lordship's stare inscrutable, until Charles decided to ask what had long now bothered her; she may as well anger him more.

"For that matter, why do you allow your steward and servants to insult the Duchy with rank impudence, my lord, when it is clear you are not yet Duke?"

Wellesley's lips tightened. "I need not answer either brash question." He scowled. "But because I do not wish either brought up again, *ever*," he stressed, "I will answer you this once. Only once."

Charles gulped.

"My men know I am less than eager to become the next Duke." He grimaced. "For reasons that do not concern you." His eyes flashed. "When we arrived at the Abbey they believed it time I got used to the idea, given my father's ailing health, and so took to addressing me as His Grace."

He'd flinched upon saying the title aloud, emboldening her to probe further. "But that does not explain why *you* suffer their abuse, sir, only why *they* do it."

"Yes, Charles." He spoke through his teeth. "Yet that is all I will say on the subject." He inhaled, nostrils flaring once more.

"Men as faithful as mine, as steadfast as Cuthbert, will always have my respect, regardless of insult."

She was still shocked that a future Peer of the Realm should so lower himself before such ruffians. "I see," she said, not really seeing at all. "Yet a woman who dares address you as Your Grace is . . ."

"Women cannot be trusted, Charles."

She let out a hiss of hot air as fresh rage bubbled inside her —with nowhere to go.

***

Wells watched her stick out her chin at him. It aroused him, that pert little chin of hers, and he was pleased he'd managed to provoke her. "Now be a good girl and come sit on my lap, that I might pet you a while before I take you to bed. I've a mind to finally debauch you tonight, as punishment for your ruining my game."

The way she bit her lip, glowering at him, aroused him only more.

She grudgingly seated herself on the edge of his lap, still stewing, he could tell, before he turned her to straddle him, hands busy at her shirt, quick to bare her stays. She remained stiff and stubborn.

"What, no kisses tonight, Fox? And here I thought we'd moved past your mulish reticence. I thought you'd come to like me just a little."

"I like you less tonight, sir." Her tone was flat.

"Because I tell you women cannot be trusted?" His lips met the valley of her breasts. "I know it to be a fact, Charles, else I should never have left London. Women all profess one thing, then do the opposite. I'd not trust you with my life for a second, girl." His hands, gripping her backside, pulled her to his crotch.

"Yet you trust me with your sex, sir." She leaned in and bit his ear, making him wince. "You trust me with your hearth, your bread." Her mouth moved to his neck, nipping flesh harder still. "You'd trust Cuthbert with your life but not just any man, meaning not all men are created equal either." Her teeth now traced the swell of his Adam's apple, dipping to his windpipe, where so positioned he felt she might crush it with her jaw. "So how is it you claim all women are the same, my lord?"

Wells inhaled a breath; her words were argued well. Rationally. They gave him pause. "Because Eve, my dear, brought Adam's downfall."

"Eve, my lord, gave Adam the *world*." She lifted her head to face him. "Would you rather discover the world, Lord Wellesley, in all its exquisite, complex wonder, or remain eternally a babe in Eden?"

His pulse quickened. "I did not say I regretted Eve's decision, woman."

"Good," she told him, "because I thank her for it every goddamn day."

And then her lips met his in a dark and daring kiss, obliterating all further talk, until he carried her to his bed. There, he stripped her of all clothing and laid her out, his thoughts single-minded in purpose. He was done waiting. If she wished to embrace Eve's downfall he would show her this night how that downfall happened, and she would thank him for it after.

His knee pushed her legs wide as his hands gripped her hips, lips meeting one breast, making her gasp. Then he leaned in close, his breath at her ear caressing, "You're ready, Fox, and I'll no longer wait. Tell me you are Eve and I will give you Adam."

In answer she arched her back and pulled him down, her nails scoring through his clothes to draw him closer, her mouth on his own her sole answer. His Fox, it seemed, gave in to him at last.

His hand slid inside to test her, finding her willing, eager even beneath his touch. He stroked her there while his tongue returned her kiss, testing and teasing as he brought her close but not too, wanting her at the edge when he entered, wanting to revel in her surrender. His hand stroked a rhythm till she whimpered with need, and then he undid his fall and with one thrust broke her defense, delighting in her undoing. He freed her lips to gaze down at her face, her eyes wide with surprise as he eased himself in, her mouth parting in shock and something akin to . . . fear?

He tensed, waiting, then said softly, "It hurts but once, Fox, and I promise to be gentle. Move with me, Charles. Let Eve's body feel."

And she relaxed—he could feel her body give as he opened her to him, taking great care, though he wished only to plunder her depths with abandon. He steeled himself to ease her in slowly, his hand returning to work her core, rewarded by another gasp as he felt her open more. Eyes locked on her face, he increased his pace, checking again for more pain, but her fear had now vanished, replaced by wonder as he finally let go his restraint. He took her less gently as she took him now eagerly, open to the experience. When she shuddered under and around him, his own response was near to desperate as he pulled out in haste to spend across her belly, collapsing atop her in a heap.

Wells lay there breathing shallowly, his mistress's chest rising and falling beneath his weight. When her hand crept up to fondle the curls at his nape, he moaned, content to suckle at her breast.

"My lord," she whispered, "I did not know it would be like this."

He shifted his weight, then rolled off her, slaked. "I did not hurt you?" His hand plied the stickiness at her belly, kneading his seed into her skin.

"No." Her hand joined his in play. "You did not hurt me."

They lay there a moment more in silence, until she ventured at what felt like forgiveness.

"Thank you for waiting, my lord. I do not think . . ." She struggled for words. "I do not think I should have been so willing had you . . ." She swallowed. "I am grateful you did not force me sooner, Lord Wellesley," she said more formally. "It is no small thing for a woman to give herself to a man and I—"

His lips took hers in a searing kiss. "I know it is no small thing, Charles, but it is no terrible thing either I hope you now see. It is a joy between man and woman—the knowledge Eve longed to gain." He looked her in the eye. "There is no shame in such knowledge, Charles. I hope you will no longer feel shame in being my mistress."

She smiled then, timidly curling herself into his body. "I shall try, my lord. And I shall try to like you more too, now that I may enjoy you." Her eyes sparked up at him, filling him with delight.

He drew her closer. "That pleases me greatly, Fox, and the more you please, my dear, the greater my wish to please *you* in return." His lips suckled a tender place at her neck until he felt her melt deeper into his arms. Until her hands moved to undress him, eager to press her flesh to his own, as if his mistress relished his naked self, just as much.

CHAPTER NINE

C ome morning Charles was roused from sleep to feel Lord Wellesley's manhood pressed hard against her backside, as it had been nearly every morning she'd awoken in his bed. Only this morning she knew he'd not hesitate. This morning he'd make good on past threats, which made her shiver with anticipation.

She could not believe how much she'd enjoyed him last night.

Wellesley drew her to him, then slipped a hand between her thighs where she was wet still from desire. He'd taken her more than once and he'd take her again, it seemed, with one thrust entering from behind this time, the position new to her, the sensation shocking. He stroked her with alarming skill as she cried out in surprise, making him press only harder, deepening his entry, his breath at the nape of her neck soon nipping skin as he grew in size.

Before she knew it, Lord Wellesley had rolled her onto all fours, arse up like a mare in heat, and proceeded to enjoy her thus.

Charles was overwhelmed by the onslaught of emotion

clamoring in her breast, for to be mounted like an animal brought lewd and loathsome images to mind. She battled her body's panic, at war with her shame and pleasure, appalled at passions she should not—could not—accept.

***

Wells had reacted instinctively, half aslumber and half aroused, for having found a warm body in his bed, he'd done what any red-blooded man would. Yet it was only after he'd spent himself across his mistress's backside, collapsing onto the bed beside her, that he realized the gravity of his error. He'd promised to go slow with this girl, yet already he abused her.

He let out a snort of irritation at himself, afraid almost to look at her lying there beside him with her eyes shut tight, breathing hard still from exertion. She lay curled away from him, hugging her knees to herself in obvious distaste.

Fuck, he silently swore to himself.

"Charles." He ventured to touch her; at least she did not flinch. "Charles, I am . . . I forgot myself in my state of half-sleep."

Still she said nothing.

"Are you alright, girl?" he gruffly asked.

She sniffed. "I'm fine."

She did not sound fine.

"I am sorry I . . ."

"Only you're not," she said, hurt. "You are not truly sorry ever, sir. It is not within a lord's purview to be sorry, and so I cannot . . . I cannot even hold you accountable for such base and beastly actions."

This, more than anything, struck a nerve. For his apology had been genuine and she'd dismissed him as if . . .

Realization dawned as to why this woman maddened him so. She did not, in truth, defer. Even in deference she remained defiant. Even in apology she oozed disdain. She did not believe him worthy of respect or trust. She held him to some impossibly high standard of behavior he would never be able to live up to, a standard no man could, and yet a part of him desperately, miserably almost, *wanted* to.

Wells remained sunk in his thoughts as his mistress stewed beside him, clearly appalled by his rough treatment. He hadn't meant to be rough, damn it. Well, maybe he had. He'd enjoyed her, after all. He liked things rough but reminded himself she was new to all of this, newer than new as he'd only just taken her maidenhood last night. Twice.

Bloody hell, he swore again.

And then he huffed with disgust, angry at himself as much as at her. He should have sent to London for a mistress instead, someone he'd not have to train. Someone less prickly and more pliant. A woman from whom he could simply take what he liked, when he liked. Someone who . . .

A face swam before his eyes from his past, followed by the face of his betrothed, whom he'd by no means loved, but whom he'd settled on. And here he had a girl at his utter command, slave to his physical desires as punishment for her crime, and he had no idea why he couldn't enjoy her more.

"I *am* sorry," he insisted, "whether you believe me or not, Fox." He took her in his arms, knowing no other way in which to prove himself to her, and began to stroke her hair.

She merely sighed into his chest, that small puff of air her sole response. Or so he thought.

"I beg your pardon, my lord, for my liberty of expression." She stiffened in his arms. "I should not have been so bold."

Yet this irked him only more—that she should foist some insincere apology now at *him*, when he knew damn well she wasn't sorry for her words one bit.

He rolled her away from him. "Take it back."

"What?" She looked surprised.

"Take back your half-wit apology."

"But my lord, I—"

"Do it." He glared at her.

"No!" She glared back.

Wells pinned her down, looming over her as he repeated the order that was now a threat. "You mock my own sincerity with an apology so hollow it rings yet in my ears." His will hardened. "Take. It. Back."

***

"You take yours back!" Charles threw at him and then flinched as his face came to within an inch of her own, eyes boring into her skull.

"Do you really want to test me, girl?" he snarled. "Or would you like me to be rougher still with you? Because I can, and will, if you continue to defy my direct orders." His tone and his grip on her wrists told her she should stop—*must* stop —before he hurt her more.

Only Charles could not seem to stop herself.

"I have no power at all, my lord." Her voice hardened, though her heart galloped in her breast. "You've already shown yourself rough, sir—cruel, even. What difference should it make were I to beg, apologize, or accede to your demands? You may own my body at present, Lord Wellesley, but you will not *ever* own my soul."

And rather than strike her, his lips crushed her in a ferocious, bruising kiss, his mouth traveling down her neck to suckle her skin almost painfully, teeth and tongue ravaging her flesh till she was shaking beneath his assault. It was as if he demanded full ownership of her, insisting some part of her acquiesce and furious that she did not. His mouth traveled lower, nipping flesh until he splayed her legs and landed there between her thighs, his tongue far from tender, but far from

98

brutal too. He was making her body relent, if not her soul, and Charles realized with damning clarity *this* was how he'd make her pay for her insolence.

Every fiber of her being was aflame, every bodily nerve lit with a burn, a hunger, she did not know she possessed. He was feasting on her core, bringing her to a point of no return, and though she fought with all her might to resist this man's effect she could not. He owned her entirely. He controlled her every physical response, the sounds emanating from her alien even to herself as she pleaded for mercy, yet he would not relent. He brought her steadily ever closer, yet never to release, and when at last she wept outright, begging for absolution, he merely pulled away to stare down at her reduced and ravished state, then took his body from her.

Charles had never felt so humiliated in her life.

***

Wells turned from his tortured mistress, leaving her precisely as he wished: desolate. Because a woman denied completion was a woman he could control.

He did not look at her again until he had fully dressed. And only when he saw the swollen tears streaming down her face did he tremble a little at what he had done, for she looked broken, all the fight in her gone. He'd wanted her surrender, and he'd achieved it. Whether she would hate him now forever was a possibility he'd not considered in his rage.

Wells paused as a voice in his head whispered he should remedy this quick, else find himself a different mistress quicker, because Cuthbert had been right: This woman would only give him hell.

He abruptly sat back down at the edge of the bed and put his face in his hands, muttering *"Bollocks"* under his breath, paralyzed by what to do or say next. He heard sheets rustle in response and imagined the ache she must feel in her loins, the searing hunger. No doubt she'd been unaware such a lurid act could even be done.

Shame overtook him. Her words did not help.

"I take it back, my lord," she gulped, voice cracking. "You have proven your point, sir, for it is true I am no more sincere in apology than you." Her breath stuttered. "My body deceives me, sir, it fails me yet again. It is a cruel trick God played on Eve, to make her the physically weaker sex. A bitter, awful trick."

For the second time that morning Wells swept her into his arms and cradled her to him, kissing the top of her head as he loosed a string of curse words into her hair. She froze in his arms yet he did not let up, continuing to mumble passionate, incoherent nonsense into her scalp, the words sounding strange and strangled even to himself. She allowed his caresses without response, until at last he felt her soften in his arms.

His mouth left her scalp to murmur in her ear, "Your master is a fool and a fiend, Fox. Though he tries to improve, he fails again and again. But I wish to be better, do better. Truly it is my honest intent. It is why I came to Cumberland: to be a better man, to leave all that is ugly behind me in London. Only I see I have not. I bring London's ugliness with me."

She stilled in his arms, remaining stiff as a board, while inside his breast Wells's heartbeat spiraled. He should let her go, only he didn't want to. He wanted this woman's fealty and respect. Shockingly, he wanted her affection and trust. He didn't know why he desired that which he did not deserve, yet he did. Forever, it felt, he was in *want*.

"Can you stand me yet, Fox? Can you learn to like me still, if but a little, after this?"

When she did not answer he comforted himself by inhaling the warm, earthy smell of her, burrowing his nose in her hair.

"Stay, Fox, and I will try harder, I swear. Stay but longer and I shall make it up to you, Charles. Only stay . . ."

"I have no choice but to stay, my lord." She spoke in a quiet, small voice. "I am your prisoner until such day as you release me."

Her words rang oddly false, though she spoke raw truth. He gripped her more tightly to him and shockingly felt her hand touch his cheek, that brief tenderness nearly rending him in two.

He kissed her, swift and sweet. He kissed her nose, her cheeks, her forehead. He did not attack her with kisses as he had before. This time he was deliberate and determined to assuage her fears for good. He felt a shiver run through her as he laid himself beside her in the bed, spooning her gently beneath the covers as he shut his eyes tight.

Wells willed himself back to the night before, to another beginning and a very different end. He willed them both back to sleep.

***

Charles left his lordship snoring lightly in his bed to hurriedly dress. She needed distance from Lord Wellesley—from all that had just transpired. She needed time and space in which to think.

She also had a job to do.

She went about her duties in a fog, her mind a maze of contradictions, not to mention the fact that she was sore. Three times he'd had her, and she felt him still. She wanted a bath: a long, hot soak to ease the ache between her legs and the greater ache in her middle. How this man could *be* so tender and terrible at once defied all reason. A man could not be both, could he? A man must choose his path, must he not? Yet her mind whispered *no*, no man or woman was ever forged so simply. Each held light and dark within as each struggled to command the wayward impulse of the soul.

Charles winced at her own recent actions—she was no paragon of virtue herself—and recalled Lord Wellesley's attempt at apology. She had scarce believed her ears, to hear him speak like mere mortal gadgie, no longer heir to a dukedom. It was the closest to sincere a lord like him might come, she thought, remembering how his lips had left an imprint at every place they'd landed, as if branding her flesh. Yet despite her mind having screamed at her to flee—*run now, fast!*—she'd simply stilled in his arms. Her heart had slowed, her gut had eased. And then, without thinking, she'd reached her hand to caress him.

What the devil was *wrong* with her?

Charles renewed her scrubbing with vigor, polishing the surface of a particularly dull marble table in an attempt to clear her thoughts. She was still furious at Lord Wellesley but equally livid at herself for not keeping her mouth shut. Had she simply bitten her tongue, he'd never have reacted as he had. She was lucky he'd not beaten her again. And yet the punishment he had meted out—the searing intimacy of it, the manner in which she'd been so unequivocally reduced . . . Charles flushed to recall the act, knowing her response had been just as base and wanton as his.

Lord Wellesley had made her recognize how readily lust could control a body—*any* body, her *own* body—for she was no less guilty than he of caving to carnality.

The thought only tortured Charles more.

CHAPTER TEN

Cuthbert had brought not only a uniform back from town that afternoon but news that Mrs. Jenkins would arrive at week's end to take over as cook, sending Charles into a fresh tizzy.

"And just where are we to put her?" She settled both hands at her hips.

"Well, seein' as you're now housekeeper here," Cuthbert's voice jeered, "I 'spect you'd know better'n me, miss."

"But we haven't . . . " She bit her lip. "We haven't even *begun* yet to air the servants' quarters, Cuthbert. I know of but one room there barely suitable for sleeping."

"Y' look right upset, miss." He grinned. "Too much for yer, is it? Better t' serve the master in bed than serve his house, eh?"

She scowled at him. "You wipe that look off your face, John Cuthbert. I'm your equal in this house, Lord Wells said so himself, so you'll address me with respect."

"True, miss, only you've two positions here, and one of 'em's neither upright nor respectful, now innit." He laughed until she kicked his shin, making him yelp, "Whadya go and do that for, damn it?"

"Because you deserved it!"

"Well you've a mite better t' do than kick folks, seein' as how this Jenkins'll no doubt wonder where Lord Wellesley's housekeeper *sleeps* nights."

Charles grew grave, for she'd had the very same thought not a second before. She steadied herself. "Apologies for the kick, Cuthbert, but you must help me find a room close to Lord Wellesley. Somewhere I may purport to bed." Her eyes pleaded with him for help.

His face softened. "Well, 'tis true the master'll want you close by." He chewed his lower lip above his burly beard; Cuthbert was decidedly unkempt. She wondered how old he truly was beneath the forest on his face, for though large in frame his body did not look or move as one much older than his lordship. He might be younger even, for all she knew.

And Charles suddenly realized she'd no idea how old Lord Wellesley was either. God help her, she knew next to nothing of the man who'd just . . .

She shook off all thought of debauchery. "Help me, Cuthbert, and I shall return the favor, I swear," she begged outright.

"And just what favor might that be, miss?" His look was canny.

She met his eyes, stating, "Butter," and knew at once he was in.

§

Later that day Cuthbert proposed to Charles that they turn a linen closet near Lord Wellesley's bedroom into the housekeeper's office. It was just wide enough for a narrow bed and table, even a small chair, with shelves lining both walls high enough to clear one's head when seated below. There was a single window opposite the door for light, with panes blessedly intact. Charles would surely freeze in such a room come winter, but given she'd like as not be sleeping in Lord Wellesley's bed it wouldn't matter. What mattered was that she'd have a respectable room of her own, where she might also store supplies.

It was perfect. There were even hooks below the shelves to hang clothes and cloak. She smiled "yes" at Cuthbert before he left to go procure the room a bed.

Charles remained in the space a moment longer, looking about her little closet with hope. She'd not had a room of her own in so long—not *slept* alone in so long—that the idea felt strange. She wondered if Lord Wellesley wouldn't desire her less anyway, now that he'd had her. Perhaps he'd tire of her, and she could keep this room all to herself. Perhaps he'd send to London for a proper mistress and she would be only housekeeper here at Almsdale. She imagined what that might feel like, to be free of him, yet was surprised to discern a tingle of dismay. Did she enjoy his attentions after all? Or was it simply her body responding, not her mind? What did she care if he bedded another woman? She was but flesh to him—he'd told her as much himself—and he but flesh to her too.

Albeit handsome flesh.

Charles exited her new bedroom to fetch a mop and pail. There was work to do aplenty before Mrs. Jenkins would arrive. Best get to it.

The new uniform Cuthbert had delivered chafed. Oh it fit well enough, the dark grey wool even properly somber. Charles at last looked like a housekeeper and need only sew herself an apron for it, yet she missed the ease of breeches. For over two weeks she'd dressed like a man, lived only with men, even been debauched by a man. It had changed her. Attired again as a woman, she felt suddenly constrained—not that Lord Wells or his men had treated her differently in trousers.

Still, she'd felt more liberated in her movement, more like their equal. Even though she was anything but *free*.

Charles had scrubbed and polished her small closet spotless and now worked on Mrs. Jenkins's room next. The servant's wing was in need of significant repairs, but one bedroom was intact enough to house Almsdale's new cook. Charles wished to make the space as hospitable as possible for the widow, knowing the cozy cottage she was leaving behind. She would find curtains and rug and a small painting even to hang in the room. She wanted Almsdale's cook to feel at home here, for she'd be Charles's sole female companion—not to mention staunch arbiter of propriety. It would not do for Mrs. Jenkins to think her anything but perfectly suited to the position of house-keeper. Nor would it do for her to witness what utter ruffians Lord Wellesley employed here otherwise.

When Wells snuck into the kitchen that evening—having successfully avoided his mistress all day—he grabbed a bowl of what he hoped would be the last damn stew he'd need ever eat. And then he went in search of his steward, hoping John might shed light on their housekeeper's current mood.

"Busy today, that one. Looks the part in her new uniform too. Picked it and the rest o' the items up as ordered. Jenkins movin' in end o' the week has her in fits though, lookin' t' find herself and the cook proper bedrooms. It's all worked out, Yer Grace. She's started in on both. All should be ready by arrival, rest assured."

Wells merely stared at Cuthbert, shocked to imagine the day had progressed so productively, normally even. It seemed his housekeeper knew how to complete her duties well. He was impressed by her efficiency, if not a little irked she'd been so unaffected by him.

"And she seemed otherwise fine to you, did she? Not overly upset about anything?" he pressed.

"No sir, ought she've been?" Cuthbert gave him a look. "You two quarrel again? I warned Yer Grace that gel were trouble, yet you insisted she—"

"John, I did not ask for a lecture. I asked your opinion as to her mood, that is all. And it is none of your business how she and I get along otherwise. It appears her housekeeping skills are admirable enough, and as to her other skills—"

"She ain't workin' out as mistress near so good, is she?" Cuthbert spoke frankly, a liberty accorded him only because of their shared past. "Y' ain't fooled me, Yer Grace. Known yer too long I have. And the offer still stands, sir, t' find you a different gel."

But Wellesley's mood only darkened. "We don't need yet another woman in this house." He snorted. "Miss Merrinan and Mrs. Jenkins will be enough. Nor would it help to have more skirts about for our fair-weather crew to leer at." He knew his men were growing bored, and boredom did not bode well with their lot.

"Fine, sir," Cuthbert ground out; his steward always knew when something ate at Wells. "You up for another match then?" he asked, though the hour was late.

"Not tonight, John, though you could use some lessons from Charles. She's damned good at chess."

His man harrumphed. "Too clever, sir. I said as much. A clever woman makes for trouble, Yer Grace, always does. Now her sister, on the other hand, she's a—"

"Her sister?" Wells had forgotten. "I should like to meet this sister of hers, and the father, Cuthbert. When are you due to deliver them food again?"

"Day after t' morrow, Yer Grace." He frowned. "Though

you'll not learn much, sir. Their old man's daft as a March hare, but Miss Eleanor's a delight." His face flushed, a fact not unnoticed by Wells. "She's the opposite o' yer mistress, that's for damn sure," he added with feeling.

"Good," said Wells, surprised by Cuthbert's emotion. "I intend to meet her myself."

❦

At long last Charles sat soaking in his lordship's large tub. As housekeeper she'd had the authority to order Cuthbert's crew to bring it to Lord Wellesley's chamber, on the pretext that Wells himself wished to bathe. But once they'd gone it was she who stripped and lowered herself in, reveling in the hot balm of water on her aching bones.

A night of lovemaking and a day of labor made for sore limbs. Only she'd not call it lovemaking, she corrected in her head. She'd call it *fucking*, as he had. It deserved the crude term.

Charles sank deeper into the water, luxuriating in its caress, letting it buoy her almost. She soaped her hair, rinsing the grime and dust of the house from every strand, then scrubbed her skin until it shone with health. She'd put on weight, she could tell, and this, too, felt good. She'd eaten well ever since arriving at the Abbey, the gnawing need in her belly lessening with each meal. She sighed, content. Regardless of what Lord Wellesley should say or do to her tonight, she had this moment, all to herself.

She relished it.

***

Wells slipped inside his room, stealthy as ever, as his mistress soaked in his tub. He'd wanted to bathe himself, the minx, and would now have to share her water. He began to strip quietly, thinking any moment she would hear him and turn her head. But she did not, or chose not to. He couldn't tell which.

"May I join you?"

She made something of a splash. "My lord, I did not hear you enter, sir. Forgive me, I'll leave you the—"

"No." He laid a hand upon her shoulder to push her back down. "No need to get out, I shall simply let myself in." Which he did, though the fit was tight. His long legs stuck up at angles to fold her smaller body into his chest. He pulled her back against him, feeling the water embrace him with warmth.

"You read my mind." He wrapped his arms about her waist, his back against the tub's hard edge.

"How was your day, my lord?" she asked—a little stiffly, he thought.

"Fine, Charles. And yours?"

"Productive, sir." She began to relax more into him as his hands slowly travelled from her waist to her chest.

"Cuthbert says our new cook will arrive by week's end." He was going to keep their conversation as banal as possible not to scare her off.

"Yes, my lord. I started readying a room in the servant's wing for her. And Cuthbert found a room for me close by your own."

"You share *my* room, Charles."

"Of course, my lord, only there's a closet down the hall but a short distance to this chamber, which will do nicely should Mrs. Jenkins—"

"—need you at night only to discover you in my bed," he finished for her. "I see you think of everything, Fox."

"It is my job to think of everything, Lord Wellesley."

"And what of your job as mistress, Charles?" He was almost afraid to ask. "Tell me, are you sore today?"

"A little, sir." She blushed. "The bath has helped." She surprised him by taking his hand to give his palm a quick kiss.

"And what is that for?"

***

"For asking after my wellbeing, my lord." Charles decided in that instant that what Lord Wellesley needed most from her this night was not more fight but more accord. Perhaps that's what he'd needed all along.

"Well, I suppose I *am* in charge of your wellbeing," he grumbled.

She snuggled deeper into his embrace, backing her hips into his, feeling him rise behind her in arousal. She slid his hands lower to her thighs, saying coyly, "I thought of you today, my lord."

"Did you?" He seemed surprised.

"Yes," she purred and felt him harden more.

"I thought of you too, Fox." His tongue dipped into her ear while one hand slipped lower still, making her slowly exhale. "All day I have sworn to do better by you, if you'll still have me."

It was another shocking attempt at apology, which made Charles respond to his touch only more. "You can be most persuasive when you wish, my lord." She twisted herself around to plant a kiss upon his lips.

He looked again surprised, and pleased. Perhaps he needed a softer woman than she, one who would accommodate and anticipate, rather than one who perpetually riled. Perhaps she could be this for him. She must at least try.

He returned her kiss with gentle pressure, his tongue questioning almost, and she responded with more intent. When she broke off, he stared at her a moment, as if unsure, until she smiled, eliciting a smile from him in return.

"I take it you are no longer angry with me, Fox?"

"I have forgiven your lordship," she told him firmly, "and mean to prove myself more than just your housekeeper." She turned around in the bath to straddle his lap, a little worried he might laugh at her for this, but he did not.

"Then I am indeed pleased, Fox." His smile deepened, hands now cupping her buttocks, drawing her only closer to his crotch until she felt him notched beneath her.

"And will this please my lord too?" She lowered herself, inch by daring inch.

"God, yes," he exhaled.

"*Your Grace*," she whispered, impaling herself now fully, "take me to bed."

***

With one swift move Wells lifted her, still joined to him, out of the tub and onto the bed, where he lost not an inch as he laid her down, throbbing inside her, wishing only to undo her utterly. He did not care that she'd flaunted the damn title. Did not care if she did it again. This time he'd give her what she wanted. This time he'd satisfy his mistress by granting her a less frustrating, and far more pleasurable, end.

He'd grant himself a better end too, he hoped: a more willing mistress in future whom he might play with more vigorously. One who would desire him as much as he desired her.

He bent his head to her lips and tasted possibility.

CHAPTER ELEVEN

Charles awoke again to the familiar male prod of morning virility, tensing a moment before a hand gripped her hip.

"I swore I'd not abuse you, Fox," his lordship's voice rumbled, "and I meant it."

She relaxed as she rolled over to face him in the bed. "You were most gentle last night, my lord." She kissed him timidly. "I enjoyed your attentions."

"Did you?" He grinned back, kissing her nose in return. "I enjoyed you too, Charles." He moved to taste her lips. "You make a fine mistress, Miss Merrinan." His hand stroked the dip at her waist. "I look forward to teaching your lovely body more ways it might enjoy my own."

She tried hard not to smile in return, but failed, his grin infectious.

"Ah, she laughs. See, she is no stone after all." His eyes crinkled. "You are beautiful when you smile, Charles." His hand stroked her cheek, making her blush.

"Please do not say that, sir." She looked away. "We are not lovers; I am but your servant in bed."

"And that precludes tenderness?" He frowned, turning her

chin to look at him. "Surely kind words between master and mistress are allowed, Charles. One needn't be in love to show affection."

"I wouldn't know sir."

***

Wells was bedeviled by her response. "Charles," he pressed, "explain your hesitation, woman."

"I cannot, sir. I know only that it pains me when you speak too tenderly."

He was confounded by her manner, though perhaps Cuthbert was right. Perhaps she *was* overly clever.

"Well I'll not apologize for that," he said a little gruffly.

"Oh I didn't . . ." She looked visibly upset. "I didn't mean it, sir. I am abysmal at this." She hid her face in his chest.

His frown deepened though he held her to him. "Charles you are far from abysmal at this." He stroked her hair. "In fact you're quite good. *Very* good I should say." He shifted himself away from her body out of sheer necessity.

"It is not the act I am referring to, my lord," she mumbled into his chest. "It is the . . ." The words rushed out. "It is the fact that emotion appears attached to this act which I neither anticipated nor wanted, and so I would beg you, sir, to refrain from tenderness lest I—"

At last he understood. "Lest you develop feelings you would rather not have, I see." He peeled her face from his chest to notice she'd blushed pink; she was more innocent than he thought.

"Charles, it is natural to feel something in return, especially for a woman as, well, passionate as yourself." He'd indulge her this much. "Words of endearment are normal between lovers, and you may in good faith call us lovers. A mistress is not a whore, I've told you this before. You are allowed to feel and enjoy yourself. But neither is a mistress more; no position is, after all, permanent." He chose his next words carefully. "Nor am I inclined to attach myself to the fairer sex, though I will no doubt be forced to attach myself in marriage one day." He grimaced. "Which is not to say a married man might not keep a mistress too," he amended, "or even his wife take a lover, should she be discreet." His hands began to rove about her body.

***

Charles mulled over his words. "I see, my lord. You will marry one day but not for love, and you will take a mistress again after marriage, but also not for love." She met his eyes. "It is surely as much burden as gift, to be born a peer, in service to both crown and family title. You are duty bound in ways we common folk might only dream of, yet duty commands you just as surely as you command us."

He simply looked at her, seeming stunned.

"You are not free, my lord, to live life as you wish." Charles felt as if she saw him for the first time. "You appear to have great freedom, and in most ways you do, yet all this time I thought myself the one imprisoned here, but you, too, are chained." She furrowed her brow. "More gilded chains by far, but chains no less." Charles lowered her eyes. "I mean no disrespect, my lord, I only just remark." She'd noticed his expression turn, realizing she'd perhaps said too much. "I shall keep my thoughts to myself, in future, please forget all I just said."

He tipped her chin up to look at him. "We are none of us free, Fox. We only pretend to be." He kissed her harder this time, urgent enough to prick in her a similar need. His eyes searched her face for recognition, demanding, "Will you run from me still, woman? Or have I tamed you at last? Answer me honestly now: Do you still long for escape?"

Her breath caught, for his eyes pooled like storm-tossed oceans, depths she felt herself pulled into, drowning. "No, my lord." Charles surprised herself, her voice a bare whisper. "I'll not run now, but I will leave you one day, as surely as you will leave me."

His face shifted almost imperceptibly. "Yes, it is the way of things, though some days, Fox, I'd give anything to take a different path." He buried his face at her neck, inhaling her before he kissed her madly almost, making her gasp with real feeling, until she'd loudly cried, "*My lord!*"

His head snapped back. "I've a name, you know." He let that sink in. "It's time you learned to use it."

She was stunned again by his change of mood yet wagered it safe enough to be bold. "Then tell me your name, Lord Wellesley." She looked him straight on. "Your name and age. A lover ought to know such things."

His eyes flashed. "Yes, a lover ought, Charles Merrinan, five and twenty. I am nine and twenty, and my name is Roland Rutherford Wellesley."

She laughed; she couldn't help it.

"And might I ask what is so funny, miss?"

"Nothing, sir, nothing at all, *Roland Rutherford*." She bit her lip. "It is only you have finally become real, you see." She continued to inwardly laugh. "Until this moment you have been but a nameless lord and master, and now, sir, you are flesh and blood."

"I daresay I've *been* flesh and blood, girl." He arched an eyebrow.

"Yes." She kissed him softly. "Yes but now there is a *name* for that flesh and blood, a name I might invoke and taste"— she licked the bob of his Adam's apple with a flick of her tongue—"and ponder and swallow and think on and—"

"Swallow, eh?" His grin was almost impish. "I like it when you swallow, miss."

"I like how you taste, sir," she answered, coy.

He laughed outright. "You're a minx, not a fox, woman! And I will taste you now, this very minute, before I take you again. If you will have me, mistress. Say you will, Charles. Do but say it."

She watched his eyes for the first time waver.

"Aye, Roland Rutherford." His name was honey on her tongue. "I'll have you, sir, if you'll have me."

Wells felt lighter somehow, his feet less heavy upon the flagstone corridor as he went in search of his steward. His head was filled with fewer details and detritus. He'd left his bed content this morning, his new mistress at last more balm than adversary. She was quite delicious, really—perfectly suited to frigging *and* to keeping house. He nearly laughed, for isn't that what a man wanted in a wife? Yet he hadn't had to marry her to get it, he'd simply taken her—better yet! He pictured his mistress as he'd just left her: tousled and tangled in the sheets, so thoroughly fucked she'd looked wanton and spent and . . . God, he wished to go back and have her again.

And why not? he thought to himself. He'd find her later today, and again have his way. Wells whistled a little tune under his breath.

Charles wondered if she weren't in for a reckoning with Lord Wellesley, because he'd suddenly become altogether too tempting; she didn't know quite how to handle or resist him anymore. How she'd gone from hating the man to now wanting the man in little under a fortnight worried her. Much.

He was becoming all too human. She wished almost he'd

not told her his name. She wished almost he'd remained cruel. *He might yet*, a voice inside her warned. He might hurt her again. He likely would. Only she wished to enjoy him too, now that he'd ignited her senses. She felt so blissfully aware of not only the pleasures of sex but of everything around her, as if the world had grown colors once more. She felt renewed purpose in her job, even in being his mistress. Or was it not joy but relief she felt? No, it *was* joy—joy in such pleasures as she had discovered.

Charles's thoughts shifted. She must write again to let Eleanor know she was well. She'd not tell her sister the particulars—she could never reveal the truth of her position here—but she could share her newfound sense of joy. And perhaps now that he might trust her more, Lord Wellesley would let her visit her family again. Perhaps he might even let her run errands in town without Cuthbert traipsing behind.

She would broach it with him carefully, for she would no longer flee, she knew this now with certainty. She would undertake to please Lord Wells, so long as he continued to please her. Charles smiled, thinking *Roland Rutherford* such a ridiculous, formal-sounding name, so ill-suited to him. She laughed, then promptly frowned. She ought to rein in her joy a little. It would not do for Almsdale's housekeeper to appear flushed and flustered. She had a job to do—her other job a private matter between his lordship and her. *Those* thoughts she'd keep to herself, locked up.

Charles made her way towards the sea room to spend her first hour there, in another place where she found joy. It had been so long since she'd felt joy that she suddenly overflowed with it, feeling it bubble up inside her.

Her step upon the flagstone now felt as surefooted as it felt light.

&.

"Yer Grace." John caught up with his lordship just as he was leaving the Abbey. "I'm headed to the Merrinans if y' wish t' join me, sir."

"Right." Lord Wells stopped short. "The father and sister. It shall have to wait, Cuthbert; I'm late enough in speaking with Adams. But give them my regards. No." He paused. "Invite them here next week, once our new cook has settled in. It will give her a dinner to plan, that I might see how well she serves guests."

John swallowed. "Sir, y' can't mean to . . . That is, I don't think the Merrinans would accept the invitation. Tea at most, but t' dine with Yer Grace, well, it weren't seemly."

"And why?" Wells frowned. "Are they not people too, John? You said yourself Miss Merrinan's sister is quite the proper lady. It is not as if I am formally entertaining either. The Abbey could not accommodate guests even if I so wished. I thought merely to allow Charles's family to see that she is cared for here."

John's mouth formed a line. "I'm sorry, Yer Grace, but it were better y' visited them instead. Her old man's not right in the head. He's muddled with age and confuses things outright. Who knows how he'd react t' bein' in a strange house, far from home."

Wellesley's frown deepened. "The Abbey is not far from the man's home, John, not if the fellow grew up here." His lordship searched John's face before capitulating. "Fine then, I shall pay them a visit instead. Now off with you. And I'll need you later at stonework. We are still short men."

John left his lordship heading to the south wall, thinking Wells was a might more interested in his mistress's family than he ought to be.

Then again, *he* was a might more interested in Miss Eleanor himself.

❧

"He wishes to . . . You mean he . . . ?" Eleanor Merrinan sat down, distraught, leaving John to fear the lady might faint.

"Just t' stop by, miss, sometime next week perhaps. No need t' worry yerself about it." He tried to reassure her.

"But he's the Duke's heir, Mr. Cuthbert, and we live in a *hovel*," she cried, her distress only mounting. "He can't see how we live. Charles would never allow it. Does she know of his intent?"

"Well, I don't right know, miss," John replied. "I spoke with Lord Wells only this morn 'bout it."

"I shall pen her a note forthwith. Have you a minute to spare, sir? Come, seat yourself and eat. I'll fetch you what is left." And she made off for a plate before he'd even the chance to reply.

Once she'd placed food before him, John watched her scribble a note to her sister, one lock of hair curling across her face which she pushed back in irritation, only to have it fall forward again. With a snort she finally removed a hairpin and stuck the curl harshly back into place.

God how he wanted to touch her. She was so lovely it made him ache just to look at her.

"There," she announced, folding the note into quarters. "If you would give this to my sister, sir, I should be most grateful." She handed him the letter and then threw him a quick smile that was like sunbeams on a cloudy day.

"Happy to, miss." He smiled back, shyly.

"Mr. Cuthbert do you think . . . ?" She hesitated. "Rather, would you say my sister is happily employed at the Abbey?" She looked at him most keenly.

"Well now"—he chewed his moustache a moment while worrying his hair with his hand—"I should think she's settled in now. Looks quite smart in her new uniform, she does. And his lordship seems pleased with her, if that's what y' mean, miss."

"Yes, yes." Eleanor seemed flustered. "But is she *happy*, Mr. Cuthbert?" Her large brown eyes pooled up at him till he thought he'd puddle right there into the floor.

"Oi, gel," he got out gruffly, "are any of us really happy?" He abruptly stood to leave. "I thank you for the breakfast, Miss Eleanor, and will deliver yer sister yer note."

Only she surprised him by saying, "Oh don't go yet, sir, please." She blushed. "That is, I have only father to talk to anymore and he is, well, he is rather poor conversation now that Charles is gone."

John froze. He'd a chance here but wasn't sure he ought to take it. However, nerves soon gave way as he ventured a shot. "Would y' like t' step out with me a ways then, walk me partway back, miss?"

She beamed in response, making him more relieved than she knew. "I should like that very much, Mr. Cuthbert. Just let me fetch my shawl."

John swallowed, his heart beating fast to think he'd have this gel all to himself a ways longer, to walk beside.

She was back in a flash and followed him out the door. Then, to his amazement and delight, she took his arm. Miss Eleanor walked him halfway back to Almsdale, chatting on about everything and nothing.

His soul soaked up each word she uttered, her voice better than butter.

☙

Charles was busy at Mrs. Jenkins's room, nearly done scrubbing both floor and walls. Having spied some passable pieces in other rooms, she would consult with Cuthbert next about filling the space with furnishings. He could help her haul them over. She stopped to survey her work, wiping her brow, when she felt a familiar prick of awareness.

Charles turned to find Lord Wells leaning crookedly against the door frame.

"'Twill be a fine chamber for a cook." He cocked his head at her before he strode across the still damp floor. "And you know well how to scrub a room, housekeeper. Only put down your rag, girl, and come greet your master properly."

She flinched at his tone, but did as she was told, dropping rag to pail only to have him pull her in for a swift, dark kiss.

"Better," he murmured at her lips, "though I like you on your knees."

"My lord, I should finish the room before dinner, sir."

"I'll not interrupt you long." He took her lips again, shoving his tongue down her throat as reminder that she obey.

Charles felt her insides burn.

"I'd have you again right here, woman." He dove in for another kiss.

"My lord, I've work to finish . . ." Her protest sounded feeble.

"Mmm, I know, Charles, but all work and no play makes for a frustrating day."

She laughed, pulling from him. "I daresay you ought to be kept frustrated some, sir." Her eyes met his. "It wouldn't do for me to give in too readily to your desires, lest you tire of me too fast."

His eyes twinkled. "Know me that well already, do you?" He pulled her taut against his body, his hands cupping her bottom to knead both cheeks through her thick wool skirt. "Very well, Charles. I'll remember your words when next _you_ need frustrating."

"You frustrate me enough, Lord Wellesley," she replied, even as his hands began to roam more boldly. She again pulled away, creating space, and for once he relented, though he kept one of her hands prisoner in his own.

"My lord." She hesitated. "There is a woman in town I think it wise I go see."

"And what woman is this, Charles?" He began to play with her fingers.

She blushed. "She is . . . experienced in matters and might counsel me discreetly on how best to . . . That is, if we are to engage more often in coupling, sir, I should like to be better informed." Her face was likely scarlet it burned so hot.

"I see." He lapsed into silence. "Quite right, Charles, and spoken like a true mistress." He kissed the inside of her wrist, flustering her only more. "I shall accompany you when you visit this woman."

"No!" She was upset. "No, my lord, I will see her alone."

He frowned. "And why, pray?"

"Why?" She was appalled. "Because if you accompany me she will know at once that you are . . . That I am . . ."

"Still ashamed of your position here, Charles?" He arched his brow.

"No, sir, not with your lordship, but in the eyes of others I cannot . . ." She swallowed. "I must safeguard my sister's reputation, sir, as well as my father's. Out of respect to them I would beg you give me leave to visit this woman on my own, in secret. I have given you my word I will not flee, but will return to you, to my position here at Almsdale."

He pulled her to him once more, fingers lazily this time unhooking her dress. "So you say, yes." He exposed her stays, his hand fast caressing her bosom. "Only I am not entirely sure I can trust you yet, Charles." He dipped his head to kiss her décolletage. "Cuthbert will go with you."

"Cuthbert," she huffed his name. "Why must Cuthbert shadow my every move, my lord?"

"Because I wish it." His tongue now probed the valley of

her breasts. "And if he tells me you behaved yourself I might even let you accompany him on a visit to your family next."

"You would?" Charles could barely contain her delight. "Thank you, my lord. I should like to see them again, perhaps on my day off."

"There are no days off, Charles." He pushed her to her knees. "And if you wish me to grant you favors you must grant me ones in return."

She was shocked and aroused, a bundle of conflict. He angled her face to look up at him, and the storm in his eyes met her own with lust.

Charles knew what he wanted, and was shocked to discover she wanted it too. It was less a chore, and more a pleasure, now, to please him. She began to unbutton his fall.

"My mistress learns quickly." Wellesley's hands gripped her hair as he inhaled a breath.

Charles bent her head and readily acquiesced.

CHAPTER TWELVE

"'T'ain't right," said Tom, banging about the pots. "They're at it all the time now. Ruttin' beasts, those two. Why should *he* get all the fun while we get none?"

"She ain't fit t' call 'erself housekeeper, orderin' us about when she's friggin' 'im at all hours. 'Tis a wonder anythin' gets done on 'er watch at all!"

"Aye, an' if he's payin' her t' keep house when she's but earnin' on 'er back, I says he—"

John cut them off. "Oi, shut up now, all o' you!" He scowled at the men. "Miss Merrinan *is* now housekeeper here and you'll treat her as such. His grace orders it. And as for her duties as mistress"—his eyes blazed—"well, that's twixt him and her, and none o' yer goddamned business."

The men all fell silent a moment before Tom piped up. "Sure, John, 'tis none of *our* business, only they're loud enough, an' often enough, as t' make it our business, y' ken?"

"Hear, hear!" and "'Tis true!" came the bevvy of retorts.

John's lips pinched. "I'll talk to him," he grumbled. "But you'd best treat that gel with more respect, 'specially with a new cook comin' on. Lest you want yon housekeeper runnin' to

Capt'n Wells with tales o' yer abuse." He knitted his brow. "Y' know how he can get, boys."

Which quieted the room, for they'd all borne his lordship's anger at one point or another.

"Well, you tell 'im we're sick of hearin' her cries o' delight at 'is lovemakin'," Tom repeated. "'Tis enough t' drive a man mad with yearnin' 'imself."

"Don't I know it," John muttered as he made a quick exit.

"My lord, please, I can't!"

"Hush, woman, there's no one about."

"Yes but I've work to—"

"It is as much your job to please me, Charles, and it pleases me to have you now." Lord Wellesley had pushed her palms up against the dark hall paneling, lifted her skirts, and undone his fall all in a matter of seconds. Before she knew it he was inside her.

Charles sucked in her next breath, hands planted against the wall as he angled her hips back towards him.

"Now, Fox"—he nipped her neck before he let his tongue trail her cheekbone—"tell me what work you still have. Tell me what housekeeping duties make it so difficult"—he thrust again —"to enjoy"—he ground into her harder—"my attentions."

The man made her moan out loud. "You cannot . . . I'm not . . ." Words failed her, for it was impossible to think coherently with his lordship inside her, demanding submission. She puddled beneath his touch, pure putty in his hands. For days now he'd taken her at will, all over the house, in impossibly indecent positions. Worst of all, she'd welcomed it. She'd wanted him as badly as he wanted her.

And clearly, this devil of a man knew it.

"Come now, housekeeper, obey my order. It is not your

mouth I now occupy, so give your report while you've breath left to speak."

And an almost guttural, low groan escaped her. Charles was furious at him and equally aroused by him, a state he knew well how to coax from her body, as she ground her hips deeper against him, urging him to give her what she wanted.

"Not yet, my sweet," he breathed the words hot into her ear, unrelenting. "Not till you've given your report. Come, housekeeper, I wish to hear you talk. Speak."

Only the sounds he rent from her were far from decent, or coherent.

&

"And . . . ?"

John was annoyed by his lordship's many questions. Wells sat by the parlor's fire, whiskey in hand, grilling him on the housekeeper's visit to the village madam.

"And I escorted her back, Yer Grace," he finished, hoping this spelled an end to the interrogation. "She's in yer room now, I should think."

John neglected to tell his lordship how surprised Mamie Griswald had been to discover Charles Merrinan on her doorstep, though by now the whole village knew the Duke's son was in residence at Almsdale. John had listened in on their conversation, his ear pressed to the door, and heard Mamie tell Charles she knew the new lord would want his pound of flesh, like any blasted blueblood. She just wished he'd come to her first.

Charles had sounded mortified to admit *she* was that flesh instead.

His lordship continued to stare into the liquid amber of his glass. "She didn't try to flee?"

"No, Yer Grace. Perfectly annoyed by me presence, sir, but

not a lick o' trouble otherwise. Dunno what you've done t' settle her, but she's—"

Wells scowled. "That woman will never settle."

John frowned. "Yer Grace, if I may speak freely a moment, sir?" He figured now was as good a time as any.

Wells nodded.

"The yobs've been makin' noises, sir, 'bout you and yer housekeeper."

His lordship's scowl deepened. "What kinds of noises, Cuthbert?"

"More like *you and she*'ve been makin' noises lately, sir." John looked pointedly at his lordship.

"Do you mean to tell me they're complaining I have a mistress?"

John worried his lip. "Yer Grace, it's less about you havin' a mistress, and more about how often and how, well, loudly you've been havin' said mistress."

Wells paused. "She is rather vocal, I'll grant you that." He grinned. "But why the devil should they care, eh? Bunch of whining ninnies, that crew, and after all I've done for them."

John leveled his gaze. "With respect, Yer Grace, you've fed and housed and kept 'em from trouble, sir, 'tis true, but there's little entertainment here, not like in London. They need a night out now and then—a few pints, a good brawl, a warm body t' bed."

Wells sighed loudly. "I am not about to procure that gang of thugs a harem, John."

"'Course not, Yer Grace." He smirked. "Only y' might, y' know, *temper* yer attentions t' Miss Merrinan some. Be a mite more discreet about the Abbey."

Wells nearly sputtered for outrage. "Cuthbert, if you so much as—"

The steward kept a straight face, though inside he chuckled. "'Course, Yer Grace, shuttin' me trap. Just . . . have a word with her, is all." And then he made for the door, but not before he'd thrown at his lordship, "That much pleasure comin' from a woman's mouth, sir, 'tis enough t' drive *any* man mad."

John grinned to himself all the way down the hall, knowing exactly how it was Lord Wells had tamed Charles Merrinan: She was a glutton for rutting same as he. The two deserved each other.

&

His mistress was asleep when Wells slipped into bed, and he had every intention of waking her but then thought better. He could wait till morning; he wasn't an animal, despite what his men might think.

He reached a hand to stroke her soft, sleek skin. Not even his London mistresses had responded so quickly, so effortlessly, to his advances. They'd been skilled and willing—they were paid to be willing—but this girl . . . He was growing stiff just pressed against her in the bed. This girl, he knew in his core, enjoyed him too. It was an added delight he'd not expected when she'd been tossed at his feet, covered in chicken shit, and it made his desire for her that much more intense. But Cuthbert was right; as more staff came on they could ill afford to continue rutting about the Abbey. Well *he* could. His housekeeper could not.

He sighed, letting his hand trace the line of her spine before he settled at the sweet swell of one buttock. Wells lingered there a moment, pressing his fingers into her flesh to make the luscious cheek dimple.

Then he took himself in hand, rather than wake her, for if he didn't relieve himself soon he'd find no rest this night. None.

&

Only it was she who woke him the next morning, peppering a trail of feather-light kisses down the middle of Wells's chest, landing at his swollen sex before mounting and riding him awake. His eyes opened, half-lidded with lust.

"My lord," she greeted, her hands tracing stomach muscle as she ground her hips along his length.

"Christ, woman." He shook the sleep from his brain. "Who taught you how to wake a man thus?"

She leaned forward, her breasts tantalizingly close to his lips. "You did, Lord Wells."

He awoke fully in that moment, grabbing hold of her haunches to urge her faster on until he could wait no more and pulled her off, spilling his seed against her thigh as she collapsed atop him, her body a warm and welcome weight upon his own.

"You lovely, lovely creature." He nuzzled her neck.

"Mmm . . ." The sound purred in her throat. "Good morning, Roland."

He flinched at so intimate an address, but then remembered he'd given her permission to use his name in bed. And so she had, only not as he'd expected.

"Charles," he warned.

She immediately resumed formality. "Forgive me, my lord. I merely missed your attentions last night."

"Missed me, eh?" He drew her closer, wrapping his arms tight about her. "I did not wish to wake you, and so, it seems, you chose to wake me instead."

"But you have woken me plenty in past." She frowned. "Why hesitate last night?"

Wells had the distinct impression his mistress was trying to puzzle out what made him tick both in and out of bed, alarmed to imagine her so cunning. Then again, she was his Fox. And a mistress was expected to anticipate her master's desires. She was learning the role. Isn't that what he'd wanted?

"The men have been complaining to Cuthbert about us."
He decided to be frank. "I suppose it gave me pause."

"Complaining?" She seemed instantly piqued. "Well I've a
complaint or two myself when it comes to that passel of good-
for-nothings who barely keep their—"

"Charles," he warned again.

"My lord." She met his eyes with disdain. "They are
uncivilized."

He burst into laughter.

"Why are you laughing?" She looked doubly aggrieved.

"Because . . ." He was in stitches. "Because you look so
appalled, woman!" He tried to calm his laughter, yet he could
not quell his mirth. "Forgive me, Fox, I am thinking only of
how . . . Well, let us be honest, Charles." He gathered his wits.
"You are rather the pot calling the kettle black, my dear."

"I do not comprehend you, my lord." She stiffened.

He merely raised a brow as his hand stroked the tip of one
pink, delicious nipple into a perfect, pretty peak, causing her
cheeks to blush a lovely hue of red.

"I happen to *like* how uncivilized you've become of late,
Charles, and only find it amusing to discover you still think
yourself—"

"Moral? Principled?" she burst out, fast removing her body
from his grasp. "It was *you*, sir, who insisted I distinguish
mistress from whore, but apparently I am no better, and you
have made me one in the eyes of all your men." She scrambled
from the bed to hurriedly begin to dress.

"Charles," he sighed deeply from the pillows, "why must
our every interaction turn so swiftly into disagreement,
woman?"

"Why?" Her eyes blazed. "Because our interactions are
based not on respect, my lord, but on abuse of power. *Your*
power. I'll not deny I enjoy our sexual congress. It shocks me
that I do, but that is not what fuels our debate. What fuels our

continued disagreement is that you see me as mere body upon which to slake your lust, rather than a thinking, feeling, being with needs equal to your own." She was vibrating with anger. "So do not call me a pot, sir, when your kettle is just as black."

His mistress abruptly turned from him and impossibly, stormed out.

Wells lay there, stunned. The way this woman took him to task was inconceivable. Why, he ought to bend her over his lap for another sound thrashing! A thought which only made his cock twitch in response as he forced the image from his mind. Why the devil he allowed her to talk to him as she did baffled, for it was not the first time she'd been so brazen in her speech —and no doubt would not be the last. Yet each time her words pushed and poked his conscience, he felt as aroused as he felt enraged, and a part of him also undeniably chastened. He wanted her to think better of him, damn it, which only maddened him more.

Bloody hell, he hissed as he got out of bed to dress and head to the south wall, to *that* pile of rubble, as far from his infuriating housekeeper as possible.

Charles stormed straight from Lord Wellesley's bed into the kitchen, where she knew his blasted men would be breaking fast before commencing the day's work. She launched herself into their midst, picking up a ladle and saucepan on her way in, before she stepped atop a chair and cracked both loudly over her head.

They fell quiet to a man, staring at her in shock.

No doubt she looked like a witch perched up there: hair akimbo, spoon and pan gripped fiercely in both hands.

"Miss Merrinan," Cuthbert cautioned from a corner.

"Don't you Miss Merrinan me, John Cuthbert." Her eyes

shot daggers at him before she glowered at the lot. "I've your attention at last and will damn well use it."

One could have heard a pin drop, the room fell suddenly so still.

"Now, you louts, listen up. I will no longer tolerate the disrespect you continue to show me. I may be Lord Wellesley's mistress, but I am housekeeper here too, and that position affords me control of the Abbey, under which roof *you* reside. So unless you wish to eat in the filthy stables where you sleep, you will behave yourselves in this kitchen, in these halls, and towards my person. Have I made myself clear, *gentlemen*?" The word was vinegar on her tongue.

They stared at her, slack-jawed with equal parts horror and horn.

"Today our new cook, Mrs. Jenkins, arrives—a respected, upstanding widow whose culinary powers will have you slobbering like dogs. And though you don't deserve to lick the pots she cooks in, you will behave yourselves in her presence or I swear to God I'll castrate every one of you in your sleep."

They continued to stare up at her, rapt, though it might have been her bosom that enthralled them most, she wasn't sure. Even Cuthbert looked impressed.

"And if a one of you so much as breathes a hint of my relations with his lordship to Mrs. Jenkins or anyone else in all of Cumberland, I'll have no qualms informing his lordship you dared lay hands on me. And *then*, gentlemen, we'll see what 'his grace' does with you. And this only after I've cut off your puny cleppets."

"Now that's not fair, lass," one of them piped up, looking confused by the word cleppets. "We've ne'er once laid a finger on yer, an' y' knows it."

She narrowed her eyes to slits. "Aye," she hissed, "yet I'll perjure myself to hell, I will. I shall knowingly swear lies upon the Holy Bible just to see you louts suffer."

That seemed to finally cow them.

"But neither am I cruel, lads, for if you promise me this, if you treat me with respect, keeping my reputation intact, I'll give you what you want most of all."

"What we want?" scoffed a voice. "Said yerself you'll not splay yer legs fer us, woman."

She bit her tongue from lashing back and instead inhaled a breath. "'Tis true, boys, I do but one man's bidding in bed and that's his lordship." It almost physically hurt Charles to say this. "However, I've arranged for the village madam to service you all, two a night she'll take for modest coin. But only if you give me your word, each of you now, that you will keep my relations with Lord Wells secret."

She'd been appalled by all Miss Griswald had told her— more appalled, in fact, that she'd not been more shocked by the woman's crass words. Because what Charles now did daily with his lordship at the Abbey was no different, really, than what Mamie did for blunt. Wellesley had told her a mistress was no whore, but from what the village madam had explained, little seemed to separate the two.

And the idea these men all saw her as such was unbearable.

She caught Cuthbert's eye, who nicked his head in tacit approval before he stepped forward to interject.

"Oi!" he shouted above the fray. "You've me word, Miss Merrinan." He looked serious. "I'll keep me mouth shut." He poked the man next to him.

"Aye, you've mine, too," the man grumbled.

"An' mine," said another.

"Hell, if there's a woman for us I'll stay mum," shouted one.

"Aye!" came shouts from several more until each man, at last, had sworn an oath.

Charles exhaled relief. "Good," she told them. "Decide

who sees Miss Griswald first, and I'll arrange she take those men tonight."

The room burst into raucous debate as she caught Cuthbert looking displeased he'd have to manage the ruckus she'd just caused. Then she quietly slipped out, grabbing a bite of yesterday's loaf for breakfast and making her way to the sea room for some blessed peace and quiet.

CHAPTER THIRTEEN

Wells rolled up his sleeves as he approached the worksite, the crack of stone being hewn punctuating the brisk morning air. He spotted Adams and made his approach.

"Put me to work, sir. I've a need for it."

"Milord, I don't know as 'tis wise for—"

"I don't care if it's wise, man," Wells stated gruffly. "I pay your wages and I'll work my own wall if I please."

"As y' like, Wells." Adams dared the informal. "Only if y' work my styan, y' work for me too, sir."

The two men's gazes met.

"I'll not have no Duke's heir do wrong by my wall, even if he's t' one as is payin' for it."

Wells's scowl tipped into a grin. "Sir, 'tis why I hired you. Now put me to work, Adams."

And with a smirk, the good man did.

Almsdale's new cook arrived at noon by wagon, her belongings stacked high behind her. Charles watched Mrs. Jenkins approach—seated ramrod straight beside Cuthbert—then remembered to pull off her hastily made apron before she ran downstairs to greet her. As she hurried across the courtyard, patting her hair into place, she passed Mr. Adams at work on the south wall and waved up to him as he waved back. And then she nearly tripped her feet, for she could have sworn she'd stared straight at his lordship's muscular back, lifting stone beside another man.

Adams climbed down from the scaffold. "Good day, Miss Merrinan."

"Mr. Adams." Charles nicked her head.

"That Mrs. Jenkins I spy, t' be Lord Wellesley's new cook?" He nodded towards the wagon.

"It is indeed, sir." Charles suppressed a proud smile. "And his lordship's not a clue how sporney he is."

"Nor you, miss." Adams's eyes sparkled back, looking her over in approval. They both knew how fine a chef Jenkins was, just as Charles knew Adams's roving eye meant no harm. The stonemason remained an incorrigible flirt, but the benign sort: married. "You'll be eatin' well now, miss. Cuthbert'll be pleased too."

"Aye." She grinned. "'Tis a grand day for us all." But her smile faded fast as she looked back at the Abbey's wall. "Mr. Adams, I could have sworn I saw Lord Wellesley . . ." Charles worried her bottom lip. "Surely he is not laboring alongside your men, sir?"

Adams winked. "Surely is." He lowered his voice. "Came out all in a fratch this mornin' and said I were t' put him t' work. Said I could even order him about." He looked near gleeful telling her this.

Charles's jaw slacked.

"Couldn't believe my ears, I know," he told her. "But he's

no dosser, miss. He's worked hard as any gadgie this day, and I'm grateful t' have him. We'll make good progress if he keeps this up."

She was still stunned Lord Wellesley would dirty his hands at stonework.

Adams met her eye. "So you make sure he gets a good rest after, miss. A hot bath I should think for sore muscles, and Mrs. Jenkins's fine supper for his belly with a glass or two of his cellar's best. I'd like Wells back at work t'morrow, if you catch my drift."

In wonder, Charles watched his lordship continue to work. He was so focused on his task he was oblivious to her presence in the yard.

"Aye, Mr. Adams, I'll turn down his bed with an extra pillow tonight. He's sure to need it." She was still staring, making Adams stare back at her.

"Well get on then, miss. Looks as if Jenkins is waitin' for you t' stop eyein' his lordship and go greet her like t' proper housekeeper you now is."

Charles startled back into action, quickly striding over to welcome the new cook inside the Abbey in order to show the lady to her room—finished in the nick of time for her arrival.

True to form, Jenkins immediately began to order Cuthbert about, telling him where to put her things, and he did not look pleased. Charles had failed to mention that Mrs. Jenkins was not only a fine cook but a bossy cook, thinking it would do the Abbey's ruffians good to have another woman here to keep them in line.

"Miss Merrinan, the room's sommit lovely, right down to its rug. You've made me most welcome, dear," the lady praised as she looked about.

"Ma'am, we are honored to have you cook for his lordship and welcome you to our staff."

"Aye," said Jenkins, "only where's t' rest of your staff,

miss?" She frowned. "I'll need a scullery at t' least, not t' mention a girl t' help me chop." Her face scrunched. "And just how many mouths am I t' feed?"

It was Charles's turn to frown. "Did you not discuss the particulars of your employment with Lord Wellesley, Mrs. Jenkins?"

"I did not." The widow's lips pursed. "I were told his housekeeper'd see t' all my needs."

Charles's heart sank, thinking Wellesley had done this to her on purpose, the blackguard.

"Well," she forced a smile, "I'm afraid his lordship failed to mention such detail to *me*, but I will discuss matters with him today in order to procure you more help, Mrs. Jenkins. There are nineteen of us currently at the Abbey, including yourself, and with the exception of we ladies and his lordship's steward, Mr. Cuthbert, the only person you need truly cook for is Lord Wellesley. The rest can eat swill for all I care," she added under her breath.

"Good t' know, Miss Merrinan." The widow grinned. "Looks like I'll be cookin' for four then, and merely feedin' t' other fifteen."

Charles smiled. "I think we shall get on well together, ma'am." She made for the door. "I'll let you unpack before I show you the kitchen."

"And your room, miss?" the widow called after her. "Should I need t' find you?"

"I shall show you that as well, yes." Charles hurried downstairs to grab paper and ink to start another long list. She intended to sit down with Lord Wellesley that evening to make a few things abundantly clear.

❧

"Madam," Wells started, his mouth crammed full of food as he simultaneously attempted to swallow and speak, for he was that hungry after the day's labor—and his palate that pleased. "You've outdone yourself, truly." He gobbled another mouth-watering bite. "I am beyond impressed." His satisfied smile made the widow beam.

"Well then, you enjoy your meal, milord. Looks as if you've earned it." She took in his disheveled state with a critical eye as Wells looked down at his rolled-up shirtsleeves and recalled the scratch marring his cheek. The scratch still smarted.

"Mmm." He tried to speak again. "Best damn meal I've had in months." He checked himself. "Begging your pardon, Mrs. Jenkins."

"No offense taken, milord." She gave him a bright smile. "Miss Merrinan said you'd appreciate my cookin', and I see now as she were right."

Only at the mention of his housekeeper Wellesley's humor turned; he was still hurt by her behavior from the morning.

"Has she seen you well settled, madam?"

"She has, sir. A fine housekeeper you've hired in Charles. Everyone knows that girl for t' good head on her shoulders. Smartest young lady for miles, t' come from sech family as hers."

But before he could ask what she meant by 'such family,' Miss Merrinan herself appeared, stopping short at the doorway to see him still shoveling food into his mouth.

She proceeded to ignore him. "Mrs. Jenkins, I came to enquire if—"

"If it were time for dinner? Aye." The widow laughed. "Only his lordship here found me first, and starvin' man that he were, set t' eatin' afore I could even set him a proper plate."

Charles scowled at Wells, who chose to ignore her too.

"Well, you let me know when he has finished"—the imper-tinent miss spoke right over his head—"and then I'll send the others up with Cuthbert." She paused. "And if you'd like to dine separately with me, Mrs. Jenkins, you may find it considerably more agreeable than sharing a table with Almsdale's *horde*."

And out she flounced as Wells continued his meal, deciding he was not done being angry at her, either.

֍

Later that evening, as Wells soaked his aching body in the delicious hot bath he'd found waiting in his room, his housekeeper marched in unannounced. She had her ledger in hand and pulled up a chair beside him.

"You might have knocked," he muttered.

"And you might have sent me away."

"I may still."

"Then I'd best be quick." She tossed him a look as he sank below the water, refusing to respond to her sass.

When he eventually came up he found her still there, glaring at him. "Go on then," he growled, "out with it."

"You did not tell me Mrs. Jenkins required a scullery and sous-chef."

"Well that's a housekeeper's job to figure out, now isn't it?"

"I can hardly figure something out when I am denied information, my lord."

"Really?" He raised a brow. "And here I thought you clever, Charles."

He watched her swallow, as if debating her retort.

"We are going to require additional staff, my lord, if you wish to see Almsdale restored sooner rather than later."

Wells found her formal tone amusing.

"There will be more laundry now, and if I'm to prepare more rooms, I shall need help cleaning. I will need at least two more girls to handle this work, plus the two Jenkins needs in her kitchen, and if you wish to entertain, my lord, we will need footmen as well, for I do not think a single one of your men capable of—"

He cut her off. "I shall *not* be entertaining." Then he promptly sank back underwater and remained there a good long while. When he resurfaced, he saw alarm etched on her face.

Wells could hold his breath for ages. What he could not always hold was his tongue. "Why must you pester me with household details, woman, when I wish only to relax in my bath?"

She harrumphed. "I beg your pardon, my lord, for simply doing my job." She got up to leave. "I take it you approve the cost of hiring four additional staff?"

He waved her away, closing his eyes. "Yes, yes."

"And I may hire whom I like without receiving your approval first?"

"Yes, of course. You're housekeeper here, aren't you?" He was in no mood to discuss matters further.

"Very good, Lord Wellesley, enjoy your bath." She closed the door with a pronounced slam as he filled his lungs and sank back under, the water drowning out her angry footsteps receding down the hall.

CHAPTER FOURTEEN

Wells awoke early, sore but refreshed, and eager to return to the stone. It had felt bloody good to work his body yesterday, and he meant to do more. Just as he'd worked alongside his crew at sea, he'd work here, too, on the Abbey. He was able-bodied enough, and hell and devil if it wasn't better to tire oneself with physical labor and in so doing, tire one's infernal mind. Besides, Adams's men had warmed to him some by day's end; they'd see today he meant to pull his weight. His pitching in would also see the job finished that much faster.

He'd grabbed a slice of cold meat pie from yesterday's dinner before heading out, passing Jenkins in the hall, who told him he should come back in an hour for proper breakfast for *my, but don't his lordship rise early!* He'd merely winked at her, mouth full, to indicate he would. Wells thanked his lucky stars Charles had found him such a fine cook—and good riddance to Tom's sodding stews.

Only then he thought of his housekeeper, wondering how she'd slept on her hard little bed last night, in that drafty closet room of hers. Cold, no doubt, without hearth for heat. He felt a twinge of guilt before he quashed it, imagining she'd learn to curb her tongue now that she knew *his* bed at least was warm. In fact, he would insist she come to him with an apology that included a good fuck, which he'd deny her out of hand, making her regret her words to him that much more. She must learn her words bore consequences not even her body could repair—and just see how long she held out. He gave her another day at most before she came begging him to bed her, for his mistress was a hoyden, through and through.

"Milord," exclaimed Adams in surprise. "Joinin' us again, sir?"

"I am," said Wells. "The sooner we finish the better, and if that means I put my back into it, so be it."

Adams looked him over. "Glad t' have you. 'T'ain't often a workin' man finds a blueblood willin' t' break a sweat."

"I spent some years at sea," Wells offered, "and I can tell you she cares not a whit what blood you're made of. She'll swallow a man on a whim only to spit his bones to shore."

"That where your London fellas come from?"

"Indeed," said Wells, smiling. "A rough but loyal crew. I swore I'd give them work in the off season, but they'll set sail again come spring with a new captain; my days at sea are over."

"Glad t' hear it, sir." Adams grinned at him. "For you ain't half bad here on land." He tipped his hat to Wells before hollering to his men, "Lord Wellesley's back, lads, so make sure he gives as good as he gets!"

A few stoneworkers looked up to nod at Wells, who'd already rolled up his sleeves, preparing to prove his worth again today, even if a certain housekeeper didn't see it in him.

Charles had a few girls in mind for laundry and housemaid but had needed to confer with Jenkins as to scullery and kitchen help. With names in hand she next sought Cuthbert, only to be told he was working the south wall. So out she went, greeting Mr. Adams for the second day in a row.

"Mornin', Miss Merrinan," he called down to her. "Fancy seein' you again, lass."

"Yes, Mr. Adams, duty calls." She made a face. "Is Mr. Cuthbert here? I need a word with him, if I may."

"You may, and he is." Adams hollered over his shoulder, "Cuthbert! You're wanted!"

The steward looked up from his work, even as Lord Wells did too, his eyes meeting Charles's for no more than a second before he turned his back to her.

She felt her cheeks pink and hoped Adams hadn't noticed.

Cuthbert climbed down. "What's it now?" he grumbled.

"I need to go into town."

He merely glared at her.

She glared back. "Will you take me?"

"No." He scowled. "I'm in the middle o' somethin'."

Her own frown deepened. "Then I shall go myself," Charles announced, spinning on her heel to march off towards the stables, thinking she'd show the steward she'd manage just fine without him.

"Now wait just a—!" he yelled after her, his footsteps fast following.

***

A few minutes later and John was back at the wall.

"Yer Grace?" he called up to his lordship, who expelled an oath before swinging himself down from the scaffolding.

"Speak, man."

"Yer housekeeper insists she needs t' go to town, sir." John kept his voice low, nodding towards the stables. "T' see about the new help, hirin' the staff you agreed to. Only I can't take her now meself and—"

"Blasted woman," Wells huffed. "Let her go, John, but have her tailed. Put Fergus or Pinky on her. I don't think she'll bolt, but nor do I trust her entirely either."

"Yes, sir." He nodded. "Pinky 'tis."

"And John . . ."

"Sir?"

"Have Pinky see me after. I'll want a report."

John nicked his head in answer before he took off for the stables again, thinking that if Adams had overheard their conversation he'd wonder why his lordship took such interest in his housekeeper—and why his steward addressed his lordship as 'his grace.' Though if the man were smart, he'd forget whatever he'd just heard.

Charles felt glorious in the saddle, on the road, alone. She hadn't ridden in years, and the mount she'd been grudgingly given was a sweet old mare that barely needed handling. The horse plodded along at an easy pace while Charles took in the fresh fall air and raucous birdsong. She relished the fact she was at last outside the Abbey's walls—without Cuthbert stuck at her side like an ornery burr.

That she was being followed did not surprise her; she'd expected as much. But even this did not irk Charles. She had no need to flee if Lord Wells had lost interest in bedding her, because now she might be wholly and truly housekeeper of Almsdale, a respectable position with respectable pay. She could save her earnings till she had dowry enough for Eleanor and a bit left over for herself. And she'd have help about the Abbey soon too. She'd not be the only one scrubbing furniture, walls, and floors. Eventually, she'd do no scrubbing at all but simply manage her staff. That, after all, was what a real housekeeper did.

She urged her steed on, nudging the old mare into a trot, then a canter, and finally, feeling reckless, pushed her into a gallop. Only after a minute or two her mount balked at the exertion. Charles let her fall back into her steady amble. She'd not tax the poor creature more on such a glorious day as this. She could enjoy a slow ride too. After all, who knew when she'd be allowed out again on her own. Or perhaps she might steal a better horse next time to go joyriding on a day when Lord Wells was absent. Though when that might be . . .

No, she chastised herself. She'd not steal a horse, she'd simply borrow one. She would not add horse thief to her list of crimes.

Her thoughts reverted to Lord Wellesley at the south wall this morning, working alongside Adams's men. Who the devil did he think he was, laboring like a commoner? He did not behave like a duke's son, and she felt further stymied by his actions. Why he'd left London in the first place was a mystery still, not to mention why he'd brought such a rough crew of men with him. As to why he'd roll up his sleeves like a field hand, lifting stone . . . She could not fathom the man.

Yet the vision of his bare forearms resurfaced in her mind. She felt a small ache in her middle, realizing she'd missed his touch last night. Not his anger, not his prodding, and certainly not his pompous behavior—just his touch.

Charles sighed, irritated with herself for thinking of Lord Wellesley at all.

❦

Wells heard the clatter of hooves in the courtyard and looked up, surprised to see both Charles and Pinky ride in on their respective mounts. He grimaced to imagine why the devil Pinky now accompanied her back, but he willed himself not to react. He'd find out later.

Still, his mistress looked good on a horse, confident even. Cuthbert had done right to give her an old nag, but she sat the beast well. And she'd donned his old breeches again, making her shape that much more . . . He shook off the thought. Where the deuce had *she* learned to ride? Did all Cumberland women know their way around a horse? He found that hard to believe, especially given Cuthbert's description of her family. Wells clenched his fists as he heard whistles and catcalls from Adams's men. Charles had just dismounted and damn but if those breeches didn't hug her arse tight.

Adams barked his disgust. "Leave off," he shouted, glowering at his men, "or I'll box ears myself." Then he called down to Charles, "Beg pardon, miss. They're not used t' seein' a lass dressed as a lad."

"No offense taken, Mr. Adams." She smiled up at him, bold as could be. "Were a side saddle in sight I'd have kept my skirts, but as it were, I'd no choice but to straddle my mount."

Wells heard the men around him suck in their breaths while his face burned. She'd meant those words for him, he knew.

He ushered a swift rebuke. "You'll don skirts if you want to keep your position here, woman." His voice thundered across the courtyard. "No servant of mine parades her wares about my Abbey like a common strumpet."

Charles blushed crimson at his dress down, bobbed a meek, skirtless curtsy, and scurried inside the Abbey.

Adams caught his eye as Wells muttered, "She's a mouth on her, that one."

"Aye," the mason said with a smirk, "that she do."

And they all returned to work, Wells seething inside while still aroused by her figure—along with half the men beside him no doubt too.

CHAPTER FIFTEEN

Charles wanted to murder him for the humiliation she'd just endured, yet she'd no one to blame but herself again. It had simply popped from her mouth, that bit about straddling her mount, and it had been true too, damn it. She knew perfectly well how to ride in skirts but not in a man's seat. She'd had no choice but to don breeches. What's more, she was respected enough in Cumberland that no one had commented the entire stretch she'd ridden through the village. Yet here, in front of Adams's men, all of whom *were* her folk, she'd been called out harshly by his lordship. Why, he'd all but ruined her reputation with his words, the blasted, self-righteous, conceited devil!

As she stood in her small room hastily fastening her dress, she wiped angry tears from her eyes. Nothing had gone right from the moment she'd tried stealing those two lousy chickens from Lord Wellesley. *That* had been her true moment of ruin, and perhaps she should simply embrace it. She was a fallen woman, after all: forced to become his mistress even if he'd not taken her by force outright. Was there really any difference, mistress or whore? Charles thought she'd reconciled her shame in this, but now Adams's men would think her a 'hoor' instead of a lady. Even Mamie Griswald had used the term during their talk.

Charles winced, for Mr. Adams had always treated her family with the utmost respect. She hated to think he, too, would think less of her now.

"And that's it then? She found you out, you oaf, and invited you to ride back with her?" Wells had nearly finished grilling Pinky, though his mood remained foul—despite having enjoyed another of his cook's fine dinners.

"Aye, Capt'n. Kept me distance the whole time, I did, but she's no fool, sir. Knew I were skulkin' behind. Likely didn't think you'd let 'er out alone anyways."

Wells snorted. "Likely, yes. And she merely visited prospective staff, she didn't try to visit her father and sister?"

"No sir. Kept t' her work, she did, an' didn't dally neither. Even tried t' make the ol' mare run, she did." He laughed. "But the beast weren't 'avin' it, slowed right down again."

Wells pictured Charles urging her aging mount into a gallop and almost smiled. "Alright, Pinky, you may go. But next time I ask you to tail someone you'd best do it right."

"Sure, Capt'n. Only honest, sir, she's got eyes in the back of her head, she do. That woman's like a—"

"Enough, Pinky. Go."

And out the fellow went.

Wells leaned back in his chair and took up his whiskey again. Should he speak with Charles? Or let her stew another night? Would she seek him out, to report on the new staff? He was mulling precisely this when in she walked.

"My lord." She curtsied low.

"Miss Merrinan," he answered clipped.

"I've procured the additional staff you approved, sir, to start next week. I'll need to ready two more rooms with Cuthbert's help, if you can spare him or another man to assist me in the coming days."

Wells nodded.

"I should also like . . ." She faltered. "I should also like to request a side saddle, my lord, for when I need to ride into town on future errands."

He let her stand there a moment longer in her humiliation before he told her, "In future you will take the wagon into town."

She bit her lip. "My lord, there is but one wagon here and it is often in use. A side saddle might be used by others, not just myself, should any staff need to—"

"Do you mean to tell me all the women of Cumberland ride as well as you, miss?" He arched his brow.

"No, my lord," she ground out. "I merely meant to say that any saddle purchased would benefit more than just my—"

"Your unseemly display before a crew of men today will not go unpunished, Miss Merrinan." Wells willed himself to remain in control. "Therefore, you will use the wagon in future and you will *not* ride publicly astride a horse again while in my employment."

Her mouth tightened.

"For someone as concerned about her reputation as you claim to be, I was surprised by the brazen behavior you displayed this afternoon."

She again bit her lip.

"Have you nothing to say for yourself, miss?"

Her eyes flashed up at him, burning. "No, my lord," she gritted. "Would you like another bath brought to your room tonight, sir?"

"Yes," he told her. "You may go now."

And out she went, slamming the door behind her.

Wells leaned back in his chair, tension draining from his body. God but he wanted her again, badly. He told himself he didn't, that he wanted her apology well-and-good first, but the image of those sweet hips of hers sashaying across the courtyard in his breeches . . . He felt his trousers tighten. No, he'd make her wait. She'd come begging before long. She wanted him as badly as he wanted her.

Although a tiny voice inside his heart warned that maybe she did not.

John stood in the shadows, enjoying his evening pipe, as he watched Miss Merrinan enter the courtyard. She hung a blanket over the clothesline and swung at it halfheartedly before she increased her pace. Soon she began to beat at the cloth with such vehemence that she was fast enveloped in a cloud of dust, forced to back away, coughing and hacking from the plumes.

"There now, miss." His voice made her startle as he approached. "What's all this so late at night?"

"Needed . . . airing out, Cuthbert." Charles gasped to catch her breath. "All the . . . blankets do." She gulped more air.

"True, but can't it wait till the morrow, gel?"

"My room is rather cold, Cuthbert," she wheezed.

"Right." He frowned. "Only I thought that room were more for show than use, miss."

"Well, it's being used now." She began to beat the blanket with renewed zeal.

John stood there a moment longer. "You fightin' again with his grace, Miss Merrinan?"

"That is none of your business, Cuthbert."

"'Tis me business t' know his grace's mind, miss."

"Then go ask him yourself."

"I might just," he shot back.

"Good!" she fumed.

"Fine!"

And off he stormed, only to turn right around and stomp right back. "And y' might try bein' a mite more agreeable, miss. His grace ain't always the easiest man t' serve, but he's one o' the fairest and most decent masters I've ever—"

Charles swung her paddle at his head, making John duck fast.

"Fair?" she shouted. "Decent?" Her eyes flashed and her bosom heaved with exertion. She was quite the sight.

"Did you hear what he called me today in front of Adams's men, sir? *Did* you?"

"Well now, all I know is that you—"

"He called me a strumpet, Cuthbert! He *made* me into one and now he's publicly called me out, ruined me with one word. One bloody word! How will I be able to look my sister in the face after this, or my father?"

John winced.

"Mr. Adams has always respected my family, but after today, he and everyone else will think me no better than the whore Lord Wellesley forced me to become. Because he did, you know. He gave me no choice but to bed him in payment for two goddamned chickens. So he may be a fair and decent master to you, John Cuthbert, and to his men, but to me, a woman, he has been nothing but cruel and detestable from the start."

John took umbrage at this. "Now look here, miss. From what I heard today, 'twere yer own words as forced his grace t' call you out. Now I'll grant he could've used a different term, but y' baited him, gel, just as you've baited him before. A bit less sass and a bit more respect and you'd see a changed man for sure. For y' can't speak to no duke's son the way y' do, Charles. 'Tis a wonder he's not throttled you already."

"Throttled?" She gaped. "He beat me, Cuthbert, whipped me with his belt! And *you* are one to speak, with you and your men all calling him *Yer Grace* to his face. How is it you are allowed to disrespect his lordship but I am not?"

"What we call him ain't none o' yer business." He narrowed his gaze. "But the way you goad him, woman, Christ," he muttered. "No wonder he called you a strumpet. You're incorrigible."

And her face fell, the corners of her mouth beginning to tremble almost, making him sense she was trying most hero-ically not to burst into tears. Against his better judgment, John pulled her in for a hug.

"There now, miss, I'm sorry I said as much. Go and have a good cry, you're no less if y' do." And weep she did, the flood-gates opening upon his coat as he awkwardly patted her back.

"I don't know what is wrong with me, Cuthbert," she told him through her tears, her voice muffled into his chest. "He makes me so angry, all the time, and yet he also—"

"There, there," he shushed her. "'Twill all be better come mornin'. He'll forgive you, miss, he's not a bad man, I know he's not. Only he's not like us, you ken? He's a duke's son, Charles. Raised t' command, t' order. He knows no other way t' be. You keep pushin' him as you do and he'll lose his temper for good one day."

"I know." She sniffed, pulling her face away to wipe her eyes and straighten her apron. "I know it, John." She spoke more quietly. "Only I don't know how to stop myself. He goads me in ways I—"

"Miss," he told her more firmly, "I've known Lord Wells me whole life. We grew up together. I've sailed half the globe with him." Her eyes grew wide at this. "He's like a brother t' me." John was careful how much he told her. "He's a good man, despite his flaws, and the finest ship's captain ever. He'd never harm you on purpose, miss. I know he cares for you."

"He doesn't, John." She was adamant. "I am just a body to him."

"And he's a body t' you, gel, don't you deny it," he scolded.

She looked briefly chagrined, then stuck out her chin at him. "I don't. I admit I enjoy him. That is not the . . . That is not the source of my anger," she finished.

"Nor the source of his," he said softly. John took a breath. "Which begs the question, Miss Merrinan, as to why the two o' you is so often so angry with one another. When were it just the body y' each craved, you'd be satisfied enough, eh?"

And she reacted with a start, as if she were about to retort. John chose that moment to quietly slip away and leave her to her airing. He watched her take up the paddle again to beat at the blanket with less vehemence this time—with more measured, focused intent.

He hoped the gel had heard him.

§▲

"Yer Grace?" Wells heard Cuthbert call through the door.

"Enter, John," he answered from his bath.

"Pinky's report satisfy, sir?" His steward strode in.

"Yes. Couldn't keep hid long from her though." His eyes met Cuthbert's. "You should've sent Fergus instead. Pinky's still green."

His man nodded. "Next time, Yer Grace, Fergus 'tis."

"Only there won't be a next time, John." Wells grimaced. "She had the audacity to demand from me a side saddle tonight, as if I'd agree to let her ride about anytime she liked. The gall of that woman."

"Well now, Yer Grace, t' be fair, we've only got the one—"

"Wagon, yes. She said as much herself. Don't you dare start defending her, John."

"Weren't about to, sir." Cuthbert chewed his lip. "Only

after the dress down I heard you give her today in front of Adams's men, is it any wonder she——?"

"It's a wonder I haven't tossed her arse out." Wells stepped out of the tub in a spray of flung water.

"Yer Grace," Cuthbert started in again, "I've just come from Miss Merrinan beatin' a blanket half t' death in the courtyard, so I 'spect she's more'n sorry for the trouble she caused today."

"Sorry? Oh I doubt that." Wells snorted. "Sore more like it. She's not apologized yet for her behavior, John, and I'll not tolerate a servant who doesn't know her place."

"And don't I know it," his steward grumbled.

Wells shot him a look. "Watch your tone, John. I know damn well what you're thinking and it——"

"Beggin' yer pardon, Yer Grace, but y' don't know a damned thing when it comes t' me or that gel."

"What the devil makes you think you can speak to me like that?" Wells was stunned.

"'Cause it's the truth, and 'cause I swore an oath t' yer father, Roland Wellesley, that I'd serve you honest and true. But I'll not lie t' you, not even when it suits Yer Grace."

"Fine," Wells growled, which was as much permission as he'd grant his friend and steward.

"She's a wreck, sir, she is. Cried her eyes out just now on me shoulder—you can see yerself the stain she left."

And sure enough, Wells spied the wet spot on John's coat.

"Said you'd ruined her for good, callin' her a strumpet in public like you did. Said you'd made her into a whore and she'd not be able t' look her sister nor father in the eye no more. Said Mr. Adams'd lose all respect for her family."

"Nonsense." Wells roughly toweled himself dry. "She is exaggerating, as women do. And being purposefully emotional in order to manipulate you into feeling sorry for her, John."

"I think I'd know the difference, sir, 'twixt some London lady's manipulations and a Cumberland gel's honest hurt."

Wells quietly fumed.

"She cares for you, clear as day, and even if you don't, you've a duty by her." Cuthbert raised his hand to stop Wells from interrupting, because he'd been about to open his mouth in protest. "You've a duty by her as you took her honor, sir, so you must ensure her reputation ain't further sullied. It's all that gel's got in this community, and though her family's dirt poor they were once of some class. I see and hear it in her sister's every word and breath. Those two were raised t' be ladies, good as any, and what happened to 'em I couldn't say, but I will say this: Charles Merrinan weren't raised to take orders, Yer Grace, and it's fallin' hard on her to take 'em from you now."

Wells was only slightly mollified. He knew he had a responsibility to his mistress, but neither did Cuthbert have the right to needle him like this. He knew she was educated, spoke well, rode well, played chess well. If she *had* been raised a lady then why didn't her family live accordingly? Why thieve chickens from his coop in the middle of the night?

He grudgingly told his man, "I shall take your words under advisement, Cuthbert, but right now I intend to get some sleep. See to it you help Miss Merrinan ready the rooms for the new staff tomorrow. And the next visit you pay her family, I will accompany you."

"Yer Grace." Cuthbert nicked his head in exit, leaving Wells suddenly less offended and perhaps more spurred to action. Perhaps he ought to reevaluate his housekeeper's position, not only at the Abbey, but also in his bed.

CHAPTER SIXTEEN

C harles had very little time in which to ready the two additional servants' rooms needed for more staff. These were in even worse repair than Mrs. Jenkins's had been. Cuthbert and Pinky were repairing the windows in both as she hunted for furniture. Two beds were needed in each, narrow ones at that, and if she didn't find any that fit she'd need Cuthbert to build her some. Tomorrow. Oh, it was a headache to be a housekeeper!

Yet she was eating well—they all were—thanks to Mrs. Jenkins. The Abbey's new cook, at least, was a bright spot in the house and Charles was grateful for the female company. She'd avoided Lord Wells since their last fraught conversation, and she'd avoided Cuthbert too, embarrassed by the tears she'd let flow on his shoulder. He was a decent enough fellow, she'd decided, and his crew of men also more decent than first assumed. They certainly treated her better now that she had introduced them to Miss Griswald. Charles would need to pay the village madam a call again to find out how well *that* arrangement was going.

She was surprised, however, that his lordship continued to

work the south wall alongside Adams's men. She thought by now he'd tire of such hard labor, but it seemed he'd tired of her instead. It had been three days since she'd last shared his bed—not that she minded. And not that she'd be able to anyway, now that her courses had started. It was an added nuisance to wash the bloody rags, but at least she wasn't with child.

And thank heavens for that.

Cuthbert had also brought her another letter from Eleanor, which she'd devoured, relieved Father was well and that the food they'd been receiving had begun to fatten him up. She had the distinct impression his lordship's steward enjoyed making deliveries to her sister, as if he were a little sweet on her. She certainly hoped not. Cuthbert may be rough around the edges, but underneath his gruff exterior he was a virile enough young man—and gentleman enough to court a woman properly, unlike Lord Wellesley.

Only she did *not* want Cuthbert courting Eleanor. She had greater plans for her sister.

Wells was accompanying his steward to the Merrinans, not quite an hour's walk east of the Abbey. It was early and they moved at a brisk pace, Cuthbert with basket in hand while Wells read the letter only grudgingly handed him, as it was intended for Charles's sister. John had protested the invasion of privacy, but Wells had insisted, ignoring his man's deep frown.

"'T'ain't right, sir," his steward had muttered. "That were given me in good faith I'd deliver it t' Miss Eleanor."

"And deliver it you shall, John," Wells had replied. "I am simply reading it before you do."

"Oi, sir, readin' a private letter not meant for anyone's eyes but—"

"Enough!" he'd ground out.

And Cuthbert had blessedly shut his trap.

Eleanor,

You cannot know my relief to receive your letter! It eases my heart, though your loss is keenly felt. I hold out hope Lord Wellesley will grant me leave to visit soon, but I must be patient, as he is not an easy master to read. I try, for the sake of us all, to remain in his good graces so that he continues to feed you and Papa this winter. That is my sole aim and desire, though I have surely offended him once too oft. I have vowed to do better and be better as housekeeper, but some days it is like a storm blows through me, Ellie. I wish I could be more even-tempered like you. I wish for so much in this world, too much, I know. Mama would scold me for even writing such words, but whom else can I confide in? I am lonely, sister, and dearly miss your counsel. Lately, I find myself in sore need of it.

So, Charles was lonely. And wished for far too much. Well, he was lonely too; lonely enough he'd taken her on as mistress. And God knew he wished for what he'd never get in this life: his freedom.

Mrs. Jenkins, at least, has me feeling less maudlin, for I am no longer the sole woman here at Almsdale, and there is comfort in that, as well as in her dishes. Lord Wellesley is pleased with her too. Next week I will have more help: Ginny Maines for laundry, Ruby Barrows for housemaid, and Clarice Helmsworth and Marta Brooks for scullery and kitchen. All girls I can depend on. And so the Abbey slowly becomes a house befitting of a future duke. It is hard work though, Ellie, work I was not raised to. I manage as best I can, but some days when I think of Mama and all she dreamt for us, I ache.

Yet I must share with you my little plan, and believe me when I promise it will indeed come true. I shall set aside my wages for as long as possible. You will have a season, as Mother always wished, to

*find yourself a good and honorable match. And when you do, you will
become the lady you were born, whom you were always meant to be.*

A season? Wells paused in his reading. What the devil was
she talking about?

*I hope Cuthbert delivers you this missive soon. And that he is
respectful when he visits. He is coarse, but kind. I think I might call
him friend now, as much as any man might befriend a woman. He
looks out for me, though, which is more than I can say for Lord
Wellesley. Him I take great care to avoid.*
Kiss Papa and write to me soon, I beg—
Charles

***

John watched Wells refold the letter and roughly hand it
back.

"And?" he asked.

"And what?" his lordship snapped.

"You find what y' wanted, sir?"

"I found she despises me and is quite fond of you," he said
tersely.

John grinned. "Well I'll be . . . Clever girl, t' realize old
Cuthbert ain't the demon she thought."

"Oh no." His lordship chewed his lip. "She considers you
her friend now, and me the devil himself, to avoid at all cost."

"Well now, sir, I'm sure she don't mean half o' what she—"

"What reason should she have to lie in a private letter to
her sister?" He sounded hurt.

"I told you not t' read the letter."

"From now on you are to bring me all her correspondence,
including that of her sister," Wells ordered.

"I will not!"

"You will, as it is my direct order, John."

"It's abuse o' power, is what it is."

"You swore an oath to me, Cuthbert."

"Oi," he said, disgusted, "I did. Only that oath ne'er said I had t' keep me mouth shut." He increased his steps, looking to lose his lordship behind him and furious at Wells for such behavior. He was better than this, ought to be at least, because for this gel to get under his lordship's skin was a sure sign Wells was not himself.

Yet there was Miss Eleanor, gliding towards him, a vision to behold. John promptly forgot all about Lord Wellesley.

"Mr. Cuthbert!" she exclaimed, swiftly taking his arm to walk him towards the house, not at all noticing his lordship some paces back. "So good of you to come, sir. I just put the kettle on before I went to fetch eggs. You'll have a bite with us, won't you?" She looked eagerly up at him.

"Don't mind if I do, miss." He smiled back, pleased as punch she took his arm so readily now. And then he remembered Wells, stopping dead in his tracks.

"Is something the matter, John?" she asked.

"*John* already, is it?" came a voice from behind them, making Eleanor whirl about. "Didn't realize you were on a first-name basis already, Cuthbert." Wells spoke cuttingly as John hastened to make introductions.

"Lord Wellesley, if you'll allow me, sir, this is Miss Eleanor Merrinan, sister t' yer new housekeeper, Charles Merrinan."

Eleanor's eyes grew wide. "My lord." She sank into the lowest curtsy John had ever seen a woman accomplish— holding it—until Wells gave her leave to rise.

"Please, Miss Eleanor, there is no need for you to prostrate yourself so."

She rose, her face flushed. "Will you join us, my lord, for breakfast? We would be honored to have you as our guest."

And she bent her head again, meekly almost, making his lord-ship only more uncomfortable, John could tell.

"The honor, I am sure, is all mine, Miss Eleanor. Pray proceed." Wells waved her forward, though she no longer took John's arm but hurried up the hill to the house, no doubt wishing to reach her father first in order to prepare the old man for visitors.

Only it wouldn't have mattered either way, because Mr. Merrinan already sat at the table, drooling, when they entered the house. He looked up bleary-eyed at Eleanor.

"Charles, dear, that you?" he asked.

"No, Papa, I am Eleanor," she corrected. "Remember, Charles works at the Abbey now, for his lordship."

"For his grace?" The fellow was confused, as usual. "What-ever does she do there, Ellie?"

"Not his grace, Papa, his grace's son, Lord Wellesley. She is his housekeeper, Father. Now look sharp, for Mr. Cuthbert has brought Lord Wellesley to visit us this morning. You are to address him accordingly, yes?" She nudged him again. "Father?"

Only his eyes had sunk in on themselves, all their light extinguished, as his chin dropped, in another stupor.

Eleanor looked to John, who smiled with reassurance, before she turned to Lord Wells. "You must forgive my father's lack of decorum, my lord. Ever since our mother's death he's not been himself. He shall revive again as soon as I serve break-fast. I beg you, please be seated. I shall have plates ready in no time." She curtsied again, hurrying out.

John sat down and indicated his lordship ought to do the same.

***

Wells followed his steward's lead, seating himself across

from Mr. Merrinan and looking about him in some shock. There were barely any furnishings in this house. In fact, it looked as if the very rugs had been sold from underfoot, in a home run down but decidedly more grand than he'd expected. It looked like a rural magistrate's house, or a clergyman's, roomy enough and hewn of stone, with a slate, rather than thatched roof. No wonder Adams had been by for repairs in past.

The walls were cracked, though patching had been attempted, and faded plaster showed where paintings once had hung. Even the curtains were few and far between. His Fox had not lied; this dwelling confirmed her family had been starving.

Miss Eleanor returned with tea, but no milk or sugar, and out of politeness Wells did not remark. He'd keep his mouth shut this visit, for Charles's sister was behaving with perfect grace; he'd make damn sure he did too.

Mr. Merrinan in that moment perked up, his eyes meeting Wells's with surprise. "Wellesley?" he asked. "That you, man? How the devil do you look so young, sir, when I am grown so old?" He laughed.

Wells frowned but Cuthbert interrupted before he could reply. "Mr. Merrinan, sir, 'tis his grace's son come t' visit, not his father, the Duke. Lord Wellesley's restoring Almsdale Abbey, sir, where yer daughter, Charles, is now housekeeper, remember?"

"Housekeeper?" The old man's bushy brow knit with consternation. "Charles ought to be married and settled by now, not working as someone's housekeeper." He harrumphed. "Who does his grace think he is, employing my daughter as if she were some common—"

Eleanor rushed in. "Father!" she hissed from the door. "You will address Lord Wellesley respectfully, sir, or I shall send you to your room." She threw Wells a worried glance. "Charles is fortunate to have the position she does at the Abbey and Lord

Wellesley has been kind enough to keep us both fed, so you"—
she almost lost her temper—"keep your thoughts to yourself,
Papa." She nearly spilled the cup she pushed at him. "Drink
your tea," she hissed again, apologizing profusely, "My lord, he
is not of right mind anymore, you mustn't take what he says
personally. I am terribly sorry if he offended in any way, truly."
Her gaze pleaded.

Wells smiled kindly at her. "No offense taken, miss. I
promise not to mind a thing he says, have no fear."

She breathed a sigh of relief before disappearing again into
the kitchen.

Wells met Cuthbert's eye. "I see now what you meant."

His man nodded. "He's right befuddled, he is."

Yet the old fellow was back within moments. "Duke's boy,
eh?" Merrinan eyed Wells closely. "I remember when he was
but a lad, came to visit us he did, ran around with Charles out
back." He again laughed. "All grown up I see." He sank back
into thought. "Eleanor, where is Mother?" he suddenly called
out. "She ought to be here with our guests. Go and fetch her,
dear. And where is Charles? That girl is never where she's
needed. She'll be the death of me, she will."

Eleanor returned bearing food, serving Wells first and then
Cuthbert. "Father, Mother is not well, remember? And Charles
is tending to her, so you must entertain our guests. Be good,
now, and I shall bring your plate."

She looked to Cuthbert, who took it upon himself to
speak.

"Mr. Merrinan, it's right fine weather we're havin' this fall,
wouldn't you say, sir?"

"Weather?" The old man glared at Cuthbert. "The
weather is beastly out here, man. Stole my wife it did, took her
from me, my love." His eyes filled with tears, making Cuthbert
look as though he rued the words he'd just said.

"Tell me, sir, did you know my father, the Duke of Allendale?" Wells interrupted, hoping to divert the old man's thoughts while curious as to his past.

"Know him?" Merrinan scoffed. "Served beside him I did! Two bloody campaigns!" He shook his head. "Tell me, does he love his hounds still? The man could talk for hours on end about his—"

"Father." Eleanor glared daggers at him as she put down his plate. "Eat," she urged, and then stepped away, asking, "More tea, gentlemen?"

"Don't mind if I do." Cuthbert smiled at her.

"No, thank you, miss, though breakfast is delicious." Wells did his best to remain polite, yet he was disappointed she'd interrupted the old man's ramblings.

"Where the devil is Charles?" Merrinan suddenly looked up. "Charles! Girl, where are you?" he shouted with more force.

Eleanor rushed over. "Papa, keep your voice down, we've guests. Charles is not here, she's tending to Mama. You mustn't shout. It is unseemly."

Wells suddenly felt bad for this girl, to have to manage her old man, though it was also a labor of love, he could tell.

"Your daughter, Charles, is a fine woman, Mr. Merrinan. She keeps house well and plays a keen game of chess," he told him.

"'Course she does, smart as a whip," he answered, frowning. "Taught her myself, I did. Knows Latin, Greek, and French as well. She'll make you a fine wife, Your Grace. Would please your father immensely, I'm sure. Glad we had this talk."

Cuthbert's jaw dropped as Eleanor's face turned beet red. The sudden silence in the room was deafening until Wells rescued the moment, looking at Eleanor with assurance before he turned to her father.

"I am honored, sir, that you should find me worthy, and

promise always to take care of your daughter, you have my word." He ignored his racing pulse.

Charles's sister exhaled a breath even as her father's face relaxed, sank to the table, and with a crash, landed in his plate, a jagged snore erupting. She gently removed the plate from under his face and motioned to Cuthbert for help. The two of them each took an arm to drag him from the table into the next room, where they gently laid him upon his bed.

Wells, meanwhile, shook his head at the thought that this confused old man considered his daughter worthy of a duke's son. And then he felt bad for deceiving the befuddled fellow, even if it had seemed best to lie in the moment rather than upset him more.

When Eleanor returned with Cuthbert she still looked pained. Wells decided to speak with her alone before they left.

"Miss Eleanor, would you do me the honor of a walk about the garden while we leave John to clean up?"

"Why . . ." She turned to Cuthbert in confusion, who merely nicked his head in accord. "Why, of course, my lord, allow me to fetch my shawl."

"Yer Grace." Cuthbert pulled him aside. "Be gentle with her, please. She's not t' blame for her old man's daft words."

"Of course she's not to blame." He frowned at his man. "What do you take me for, John?"

But Miss Eleanor had already returned to wait by the door, and Wells followed her out, leaving Cuthbert standing there with a worried expression plastered to his face.

"Thank you for being so gracious just now with my father, Lord Wellesley," Miss Eleanor began. "He does not know whereof he speaks. I am so grateful my sister was not present to witness his . . ." She clearly could not bring herself to say it. "It would have embarrassed her greatly, I am sure."

She looked at her feet as they walked, Wells accompanying her in a slow stroll about the house exterior, noting both the rot in the eaves and a gaping hole in the barn roof. He clasped his hands behind his back, as a gentleman would, and she walked careful of her step, with absolute propriety. He understood now why Cuthbert had called her a lady, for she truly was nothing like Charles.

"Miss Eleanor, it must be difficult for you, all alone here with your father, to care for him as you do. I admit I am sorry for having stolen your sister, as it were." Wells grimaced a little as he said this.

"Oh no, my lord!" she effused. "We are extremely grateful for the position you've given Charles, truly. She is not like me, you see, and it has stifled her some, to be stuck here with the two of us." She smiled at him, appearing to relax some. "She is much livelier than I, more . . . spirited. So I am glad she has something to occupy her, an entire household to manage, no less. It is surely challenging work, but Charles can do anything she sets her mind to, my lord. Why, without her I don't know what we would have done when Mother . . ." She again looked down at her feet. "Forgive me, my lord, I do not mean to prattle on so."

"Pray continue, miss. I could not agree more with your assessment of your sister's abilities. I can only presume you miss her greatly."

"Oh I do, sir. But Mr. Cuthbert's visits help, for he is kind enough to bide a while when he comes. And when he delivers Charles's letters it's as if she visits me herself."

The smile she beamed at him was so genuine, so radiant, he felt his heart warm to her. No wonder John was so enamored.

"Cuthbert is the best man I know, Miss Eleanor." He surprised himself by the force of his words. "He is like a brother to me, for I have no siblings."

"None, sir?" She looked shocked. "Then I am glad you have a friend in John." She smiled again. "For to be without a friend in this world . . ." she trailed off. "It is indeed a sorry fate."

"I am glad your sister has you, miss." He smiled back. "She is lucky indeed."

They lapsed into silence, but it was not an awkward one, and then Miss Eleanor wagered more.

"My lord, if I may be so bold as to ask you . . ."

He nodded.

"I know my sister can be outspoken, Lord Wellesley, and her letters have implied that you and she have been, well, in disagreement at times."

He flashed his eyes at her.

"I do not mean to disparage you, sir, in saying this, truly. I meant only to ask if you might be patient with her, my lord, as she has not had it easy." Eleanor dropped her gaze. "Were it not for Charles, Lord Wellesley, we'd never have survived our escape from London I am sure."

"London?" He raised his brow. "You lived in London before coming here?"

"Why yes." She frowned. "How else do you think my sister came to be so accomplished, my lord?"

"She said she was a native of Cumberland, miss."

"And so she is, sir, so are we all." She blinked at him. "But we spent winters in London, with my mother's family, and only summers here."

It suddenly made sense. "And when your mother passed, you no longer went back?"

A shadow crossed her face. "She passed away here, sir, in childbirth. When we returned to London, to her parent's house, they . . ." She faltered. "It is in the past, my lord, and we are simply grateful to be a family still." She smiled at him once more. "Charles was scant fifteen at the time and I but ten, so she mothered me, you see."

"I am sorry for your loss, Miss Eleanor. Your father must

have loved his wife very much, to have been affected so deeply by her death."

"Yes." Her smile pinched. "She loved him enough to . . ." Yet again she stopped herself. "It was so long ago, my lord, it seems another lifetime I am sure."

Wells could tell she was done talking. It was also time he left.

"I must return to Almsdale, Miss Eleanor. Business awaits, I'm afraid." He brought her hand to his lips. "Tell Cuthbert I have gone, he needn't catch up. Let him finish in the kitchen for you." He winked at her, making her eyes widen. "You might even offer him another cuppa," he continued, "for he likes to sit and chat, especially with a lady as pretty as yourself, I'm sure."

Which made her blush and fumble another deep curtsy, as Wells hurried off to make his way back to the Abbey, a multitude of thoughts crowding his mind.

CHAPTER SEVENTEEN

Wells made no mention to Charles of the visit he'd paid her family. He'd enough to chew on from his conversation with Miss Eleanor—not to mention the strange ramblings of her father—to keep his mind busy even as his hands labored at the south wall. That his mistress's family had been of some repute in the past was now abundantly clear. That she was still an obstreperous hellion was another matter.

He kept his distance, and she hers, their only communication now relegated to household matters. He noticed she'd nearly finished with the staff rooms, and he'd put in solid work every day alongside stonemason Adams's men. Thus progress, at least on the Abbey, was being made.

Yet at night his bed was empty, and the fact that she slept but a few doors down the hall was a temptation he'd nearly succumbed to several times. It would be easy to slip into her room and kiss her into submission, carry her back to his bed, kicking and screaming even. Only he wanted her to come to him. He wanted her apology and her admission of guilt. He wanted her to desire *him*, and in so doing, willingly give herself to him again.

And still she did not.

꒰꘩꒱

Cuthbert grudgingly handed Wells another letter.

"'T'ain't right, sir," he grumbled again.

Wells merely glared back. "I'll be the judge of my own conscience, John. Wait while I read it, then you may give it to her."

Dearest Charles,

How your words fill me with joy, sister! I am so grateful for your news, yet I have news of my own this time. Imagine my surprise the other morning when Lord Wellesley himself arrived alongside Mr. Cuthbert. I nearly died of shame that he should enter our lowly home. Yet he behaved with such absolute decorum, as if to sit and breakfast with us were the most natural thing in the world! He was kind to Papa, too, whom you can imagine said all manner of disagreeable things. Yet Wellesley treated him with the utmost respect. It made me nearly weep, to see a lord such as he regard our father with such gentleness.

He'd made a good impression on the sister, at least.

So I cannot in good faith comprehend, Charles, why you disparage his lordship in your letters. He struck me as the very picture of nobility. He admitted, even, that John Cuthbert was his best friend. Imagine a lord and layman friends! He took me on a walk about our sorry garden—can you picture how absurd it must have looked? Frumpy me promenading the Duke of Allendale's handsome, charming heir. It was a scene from a fairytale almost! And yet your letters tell of a very different man who is anything but a prince, and I cannot reconcile this with the lord who came to visit. Perhaps I only dreamt him after all, because Lord Wellesley was not the least bit

awful, sister. So you must explain your low opinion of him, Charles,
else I shall not believe you.

Low opinion, eh? What the devil had Charles written to
her sister about him?

Father is well, the chickens lay daily, and . . .

He skimmed ahead.

. . . as to your offer, I must refuse. You cannot save every penny you
earn solely for me. Why do you not see yourself also someday wed? I
love you more than anyone in this world, Charles, (except for Papa,
of course) yet you baffle me at times. I suspect you baffle others as
well. Lord Wellesley must surely find you a difficult housekeeper if
you question him at every turn. He is heir to a dukedom, Charles. You
cannot speak to him as if you were his equal when clearly you
are not.

Write to me soon! Ever yours, Ellie

Wells carefully folded the letter back into its original creases
and handed it to Cuthbert without a word. Then he leaned
back in his chair, mulling. At least Miss Eleanor thought highly
of him. Yet she'd no reason not to. Charles, of course, had
reason in plenty, reasons he knew all too damn well. No
wonder she'd been desperate to become anything *but* his
mistress. Miss Eleanor would be horrified if she knew the truth.
And no wonder she'd reacted with such horror when he'd
publicly chastised her before Adams's men.

He sighed. Perhaps her sister's letter would make Charles at
last see reason, for she could not continue to speak to him as
she did. She must submit to his will or he'd have no choice but
to cast her out and find himself a new mistress—and new

housekeeper—because she tempted him too much, even traipsing about the Abbey in that dull new uniform of hers.

The trouble was, Wells did not want just any mistress anymore. He wanted *her*, bloody hell.

❧

In between her work, Charles read over her sister's letter, still shocked his lordship had visited her family and still stewing over why the devil he had. Did he somehow mean to injure her further? Or was he simply making sure she'd not lied to him about her father and sister? Perhaps he was simply curious? He couldn't be. He was too self-centered for that. She'd need to query Cuthbert, for if the steward truly were a 'friend' to Wells, as Ellie had written, he'd have some opinion as to why his lordship had sought out her family. Why indeed! And devil take the blasted man for even occupying her thoughts!

Truth be told, Eleanor's letter had only inflamed Charles's own roiling temper more. She remained disgusted at herself for wishing Lord Wells *would* demand his gratification. It had been days since he'd done so, and she ought to be relieved. Instead, she missed the wicked ways with which he disturbed her work in the middle of the day: passionately crushing her up against a wall, a table, or even splaying her out across the floor.

She grew flushed just picturing past encounters, at war with herself for reliving such lustful, primitive acts. Because tender or cruel, she'd relished Lord Wellesley's attentions, so what did that say about her? Surely her parents had not been so rough in their lovemaking. She remembered them softly touching one another during the day—secret, gentle touches—nothing remotely lewd. She could think of no more loving couple than her parents. Indeed, her entire understanding of romantic love was based on the model of their marriage and precisely what she wished for Eleanor someday.

She, alas, would never be so lucky.

🙘

Wells had just slipped the shirt off his head that evening when he heard a knock at the door.

"Enter," he called, expecting Cuthbert.

Yet it was his housekeeper instead who marched inside, making his heart skip to think she might relent at last.

"My lord, have I leave to speak?" She bobbed a proper curtsy with her question.

"You do." He motioned her to continue before removing his boots.

"The rooms are ready for tomorrow's arrivals, sir. I've arranged for Cuthbert and Fergus to fetch the new help and have given your men strict orders not to hassle the girls." She paused. "Although it might impress them even more, my lord, were you to reinforce this yourself."

"Done." He began to unbutton his fall.

She swallowed, looking away. "I also received a letter today from my sister, sir, who informed me you visited her and my father this week."

"I did."

She rushed to speak. "I should like to thank you for the kindness she wrote you showed our father given his infirmity. He is not the man he once was, my lord, and she tells me you were most respectful towards him despite his own lack of courtesy." She swallowed again. "I am sure it brought him great pleasure to have you visit, Lord Wellesley."

"It brought me pleasure too, Charles." He spoke without emotion, looking straight at her enough that she blushed. "Your sister was perfectly delightful and your father, in his way, quite the gentleman." Wells flashed her a small smile.

She wagered a timid one in return. "He was once, my lord, a gentleman, and both soldier and scholar, sir."

"And your mother?" he asked.

"A lady, sir, of the finest caliber." She hesitated. "Theirs was a love match, which is why he took her passing so hard. We believe he suffered a fit upon her death, likely apoplexy."

"I see." He chose not to press her more.

"My lord, I should also like to offer an apology for the manner in which I behaved before, in the courtyard regarding the saddle." She hurried to finish. "I should not have spoken as I did, in such coarse terms, nor responded as I did to your lordship's chastisement." She looked down. "Were my mother alive she would find great fault in the manner in which I have behaved, and I give you my word I shall improve my behavior in future." He watched her hands ball into fists at her sides. "It is not easy for me, my lord, to serve under your . . . direction."

His mistress's apology had come, but not as he'd expected. She'd not thrown herself at his feet, begging his forgiveness, nor had she thrown herself into his arms, begging for his bed. Instead, she'd humbled herself rather nicely, owning up to her errors. Wells was not sure how to respond.

"Apology accepted, Miss Merrinan. Your sister asked that I be forgiving of your . . . spirited nature, I believe she called it." He exhaled a breath. "It is not something I wish to quell in you, Charles. It is something I admire, even, in you." He searched for words. "But I have a role to play, a role which demands obedience and respect here at Almsdale. And if I show you too much favor, tolerate too oft your impertinence, then I become weak. And I cannot show weakness before my subjects. It is a role I must take seriously, Charles, even if I am not yet the Duke of Allendale—and even if it gives me little pleasure to imagine myself one day Duke. What pleasure I have found here, has been only with you, lass, in your arms."

He watched her eyes grow wide—likely at his slip in speech

—for that word *lass* had again tumbled from his lips as if he were a wholly different man. He upbraided himself as her dark green irises stared deep into his eyes, as if she wished to devour him with her gaze.

And then she bolted from his chamber, footsteps pounding down the hallway's flagstone like a spooked colt. Unbelievable!

Wells shook his head in arousal, confusion, and then sheer frustration. Maybe he did, in fact, need a different mistress. He'd tell Cuthbert as much tomorrow—see if his man couldn't find him a simpler, pretty enough village girl. Because Charles Merrinan was too much for him to handle. He didn't care anymore how well she argued, or how well she fucked. He could not comprehend this woman's behavior, nor would he likely ever.

***

Charles scurried down the hall to her closet of a room and slammed the door shut with a bang. The hammering in her heart was so loud, so deafening, she thought the poor organ might expire in her chest. She could scarcely breathe for her heart's terrific pounding. She wanted to run straight into Lord Wellesley's arms and crush her body to his. Yet she could not, dared not, let him see her so completely overcome by his words.

His tenderness, this time, had torn her open. Charles felt more alone than ever before.

ACT II

ENVY

Jealousy is bred in doubts. When those doubts change into certainties, then the passion either ceases or turns absolute madness.

François, Duc de La Rochefoucauld (1665-1678), from *Moral Maxims and Reflections* no. 33

CHAPTER EIGHTEEN

"And the table linens, what few of them are usable, are stored here." Charles opened another cabinet to show her new staff. "Cutlery below. In time, there will be more of everything, but for now we must make do with what is here. I am sure we shall discover more as we begin to unlock the secrets of this house." She smiled at Ginny and Ruby, who stared back wide-eyed. She knew the two girls had never stepped foot in a place so grand as the Abbey, for despite its disrepair it had once been magnificent. No doubt in their eyes, it still was.

"Now," she continued, "you shall have a Sunday off every two weeks, though we will stagger those weeks to ensure there are always enough hands here to—"

"Miss Merrinan!" Fergus's voice bellowed from below the staircase. "Quick now, there's been an accident at the wall!"

Charles's pulse raced as she turned to the girls. "Stay here, explore at will. If you hear calls for help, do whatever is asked of you."

And then she ran.

The scene that greeted her was sheer chaos. A section of

scaffolding had collapsed at the south wall, and men were pinned beneath it. Charles could see limbs only, the able-bodied grabbing beams and planks, anything with which to brace and lift the weight of rock off those still trapped. She hadn't time to despair, she simply rushed to find Cuthbert, telling him, "I'll have the girls prepare the main hall to receive injuries." And she was off, again.

Charles issued commands to whomever she found, telling Fergus to ride as fast as he could for the village doctor. Her new staff made off for linens and water. She bid them find liquor, too. Her mind spun with the magnitude of the disaster as she prayed to God no one had been killed. Broken limbs were a surety. They would need splints, so she ordered Tom to break an old chair. She was so focused on what must be done that with a gasp she realized she'd not seen Lord Wells. Her heart leapt in her throat as she again made for the south wall, assuming he'd been at work there, too.

"John!" She found Cuthbert again. "John," she repeated, "where is Wells?"

He stared at her a moment. "He's fine. Where's the bloody doctor, woman?"

"Fergus rode for him, and my girls are readying supplies to set bones. Bring the injured into the main hall. Tom's hauling in beds and cutting splints."

He nodded, as if relieved she knew what she was about. And then he nodded in the direction of his lordship, whom she could see was bloodied but standing, working alongside others to frantically pull rubble off planks.

Her relief was palpable. "What can I do, John?" She turned back to Cuthbert, resolute.

"Ready yer girls for blood, Charles." He looked grim. "Tell 'em not to faint. And fetch liquor t' ease the pain."

Not a one of her girls had fainted, and not a one had failed her either. They'd had trial by fire their first day here, her new staff, and proved themselves more than capable—they were Cumberland hale and hearty. Charles took a moment to catch her breath and survey the room, soft moans punctuating the quiet that had fallen after the last man had been treated. There'd been but one casualty and only two limbs lost. The rest were breaks, cuts, and bruises. No worse injuries, when it could have been far, far worse, she knew.

She walked the room once more, checking that each man was calm, resting. Those that would eat had been fed, and she'd ordered the girls to sleep in shifts to make sure someone was with them at all times. Dressings would have to be changed, especially for the hand and leg that had been lost. The smell of burnt flesh from cauterizing stumps still filled her nostrils as she shuddered, trying to bury the lurid visions and the haunting sounds of screams.

Instead, she made her way to the parlor—the sole room in the house acceptable for guests—where she found Cuthbert, the doctor, and Lord Wellesley, deep in conversation. When she entered, all three looked up at her, his lordship motioning her in.

"How are they, Miss Merrinan?" Dr. Ambrose asked.

"Resting, sir, all. I've put Ginny on first watch. She'll see that bandages are changed as you directed. They've been given food and drink."

"Your girls did well today, Charles," the doctor told her, "as did you. Your father would be proud."

"'Tis no less than what any would do, sir."

"Aye," he smiled kindly, having known her his whole life, "but it were a wise man as hired *you* t' be housekeeper here." Ambrose turned to Wells. "I'll be leaving now, Lord Wellesley, but will return come mornin' t' check on our patients. There's naught else can be done for them tonight."

"Thank you, Doctor." Wells stood from his chair. "Cuthbert will see you out."

As the steward led the doctor away, Charles finally looked at his lordship. It hurt her to see him still bloodied and bruised. Without a word, she took his hand and pulled him behind her.

"Where are you taking me, woman?" He sounded exhausted.

"To your room, my lord. You need tending."

Lord Wells let her guide him by hand to his room where she made him sit upon his bed before going immediately to the washstand.

Slowly and gently she cleaned his cuts and scrapes. He had a deep gash above his right eye and winced as she dabbed at it, wincing even more as she worked to rid it of stone dust.

But when she unbuttoned his shirt and saw the bruising along his chest, noting how tender his left ribs were, she inhaled sharply. "Did you let the doctor examine you, Roland?"

His eyes met hers at the sound of his name.

"No need," he mumbled, obviously in pain.

Charles bit back her anger. "He will see you first thing tomorrow, my lord."

***

"Charles—" Wells tried to speak but she stopped him short, his mistress stubborn as ever.

"Do not argue with me, Lord Wellesley." She remained firm. "You are no good to anyone hurt, sick, or dead." She let out a huff. "And this likely needs stitching, damn you." She cleaned the gash at his abdomen with her cloth. "Why did you not seek the doctor's help?"

"Because he'd worse injuries to treat, woman, now stop

fussing." He didn't like feeling vulnerable before her. He didn't like when she had the upper hand.

She met his gaze with a look like flint. "It is my job to tend to you, my lord, and I will do my duty by you, whether you want me to or not."

"And what of your other duty to me, woman? Your other job which you have neglected entirely of late?" He could no longer hide the hurt he felt at her rejection.

"I am available any time you desire me, my lord. It is *you* who have not sought my company."

"Liar!" He hissed at the same moment she dug deeper into his gash. "Damn it, Charles, that stings!"

"Forgive me, my lord." She again made him wince. "I need to clean it."

"You wish to hurt me," he grumbled.

"No, Roland, you are hurting yourself."

She'd said it so softly Wells almost hadn't heard her, and then he moaned, for she'd turned the cloth to his face, one hand palming his cheek as the other gently wiped blood and dirt from his neck. He wanted so badly to kiss her he ached.

She continued her gentle ministrations as he closed his eyes in pleasure and pain, relishing the touch of her hands on his skin again. And when she carefully removed his shirt altogether, checking his ribs all the way round, he found her touch almost excruciating, searing. It felt like ages since she'd touched him thus, and he longed for so much more.

**

Charles knew she ought to leave—ought to simply bandage his ribs, tuck him into bed, and then check on the men downstairs. But she couldn't bring herself to go, not yet, not after touching him again after so many days of distance. She wanted to bury her face into the crook of his arm and inhale his musky scent. She wanted to pepper his body with kisses, as he'd attacked her that morning, ages ago. She wanted to hold him to her breast, stroking his unruly mop of hair while curled beside him in his bed. She *wanted*.

And this want, it seemed, had a will of its own, for without her bidding Charles's lips graced his lordship's forehead, his eyelids, nose, and cheeks. Her lips landed at his own as he gripped her fiercely to him for a far deeper, darker kiss.

"Charles, I am not . . ." His eyes met hers. "I am no good at this, lass, but I want you, *need* you tonight."

"Roland." She spoke his name as her hand stole back to his cheek, stroking.

"A man is dead because of me, Charles, and two others have lost their limbs. And now I . . ." Lord Wellesley's face said it all.

"Of course I will stay, my lord. I will always stay if you ask me." Her lips brushed his again, eliciting another low groan from his chest, before her hands reached down to help him from his trousers. She backed off the bed to lower herself between his thighs, not once taking her eyes from his face, until she bent her head to gently kiss his sex, tenderly taking him into her mouth.

She watched a tear roll down his cheek, surprising her greatly, even as he swelled beneath her tongue. She took him sweetly, lovingly almost, until he spilled himself into her, his release too fast, uncontrolled. And then Charles simply slipped out of her dress to crawl into bed beside him, bringing Lord Wells to her bosom, to cradle him to her. She held him there all night, knowing he needed comfort more than anything else.

She needed him too.

Charles awoke with a start and sat bolt upright. What if she'd been sought in the night and not found in her room, nor found this morning either?

An arm reached to steady her. "It is early yet, Charles. No one missed you."

"My lord, I must return to my room. If something happened to one of the men . . ."

"I checked on them already. All is well."

"You did?" She was stunned.

"Around midnight, after you fell asleep. Whatever girl you had on watch was up and tending to them. You did right to hire more hands when you did, woman."

She flushed at his praise. "Thank you, my lord."

"What happened to *Roland*?" He tipped her face to look at him, and she flinched to see his bruises in the daylight.

Charles carefully traced the gash above his eye. "Promise you will let the doctor look at this, and your ribs, Roland." She ventured his name again.

"Does this mean you care for me after all, Fox?"

"Of course I care for you." She frowned. "Do you think me heartless, sir?"

***

"Do you think *me* heartless, miss?" Their eyes locked and then Wells cupped her breasts, whispering, "I've missed you, Fox." And he had, terribly.

"I've missed you too, sir."

"No more *sir*, not in bed." He nipped her ear, then suckled the lobe, drawing another gasp from her lips. "I like it when you are sweet, Charles, and you were ever so sweet to me last night, lass."

Only she gently pushed him onto his back. "Shall I show you how else I can be sweet, my lord?"

His mistress's eyes flashed as she straddled his waist.

"Charles." He flinched, his ribs still tender.

"Yes, Roland?" His name was a caress as she notched herself above him.

"Go easy on me, Fox, I am sore yet."

"I'll be ever so gentle, *sir*." She slowly slid herself down his length, placing barely any weight upon his lap.

"Christ, woman." He sucked in his breath.

"Slow and steady, Captain."

"How the devil . . . ?"

"Cuthbert your first mate, eh?" She grinned. "He spilled the beans about your seafaring ways." Her smile deepened. "I knew that crew of yours were pirates, Wells, making you the prince of thieves."

He gasped again to feel the slow burn of her, achingly hot and sweet. "Aye, lass." He smirked. "And you my bounty, Charles, a most fine treasure to keep."

CHAPTER NINETEEN

A package from London had arrived early by post, and along with it another embossed ducal missive John delivered to his lordship, curious as to its contents.

"Leave the box, Cuthbert, I'll unpack it later." Wells had a gleam in his eye.

"And the letter, sir?"

His lordship grimaced. "Leave that for later, too. I'll not have my mother ruin a perfectly good day. And John," he added as he exited his bedroom, "give my regards to our housekeeper's family. I'm sure they'll be pleased to see her."

Lord Wells headed for the south wall, to put in his labor before what looked to be a gathering storm, while John hastened to the kitchen in search of Charles. Along the way he pondered his master's mood, for his grace had gone from foul to fair-tempered ever since the accident. John suspected Wells had made good again with his mistress, though he'd heard not a stitch more grumbling from the men, nor fresh complaints from the new girls, regarding loud 'activities' about the house. In fact, now that more staff had come on, Charles seemed positively rosy herself.

Which made him think of the housekeeper's sister, picturing *her* rosy demeanor. He wished Miss Eleanor were his to keep warm nights, engaged in all manner of sweetness.

"Ready, Cuthbert?" Charles sidled up, disturbing his reverie. "You do realize I might deliver this basket myself, sir."

He sniffed. "His grace don't trust you that much, miss. I don't care how well you two now get along." He pinned her with a look.

"We get along just fine, yes." She grinned back. "Fine enough that *his grace* is now letting me visit my family. So I dare not pick another fight with him, and least of all with you, John, who have been so kind to my father and sister."

John blinked, afraid she'd read his thoughts about Eleanor, but then he straightened his spine. "'T'ain't hard bein' kind t' folks what deserve it, miss." He grabbed the basket waiting on Cook's broad work table. "Come on then, let's not dally."

The walk went by quickly, and Charles reveled in the familiar steps that brought her ever closer to home. She was a little anxious, truth be told, for she'd not seen Ellie nor Papa for over two months. She also feared her face might give away too much of her new life at Almsdale; lately, she had only to think of Lord Wellesley before her skin prickled with awareness. Yet the moment she saw her sister standing at the doorstep, all fear vanished.

She rushed to embrace Eleanor.

"Why Charles, let me look at you, sister!" Ellie held her at arms' length a moment. "Most proper indeed in new house-keeper dress—it suits you well."

"And a fine job she does as housekeeper, too," Cuthbert added in an uncustomarily friendly manner.

Eleanor granted the steward a warm smile. "Come in, both of you, come and sit."

Within seconds it was as if no time had passed, and Charles greeted her father with a bear hug. "Papa, I've missed you so!" She almost wept her relief into his shoulder, the old man so stooped now she stood a full head taller than he.

"That you, Charles?" He looked at her and blinked. "Where's Mother got off to? I don't know why you are so happy to see me, girl, when but an hour ago you beat me roundly at chess."

Charles laughed. "Of course I beat you, Father. I learned from the best." She again hugged him to her tightly, not caring what reality his poor, befuddled mind might currently live and breathe.

Eleanor returned with tea to pour them all cups, then took Charles's hand across the table, squeezing it a little. "Now sister, you must tell me everything that has happened these long weeks past."

"Ellie, I've written everything in my letters. There's not much else to tell."

"I don't believe that for a minute." Her eyes met Cuthbert's. "John here says you've turned a new leaf with his lordship. Says he fancies you reformed." She winked at Cuthbert, who looked mildly horrified by her candid manner.

"Did he now?" Charles shot daggers at John. "*Reformed* is an awfully charged word, Ellie. Though I believe it is Lord Wellesley who is changed since the accident at the south wall."

Cuthbert met Charles's gaze a little sheepishly before he set down his cup. "Well, as I've a leakin' roof to tend to in the barn, I'll leave you to it." He again smiled at Ellie, who smiled right back. A look not lost on Charles, *that*.

"Thank you, Cuthbert," she told him. "We'll not be long. The weather's looked ominous all morning, so we ought not dally."

"Oi." He nodded. "Storm's a brewing." And out he strode.

Eleanor immediately launched in. "You look well, Charles, and well fed too. It must be Mrs. Jenkins's cooking. Your cheeks are flush with health and . . ." She peered more closely. "But you are blushing, Charles. It is not health but something else which makes you glow. What has you blushing, sister?" She frowned. "What is it you are not telling me?"

Charles briefly panicked. "Nothing. I am simply overcome with joy to see you and father again." She quickly changed tack. "And I blush, I think, to witness your response to John Cuthbert." Charles met Ellie's eyes with resolve. "What is it you are not telling *me*, Eleanor?"

***

Eleanor felt her own cheeks pink. "I assure you, Charles, I am merely grateful for John's company." She looked away. "You know what poor conversation Father is. John, however, listens to me, treats me like a thinking, feeling human. So of course I've grown somewhat . . ." She broke off. "Well I admit I am a *little* fond of him, I suppose."

Her sister's eyes narrowed. "Eleanor Merrinan, you must not allow yourself to grow any fonder of the man, promise me." Charles's tone was terse. "Cuthbert is decent enough, I'll grant, but he is not of your caliber, Ellie. You are a lady, despite how you live, and you must not forget it. You will marry an upstanding gentleman one day with a respectable title, ample means, and—"

"Stop, Charles," she got out, her ire rising. "Stop at once. *You* are a lady too, yet embrace instead now your position in service to Lord Wellesley. You cannot insist on something for me which you do not insist for yourself, nor may you decide who it is I do or do not grow fond of."

Her sister stared at her in shock, and Eleanor barely knew

herself for the words that had so rashly tumbled from her mouth. She watched Charles pause her response, and in that pause Ellie felt awash with such concern and dismay she could stand it no longer. She burst into tears.

"Oh Charles, I do not wish to argue! You have only just arrived and already we are fighting. I don't know what's come over me of a sudden, only I couldn't bear it if you were angry with me. I didn't mean it, truly. I only meant that I . . . that since you left I've . . ."

Her sister gripped her hand. "You've grown up, Ellie, I see that now. It is *I* who must apologize."

Eleanor hastily brushed back tears.

Charles continued. "I left you all alone, not by choice you understand. I am sure you figured that much out. Lord Wellesley has not trusted me till now to visit, else I would have come sooner, believe me. But perhaps it's been good for you to fend for yourself here with Papa. I am proud you stayed strong in my absence, proud even that you now take me to task." Charles finally smiled. "Let us not argue further, Ellie. My time here is short; I wish only to spend it with you happily."

"As do I, Charles," Eleanor exclaimed. "Nor do I blame you for what happened. I can scarce complain when we are well fed and nearly stocked for winter." She looked down a moment. "I worry more for you than us, Charles, on your own with all those men at the Abbey. John tells me they are harmless, but I know how you turn heads."

***

This was too close to the truth for Charles. "Ellie, I assure you, as housekeeper of Almsdale Abbey no one dares to disrespect me."

"And Lord Wellesley?" Eleanor asked, not yet appeased.

"Your letters describe him so varyingly I hardly know what to think of him. His visit to us was rather odd, was it not?"

Charles swallowed. "He puzzles me, yes. But so long as he is happy with my work and keeps you and father fed, I cannot complain." She hoped this would spell the end of all such talk.

It did not.

"But your letters gave the impression you did not like him, and then they gave the impression that you did, and I am confused, is all, when you of all people rarely——"

"Eleanor." Charles took great care to compose her face. "I do not wish to discuss Lord Wellesley more. He is my employer, that is all. It matters little what I think of him and only what he thinks of me. And I *certainly* do not entertain thoughts of whether or not I like the man!"

***

Eleanor stared at her sister in surprise. Charles only ever raised her voice when inflamed, and the sentence she'd just uttered sounded altogether impassioned. Yet she knew better than to poke a dragon.

"Of course, Charles. I meant nothing by it, truly. He is a duke, after all, or as good as one. Forgive my indiscretion, please."

"Oh Ellie, it is no indiscretion. It is only that——"

Mr. Cuthbert returned just then with a worried look on his face. "Beg pardon, ladies, but we ought t' leave at once." He looked at Charles. "Storm's headed quick; we'll need t' make haste t' outrun it."

Charles peered out the window at the darkening sky and at once rose from her seat. "You're right, we must leave. Yet I almost forgot." She pulled a small bag from her pocket. "A gift for Papa, Ellie." She handed it to her. "Will you remember how to brew it?"

Eleanor was confused until she pressed the item to her nose. "Of course I remember! Oh, he'll be overjoyed, Charles! It will bring back such fond memories of his days debating books in London's coffee houses."

Charles kissed Ellie on both cheeks, kissed their still-sleeping Papa goodbye, then followed Cuthbert out the door, the wind whipping her skirts into a frenzy.

Eleanor watched them both disappear down the path.

***

In no time at all their clothes were soaked through, the wind driving the stinging drops straight thought their cloaks. John took Charles by the arm and held on to her tight, dragging her behind him so they'd not lose each other in the torrent. He could barely see the path, which had already turned to mud, and the howling gale chilled him to the bone.

Still they soldiered forth. There was nothing else for it.

It seemed like an eternity of walking, the storm slowing their progress and the wet earth growing more treacherous as sections of trail washed out. At one point Charles tripped and fell, John yanking her back upright. He fell once too, pulling her down with him. They were muddied and muddled but knew better than to stop, for there was no shelter along this path, only the fells to either side. Their sole hope was to reach the Abbey.

And they nearly did before Charles slipped again and went reeling back, taking John down with her. He landed hard on his arse, but when he shook off the fall, he saw she'd landed dead on her head. And looked dead, to John, who in shock picked her up and simply carried her the rest of the way back. He prayed she'd only knocked herself cold.

When the Abbey took shape in the distance at last, John picked up his pace, then spied a figure heading towards them through the deluge. It was Lord Wells, shouting through the gale, "John, where the devil have you been? Why the hell did you not . . . ?" He took one look at Charles's limp form in John's arms before he grabbed her from him, rushing her into the house and demanding a bath be brought to his room at once.

Men scurried to obey as John entered right behind, feeling like some soggy clay golem as he collapsed against the wall.

Fergus glanced at him and hollered, "Two baths, lads! Warm mead! An' stoke the fires!"

Outside, the storm raged and buffeted the Abbey. The windows shook and rattled, and beams creaked and sang, while inside, fires crackled and flared, exuding heat and light against the fierce, descending dark. The servants huddled in groups about the kitchen's bright, warm flames, whispering amongst themselves. The men spoke of squalls at sea, while the girls told of Cumberland storms past.

Mrs. Jenkins nodded sagely at their talk as she set soup to simmer and mead to warm. John settled his chair closer to the great hearth's warmth. It would be a long night before such storm as this was over, and likely one he'd not forget.

CHAPTER TWENTY

Charles awoke groggy, her head aching and eyes swimming before she shut them tight against the world. A voice murmured at her ear, *rest, lass,* as she sank back into darkness.

❧

"Mr. Cuthbert," Jenkins' voice snared him where he sat, "where's Miss Merrinan, sir? I've not seen her since you returned. 'Tisn't like our housekeeper t' have not checked with me, 'specially in weather like this."

John tensed. "Restin', ma'am." He took care what he said. "Fell and hit her head while we were headed back. Nothin' too bad, no more'n a lump t'morrow, I'm sure."

"Well I ought to check on her, bring her some scran." She rose from her seat before John stopped her fast.

"No need, ma'am. Checked on her meself. She's sleepin' now, said she'd let me know if she needed aught."

Jenkins frowned. "I should like t' see her anyways, Cuthbert, 'specially in that cold laal room of hers. She's like as chilled t' death and should be sleepin' with me or Ginny and Ruby, where there's a mite more warmth."

John knew it was a losing battle. "Lord Wells offered his room, ma'am, on account o' that very reason—it bein' closest t' Miss Merrinan's. He'll sleep in her room tonight instead," he added, pleased to have come up with such a reasonable explanation.

"Are you *tapped*?" Jenkins's face was pure indignation. "Why in t' world would his lordship offer his own bed to . . . 'T'ain't generous, sir, 'tis . . . Why, 'tis ledgeful, Cuthbert. Outrageous! Miss Merrinan should've been brought at once t' my chamber, sir. Have you no decency at all?"

A sea of faces turned to John, the maids looking scandalized and the men all looking sheepish; they knew why Wells had brought his housekeeper to his bed. Yet everyone expected the Abbey's steward to answer the cook, and damned if John had an explanation for Mrs. Jenkins. At least, no honorable one.

"Ma'am." He opted for charm, flashing her a half-smile. "We're an unruly lot, I fear, havin' lived here too long now without finer company such as yerself. I'm afraid I didn't think, see, when I brought Miss Merrinan in. I simply brought her to the nearest, warmest bed, which happened t' be his lordship's room. There ain't enough rooms t' go round yet in the Abbey, as I'm sure you know, or I'd've brought her elsewhere." He tried to look contrite while lying. "'Course his lordship frowned too, at first, at me behavior, he did. Only he were kind enough not t' insist she be moved. Offered to take her room himself tonight. And there ain't many like him would do as much, no indeed. Lord Wellesley's proved himself a more decent and honorable master'n most, ma'am. So I'd kindly ask you let things be. Not embarrass his lordship more by callin' into fact his house ain't ordered well enough t' offer so much as a spare bed with heat. He's doin' his best, ma'am, t' bring the Abbey back, same as he does his best by his staff, too."

Mrs. Jenkins looked only slightly mollified. "Well," she puffed, "I certainly shouldn't wish t' embarrass his lordship more, Cuthbert. But if Miss Merrinan's no better by t'morrow she'll be brought t' *my* room t' recover, eh?" Her eyes met his in warning.

"O' course, ma'am. I'm sure Miss Merrinan'll speak with you herself come mornin'." This seemed to finally settle the cook and John breathed a sigh, as did the men about him. Not a one of them wished the housekeeper ill anymore, not since she'd traded them the village doxie for their silence. After all, she'd done more to improve their lives here than their Captain had . . . thus far.

"Yer Grace!" Cuthbert's voice softly called through the door. "Supper, sir!"

Wells ushered his man in.

"How is she?" John plunked down the tray.

"Still asleep." Wells nodded towards Charles. "But she did wake, briefly. I don't think the blow was as bad as it looks, lost a fair bit of blood though. She'll have a rousing headache come morning, I suspect."

"Oi," Cuthbert agreed. "Could've been worse. Came on out o' nowheres, that storm. Thought we'd time enough t' make it back."

"Thank you for getting her here safely, John." Wells met his steward's eyes.

"O' course, Yer Grace, only I'm afraid we've another matter on our hands, sir."

"Oh?"

"Mrs. Jenkins, sir, insisted on seein' Miss Merrinan herself, and one thing led t' another 'til I were forced to tell the cook I'd brought the gel here, t' yer room. And then she . . ." He sighed. "Let's just say I quick talked me way t' keep yon housekeeper's honor intact."

"Damn these women and their incessant need for respectability," Wells ground out, rolling his eyes.

"Aye," Cuthbert muttered. "And I've worse news yet, Yer Grace. You're sleepin' in Miss Merrinan's room tonight," he told him.

"I'll do no such thing."

"'Course not, sir." Cuthbert smirked. "Only y' might at least rumple the bed in there. Y' know, make it *look* slept in."

Wells harrumphed. "Have Fergus bed there tonight. He's about my height. I wouldn't put it past our new cook to go sneaking about. I'll lock this room too."

"Aye, sir." Cuthbert was fairly grinning.

"And the visit, John?" Wells changed the subject. "Was Charles happy to see her family?"

"Yes, sir. Her sister were too, Yer Grace."

"Good."

"I'm right glad t' see the two o' you gettin' along better, sir," Cuthbert offered.

Wells shot him a look. "I take it you are no longer scouring the countryside for a different mistress for me then?"

"No, Yer Grace." Cuthbert sobered. "I happen t' like Miss Merrinan fine, sir, though I'd warn you not t' lose more'n yer bed to her."

"What's that supposed to mean?" Wells frowned at his man.

"Seen the way you looked when I brought her in."

Their eyes met.

"Am I not allowed concern for another person, John?" Wells was careful of his tone.

"Y' are, sir," said Cuthbert. "Only there's concern, see, and there's *concern*, Yer Grace." And with that, he exited the room.

Wells was grateful his man had not said more.

❧

She was coming to again, and Wells spoke gently. "Charles, how's the head? You knocked yourself silly. Can you sit up now, eat something?"

She groaned and opened her eyes, looking dizzy.

He placed an arm about her shoulders, easing her up, before he plumped a pillow behind her.

She inhaled sharply as he lowered her head back onto it.

"You've a nasty lump forming."

"Is Cuthbert . . . ?"

"Fine, Fox. Carried you back, good man."

"I must thank him."

"Later, Charles, right now you must eat." He went to fetch the tray.

She looked at him as though she did not know him. "Am I dreaming, sir?"

"No, miss." Wells smiled. "At your service."

"You are never at anyone's service." She frowned.

"Not true." He feigned offense. "I've done Adams's bidding for weeks now. If that's not service to stone I don't know what is."

She managed a faint smile. "You are the oddest heir to a dukedom I have ever met."

"You meet many dukes then, Charles?" He grinned at her.

"No." She smiled, beginning to spoon the now lukewarm soup. "I meant only you are unlike a typical peer."

"Hmm," he mused. "And pray what is the peerage typically like?"

"Insufferable," she stated glibly, making him burst out laughing.

"Why, you *have* known a duke or two, Miss Merrinan." Only he grew serious fast. "I must warn you, Charles, Cuthbert had to spin a fine tale to Jenkins in order to prevent her storming in here to check on you herself."

Her eyes widened as she opened her mouth to speak, but he cut her short. "Because she was quite upset he'd put you in *my* room instead of hers." He stifled his mirth, to see the look on her face. "I'll have you know she thinks *I* am in your cold little closet tonight, as that is the kind of future 'Peer of the Realm' I am." He couldn't help but grin. "I've put Fergus in your bed instead, never fear."

"Fergus!" she sputtered. "Could you not have sent another man, my lord? I shall have to boil the sheets to get out his stink."

"Hush, Fox." He pushed back a stray lock of hair from her face. "Fergus resembles me most; no one else would do."

Of a sudden she looked miserable. "I shall be found out one of these days, my lord, I know it."

He pursed his lips. "Nonsense, Fox, we have been inordinately discreet of late, and I'll not apologize for wishing to nurse you back to health myself."

"And I thank you for your care, Roland, I do."

Her use of his name made his insides briefly flip.

"Only my sister asked me one too many questions when I saw her, and I found it difficult to lie."

"Then why must you lie, Charles? Surely she can keep a secret. Surely with time people will not think it uncommon their lord and master's taken a—"

Her face pinched. "It is perfectly common for a lord to take a mistress, I know this, sir." She struggled. "It is simply not acceptable for *me* to be your mistress. Should I have no sibling I'd not care a fig if Jenkins found me out, but I cannot compromise Eleanor's chance at a suitable match. She must be settled before Papa is gone so that she . . ." She sank back against the pillow in exhaustion, her face suddenly drained.

"Hush, Fox." He stroked her cheek as she closed her eyes. "Your secret is safe. I shall do all I can to safeguard your sister's reputation."

"Roland," her lips whispered.

"Yes, Fox?"

"Thank you," she said, as he pressed a kiss, softly, to her forehead.

❧

Charles slept soundly the rest of that night, and at dawn, when she awoke, the fog in her head had cleared, and with it the storm outside. Beside her lay his lordship, still fully clothed, and she noticed she wore one of his shirts. Had his lordship undressed and bathed her last night? It seemed too menial a task for Wells to perform, but she couldn't imagine Cuthbert had, and if Jenkins hadn't known her whereabouts either then . . .

"Morning, Fox. How's my patient?" His hand rested gently, possessively almost, at her hip.

"Better, sir, thank you."

"Good." He kissed her cheek. "You had me worried last night."

"Worried?" She smiled. "Surely Lord Roland Rutherford Wellesley does not worry himself over his servants."

"Only his favorite servants, miss. Only those who serve him exceptionally well," he teased back.

"Exceptional?" She arched her brow. "I see your estimation of my skills has increased, my lord. Pray tell what else I must yet master to properly serve a future duke's bed?"

***

Wells felt his gut clench. "Do not tempt me with words, Fox, while you still heal. Otherwise I shall be forced to take advantage of your weakened state in ways that might only be deemed shameless."

"Shameless, Lord Wells, is your middle name."

He could tell she was feeling better.

"I should be remiss as mistress, my lord, were I not to learn every shameless act, position, and manner of pleasure to ensure your appetite is duly sated."

"Woman, you are wicked," he whispered in her ear, running his tongue down her neck till she shivered.

"I enjoy being wicked with you, Roland," she whispered back. "You are my weakness, sir."

"As are you mine." His tongue took greater liberty, until he had to stop himself from abusing her more. "Yet I am not so wicked as to ravish you while infirm." He slipped from the bed. "I must rouse Fergus, after all, and see to the boiling of your sheets." He grinned at her. "And I'm afraid it's back to trousers for you today while the mud is scrubbed from your uniform. Who's the girl in laundry now?"

"Ginny, sir. Only I think it time, my lord, that I have more than one dress to wear. You did promise me that bolt of cloth, sir."

"I did, didn't I?" He remembered. "'Tis I who've been remiss, Charles. As mistress you deserve gifts and gowns, and were we in London . . ." He abruptly broke off. "Yet I do have a gift." He quickly fetched the package that had recently arrived.

"What is this, my lord?" Charles opened the box and with a look of shock pulled back the thin wrapping paper to remove silk stockings, silk ribbons, and a chemise of gossamer thin fabric. She stared up at him, confused—as if she'd never seen such undergarments in her life.

"For you to wear, Fox, in bed." His eyes met hers. "It's what a proper mistress would wear when visited by her lover."

Charles blushed but then immediately put the things away. "I see it is a gift for *you*, then, my lord, not for me." She hastily placed the lid on the box and set it aside.

It was his turn to be surprised. "I hadn't considered . . ." He felt suddenly contrite. "Of course it is a gift for us both, I thought, to enjoy." He was no longer sure what to say.

"It is most generous of you, sir," she said politely, but he could tell she was not pleased.

"I've upset you, haven't I?"

"No, my lord." Her smile was forced. "Not in the least. Only it is time, I think, I returned to my room and assured Mrs. Jenkins of my health. And saw to the cleaning of my uniform. I would appreciate that fabric you promised me, and as Ruby is the best seamstress on staff, I will set her this task."

She moved to leave the bed and stand, but when she wobbled a step, he caught her. "Charles," he told her sternly, "clearly you are not well enough to—"

"Dizzy, sir. I need a moment is all."

"You need to lie down again."

"No," she insisted, then corrected herself. "My lord, I must return to my room now. Please."

He could tell she'd brook no argument, so with a sigh he simply hoisted her into his arms. "Very well, Miss Merrinan, but you shall let me carry you to your bed, and we shall strip the sheets before I lay you down on it."

CHAPTER TWENTY-ONE

L ater that afternoon, Wells caught a glimpse of Charles in what appeared to be a borrowed print dress; he'd not seen Miss Merrinan wear anything quite so feminine before. It was a little short, showing her ankles rather nicely, and it was a little tight, showing her figure better still, but the fact it was a patterned dress of blue gingham made the biggest impression of all. She looked like a young woman at a country dance. She looked nothing like a housekeeper, chicken thief, or London mistress. She looked like her sister almost: a respectable young lady. His breath caught, to see her thus, for she was stunning. He knew her person—her body—well, but he didn't know her like this.

Wells suddenly felt even lower for not having bought her a true gift, rather than the flimsy undergarments he'd ordered from *LeBrecht's*. He'd showered past mistresses with far more lavish purchases for far less in return than what Charles had already given him, in bed and out. Miss Merrinan deserved better.

And he realized with some shock it was not the first time he'd rethought a decision or reconsidered his behavior since her arrival at the Abbey. Her very presence here seemed forever to insist that he improve himself—which was an utterly absurd notion.

He did not need improving. *She* did.

⁂

"Miss Merrinan, I'm that pleased t' see you up and about, dearie. You had us full flaiten last night, baggin' ourselves when Cuthbert reported your fall."

Jenkins had cornered Charles, her stout frame literally blocking the closet office door as she stared the housekeeper down.

"Yes, it was quite the storm, wasn't it?" Charles smiled back, nervous. "But then, we've seen worse here in Cumberland, haven't we, Mrs. Jenkins?"

"Aye," she said, "and you'd think a Cumberland lass like yourself'd know better than t' get caught in sech storm, miss."

And here it comes, Charles thought to herself. "I do, ma'am, and I'm ashamed to admit I paid it little heed yesterday as I was visiting my family with Cuthbert. Hadn't seen them in weeks and couldn't bear to drag myself away." Her eyes met the cook's in what she hoped would be a convincing face. "I'll not be so foolish again."

Jenkins nodded. "You look right bonny in Ruby's frock, miss. Ginny should have t' mud out of your uniform by t'morrow, I'd hope."

"Thank you." Charles suspected there was more.

Jenkins did not disappoint. "You know I respect how well you've managed here on your own, miss, and I'm grateful for your recommendin' me for t' position, not t' mention how well you handle t' girls and his lordship's louts."

Charles swallowed.

"But we both know you weren't raised t' be no housekeeper, Charles, and you're smart enough, and well-spoken enough, t' more'n turn a man's eye. To turn his thoughts t' makin' you his bewer."

Charles's heart leapt in her chest.

"Which is just t' say I hope you know what you're about, miss."

Her breath caught. "Mrs. Jenkins, I can assure you I—"

Only the older woman was having none of it. "Charles, I may be oal, lass, but I ain't *that* oal. No lord offers his bed t' no servant for nowt but one reason only."

Charles winced.

"Have a care, marra, as these things rarely end well." And with that, the widow turned on her heel and walked out.

Charles remained fixed to her seat, stunned. Jenkins knew, or suspected, or suspected she knew. It didn't matter either way, what mattered was she *knew*. And yet the woman hadn't condemned, threatened, exposed or done any number of things she could have.

Charles slowly inhaled a breath. Perhaps the cook would keep her secret. Perhaps Mrs. Jenkins was not as respectable as she seemed. Either that or she'd no wish to jeopardize her position here. Maybe Charles had been mistaken to think Cumberland's rules of civility were like those of London. Perhaps folks here were more willing to turn a blind eye, to understand why a body did what it did to survive.

Either way, Jenkins knew. And if she knew, others would too.

Wells, at last, sat down to read his mother's latest missive, which was more of the same, insisting he marry. Apparently, the Duke's health was in even worse decline. At this rate, he'd need to visit the old man himself to gauge how poorly he truly fared. And yet if he did visit he ought to go now, before winter fell, or he'd be forced to wait till spring. *Blast*, he swore, thinking of the south wall and how close they were to finishing. He didn't want to return to London so soon, and he didn't want to see his mother so soon either. Of course he didn't mean to avoid his father—he loved the Duke, inasmuch as a son raised by nursemaids, tutors, and servants could love a father.

He swore again, because his mother had made mention of at least four eligible young ladies in her letter, praising one in particular. He was certain that if he made the trip to see the Duke he'd be forced to pay calls on all four prospective brides. And he couldn't stomach the thought. The Duchess was baiting him, using his father's ill health as a ruse to lure him back. He'd not go. He'd write to the Duke instead, tell him about the work he was doing here. His father would understand the urgency. He adored Almsdale Abbey, had grown up here. He'd have stayed, too, were it not for his Duchess.

Wells decided then and there to decline his mother's invitation. For a change, he would ask *her* for something instead, because there was indeed a gift he could give Charles Merrinan, an object as useful as it was beautiful. He grabbed paper and ink to scribble a quick reply, vowing to put off any London visit till spring. In the meantime, the Duchess could send him the item he requested.

Let her think what she liked.

CHAPTER TWENTY-TWO

Wells had gotten hold of Eleanor's latest lengthy missive.

Dearest Charles,
John tells me you were caught in that dreadful storm and injured. You should never have left when you did. I am angry at you, sister, for again being so reckless in your . . .

He skimmed ahead.

. . . though Papa enjoyed the coffee immensely. You should have seen his face light up! It is maddening some days to be stuck alone with him though, forced to fuel his delusions. I question, at times, my own sanity, sister. Yet I have but him to contend with, not a household like you must manage. Your job is infinitely more difficult, I am sure. . .

So his housekeeper was sneaking coffee to her father, eh? Wells read on, chewing his bottom lip.

Which is why I am unhappy with how we parted, for I fear you are upset with what I said regarding Lord Wellesley, and I did not mean to upset you, Charles, truly I did not. It is nothing to me how you should think or feel towards his lordship, because he is your employer of course, no more and no less. I am concerned only with your happiness, sister, and as one's happiness is linked to one's master (as mine is linked to Papa), I would be remiss if I did not ask your opinion, at least, of those with whom you now reside. Perhaps I am a little jealous, too, that you . . .

Eleanor wrote ridiculously long letters.

. . . and of course John Cuthbert. I should be lost, I think, without his visits, Charles, for it is not his baskets I look forward to so much as his company. Father is an empty husk now, but when I am with John it is like speaking to a ray of light, like there is hope and possibility in the world outside the four dull walls of our bleak little house.

But I ramble on, forgive me. I could write you pages and pages, while you . . .

Wells scanned to the end.

Write to me soon, Charles. Be kind to yourself and Lord Wellesley, whom I shall continue to bless for his generosity to our family. I pray for everyone at Almsdale but most especially for you.

Ever yours, Eleanor

Wells handed Cuthbert the letter, but stopped him before he left the room. "John?"

"Sir?"

"Has the old man—Merrinan—gotten any worse you think?"

"Worse, Yer Grace?" Cuthbert seemed confused. "Strikes me the same. Why?"

"Miss Eleanor writes how much he taxes her spirit, and how much your visits improve her mood."

His steward's face flushed. "Well I imagine she's lonely is all," he muttered, "what with her sister now here at the Abbey."

"Yes, I am sure she is, John." Wells stared at his man.

"That all, sir?" Cuthbert looked as if he wished to escape more scrutiny.

"Do you like her, John—Eleanor Merrinan?"

"Do I?" He seemed even more flustered. "Well o' course I don't dislike the gel, Yer Grace. She's a woman what treats me like . . . Well, like a man o' worth."

"Yes," said Wells, "I imagine she does treat you right, John. She is not the sort to look down on anyone, I think." He took care with his next words. "I had thought to send someone else to deliver her the weekly baskets, rather than continue to tax your time with this errand. But perhaps you enjoy your visits to the Merrinans?"

Cuthbert's eyes narrowed. "I do, sir."

"Then we will leave things as they are," Wells told him. "And you will continue to deliver me the sisters' correspondence, *not* that I need hear your continued reproach." His voice rose a notch.

"Oi, sir," Cuthbert growled back. "*Not* that me opinion's changed none on that front neither."

Ruby was sewing Charles a dress, an honest-to-goodness print dress that could be worn to church even—not that Charles would feel comfortable stepping foot inside a church anytime soon. She pushed the thought from her mind. She seemed to avoid a great many thoughts these days but was nonetheless grateful Lord Wellesley had approved the purchase of new dress cloth. In fact, the man had even winked at her when she'd pressed her case.

Charles pushed *that* image from mind too, forcing herself back to task. She was nearly done knitting his lordship's rowdy crew wool hats and mitts for winter, having put Clarice and Marta to work on these as well. Many hands made for lighter work, and she was grateful for those extra hands, because there was no end in sight to labor. Each day brought a new room to unearth and restore, leaving another that much closer to completion. Lord Wells claimed he had no plans to entertain at the Abbey, but eventually his lordship would. He'd host guests someday, Charles knew, and she'd not have the Abbey disappoint. London gentry would see that Almsdale was as good a house as any, better even. The Abbey would shine.

It would shine for Christmas, too, because she planned to make the great hall festive and merry; Lord Wells had given her permission to decorate. It would be a time of celebration and, Charles hoped, a time his lordship might be proud of his staff, proud of *her*. He'd been so sweet of late, ever since the storm, that she relished their moments—their nights—together as much as she now relished her position here as housekeeper.

Charles felt like she'd come into her own, at last.

Wells entered his bedchamber exhausted from his day's labors, his ribs still giving him grief. The south wall was nearly done, the men making a final push, and he'd pushed himself too. The weather had grown colder and the storms more frequent, which had made Adams put every able-bodied fellow he now had on the job. By the end of the week they ought to be finished, and when they were, Wells would be relieved to have accomplished this much, at least, towards restoring the Abbey.

The hot bath awaiting him brought him relief as he stripped and sank into the water, letting the heat ease his sore rib cage and muscles. He didn't mind the work anymore, enjoyed it even, but it had taken a toll on his body this past month. He was used to working a ship, not working stone—an altogether different sort of labor here on land. He sank deeper into the water, submerging himself entirely, resting both body and mind.

Yet when he surfaced he was no longer alone. A woman lay draped across his bed, clad in diaphanous silk, lush curves visible beneath the flowing fabric, her hair a river of coppery gold. His breath caught, for surely this temptress was not his Fox, surely she was an apparition instead. Either he was dreaming or his Cumberland mistress had turned siren—no, vixen—to rival the finest London courtesans. This couldn't be his housekeeper and yet . . .

"My lord," the creature purred, "will you not join me, sir?"

He was still unbelieving.

"*Roland*," she softly beckoned, "I wish to please you tonight."

Which made him suck in his breath and rise, dripping from the bath, as he hastily dried himself en route to the bed. He let his eyes soak her up, for she'd donned the silk stockings and revealing chemise he'd ordered from *LeBrecht*'s. To say it was a gift he had given himself, more than her, was undeniable.

He lowered himself to the edge of the bed and reached a hand to trace her shape, marveling at how she shimmered beneath the silk, how luminous it made her.

"I take it you like your gift, sir?" She smirked.

"Oh Fox, you've no idea." His hand stole up the inside of one stocking to the ribbon tied just above her knee, then moved further up her bare inner thigh.

"I feel like a proper mistress at last, my lord," she whispered more seductively, her gaze raking his naked body. "One who knows *just* how to command her master's attention." Her fingertip traced the dark line of hair down his chest to his gut, and lower still, where she took sweet hold of him, before she drew him into bed beside her.

Wells closed his eyes, not wishing the moment to end, but then opened them to feel the caress of lips, soft upon his own. She tempted with her tongue, entering his mouth with insistence as he returned her kiss more deeply, dangerously. She pressed her body to his, shifting herself over the seat of his lap to lower herself maddeningly slowly, until he was enveloped in searing heat, consumed by it. He broke their kiss to cry her name as her tongue lapped his skin like a fox licks its mate, nipping his shoulder gently, sinking teeth into flesh. All while she milked him between her thighs.

Wells wanted to die inside her, dissolve entirely, as a groan escaped his lips.

"*Whisht*," she teased in Cumbrian tone, "you have worked hard all day, my lord, do not move, do not speak. Only let me please you, Roland."

Her words elicited a far deeper moan which quickly turned to growl, for he could take no more. Wells threw her onto her back and hooked her below each knee to plunge inside her core, demanding she give her all. He took only his pleasure, all reason lost. Like a man starved, insatiable, he consumed his mistress until his craving passed, spilled hot across her belly.

They lay as one, breathing hard, his body collapsed atop her, until her hand reached for his head of curls and played there, her voice hot against his ear.

"I would have you again, Roland."

"Again, Fox?" He rumbled into her chest. "Christ, woman, I just—"

"Again, Lord Wells. My courses will come on the morrow,

so it is safe to spill your seed. Miss Griswald assured me. And I want you, my lord. I want your very essence given to me."

Which only roused him further, he could feel his loins respond again. God how she tempted, spurred, and drove him to distraction. He'd take her again, yes. He'd take her all night and into morning. His Fox would be sore tomorrow but he didn't care. If she wanted him this much then by God he'd give her his all. All of him.

"You'll regret this come morning, Charles," he warned.

"I'll regret nothing, Roland." She bit his neck. "Join me to you, do not hold back."

He did not.

By morning they were both utterly spent, Charles groaning as she awoke. She did not wish to start the day's chores, because her body was indeed sore from use. His lordship groaned also, as if hung over from lust, rather than drink. He seemed sapped of all strength, exhausted.

They looked at one another blearily, then grinned like two fools before Lord Wells kissed the tip of her nose. "Woman, you will be the death of me." He shook his head.

"Only the sexual death of you, Roland." Charles laughed as his grin deepened and he pulled her to him tight.

"Christ, Fox, you are amazing, you know that, don't you?"

"No, my lord, I am sure you have had better."

"I have not."

She laughed only more. "Oh I am certain you *have*, sir."

"No, Fox, I mean it." She quelled her laughter as he held her gaze. "No woman has ever made love to me as you do. I do not jest."

She broke from him. "I suppose no woman has ever been so foolish as to make love to you as I do, sir."

"Charles." He took her hand in his calloused palm.

"Don't." She felt sudden, inexplicable hurt. "Leave be such talk." Her finger traced the bridge of his Roman nose, landing at his full lips, where he promptly kissed the tip. "I wish only to remember how much I enjoyed you last night. Thank you, Roland."

"*You* thank *me*?" He looked incredulous. "Good God, woman, I have never in my life been thanked for—"

"Fucking, my lord?" She scrunched her lips in a smile. "Aye, well, I suppose we Cumberland lasses like a good roll in the hay, is all." She watched his eyes spark. "You've corrupted me thoroughly, *Your Grace*, down to the very words I dare to speak. I am indeed Eve, it seems, fallen for the serpent."

***

"No, Fox, 'tis you who've corrupted me." Wells laughed, hugging her closer and no longer caring how she addressed him anymore in the privacy of his own chamber. "I wish to stay abed with you all day. Don't leave me, lass."

She swatted at him playfully. "Housekeeper by day, sir, mistress only by night, and I've work to do, so leave be." She pushed him from her.

"And what if I found a new housekeeper, eh? And made you my mistress only, Charles?" He propped himself up on one arm.

"No." Her tone held an edge as she slipped from the bed, hastily beginning to dress. "That won't do, sir, and you know it."

"But surely with time you'll not want to continue such menial labor as—"

"No, Lord Wells." Her voice was firm. "I am more than some man's mistress, and always will be."

He frowned. "I never said you were less, Charles."

"Please." She turned to look at him. "Do not ruin what we have." Her expression was almost sad. "I enjoy you very much, my lord. Let us enjoy one another for as long as we may."

And with that, she slipped from his room—from his very grasp it felt like—in a hurry, it seemed, to leave him.

CHAPTER TWENTY-THREE

W ells scanned his housekeeper's letter, looking for information he did not already know.

Dearest Ellie,

I can scarce believe winter is already upon us and I have yet to visit you again. I sense your disappointment for miles, sister. I <u>will</u> try. Lord Wells has given me leave, and while it will be our first Christmas apart . . .

Christmas, bah. Why did women include so many unnecessary details in their letters? He skimmed more text.

Do you remember Christmases past in London? Perhaps you were too young to recall, Ellie. I remember them well. Mother's family would put on such a lovely show. I imagine they still do. Sometimes I wonder how our grandparents are. But I remind myself they did not want us, they wanted our obedience only. Is it any wonder mother left? I should have done the same if I were her.

He skipped another section.

. . . and I have made peace with everyone, even his lordship. He has proven himself most generous, Ellie, and I am ashamed, almost, to have written the things I did before. Though I admit he mystifies me still. Did you know he captained a sailing ship with Cuthbert? Only imagine their adventures! I am jealous at times of all men may do which is forbidden us women . . .

Wells handed Cuthbert Charles's letter without a word. What had her life in London been like? And why had her mother's family abandoned them? Surely if they'd known the state she and her sister had been relegated to they would have sent for their grandchildren, cared for them. Yet perhaps the Merrinan girls had not wanted to be cared for. Perhaps the conditions placed upon them were such that they would rather starve in Cumberland than spend a cozy Christmas in London. He could well imagine his Fox refusing assistance for pride. God knew *he'd* rather freeze in this drafty old Abbey than be squeezed into some overstuffed London drawing room making chitchat with his mother's circle of acquaintance.

Perhaps that was what appealed about his mistress: She did not fawn or simper, did not feign interest in him either. In fact, she'd resisted him to no end at first. Nor had she delusions as to their relations. He couldn't marry her, a commoner, even if he wished. No, he truly did believe she enjoyed his company. After all, she came to *him* now nights; he no longer had to threaten, cajole, or even ask. And it was damn refreshing to have a woman like him as he was. It was almost liberating after his experience in London. Hell, he'd take a Cumberland lass any day over the *Ton's* scheming debutantes. Charles Merrinan was a hidden gem, and he was deuced happy to have her.

Perhaps foolishly so.

❧

"Goose!" threatened the widow Jenkins, shaking her fist at John. "You promised me a goose, man, not a—!"

"Oi, you'll get yer goose, woman." He glowered at her. "Though I don't see as why it must be goose for Christmas when any fowl should do."

"Any fowl will not do, sir, and as I'm cook here, *I'll* decide what t' serve his lordship for Christmas dinner, his first Christmas in Cumberland, eh, and it'll be t' finest goose Lord Wellesley's ever had!"

"I am sure it will be, Mrs. Jenkins," the housekeeper interjected, having entered the kitchen to witness yet another temper flare. John knew Charles did not want staff more ruffled than they already were.

"Cuthbert," she smoothed, "I am less concerned with fowl than I am the kitchen staples we'll need to get us through winter. How are the larders looking? Shall we take stock?"

He was doing his best to still scowl at Jenkins. "Might as well, miss." He motioned Charles to follow him out the kitchen toward the Abbey's cellars, winding their way through a house they both knew far better than three months ago.

"Have you word from my sister again, John?" she asked.

"I do, miss." He pulled a letter from his pocket. "Meant t' give this to you earlier and forgot. I 'spect she'll be missin' you more'n ever now what with winter upon us."

Charles looked pained. "Has she enough peat to burn to get them through, John? Did you look?"

He met her eyes with understanding. "Aye. Checked the house too. It's chinked tight enough now, barn roof'll hold. Been bringin' her extra of everythin' lately."

She took his hand, stopping him a moment. "Thank you, John, truly. I cannot tell you how much it means to me to know—"

"Oi, now." He patted her hand in his own, feeling somewhat embarrassed. "I'd worry same if it were me own family. 'Tis only natural."

She smiled at him then, a smile that reminded him of her sister.

"Well I am grateful, is all." Charles squeezed his hand before they continued down the passage. "And your family, John? Have you siblings too?"

"No, miss," he told her bluntly. "Wells is all the family I know. The Duke took me in as a yob off the streets, been an orphan long as I can remember."

"Took you in? Off the streets of London?"

"I were but a mite then, and up t' no good it seems. Brought me home with him, the Duke did, said his boy needed a playmate and I needed a scrubbin'. The Duchess gave me a meal and I've served their family ever since."

"So you knew his lordship as a boy." She looked amazed. "What was he like, John?"

"Like?" He laughed. "Like every other hot-headed boy, miss! Same as any of us." John grinned. "Bit of a troublemaker, but loyal. When they sent him t' Eton, t' school, and I were left behind, he wrote t' me still, y' know. Never forgot me in all his years there."

"And did you write him back?" she asked.

"'Course I did." He frowned at her. "Hell, I signed up t' sail with him, didn't I? Me, who couldn't swim a stroke back then."

"Cuthbert." Charles stopped them in their tracks. "Why did Lord Wells go to sea? It is unlike a duke's heir to seek such pursuits."

John hesitated. "Wells never liked t' put on airs, miss. 'Twixt you and me, I think he didn't much want t' be born a duke's son. He'd rather his father live forever than be forced to take over the Duchy. He's always run from it, first t' sea and now here, to the Abbey, though the Abbey's part of the Duchy. Lookin' for escape wherever he can."

"I see." She mulled a minute, then wagered one last question as they reached the cellar steps. "And leaving London . . . Did something happen there to upset him?"

John debated telling her more. "He were engaged t' marry, miss, as his mother, the Duchess, has been houndin' him for years. Only the lady ran off with a friend of his, right under his nose. Wounded his pride, I think, more'n his heart."

"I see." The housekeeper looked like she might chew this bit of story a good while longer.

John would rather forget the fat mess. "But enough o' the past, miss, on to the larder now. " He lit a wall sconce and descended the stone steps. "Watch yer head. It's right low down 'ere."

Much later, Charles eagerly tore into Eleanor's letter.

Dearest Charles,
Just a quick note, sister, as John is in a rush to return. He tells me the Abbey is being transformed for the holidays and oh, how I wish I might see it! You must write and describe every last detail, promise, for then I shall be able to picture it perfectly. He says there is even mistletoe hung about. Make sure you're not caught and kissed. Though I should like to be kissed someday. Every girl ought to be kissed once before she marries, don't you think?

Charles harrumphed. Not a good sign Ellie was penning words about kissing.

But enough silliness. Father sends his love and best wishes for Christmas, not in so many words but in my translation. You under-

stand. I shall make our little dinner here the best it can be, and a far better dinner than last year's, thanks to you, sister. We grow round here now, I swear I've put on weight. John says it suits me, which made me blush that he should notice. But never fear, I've not made eyes at him. Though he is easy on the eyes, I admit. I am allowed to look, am I not? I can see you frowning as you read this, Charles, but I shall not be made to feel guilty for merely looking at a man. There. I can be stubborn, too.

Yet John is watching from the door and eager to be off. If you cannot come till January we shall simply look forward to you then. I love you, Charles, and miss you terribly.

Your Eleanor

Charles folded the letter. Her sister was most definitely making eyes at Cuthbert, for the more she proclaimed the opposite, the more it was surely true. She must ask Lord Wells to send a different man with baskets. She'd insist. For even though John was a decent enough fellow, he was no proper gentleman. A London street urchin for God's sake! Mother would never have allowed such a match for Eleanor, and it was Charles's duty to ensure her sister married well. Which she would. Just as soon as she had enough saved to launch Eleanor herself.

She sat a moment longer in her cold closet room and let her thoughts stray to his lordship in bed this morning. He, too, was easy on the eyes and her body flushed just picturing him. She still struggled to reconcile the woman she had been with the wanton she'd become, for like his rowdy band of men, she, too, now craved bodily comfort. It did not align with who her parents had intended her to be, but she could not deny how it made her feel to join her person to Roland Wellesley.

And why should anything that felt so good be in truth so great a sin? Having long trusted experience over rhetoric, she began to consider that perhaps her mother's grand pronouncements—the very rules of fine society itself—were askew. Perhaps both London and Cumberland were wrong to insist a woman's unspoiled virtue was her greatest asset. Perhaps the body, more than the mind, knew a great deal more.

She got up from her seat, eager for his lordship's touch.

CHAPTER TWENTY-FOUR

Despite Charles's best efforts, Christmas, it seemed, was anything *but* the celebration she had so carefully planned.

All that could go wrong, did. First there was the blasted goose—no goose at all but a pheasant, for which Cuthbert had nearly gotten his ears boxed by Jenkins. And then there was the snow, which had dropped so fast and furious that morning that the steward had been trapped by it, spending Christmas and the foreseeable future with Charles's sister and father rather than at the Abbey, where he was sorely needed. Sorely needed because then there was the wassail, which the girls had filled generously with apples but which Pinky, in his lunacy, had neglected to place upon a table strong enough to bear the great bowl's weight.

The day had been a disaster.

Charles had kept her chin up but was inwardly distraught. Like a string of dominoes collapsing—not least the wassail bowl—one after another of her preparations had gone awry. So when Clarice tripped and sent the Christmas pudding crashing, Charles lost her temper, laying into the girl a tad harshly. In that moment she felt she'd failed so miserably as housekeeper, she'd never hear the end of it from Lord Wellesley.

Only his lordship did not even raise his voice, surprising everyone by swiftly helping Clarice collect the spilled pudding like it was the most natural thing in the world for a duke's son to assist his housemaid.

"Angus, Bartram, and Henry, fetch drums and whistles, boys. It's time we had some music in this house, quick now," Lord Wells ordered, arranging what was left of the pudding into a pile upon the plate. And then to everyone's further amazement, he licked his fingers clean.

"Astounding, Mrs. Jenkins. No, stupendous. I must have the finest cook in all of Cumberland that a dessert should taste so good, even from off the floor." He grinned. "Well dig in then, don't be shy."

Fergus, at least, did not hesitate to grab a fistful of the stuff.

Lord Wellesley turned to Charles. "You too, Miss Merrinan. I'll not let a wee food fall, wassail spill, or other *fowl upset* ruin our Christmas Eve." He winked at her before addressing present company, leaving Charles speechless.

"When you've spent years at sea, ladies," his lordship proceeded, "you learn to appreciate what you have, rather than what you lack, right boys?" His gaze swept over his men. "Now drink and be merry, all of you!" He raised his glass.

"Here, Here!" came loud shouts, the men beginning to pound their mugs upon the table. "T' Capt'n Wells! Long live His Grace!"

In no time, tin whistle and bodhran began a brisk jig, with Angus's voice fast filling the hall. And before she knew it, every maid—including Charles—had been pulled to her feet as the unruly crew all stomped and kicked their thick-soled boots. The jig spun faster, hands clapping in increasing rhythm, girls swirling and twirling until Angus let out a resounding last whoop, the echo of his voice ringing loudly in the hall.

Thanks to Lord Wellesley, the mood had instantly, dramatically changed.

***

"Follow me, Fox." Hand held tight, Wells slipped Charles away from the merriment, pulling his mistress behind him down the hall, far from the dancing, until she abruptly stopped.

"My lord, I should like to show you something first, if I may?" She appeared almost shy.

"As you wish, Miss Merrinan." He allowed her to lead him up more stairs and down a dark hallway, then down another passage too, until they came to a door he knew well.

"Wait here, my lord," she told him, "and close your eyes, no peeking." Wells shut them tight, smiling at her order. He'd not let on he knew what lay beyond this door.

He could hear her steal about the room to light the sconces in all four corners, could picture her stoking the fire so that it blazed bright as a log shifted and flames crackled. When she returned to fetch him from the hallway, he still did not peek as she guided him inside.

"I wish to give you a gift, sir. You may open your eyes."

When he did, he squeezed her hand. "Charles, however did you know this is my favorite room in all the world?"

"You know it, sir?"

"Of course." He flashed her a smile. "I spent hours here at play as a boy. It is the shell room, a room my great-grandmother commissioned. It is why I set sail, Charles, why I chose to adventure at sea."

She looked a little put out, so he attempted to explain.

"Charles, I have loved this room all my life, but to see it now, brought back to glory . . . It is the perfect gift, the very best gift you could have given me." He traced her cheek with his finger. "Thank you, Fox, truly."

She suddenly looked down. "You are welcome, my lord."

"You must have spent hours in here, Charles." He tilted her chin to look up at him. "I must inspect your handiwork."

He began to tour the room and run his hands along the walls, across the many bumps of shells, marveling at how the room shimmered, how the mirrors reflected candlelight to give a glow to every surface. "Hmm, yes," he proclaimed. "Just as I expected. You've outdone yourself, miss. I believe this proves I hired the best housekeeper in all of Cumberland."

**

Lord Wells grinned at her, the light making his eyes dance and making Charles blush to see him so pleased. She should have guessed he knew of the room's existence, rather than think he'd be as surprised as she was to discover it. She felt a little foolish as she fetched the wine she'd hidden earlier in the day.

"Will you raise a glass, my lord, to toast the room?"

"I shall." He accepted the drink and held it high. "To Miss Charles Merrinan!" he declared.

"To Lord Roland Wellesley," she responded, their glasses meeting with a clink as each took a sip. Before she knew it, his arm stole around her waist to pull her to him, his lips tasting like wine upon her tongue.

"Yours is the best gift of all this night, Fox," he told her softly. "Shall we stay a while longer here, in this beautifully restored room?"

"Of course, sir. Only I must apologize for all the mishaps that threatened this evening's celebration. I am so very sorry the—"

"Hush." He placed a finger to her lips and pulled her

down to the floor, bringing the bottle with him. "All accidents, wholly unforeseeable. As if it were your fault the snow fell and Pinky's not fit to set a table." He topped off her glass. "I have every intention of getting you soused tonight, my dear. I want you so drunk you laugh yourself silly." He smiled at her so warmly she felt her heart skip a beat. "I like it when you laugh, lass."

She tried to suppress her smile but could not. "I think you merely wish to take advantage of me, Lord Wellesley."

"I'd do no such thing," he feigned hurt.

"You do such things all the time, sir, and you know it," Charles teased back.

Lord Wells grabbed her for another satisfying kiss, this one longer than the last, until he broke off. "Woman, you distract me so much I forgot entirely my gift to you! Close your eyes at once, Charles."

She did, shutting them tight while not a little afraid of what he would give her. Something smooth and cool fell into her palm and she felt it a moment with her fingertips, perplexed. "May I open my eyes, sir?"

"You may, Charles."

She looked at the object in her hand with surprise, turning it over gingerly almost and flipping open the lid to reveal an exquisite timepiece with inlaid mother-of-pearl numerals. There was a compass in one corner and all twelve months engraved about the facing. And on the exterior case, the initials CW, making her furrow her brow.

"Do you like it, Fox?"

"I . . ." she began. "It is . . ." She thrust it back at him. "Lord Wellesley, I cannot accept your gift. It is much too fine, and far too—"

"Don't you dare, Charles." His tone threatened. "You may not return a gift. And it is not too fine, it is practical instead. I specifically chose a useful gift for you, nothing overly pretty, because I suspected you'd reject finery. So no protest," he insisted.

She remained dumbstruck.

"Go on, then," he goaded. "Am I not to receive thanks?"

"Oh, Roland!" She threw her arms about him, forgetting all sense of decorum. "Of course you have my thanks, my warmest thanks, though I still say it is too fine a gift, however practical. It is much, much too beautiful for the likes of me."

***

Wells shushed her with his lips. "Do you not wish to know why it bears the wrong initials?" he prodded. "I thought you'd wonder at that W."

Her pretty brow dimpled. "Why yes, I suppose it ought to be the letter M instead."

"Drink up, Charles, and listen." He poured them each more wine before he leaned his head back to gaze up at the ceiling, the constellations high above them shimmering in the shadowy light thrown by candle and fire.

"The piece belonged to my father's brother, my uncle, Carlton Wellesley. You share his first name, see, for they also called him Charles, and though I never knew him, I heard many a rousing tale of him growing up. My father kept this pocket watch, his brother's, on him for years, because it saved his life in battle. Turn it over and you will see the dent, there on the back, where a musket ball hit the timepiece rather than pierce my father's chest."

Charles ran her finger over the indentation.

"Uncle Charles bid his brother take the watch from his breast pocket as he lay dying on the battlefield, and no sooner had Father tucked it into his own uniform than he was shot and hit too, right at the exact spot. So the timepiece, you see, is not a little lucky. When I went to sea, Father gave it to me in hopes it would protect me on my travels, which it did, for I stand on land today, in safe return. And I wish *you* to have it, Fox, that it might protect and keep you too."

Only upon hearing the end of his tale, his mistress looked so appalled she again thrust the timepiece back at him, exclaiming, "Surely you cannot expect me to accept a family heirloom, my lord. You must take it back, I insist."

Wells pursed his lips. "Miss Merrinan, I have given past mistresses more lavish gifts for far less than what you have given me these months in companionship. I shall be insulted if you do not take it, and God willing, remain protected by it. I am no longer adrift at sea but settled here now. And besides, you share its owner's first name. Flip the W on its head and you'll have an M for Merrinan."

Yet despite his attempts at levity she remained distraught. Wells drew her to him, settling her between his legs there upon the floor, resting her into the hollow of his chest. "Charles, do not be stubborn. You would be angry if I'd given you some fancy bauble instead, would you not? Is this not a better gift for my mistress-cum-housekeeper, my wicked chicken thief?"

"You needn't have given me anything, sir." She finally spoke, her voice quiet. "You have fed my family and paid fair wage—trade enough for services I admit I now enjoy."

"So you enjoy me, Fox? Now that, see, is another gift you have just given me!" He laughed outright. "I enjoy you too, lass, very much. Sometimes a bit too much, I fear."

"What do you mean, too much?" She twisted around to look at him. "Roland, how many mistresses have you kept besides me, giving them overly generous gifts? How many women have you enjoyed over the years?"

He hushed her with his mouth. "None as much as you, Fox. I swear I have enjoyed none as much as—"

She harrumphed. "I am sure you said that to each of them."

"Jealous, are you?" He smirked. "I must say, Jenkins is quite a good dancer for a woman her age, handsome still too. Maybe I'll try her next."

Charles struggled to escape him, but he held her fast between his legs. "And Ruby is quite pretty, you know, though a tad simple for my taste. I like a woman with some fire in her."

And this time she did manage to wriggle free, fleeing to the opposite end of the room with a wild gleam in her eye.

"Ah, my mistress disobeys me yet again, and here I thought I'd tamed her."

"Tamed me, sir?" She thrust her chin at him, sending a jolt through his loins. "I merely let you *think* me your pet."

"Minx!" He lunged for her, chasing her about the room until he'd caught and wrestled her to the floor, her laughter infectious as they laid in a pile of limbs, tangled and teasing, both catching their breaths. Charles finally dusted herself off to go fetch them more wine.

"You shall ruin my new dress," she told him primly, straightening her skirts before pouring them each a fresh glass. "Now tell me about this room, please. I wish to know why it was built and what the many details all mean."

"Very well." Wells patted the space beside him on the floor for her to join. "I promise not to tear your pretty dress, Charles, only give me your new timepiece, so I might explain."

***

Charles handed him the watch, already feeling its loss from her skirt pocket, for it truly was a beautiful gift.

Lord Wellesley opened it to show her the compass. "Here you see the four corners of the earth, and here in this room the same four directions in each far corner. The constellations are positioned in this ceiling as in the night sky, and the shells were all collected from travels around the globe my grandparents embarked on."

"Both? Your grandmother traveled too?" Charles was amazed.

"She did." He grinned. "Sailed alongside Grandpapa on his many expeditions. Quite the hellion, or so I was told."

"Oh how I envy her!" Charles burst out, forgetting herself. "What is it like, Roland, tell me, please! What is it like on a ship at sea, miles and miles from everyone and everything you know?"

"Frightening as hell and invigorating as nothing else, Fox," he answered, staring deep into her eyes. "Freedom near boundless, yet with it near constant fear of death. The sea shows no mercy when she is angered, and a man can be driven mad out there, with nothing but blue sky and blue water reflected back, day upon day. And yet at night, to see the stars, Charles, is the most magnificent, most humbling experience imaginable. To gaze at all those lights and realize just how tiny, how insignificant you are on a ship in the middle of such vast space . . ." He stopped himself, his voice almost wistful.

Charles closed her fingers over his own, pressing his hand to hers.

"I shall take you one day, so you can experience it yourself," he told her, impassioned. "I'll take you with me like Grandfather took Grandmother. You must sail the ocean too, Charles."

"Do not make promises you cannot keep, Roland." Charles swallowed her pain. "I beg you, don't."

***

"And why should I not keep my promise?" Wells was hurt by her words. She perplexed him anew, this woman. She forever surprised.

"Because you cannot, and we both know it." Charles sounded sad but by no means angry. "Take me with you now instead, my lord. Hold me in your arms and whisper in my ear stories from your travels, your adventures. Let me experience those wonders through your words, Roland. Take me with you, please," she begged.

And the look in her eyes so beseeched, he'd not have denied her for the world. He gazed at her with such tenderness he made her look away, as if she were embarrassed by his feeling. He settled his mistress deep into his arms and began to regale her with stories of daring and despair, of longing and loss. Of tempests and tall ships marooned and tossed.

She softened in his arms as Wells minced no words. He'd no reason to lie and so told her everything now: the sorrow, the pain, and the terror alongside moments of awe and joy. He even told her of his vow to his men made deep in the East Indies that day they'd threatened to mutiny. He'd ordered the ship straight into danger to rescue a royal lady—and as a result, now suffered their taunts as 'their grace.'

Charles listened rapt; she did not interrupt or interject. At times he heard her gasp in surprise, but mostly, his mistress soaked up his words. He felt as though he could tell her anything, anything at all now, and she would accept him no matter what devilry he revealed. He wished, suddenly, to reveal everything about himself to her—every last cowardly act or heroic feat. She was like a raft upon which he might be buoyed and saved.

That night in the shell room he did indeed wish to whisk Charles away to sail off to some far-flung island where they would be no longer master and maid, but simply Adam and Eve in God's garden: two halves of one whole, without shame or reproach. Free from scrutiny.

Wells wished to keep Charles all to himself—to *be* a better, more noble self. If only he knew how.

CHAPTER TWENTY-FIVE

John imagined things could be worse. After all, the gale had trapped him with Eleanor Merrinan for Christmas, not some snow bank somewhere he'd like as not freeze to death. He was used to storms at sea but this was something else entirely. He'd never seen so much snow in all his life. He wondered, briefly, how Lord Wells was faring at the Abbey and then promptly forgot about him; his grace's housekeeping mistress was competent enough to see the Abbey through both holiday and snow.

He snuck another peek at Eleanor, who was busy unraveling a moth-eaten wool shawl he held stretched between his thick hands. She worried her lip while she worked, making him want to kiss the pretty pout so badly he'd nearly dropped the shawl a few times already. He constantly had to keep himself in check, in the presence of this lady. For he still thought of her as one, even though she waited on him the same way she served her father. He wasn't used to such attention. He wasn't used to being alone in a small space with a woman either, forever bumping into her. Of course her old man was with them too, but the sad fellow existed on such a wholly different plane it felt to John as if Merrinan himself were but furniture and he were in truth alone with Miss Eleanor, unchaperoned.

Except, that is, when Merrinan had one of his fits, yelling and flailing and gnashing his teeth. It was on those occasions when he relived his wife's death that he acted so out of character. John had seen it twice now and felt deeply for poor Eleanor, who managed her father as best she could during these episodes. Once, his wild gestures had knocked her flat to floor and John had barely stopped himself from throttling the old man. He'd forcibly removed him from her presence and locked him in his bedroom, yet by the time he'd returned she was back on her feet, dismissive of the incident. She may not have her sister's temper, but Eleanor was no lightweight. She couldn't be, to live alone with her father as she did.

"John." He thought he heard her voice. "*John.*"

"Beg pardon, miss." He looked up. "Lost in thought I s'pose."

"And just what thought might that be, sir?" Her wide brown eyes were luminous in the firelight—eyes a man could get lost in.

"Oi, naught what needs concern yerself, miss." He might have blushed; he did not wish to reveal the nature of his thoughts or feelings to her.

She frowned. "I should think *I* may be the judge of that, sir. You needn't treat me like a child, you know."

"Why, I . . ." John was distraught. "I meant no offense, miss, truly. 'Twas only work at the Abbey I were mullin', and surely 'tis borin' t' one such as yerself."

She cast him an earnest look. "*Nothing* is boring to me, John, absolutely nothing. You see how I live out here with Papa. Can you tell me, honestly, that I should ever be bored by anything you might say?"

He'd not thought of it that way. Come to think of it, she was always making him think of things in new ways.

"I beg yer pardon, Miss Merrinan, for assumin' anythin' at all, you're right. Only I'd rather speak o' things other'n work when I'm with you, miss. Finer, better things."

"Like what, John?" She smiled again, more warmly still, and his heart wrenched to see her face light up. "And I must insist you call me Ellie, please, as there is surely no need for formality here."

It was his turn to frown. "No miss, I won't. Lord Wells— not t' mention yer sister—wouldn't stand for such behavior, and I'll not—"

Her hand snaked out to grip his warmly as he glanced down at it in alarm.

"John Cuthbert, look about you, sir. Neither Lord Wellesley nor Charles is here right now, and I have given you permission to call me by my name. Now will you or won't you be man enough to do so?"

He stared at her in shock, seeing yet another side to this woman who with each passing day revealed she was not one to trifle with. "Very well, Ellie," he grumbled, looking away. "Only I still don't think it's right t'—"

"Well *I* think it is perfectly right, and it pleases me to hear you say my name, John." She squeezed his hand. "Now sit closer, I beg, that you might block the draft from the door with your great hulking frame, please."

Her eyes twinkled with mirth, for it had become their running joke in the storm that Cuthbert keep her and her father warm by simply standing his bulky self in front of drafty windows.

John did as she asked and pulled his chair nearer to hers, a little closer than was necessary so he could smell the sweet scent of her. She, meanwhile, put down her skein and took the half unraveled wool from his hands, setting both aside before she smoothed her skirts and laid her head upon his shoulder, as if it were the most natural thing in all the world.

"I shall use you as a pillow too, John, if you don't mind. See how useful you are?" She teased him with another smile. "Tell me a story, please, any story at all."

And John Cuthbert, nearly frozen with surprise, was not so shy as to let an opportunity like this one pass him by. He slipped an arm about her waist and drew her closer still, hearing her exhale the softest little sigh. Then he mustered a deep, warm voice and told her of his adventures at sea with Lord Wells, lulling her into visions and dreams most fantastic, he hoped, until she'd closed her eyes in sleep.

&.

"But surely yer lordship can't mean to . . . !"

Clarice stood nervously twisting her apron next to Marta, both girls hovering behind Lord Wellesley, whose sleeves were rolled up, forearms plunged into soapy dishwater, as Charles watched from the doorway. She folded her own arms and secretly grinned to herself.

"Of course I mean to," he snapped at them. "Now out of my kitchen, both of you. It is St. Stephen's, for God's sake, and you are in my way," he ordered.

To which they scurried out, quick as could be.

Charles snuck up behind him, casting a furtive glance towards the door before slipping her arms about his middle to whisper, "I like you on my staff, Roland." She deliberately used his name. "You make a fine scullery, my lord."

To which he spun about, soapy arms fast drawing her to him. "Command me today, Miss Merrinan, while you still may. Tonight, too, whatever my mistress asks shall be hers."

And Charles blushed to think Lord Wells would do *her* bidding this day too. She kissed him hard. "I shall spend the day in thought, sir, as to how you might please me this night, for I'll expect no objections, only strict obedience."

"Just you wait, Fox." He kissed her fiercely. "I will not disappoint."

*

For the rest of St. Stephen's, Wells remained as good as his word, shocking Mrs. Jenkins most of all, that he should commandeer her kitchen. He fried them all eggs for dinner, he scrubbed sheets for Ginny in the laundry; he even beat rugs for Ruby.

As for his crew, they knew the drill, for he'd served them on St. Stephen's even at sea, hauling rigging and swabbing decks. They laughed and jeered at him good naturedly as he went about their tasks, telling him *he were better on a ship, aye, than here on land, useless blueblood!* To which he played along, cussing and cursing them roundly, telling them they were worthless good-for-nothings he'd fire on the morrow. They could rot in hell for all he cared!

It was a game played and enjoyed by all, most especially Wells, for it was the one day each year he could pretend to be one of them, when he could forget all about the damn Dukedom. He reveled in belonging, if but a little while. It felt briefly as it had on his ship, when his crew had been his family. He'd missed that.

*

That night, Charles snuck into his lordship's room to slip into his bed.

Immediately, he grabbed her to him. "You've an hour at most, miss, before St. Stephen's ends. Speak now what you desire of me, Fox."

She hesitated, for all day she'd been mulling what she wished from him. And the longer she'd mulled the more she'd come to such a simple request she knew it was impossible for him to fulfill. But she blurted it anyway, because he'd pleasured her body enough in past it was not as though she needed more of *that*. What she desired was something far more intimate, which he'd never be able to give her, even if he tried.

"I wish you weren't the Duke's son, my lord." She told him in a rush. "I wish you were a village gadgie instead, a simple lad to court me. Treat me like your equal in bed tonight, please; I do not wish to be your mistress. Make love like a man loves a woman. Can you do that, Roland? Sir?" He suddenly struck her as far away, and she feared her words had upset him.

"I meant no harm by it, truly you needn't . . ." Charles struggled. "If it displeases your lordship then you needn't play along. I should be content if you merely—"

His lips silenced her swiftly, passionately. He stole her breath away.

"I shall try, Fox. I shall try my best to be that man. I wish I were but a simple lad and not the future Duke. I wish I could steal you away to some snug little cottage, to a life of simple harvests, children tall as weeds, memories grown ripe with age."

She kissed him quiet. "Then give me that, Roland, pretend we have that life. Just for tonight, I beg. Tomorrow I am your mistress and you my lord, but this night be master of none, stonemason only."

"Aye and you but my lusty village lass." He grinned at her, his mood lifted, even as his lips caught her own in a kiss that lasted through the night, tasting of freedom.

❧

John dried the dishes as Eleanor washed. It was St. Stephen's so he'd insisted on helping. He still found it hard to call her Ellie, but he'd tried a few times, her name on his tongue altogether too sweet. She was telling him something, talking again, but he'd not heard a word, his eyes drifting to the nape of her neck bent over the sink, the tendrils of hair curling there like pea shoots in spring. How he longed to reach out and . . .

With a crash the plate dropped to floor as John, horrified, looked down at his feet. Why the devil had he let it slip from his hands? He bent at once to collect the shards but then knocked into Eleanor, who'd bent down too, their foreheads colliding in a bump that sent them both reeling backwards.

"Ellie!" he exclaimed, rushing to pull her back up, his hand reaching out to touch her scalp tenderly, fearing he'd injured her.

She rubbed her head, wincing a little, before she laughed at him. "'Tis nothing, really," she declared. "The kitchen is too small for you; I told you not to help me in here."

Yet his hand, still at her soft hair, wouldn't let go, as he found himself tracing her cheek with his finger, then tracing her lips. His hand had a will of its own.

Her eyes widened in surprise.

"Eleanor, I'm that sorry," he told her, hand still on her lips when she suddenly pressed her mouth to his fingers and kissed him there, her lips soon kissing the palm of his hand, heat searing his flesh.

He could stand it no more. He took her face in both hands, drawing her to his mouth, where he kissed her hard, insisting she open to him and she did, her own hands wrapping about the back of his neck to draw him closer, too, as his tongue searched and found hers willing.

They kissed greedily, then tenderly almost, before he wrenched himself away and fled the room, quickly donning his coat to head straight outside into the swirling, white-cold air, to where he might at last catch his breath.

CHAPTER TWENTY-SIX

D*earest Charles,* Eleanor's letter began as they all did. Wells settled into his seat by the fire to read.

No doubt Christmas at the Abbey was a sight to behold for all the effort you wrote of. Our own celebration was quiet, though John's presence brought merriment this year. He truly is the sweetest man, and I admit I miss him already, though he sits here as I write. He leaves tomorrow as he believes it safe again to travel. Though I fear there is another reason he is now eager to leave, a reason you will think I should regret, but I do not. I regret it not a bit. I kissed him, you see, just his hand, nothing more. It was all very chaste. Only then he kissed me back, Charles, and it was glorious, his kiss! It was as if the world stopped and there were no other souls on earth but he and me.

You are surely angry, sister, but I do not care if you are. I must be honest with myself and with you. I am in love with John Cuthbert, and nothing you say will alter my feelings towards him. I do not know if he loves me in return, but even if he shouldn't, it is the most remarkable, wonderful, feeling, Charles. Someday you will experience it too, I am sure, but until then believe me when I tell you nothing can compare to such a kiss. Nothing!

Wells paused in his reading, for it felt like a breach of confidence to read so intimate a declaration from Eleanor Merrinan regarding his steward, John Cuthbert. He was taken aback by both her passion and innocence; Charles had indeed managed to hide much from her sister. Yet Eleanor's heartfelt sentiment towards Cuthbert also struck a nerve. Wells worried his steward might in truth be in love with the girl—Charles would not be pleased. Nor did he want John rushing into marriage, stolen from him when he needed him here at the Abbey. He was his righthand man. He trusted John with his life, could not imagine life *without* him, truth be told.

With a sigh he read on.

So that is my news, judge me as you see fit. I understand now why Mama left her family to be with Papa. There is no stronger pull in all the world, Charles. And only think, sister, had our parents not eloped, there'd be no you or me. So in the end, what is wrong and what is right is only our perception in the moment, is it not? I am not ashamed to have kissed John Cuthbert. No one can tell me something so wonderful could possibly be so wrong.

Write to me soon, Charles, or better yet, now that the snow is passable come see us, please. It would do Papa good, and as for me, I need you more than ever, for no one counsels so well as you. Only do not counsel me from John, I could not bear it. Do not tell me I am foolish and naïve, as I know I am both and frankly do not care.

Love, Charles, cannot be ignored. I will embrace it.

Ever yours, Eleanor

Wells folded the letter, glad for once that Cuthbert did not read these missives too. Should he broach the matter with Charles, or let her come to him? He wasn't sure how she'd react to her sister's declaration, but he suspected that if he now forbade Cuthbert to visit Eleanor Merrinan the man would outright revolt. He'd known John long enough to recognize when not to cross him.

No. Any interference in this would have to come from Charles herself regarding her sister.

These Merrinan girls are trouble indeed, he thought to himself. And yet, for all the trouble they were, there was something about the two . . . It was absurd, almost, that he and John should both gravitate to these two sisters.

❧

"Oi, sir, 'twere a humble celebration, but Miss Eleanor and her father are well stocked for winter. Had the snow not come on so hard I'd like as not've made me way back in time."

Wells had called for Cuthbert to report on his absence. They were alone in the parlor as he did not wish their conversation overheard.

"John, I do not blame you for the storm. I wish only that you'd been here to witness the pudding debacle and Pinky's wassail disgrace. I must say it was rather lively here that night." Wells smiled to recall the evening.

Cuthbert eyed him closely. "And Miss Merrinan, sir? How'd she take all the upset? I imagine she were right peeved t' see her hard work unravel afore her eyes."

"She came around, John." Wells smiled to himself. "I think she's settled in nicely as housekeeper."

"Has she now?" His man's eyes sparked. "Think you've tamed her then, Yer Grace?"

Wells frowned at his steward's needling. "Yes, John, I believe I have. She serves me well and willingly now in both capacities."

Cuthbert snorted.

"And may I ask how you got along with her sister, the lovely Miss Eleanor, trapped as you were in that house with barely a fitting chaperone in her father?" It was time to pry.

"Fine, sir," his steward grumbled, looking down.

"Nothing untoward happen, did it, John?"

"No, sir," the man mumbled, clearly itching to leave.

"Good. Because if word got out that any man of mine took advantage of a village girl—"

Cuthbert suddenly met Wellesley's eyes. "Oi, and you're one to talk."

"John I *am* one to talk." He remained stern. "My agreement with Charles is quite different and you know it."

"Is it, sir?" Cuthbert's gaze was hard. "Y' stole a great deal more from her than she from you."

Wellesley's face darkened. "You forget your place, John."

"Sure, Yer Grace." Cuthbert did not back down. "Way I see it, though, y' need remindin' that you've a position t' uphold here too. And if I recall, as lord o' this here Abbey you've an even greater duty than my sort t' be honorable to ladies."

"A thief is hardly a lady, John," Wells bit back, feeling provoked.

"'Course, Yer Grace, I thought her but a thief too at first, only by the time y' took her honor, sir, y' knew full well she were a lady."

Cuthbert abruptly strode out, leaving Wells livid.

The very next day, Wells demanded his steward hand over Charles's response to her sister. Cuthbert did, grudgingly.

Eleanor,
I scarce know what to write you, but I shall visit as soon as possible,

only until then promise me you will not kiss John Cuthbert again. Swear it, Ellie, not until we've had a chance to discuss this change in you. Give me your word, sister, because it is a serious matter, more serious than you know, with greater repercussions than you know. And though you may think me innocent of such matters, I am experienced enough to have kissed a man and rued the day myself. But I shall leave that talk for when I see you.

Rued his kiss? Really? Wells sat up in his chair, gripping the letter tight.

I am grateful you and Father weathered the storm, and grateful Cuthbert thinks you well stocked in food and peat. I do not blame him or you, Ellie, for what happened over Christmas. I ask only that you not encourage him further. If he cares for you at all, he will keep his distance, respectably. I ask only that you also do the same. Would that I were home with you and not so far away! Mother would be so displeased with me right now, I cannot bear to think on it. She would be displeased on so many counts I cannot even tell you them all, for you would surely think less of me too. Some days I think the very worst of myself, yet at other times I feel just as you wrote: 'what is wrong and what is right is only our perception in the moment.' There are moments, Eleanor, when I have fallen very low. There are moments, too, I'd not trade for all the world.

I shall try to come by week's end, and come alone, that we might speak. Until then, Ellie, I beg you to remember the love of your family. To love a man is one thing, but men's hearts are too oft fickle. Father and I will never abandon you. Our love for you is absolute.

> *Charles*

Wells handed Cuthbert back the letter, saying not a word, nor did his steward, who simply took it and walked out. And which damn kiss did Charles rue? His, or had she kissed another? He thought it unlikely she'd been with any man before him; she'd been a virgin after all, but perhaps she'd had a village beau. And as for fickle, well, he could say the same for women—more so! London had taught him firsthand just how fickle the female heart could be.

Wells sat a moment longer in his chair before the parlor's fire, mulling the situation between Cuthbert and Miss Eleanor. Charles had said not a word to him, not even hinted aught was amiss. She was likely waiting to speak with her sister first. Perhaps he should accompany her on her visit, occupy her old man so she could talk to Eleanor unencumbered. He didn't want Cuthbert tagging along, and if he were honest with himself, he didn't like the idea of his mistress traipsing through that much snow on her own either, not after the accident she'd had the last time she'd gone home.

Yes, he would accompany her. It was for the best.

"My lord, I really don't see why you need to accompany me."

"Humor me, woman."

"I believe I do nothing *but* humor you." Charles frowned, irritated Lord Wells still did not trust her enough to call on her family alone.

"Then you may humor me further." He took her arm, the basket in his other, and proceeded to march her through the Abbey's snowy courtyard. It had been two days since she'd received Eleanor's letter.

Two terribly long days.

"They are surely staring at us," she whispered at him.

"Who, Charles—staff? I doubt very much they've pressed their faces to frosty windowpanes in order to spy on us, not when there's work enough inside to keep them busy." She felt his grip tighten. "You worry too much."

"You worry too little," she grumbled, but by then they'd left the courtyard and were on the snowy path heading out. Slowly she began to relax, the air crisp, the sun glinting diamonds off the snow, her arm tucked warm into his lordship's own. How could she not enjoy the moment, as it were? And yet . . .

"I shall occupy your father if you like, Charles, that you might converse with your sister in peace. Can he play chess still? That ought to divert him from making a scene."

"Did he make a scene when you visited before, sir?" She was mortified by the thought. "I do hope not. It so embarrasses Ellie when he does."

"Not too bad, no" his lordship reassured, "though I imagine he can be worse." She thought Wells looked a little sheepish telling her this.

"He can be difficult, yes. I wish sometimes he'd . . ." She stopped herself. "Never mind, sir, he is who he is now. It is no one's fault."

***

Wells took care not to reveal how much he knew from her letters. "He must have loved your mother very much," he probed, "to be so affected by her death."

"Yes," she answered, "and she him."

Only she did not elaborate, tromping on in silence through the snow for some while longer.

After a time he hazarded to speak again. "And what of your plans for your sister, Charles? She is old enough to wed, is she not? Has she a beau, perhaps a suitor in the village?"

She looked at him with surprise. "Why do you ask, my lord?"

"Why?" he feigned. "Why, that is what women talk about, is it not?"

"You did not ask the same of me." She sounded hurt.

"You did not, upon our initial encounter, make the same

impression your sister did when I first met her." He chose to be honest, though she walked on more purposefully.

"Charles . . ."

"It is nothing to me, sir."

He could tell that it was.

"Eleanor ought to have a suitor by now, it's true." She revealed more. "She is twenty. She is well bred. She ought to have a season in London and I intend to give her one just as soon as I have means."

"I see," he replied, not seeing at all, for why in the world would her sister need a London season to make herself a match?

"And I appreciate your offer to occupy my father this morning, my lord, as there are things I wish to discuss with my sister in private."

"I shall be happy to." He meant it.

"And I would appreciate if you did not interest yourself further in my family's affairs."

"I beg your pardon," he uttered, irked. "I meant no disrespect in asking about your sister, Charles."

"I realize that, sir, but it is unseemly for a person of your status to concern himself with servant affairs, and so I do not—"

"Charles, surely you realize you are more to me than mere servant."

She stopped in her tracks and looked at him. "No, my lord, I am merely your servant in bed. But a mistress is still a servant, so I would prefer you not cross that line by—"

"Damn it, Charles." He grabbed her arm so she'd not stomp off. "You are more to me and you know it!"

Only he saw in her eyes that she did not know, not at all, for she looked at him so queerly he felt a shudder twist his soul.

"Please do not pretend, Lord Wellesley." Her eyes betrayed hurt. "I have told you before that such tenderness is painful to me. I appreciate your concern, truly, and the kindness you now show me, but we both know full well what I am to you. There is no need to lie. In fact, I would prefer if you did not."

He was shocked, for her words, much as he disliked them, rang true. He might well feel more for her than he should, but he could never act upon those feelings in any meaningful way and so to proclaim them, honestly or not, did her no good—and might only do her harm.

"Forgive me, Charles, you are right, of course." He took her arm brusquely again in his own and began to walk them up the path towards her father's house. "I'd no right to speak as I just did. I'll not let it happen again, you've my word."

And though it appeared to pain her to say it, she agreed. "Thank you, my lord." She squeezed his arm even as the door opened to Miss Eleanor, eyes wide with joy, warmly welcoming them in.

❧

"You're a damn fine chess player, boy," Merrinan proclaimed for the umpteenth time as Wells slid his piece across the board. "As good as Charles, I'd say."

"You taught your daughter well, sir." Wells smiled at the old man. They were seated in Mr. Merrinan's sparse kitchen, at the sole table in the house.

"Not my daughter, fool, Charles Wellesley." He scowled at him.

"You knew my Uncle Carlton?" Wells asked, thinking the gentleman quite batty.

"Knew him? Christ, boy, served with him *and* your father. Two bloody campaigns! Two campaigns . . ." He sank in upon himself, lost again in thought.

Wells was confounded by this fellow's ramblings. Merrinan had mentioned before having served alongside his father, the

Duke, but that he'd known Uncle Charles, Lord Carlton Wellesley himself . . . The coincidence was too much, not least because he'd just given his uncle's timepiece to this man's daughter.

Merrinan's head snapped back. "What date you set?" he announced, moving another piece across the board, and not a bad move either.

"Date, sir?" Wells was again confused. How the devil his daughters managed his nonsense was a wonder. He'd go mad if he had to spend his days attending this dotty fellow.

"Wedding date, young man." Merrinan ruthlessly stared him down. "I've not forgotten your promise to my daughter, sir, and while her dowry isn't much, I've a little set aside, same as for Eleanor."

Wells could not believe Merrinan still thought him betrothed to Charles. "Ah yes," he faltered, "the wedding." He swallowed, deciding that to play along again was better than to rouse the old man's ire. He only prayed Charles would be spared such talk later. "We thought to wait until spring, sir," he lied.

"Spring, eh?" Merrinan nodded. "Always best for weddings, unless of course you need wed sooner." His look held mischief. "My Addie now, I married her in haste for that very reason, sir. Couldn't keep her hands off me, nor I off her. What a woman she was, Adelaide. God rest her soul." And suddenly his eyes began to swim, uncontrolled tears streaming down his sunken cheeks as his face fell to his hands.

Wells looked at him in shock, imagining Charles's indignation should she learn her mother had been compromised before marriage. He was suddenly alarmed by all he knew, or thought he knew, of this man's story—by the heartbreak felt so keenly still ten years since Merrinan's wife had passed.

He awkwardly patted the fellow's shoulder. "Can I fetch you a drink, Mr. Merrinan, or would you like to lie down a spell, sir?" He tried to think how Charles or Eleanor might handle the situation.

"No." The old man lifted his tear-streaked face to Wells. "Only promise me you'll never hurt my daughter, Wellesley. Promise you'll care for her always, love her always. *Promise*," he insisted, grasping Wells's hand in a surprisingly strong grip. "Swear it, boy," he repeated, his grip by now a crushing demand.

And Roland Wellesley, unable to articulate anything else, simply told him, "Yes."

CHAPTER TWENTY-SEVEN

"I am not angry with you, Ellie," Charles assured her sister, "I am merely stunned, is all, that you should have, well—"

"That I should have feelings for John?" Her sister's eyes flashed. "I know you think him unworthy, Charles, so beneath me that you will never see what I—"

"I do not think him unworthy, Eleanor. I happen to have a great deal of respect for Cuthbert. That is not the issue."

"Then what is the issue, Charles? I do not understand why you cannot be happy for me. Why you cannot—"

"Eleanor," she snapped, "I am unhappy not because of your feelings but because of what those feelings mean for your future."

"But so long as—"

"Let me finish, sister." Charles steadied herself. "I made a vow to Mama that I would care for you and see you set in life. And I do not take my vow lightly. She would have wanted more for you, more than what John Cuthbert offers. Ellie, consider for a moment who he is. Did you know he is an orphan, without family? That Lord Wellesley's father, the Duke, took him in as charity? He has no property, no standing in society, he has only the goodwill of his grace, the Duke, and his position at the Abbey as Lord Wellesley's steward, on a salary I imagine can't be all that much more than mine. Were you to marry him, where would you live? How would he support you and any children you might someday have?"

Eleanor looked defiant. "I should think we'd find a way, Charles, and that it would be no worse than living here alone with father as I do now."

Charles glared at Ellie. "So it is escape you seek then? Perhaps you are less enamored of John Cuthbert and more of the chance to leave father and this house?"

"That is unkind and you know it!" Eleanor pushed back. "I would never abandon Father, ever. I would simply take him with me, or John live here with us. He is used to Papa already. He is not bothered by him. And besides, it is not as though *you* have any intention of returning soon, what with your new position and . . ." She abruptly stopped herself.

"And what, Eleanor?" Charles was surprised at how heated their argument had grown.

"And your own feelings for Lord Wells," she threw at Charles in a fit of temper, only to immediately retract it. "Forgive me, Charles, I did not mean—"

"Don't you dare speak a word more to me, Eleanor." Charles's voice was brittle. "I am leaving now, and I will not be back."

"Charles, please, I didn't mean it, I swear I—"

But she was too enraged to utter a word more for fear she might strike her sister outright. She could not bear to look at Ellie, all high and mighty in her newfound love, clueless as to what had been sacrificed for her, done for her.

"Charles!" Eleanor looked distraught. "Please!"

But she continued walking. She did not even consider his lordship remained yet inside with Father, hunched over a chessboard. She continued walking at a furious pace, her insides roiling with rage, sorrow, and beneath it all, a merciless knot of growing despair and creeping, insidious envy.

§

"Miss Eleanor?" Wells took one look at the girl's face and knew something was wrong. "What has happened to distress you, miss?"

He watched her swallow her pain. "I have quarreled with Charles, my lord, and I fear—"

"Fear?" He was now concerned. "What is there to fear, miss?"

"I fear I have wounded my sister irreparably, sir, and she will never forgive me now, *never.*" And before he knew it, she'd covered her face with her hands, trying to hide from him.

"There now, miss, surely 'tis not so bad as that." He procured her a handkerchief, which she took without question. "I am certain your sister will forgive you, whatever your quarrel." Wells awkwardly patted her arm.

"She won't." Eleanor sniffed into his kerchief, allowing him to guide her to a kitchen chair. "Not Charles. She is not so forgiving. She is stubborn as a mule when hurt."

"She loves you immensely." He'd read enough of their correspondence to know this without doubt. "I am certain she will come round."

The girl only sighed more deeply.

"Where is she now—your sister?"

"Gone, my lord. She did not wait for you."

"Do you wish to tell me about your quarrel?"

She shook her head no.

"Do you wish me to sit here a moment longer with you?"

She nodded yes.

"Tea then?" he ventured, not quite sure how to deal with a

distraught female, as he'd barely known what to do with her distraught old man.

"Oh!" She let out a gasp. "Yes of course, sir. I shall make us a pot at once. Do forgive me, my lord, I seem to have lost all sense of—"

"Miss Eleanor, I mean to fetch *you* tea, not the other way round." He gave her a little frown. "Now sit a moment and collect yourself."

When she tried to rise he insisted, "That is an order, miss," and she stayed put.

Wells put on the kettle and found the tea, busying himself in the ramshackle kitchen, thinking. No doubt they'd been arguing about Cuthbert. He would have to speak with Charles on the matter—sooner than later it seemed.

Yet when he arrived bearing the tray Miss Eleanor looked no better. In fact, the girl looked worse. He poured her a cup and carefully pushed it towards her.

"Drink," he ordered softly.

"Lord Wells . . ." she began and then promptly broke off.

"You may speak freely, miss, I'll not take offense."

"Do you have feelings for my sister, sir? Have you . . ." She could not meet his eyes. "That is"—she nearly trembled to say it—"have you . . ."

He wouldn't let her. "Your sister is an excellent house-keeper, Miss Eleanor, and excellent person. I have the highest regard for her, that is all." He said this as matter-of-factly as humanly possible, knowing Charles would kill him if he did not.

"I know that sir, that is not . . . That is not what I meant." She inhaled a deep breath. "Do you have feelings for her the way a man has feelings for a woman, my lord?" She boldly met his eye.

Wells blinked, nearly cracking under this woman's gaze.

She had her sister's willpower, alright, and for an instant he didn't know what the devil to tell her.

"Miss Eleanor I . . . cannot answer you that," he choked out.

"And why not?"

"Because I do not have your sister's permission to speak," he finally said.

"You are a Peer of the Realm, Lord Wellesley." She had suddenly grown calm. "You do not need anyone's permission to speak, sir."

He bit his tongue. "Be that as it may, miss, I gave your sister my word that I would not involve myself in her family's affairs. In fact, she made me promise her no less as we walked here today."

"And why is that, Lord Wellesley?" She continued to probe, disturbing him not a little by how swiftly her mood seemed to shift.

"Because she felt it unseemly for a lord to involve himself in his servant's private life." Wells could not seem to lie to her, try as he might.

"I see," she answered. "I believe you have just answered my question then, my lord."

"I have?"

"Yes," she declared, remarkably now at ease. "It appears that you and my sister both have feelings for one another which you are neither willing, nor able, to admit. And I have unwittingly poked a hole in my sister's well-worn armor, for which I must now pay a very dear price."

"Miss Eleanor . . ." He tried to protest, but she merely held up her hand to still him.

These two, he thought to himself, *recalcitrants*.

"No, Lord Wellesley." She shook her head at him. "I do not wish to hear more, as it will only put me in worse straits with Charles. I shall simply imagine what has transpired between you these past months and shall endeavor never to bring it up with her again." She looked suddenly exhausted. And then, in a rapid turn of mind, burst out, "May I ask what you pay your steward, my lord?"

"Cuthbert?" He was astonished. "That is hardly your business, miss, though you may ask him yourself how much he—"

"Is it enough to live on, sir, were he to take a wife, to have a family?" she persisted.

"Well I should think so, yes. And if I know John, he's likely put funds aside, a nest egg as it were, for the day he leaves me, though I'd be loath to see him go." He eyed her sharply. "If you mean to steal my friend *and* steward from me you've another think coming, miss."

She held her ground, oblivious to his threat. "I mean nothing of the sort, Lord Wellesley. I mean only to keep your steward here with you, by your side. And *I* forever by *his* side," she added quietly to herself. Then, standing up, she gave him a peculiar little smile. "Thank you so much for visiting, my lord. You have been most kind again to Father, who surely enjoyed the chess game very much. But if you'll excuse me now I have a rather important letter to write to my sister, and if you do not mind, Lord Wellesley, I shall deliver it to her myself on the morrow."

He stood quickly, bowed slightly, then made his way out the door, down the path, and onto the main footpath. He walked the entire way back in disbelief at Charles's sister. Whoever had raised these Merrinan girls had been astonishingly negligent in teaching either one of them the deference due a duke's son.

Termagants, he muttered to himself. *Both of them.*

That night Charles came late to his lordship's bed. So late, in fact, that he was deep in sleep. She'd been so wounded by Eleanor's blithe comment she'd wanted to hurl something at her sister, shatter a dish, strike her even. She'd been horrified by her overreaction, yet too proud to admit the source. *Pride goes before a fall,* her mother had warned her often. *You'll hurt only yourself, daughter, if you don't learn to let a thing go. Do not be so proud you cannot ask for help, or admit when you've been wrong.*

Well she'd been wrong alright. She'd been wrong to assume she could guard her soul against Roland Wellesley. And she could admit that what her parents had found with one another was a love so rare as to be impossible to repeat.

As Charles slipped beneath the covers, she was careful not to wake his lordship. She snuggled against his warm, bulky frame, craving his person now more than ever. She closed her eyes and pretended it was Christmas and they lay in the shell room once again. In her mind she heard his rich, sonorous voice tell her his fantastic stories; she wasn't even sure they'd all been true. It had been magical to lie on the floor staring up at the star-studded ceiling, as if she stood on a ship under a constellated sky with he her captain, ferrying her off into adventure.

She loved how they'd merely spoken, too, that night; they'd not made love at all. She had felt a knot in her gut unspool only to reel her deeper in, binding her to him more firmly than ever. She'd wanted to remain in that room with Roland Wellesley, suspended in time, in a life she might never lead but could imagine in that moment, with him. His voice at her ear had filled her with such warmth and trust and longing she knew she would pay for it with her heart, but that night, just briefly, he'd been hers and she his.

Already, the memory was bittersweet.

CHAPTER TWENTY-EIGHT

D espite his better judgement, Wells unfolded Eleanor's letter to Charles.

My Dearest Charles,
I know we have quarreled and I hate it so. But I also know you are too angry with me to visit or write, so I've no choice but to unburden my conscience in this letter instead.

Wells almost folded the note back up, hearing John's voice berate him; he quashed it and read on.

I do not presume to know what you have endured since the night you left us to steal two chickens. I curse the day you did, for ever since we have been parted, and by more than mere distance it seems. You write me only half truths, I can tell, nor do I insist you tell me all. But I despair that you have taken upon yourself responsibility for my happiness at great cost to your own. It is not right, sister, and I will not accept it. You have sacrificed much for me and Papa, too much, and I hereby absolve you of your burden. I am old enough now to make decisions of my own, to steer my own course. Father remains a burden, of course, but he is both our burden, which you shall not bear alone, not so long as I live. So Charles, I beg you let go this notion of a London season for me. How many years must you toil for Lord Wellesley before you save enough to make such a thing happen? And why London again, after how shabbily that city treated us? I'll not return to Mother's family, nor will you, and without their support, no season can happen for either of us, you know this.

Charles had spoken before of giving her sister a London season, but who exactly were these grandparents of theirs? Wells felt a creeping unease as he continued to read the letter he'd conveniently accepted from Eleanor on Charles's behalf. He'd sent Cuthbert to accompany the young woman back to her father's house. She'd been disappointed not to see Charles, but he'd been unable to convince his housekeeper to speak with her, despite the fact Eleanor had traipsed all the way to the Abbey herself.

As for John, I intend to ask him how he feels, for though I shudder to imagine he does not care for me, I am not so foolish as to mope about, waiting for a sign from him either. I shall ask him outright his intentions, and upon learning them decide what action next to take. You see, Charles, I learned from you one must indeed at times act, however rashly, in order to move forward in life. Had you not acted all this time on our behalf, Papa and I should surely have perished. And though I rue the day you poached those chickens, your action that night set us both on new paths: I should never have met John Cuthbert, nor you Lord Wellesley. Do not be angry that I write it, Charles, because it is the truth. And his lordship is an honorable man. I cannot but think him otherwise when all he's done and said thus far indicate no less. And though we both know he cannot be more to you, I would hope you may depend on him as something of a friend. I love you and beg your forgiveness for my words.

Yours, Eleanor

Wells needed to sit down. He felt a wave of guilt for being privy to this girl's thoughts, intimate as they were, and an equal stab for what she'd written this time—that her sister trust *him* to be an honorable friend when he had acted anything but honorably towards Charles Merrinan from the start.

He swallowed hard. He'd been an utter heel to force Charles to become his mistress. She might enjoy him now, but he well recalled the look of terror on her face that first night he'd demanded she strip and bathe before him, and later when he'd . . .

Yet he pushed those thoughts from mind, deciding right then this was the last letter he'd read. He could no longer stand to see himself through Eleanor Merrinan's eyes when he knew full well he wasn't honorable in the least. Hell, he'd long eschewed the very notion of being a proper gentleman, else he should never have run off to sea and abandoned his duties, to his mother's enduring dismay. But to have such a lady as Eleanor think so highly of him when in reality he was so base, well . . . Were he to continue reading her correspondence he should feel only more guilty.

Wells further berated himself. Was it any wonder his betrothed had eloped with Lord Hawlings rather than marry him? Perhaps she'd seen through his act and seen him for the cad he was. Perhaps she couldn't stomach the thought of marrying a future duke who would bed her for an heir and then leave her for years at a time, gallivanting about the globe and taking mistresses as he pleased. He'd not be the first peer to do so, but reading the Merrinan sisters' letters had put him in the uncomfortable position of *feeling* what it was to be a woman, at the mercy of men, beholden to them for their happiness, for their very existence. It was an uncomfortable, unexpected feeling he did not enjoy experiencing in the least.

Wells rose from the chair to deliver Charles her sister's letter, wondering how she'd react to Eleanor's words. She'd not visited him since the disagreement with her sister—or if she had she'd left too early for him to notice. He'd not gone to her either, recognizing she needed space. Yet he'd missed her, missed her even now. As much as he hated himself for his behavior towards his housekeeper, he still wanted her in his bed, desperately almost wanted her in his arms. Like a man parched for water, now that he had sampled her elixir, there seemed no going back.

"John . . ." Eleanor hesitated slightly, her arm still tight about his own, her father's house faintly visible on the horizon. John had jumped at the chance to accompany Eleanor back after she'd delivered her letter in person at the Abbey, though he'd not been pleased that letter had fallen directly into Wellesley's hands. Charles had stubbornly refused to see her sister. *Fool gel.*

"May I speak freely with you?" Ellie continued. "You won't take offense?"

"'Course not." John pulled her closer. "I should never be mad at you, Ellie." And in that instant he truly could not fathom being cross with her. Ever.

"The other day, when we, when you kissed me, did you—?"

"I should never've been so bold, miss. I do beg your forgiveness." His heart pounded in his chest, the words feeling clumsy and rushed.

"No, I did not think you bold at all, John. That was not my question, quite the opposite."

"The opposite?" She amazed him. Utterly.

Eleanor stopped him in his tracks. "John Cuthbert, do you have feelings for me, sir?"

He nearly tripped his feet. "Ellie, love, y' know I do!"

"Only I do not, you see, *know*, because we've never spoken

of our feelings, John. We have kissed but once, and it is important for me to truly know how you—"

Yet already, his lips were upon her something fierce, her words silenced with such strength of feeling he worried almost, that she might faint.

When at last he broke off, his voice sounded harsh to his ears. "That answer yer question, woman?"

"John," she exhaled his name, collecting herself, "I should like to hear you say it. Not just kissing, but . . . words."

He struggled. "Miss Eleanor . . ."

"Ellie," she corrected.

"Ellie, you're the, why, the loveliest woman I've ever known, miss, and I've known women, plenty of 'em. I'll not lie t' you. But none've ever made me feel as you do." He fumbled to find words. "Yet I'm no . . . I'm not yer equal, miss, anyone can see that. So t' declare meself, t' court you properly, why, it'd make a fool o' you, and a lowlife out o' me, and I'll not do that t' either of us. You deserve better'n what little I can give. I'm sure yer own sister would say the same if she knew the half o'—"

"You leave Charles out of this, John Cuthbert." Her tone tongue-whipped him. "This is between you and me and not another soul in this world, do you hear me?" Her eyes blazed at him, lighting a flame inside his soul he tried desperately, abysmally, to squelch.

"I meant no disrespect, Ellie. Meant only t' say that others, too, wouldn't look kindly on me courtin' you, and I would court you, Ellie, y' know I would. I'd not ask for yer hand without first—"

"You'd ask for my hand then?" Soft, doe eyes suddenly flew to his face, searching.

"If I were a different man, if I'd means or a name or, well, anythin' at all t' offer you o' course I would, Eleanor. I'd be a damn fool not to," he ground out, impassioned.

"Good." She let out such a satisfied huff of air he simply stared at her in awe a moment, disbelieving. She then took his arm snugly in her own and began to march them along, back towards her father's house. "I should like you to court me, John, and after a reasonable amount of time, you may ask for my hand."

He was dumbfounded, abruptly stopping them. "Ellie, y' can't—"

"Can't what?" Her look burned a hole in his chest. "Do you think I am not serious, John? Do you think me so changeable, so inconstant, that I would ask you to court me and then refuse you in the end? Because if you think that of me, John Cuthbert, I tell you now I am not that woman."

He was nearly speechless. "Ellie, love," he told her, "I'd never think that of you, honest. Only I've naught t' offer you but what some other gentleman couldn't offer in plenty, giving you what you deserve, miss, which is—"

"John, *you* are what I want. And if you offer me yourself, I shall need for nothing else. What have I now that is so precious I cannot lose it?" she beseeched. "I have but only myself to give you, too, and if you would have me, I can imagine no greater gift than—"

Yet already he had her in his arms, kissing her with a madness, a need more overpowering than before. And this time, she matched his longing kiss for kiss, shocking him even more.

It was a long time before they made it indoors.

❧

That night Charles lay in bed alone, thinking. She'd nearly burned her sister's letter in disgust. No, not in disgust, in despair. Ellie was a fool to throw herself away on Cuthbert of all men. She was young and silly, ignorant of love's dangers, to be wooed by a rotten, measly kiss. How could one kiss turn her sister into such a *simpleton?*

Yet Charles knew how. She herself had been reduced by a kiss before, and the memory of that kiss, of *where* she'd been kissed, haunted her still. Lord Wellesley had proven again and again just how much a person could be ruled by the body, how *she* could be ruled. She wasn't proud of herself, but Charles understood herself better; she didn't want Eleanor to learn the same lesson.

Her sister must be made to see reason. She'd talk to Cuthbert tomorrow about it, not his lordship, for Wells, no doubt, cared little whom her sister married. Though like as not he'd prefer his steward remain unattached. Oh how she wished Cuthbert had not been the one to deliver Eleanor those blasted baskets! And yet without those baskets . . . She shuddered to imagine her family this winter without food.

Charles tossed and turned on her hard little bed, unable to sleep. Her closet room was always cold. As soon as the hot water bottle cooled she felt the chill creep into her bones. She missed his lordship's bed. *He* was warm. *He* knew how to drive away her fears and sorrows with kisses and caresses. Roland Rutherford knew just how to comfort.

In a flash, she threw off the covers and jumped out of bed.

***

Wells felt something cold wriggle against him for warmth, burrowing itself into his chest. He closed his body around the insistent beast, pulling it closer to him, warming it, until a kittenish sigh was heard, and lips felt, all along his breastbone. The creature snuggled deeper into him as he kissed the top of its head.

"Closer," he told Charles, smiling. And if possible she wriggled in more, her entire body now pressed into the hollow of his own.

"Your feet are cold," he grumbled.

"I'm sorry." Her breath was hot against his chest.

"Don't be, Fox. I've missed you."

"I've missed you too," she started, "only don't speak, Roland, please. Just hold me, will you?"

"Not even a story?" He drew her closer.

She stilled a moment. "Perhaps a story, yes."

"Good." He squeezed her till she gasped. "For there once was a lass named Daisy, a very buxom lass, who'd her eye on a lad named Tom, who was so well endowed he . . ."

She was suddenly shaking in his arms. "You lummox, you!" Her head lifted from his chest in laughter. "Not a *naughty* story!"

"Why not a naughty story?" He kept a straight face. "Do you not wish to know what Tom did to Daisy?"

"Lord Wells, you are the most incorrigible man I have ever—"

"Or would you rather I *show* you what Tom did to Daisy?" His hand slipped low, gripping one lush bottom cheek.

"My lord!" she protested.

"Well, do you?" He began to knead the delicious swell of flesh.

In answer she sank her teeth into his shoulder as he let out a rush of air and smacked her buttock, only to murmur *"I thought so"* into her oh-so-soft hair.

CHAPTER TWENTY-NINE

"And just when am I *free*, sir, to enjoy books? I do not recall being granted any time off." Charles arched her brow at Wells.

He'd caught her leafing through the library, when she was supposed to be dusting its shelves. Wells threw caution to the wind. "Yes, well, that was before you proved yourself . . . amenable."

"So now I am allowed a day of freedom every two weeks, like the rest of your staff?" she pressed.

He hesitated. "Yes."

"Then I shall set aside a few books for that day." She took the one she'd been skimming and added another, then several more, until she'd built a tall pile upon the table.

"Just how much reading do you intend to do, woman?" Wells frowned at her stack.

"I must make up for lost time," she blithely answered.

"Surely with your father the village schoolteacher you—"

"We had to sell every book we owned, my lord."

"Ah." He was embarrassed, but only for a moment. "You

might read to me in bed, you know. To make up for that lost time."

She put a finger to her lips and pointedly glanced towards the open door.

"Charles, if even Jenkins suspects our nocturnal pursuits I hardly think—"

"The girls do not, sir." She kept her voice lowered. "And I should like to keep it that way lest we put ideas in their heads." Her eyes were adamant. "I see the way they flirt with your men, and I'll be damned if my staff—"

"*Your* staff, I daresay, are kept on a very short leash. And you rather handily remedied my crew's yearnings for female company the day you introduced them to the village madam."

"Well yes, Mamie has proven quite effective."

"So they've no need to go chasing skirts."

"Men will always chase skirts, my lord, especially youthful, pretty skirts."

"Ruby is rather fetching, I'll admit." Wells smirked.

"Stop baiting me!"

"Surely you're not jealous, Charles."

"Don't be ridiculous," she huffed. "But when you tire of me, you may *not* have Ruby, Lord Wellesley. I will insist you send to London for your next mistress. I won't have you ruin another Cumberland girl."

"I'll never tire of you, Fox." The back of his hand caressed her cheek.

"You will, sir." Color rose to her face. And then she physically began to propel him towards the door.

"Oh, ye of little faith." He inwardly laughed, letting her.

"Oh, ye of little decency," she grumbled from behind, steadily pushing him out.

Suddenly Wells twisted her about to face him, his hand on the back of her neck in a grip that left no question. "I meant it, Charles. I shan't tire of you, ever."

She stilled beneath his grasp.

"Must I prove to you my ardor?" He ground his hips against her skirt as his foot slammed the door now behind her, pressing her up against its hard, wood panels.

"My lord . . ." Her protest sounded weak.

"You forget who I am, woman."

***

Charles's breaths came fast, her body lit from within. It had been a long time since he'd taken her like this, in the middle of the day, interrupting her duties. Her heart thudded in her chest as her legs wobbled almost, unsteady.

"I have not forgotten, Lord Wellesley." Her eyes met his in a blaze of heat.

"Prove it," he ordered, tightening his hold on her neck.

Charles's hands fell to his fall, fumbling to release him, while he pushed her to her knees, demanding she obey. He angled her head back to give him what he wanted, and she took him as deep as she could, her ability to control his pleasure as arousing as the grip he maintained on her head.

When he'd done, he sounded winded, pressing his forehead a moment to the door. Then he made her stand and lift her skirts as he pushed her shoulders into the hard wood, pulling her hips towards him. He slipped a hand between her legs and began to work her in earnest, until Charles was forced to bite back a scream.

"Do you still say I'll forget you?" He stared into her eyes, his gaze piercing.

"My lord," she begged, panting. Her mind was a mess, her body a wild and greedy thing.

"Say it," he urged, his hand stroking her into submission.

"*Roland* . . ." she pleaded.

"Say you do not doubt me and I'll grant you your release."

She met his eyes in desperation.

"I cannot . . ." she started, but he pressed her more deeply to the door, his body pinning her now beneath him as his hand plundered her core and her pleasure mounted, the pressure so exquisite and full she . . .

"I don't doubt!" Charles gasped as he pushed her over the edge, supporting her breaking, shattering body while tremors shuddered through her.

He gave her a moment to regain her senses, then gently pulled her skirts from her hands, unballing the twisted fabric from her fists.

His lordship lovingly bit her lip. "Finish your dusting, housekeeper." His ensuing kiss scorched her soul. "And remember who you serve in this house." He slid his hand to her bodice, squeezing one breast through her dress. "I'll expect you in my bed tonight, willing and eager. *Unquestioning.*"

As the door clicked shut Charles slumped to the floor, exhausted and inflamed. She was stunned by the encounter and thought briefly of Eleanor, of how little her sister knew of men. She was flummoxed by her own response to Lord Welles-ley's behavior, for here she was again, as aroused by his rough treatment as she was his more generous nature. Tender and cruel, her master.

She adjusted her skirts and returned to her work, her legs still unsteady and her heart in knots. Charles did not peek inside anymore books.

It struck Wells that evening that he was, perhaps, content. Ever since the disaster in London he'd been restless, on edge some-how, and yet tonight, seated in his parlor by a warm fire, a glass of fine claret in his hand, he felt calm. The south wall had been repaired just before the snows hit. The men injured in the collapse were healing well, and come spring Adams's crew would begin work on the north end. What's more, the Abbey inside was slowly being transformed. Cuthbert was the perfect steward, Jenkins the perfect cook, and Charles Merrinan the perfect lover. He smiled just to think on her. Every interaction with his housekeeping mistress these days brought a smile to his face, even when she balked at his requests. Even then, frustrated by his teasing, her eyes told him she was his. His Fox wanted him now, just as much as he wanted her.

He leaned back in his chair and took another sip. Life was indeed good. He was not being tossed about on a ship, he was not being harangued by marriage-hungry harpies in London drawing rooms, he was not being forced to dance with dull debutantes at crushing balls. He was his own man, in his own home, surrounded by competent, willing staff—and a damn fine mistress. Which set his thoughts drifting towards what he'd made Charles do in the library this afternoon, and what he might do with her tonight, when she presented herself as ordered.

"Yer Grace?" Cuthbert's knock interrupted.

"John." He motioned him in.

"A word, sir?"

Wells nodded.

Cuthbert stared awkwardly at his feet. "I should like permission t' ask Miss Eleanor Merrinan for her hand in marriage, sir."

Wellesley's fine mood disintegrated.

"Marriage, John?" He ground his teeth.

"Not just yet but soon, Yer Grace. We've been courtin' these past few weeks and—"

"And you cannot wait a few weeks more, John? A blasted year perhaps?" Wells's heartbeat spiraled. "We have only just gotten here, for Christ's sake, and I should hate to lose the excellent steward I find I have."

"Yer Grace," Cuthbert's tone sobered, "y' needn't lose me if I marry. Y' know I made a vow t' yer father that I'd always—"

"Yes and now another vow, to a woman no less, one who will surely—"

"Beggin' yer pardon, Yer Grace, but Miss Eleanor's not asked that I leave my position here, sir. She asks only that I—"

"But if you're not living here, John, then you're hardly my steward, now are you?"

Cuthbert inhaled a breath. "It's just we see no reason t' wait when we both know it's what we want."

"She won't bed you till you marry, is that it?" Wells grimaced. "Well then."

"You watch yer tongue, sir." Cuthbert's tone cut.

"Oh I'll watch my tongue alright, because it sounds to me like you want what I have with her sister, John, only Miss Eleanor's too good to lower herself, or else you think too highly of her to—"

His steward's rage was palpable. "Wells," he ground out, "you've no right t' speak of her so and no right to treat me like a—"

"Like a friend, John? Damn it, man, I *am* your friend, and as such I've every right to tell you what I think. And I think you're rushing into this. I know you want her, any fool can see that, and no doubt she wants you too, but marriage is . . . It's an impediment, John, an obstacle. A legal contract not easily broken. What if you tire of her once you've had her, eh? Have you not tired of other women before? Then what? And what if she wishes to leave Cumberland? What if you—"

"Yer Grace," Cuthbert spoke through his teeth, "seems t' me as though everythin' you're describin' applies more t' *you* than me, sir." His eyes hit Wells hard. "I've not said I'd abandon me post here, and Eleanor wishes t' stay with her father. I'd simply live with 'em there, rather'n here. And when her old man passes I'd move her into the Abbey with me. Why, she could have a position here, same as Charles."

"Oh I doubt very much Charles wishes her sister to work alongside her."

"Then Ellie can take her sister's position as housekeeper when y' tire o' yer mistress," John snapped.

Wellesley's thoughts turned ominous. "And what makes you so certain I will tire of Charles, John?"

"'Cause y' said it yerself, sir. And as you've had her often enough, and long enough now, seems t' me you'll be tirin' of her sooner'n later. Seems to me, the moment the Duke passes you'll be forced t' marry some lady o' the *Ton* and then Charles Merrinan'll want nothin' t' do with you, sir, mark my words. For she sure as shite ain't the sort o' woman who'll share Yer Grace, that she will not."

Wells saw red. "Out," he ordered, his anger barely contained. "Get out, John, before I say something to you I will regret."

His steward glared at him, turned on his heel, and left.

Air escaped Wellesley's lips in a slow and painful hiss; he hadn't known he'd been holding his breath. He hadn't expected the evening to end like this.

When Charles slipped into his lordship's bed that night, full of delicious anticipation, she could tell things were amiss. He remained sullen almost, turned on his side, though she knew he did not sleep. By now she recognized the even cadence of his breathing when in slumber; this was not a man at rest.

Gently she touched him, yet still he did not respond. "Roland," she whispered, pressing her body to his, "tell me what is wrong."

She heard him exhale before he turned to bury his face

between her breasts, letting her stroke his thick curls. He breathed her in, pulling her to him.

"Do you wish to tell me what is troubling you, my lord?" she asked, careful.

He shook his head.

"Then let me comfort you instead." She kissed his forehead, his lips, then slowly made her way down his body, kissing every inch of him, until he could stand her kisses no more, it seemed, and simply rolled atop her, spilling what felt like bitter sorrow into the belly of her embrace.

CHAPTER THIRTY

And then the unthinkable happened. Wellesley's mother, the Duchess of Allendale, arrived the very day the snows began to recede. And she did not arrive alone, for in her carriage was a perfectly respectable, no doubt utterly biddable young lady.

Miss Evangeline Mowry, daughter to some viscount, was clearly there for one reason only: to be offered up as bride.

Beside himself, Wells paced the parlor, still the sole room fit for guests. "Mother, I cannot fathom why you'd—"

"Roland, dear, I *did* write, only I imagine the post was delayed by the weather. We left London as soon as the roads were passable so I assumed . . ." She made a face. "Well, I'd forgotten how long it takes for everything up here to *melt*." Her eyes flitted to her soiled hem.

No doubt the audacity of his muddy courtyard to sully his mother's dress had infuriated the Duchess, but as always, she did not show it. Instead, she let him feel it. He grimaced, still disbelieving his mother was here. Of course she'd bloody show up on his doorstep without a word of warning. But to have brought a stranger with her, without damn well asking . . .

"And I could hardly leave Miss Mowry behind, dear, not when I'd promised the poor girl's dying mother I would look after her only daughter." She pursed her lips at him. "The young lady is grieving, Roland, you must be kind to her. It was quite a shock."

"No more than the *shock* of you bringing her here, Mother," he bit back, grateful the miss had been brought to the kitchen for some repast and so spared their conversation. Apparently, the young lady did not travel well.

"And if she is still in mourning why, pray, does she not wear black?" His eyes met his mother's, whose sharp grey orbs mirrored his own: defiant.

"I find it cruel to force so beautiful a young woman as Miss Mowry to don somber hues, Roland." She barely cracked a smile. "Especially when less austere colors are perfectly acceptable here in Cumberland at least."

He knew what she was about. "Well I promise to give her a wide berth, *Maman*, considering how keenly she must still suffer her mother's loss." His eyes bored into her. "I expect you, alone, to console her in her mourning."

"Me? Goodness, Roland, everyone knows a well-bred gentleman like yourself is the greatest balm to a lady in grief. You, more than anyone, I am sure, will take her mind off matters and bring some color to her cheeks." Her smile dazzled like a bright, cold gemstone.

"Shall we continue this little game, *Maman*, or must I be blunt?" Wells's lips formed a line. "I will not marry Miss Mowry."

"Your father is on his deathbed, Roland, and the Duchy needs an heir."

"If he is on his deathbed, Mother, then why in God's name are you *here*?" His voice cracked.

"Because you leave me no choice, son," she snarled back, matching his temper. "Had you not bungled matters with Lady

Camberly, I shouldn't need to be here, dangling another bride before you."

"You know deuced well I was willing to marry her, Mother. It was *her* choice to leave me at the altar like some cuckolded—"

"Yes, yes, she hurt your pride. But you needn't have run to the ends of the earth like some wounded pup. You could have stayed, allowed the scandal to blow over, then chosen some other girl. But instead, like the whelp you remain, you hide here in Cumberland, where the weather is as foul as—"

"Do not disparage the Abbey, Mother, because I have every intention of remaining here for eternity."

"Roland, you have a duty to your father, a duty to family, and a duty to perform as future Duke, which is why I—"

"You can shove the Dukedom up your arse, *Maman*." Her eyes grew wide at his coarse words. "Because I will not move back to London and I damn well will not, I repeat, *will not* marry Miss Mowry. I don't care how substantial the woman's bloodline or dowry."

His mother glared at him, her eyes shooting daggers.

Wells glared back, just as ferocious.

And then, without a word, the Duchess strode from the room, her back ramrod straight and her exit sharp as glass. She'd punish him for his last comment, he knew. His mother knew well how to punish her only son with the slap of ungodly, awful silence.

She was inhuman.

❧

Charles was in fits. Never would she have expected Lord Wellesley's mother, the Duchess of Allendale, to arrive so unexpectedly, so imperiously. With another lady no less! And two ladies' maids! Not to mention their carriage driver and footman. That would mean six more mouths to feed, six bodies to sleep, six linens to lay, six more sets of everything to wash. Her mind was overwhelmed by the labor this would mean for her staff, the unfairness of it. Because the Abbey was not prepared for guests. And she'd let his lordship know it.

She went in search of him but heard only angry voices from the parlor and thought better than to interrupt whatever conversation Lord Wells was having with the Duchess. She tiptoed away in search of Cuthbert, the next best man to accost, yet he, too, seemed equally distressed.

"It's just like her t' do this to us, miss, just like her grace. Reason Lord Wells went t' sea, she was. Domineerin', overbearin', smotherin' sort o' woman who never gave her son a moment's peace, and now look. Back at it she is. Willin' t' make the miserable long journey t' Cumberland t' get what she wants." He nearly snorted his disgust. "You mark my words, Charles, she'll have him married come hell or high water. She don't give up, that one, as stubborn as he, and when the two go at it . . ." He shook his head, scowling.

Cuthbert had a wealth of knowledge when it came to Lord Wellesley's family, Charles could tell, but she'd not be distracted by this now.

"Never mind all that, John, we've more pressing matters: finding beds for six unexpected guests."

"Christ," he muttered. "Where the devil are we t' put 'em all?"

"I don't know, Cuthbert, you tell me!"

The two argued at length as to who should go where, until Charles got her way.

"John, we've no choice but to give Miss Mowry Mrs. Jenkins's bedroom, and put our cook with Ginny and Marta, and their two ladies' maids in my cold closet. Ruby, Clarice, and I will simply take a spare room somewhere and ready the space as best we can—sleep amongst the cobwebs and mice if need be. We can work up the room while we're in it, I suppose."

"Oi." Cuthbert nodded. "His lordship can bunk with his men. He's used t' sleepin' in hellholes and ships' galleys. Her grace can take his chamber."

"When he rebels, I shall tell him that was *your* idea, John."

"You go right ahead, miss." His eyes gleamed.

Yet Charles already felt beat, and the guests had only just arrived. This visit would test her mettle, and test his lordship no doubt too.

"Cuthbert?" She ventured.

"Yes, miss?"

"Is there anything else I should know about the Duchess? Anything I ought to anticipate?"

He chewed his lip. "She's more stubborn than her son, Charles, and always gets her way. Mind you stay on her good side, and all will be well."

The Duchess's good side, eh? Charles thought. *Which side is that, pray?*

Yet she was accosted by the lady herself not a minute later in the hallway, with barely enough time to collect her wits.

"You." The Duchess's gaze swept critically over Charles. "Tell me where I may find the housekeeper. I've no idea where she's put us and my son is behaving like a, well, like a disobedient *child*."

Charles dipped into a low curtsy, her heart racing, for the strikingly tall, slim woman before her was altogether severe and imposing. Most disconcerting of all, however, was the fact she shared her son's eyes: the same intense slate grey.

"Your Grace, I am housekeeper here and beg your pardon for the delay regarding rooms. Yours shall be ready momentarily."

"*You* are Almsdale's housekeeper?" The Duchess's brow

280

rose a fraction as she literally looked down her patrician nose at Charles from her impressive height.

"Yes, Your Grace." Charles straightened her spine. "I apologize again for the delay, but as you have surely surmised, we did not anticipate your visit." She met the Duchess's eyes without wavering.

Her grace narrowed her gaze. "A housekeeper is always prepared, *always* anticipates, girl, but then, you look barely old enough to run a stand at market, let alone the Duke's Abbey." Charles winced at her tone. "And where is your chatelaine? You look like a maid. Was there no one in Cumberland more qualified for the position of housekeeper?"

"Your Grace, I take great pride in what my staff have accomplished thus far. Perhaps you failed to notice Almsdale Abbey remains in *great* disrepair." She knew she bordered on impertinent but inwardly Charles fumed. "So I apologize again that we are as yet ill-equipped to entertain guests."

Her grace blinked. "Quite the mouth on you too." Her eyes bored deeper into Charles. "What is your name, Housekeeper?"

"Merrinan, Your Grace," Charles spoke with pride. "Charles Merrinan."

"Charles Merrinan?" The Duchess looked appalled. "Squire Merrinan's daughter?" She shook her head, as if disbelieving. "Why, let me look at you, girl." She suddenly beamed at Charles, reaching out to physically turn her about, in a manner so familiar she made Charles flinch. And then the Duchess pulled a lock of hair loose from Charles's head kerchief to twirl about her fingers.

"By God!" she exclaimed. "Same hair, like spun gold. Nearly drove my husband mad." Her eyes held a faraway cast.

"Your Grace." Charles took a step back. "I am sure I do not understand."

"But my dear girl"—she gave her another brilliant smile—

"I knew your parents. Knew your mother well indeed. Adelaide Enright came out but a year after my own debut and caused quite the stir back then. Only had eyes for your father, of course, determined to have only him . . ." Her voice trailed off. "But tell me how he is, dear. I am sure it was very hard on you all when your mother passed."

"You knew my parents?" Charles simply stood there, rooted to the spot.

"Yes, why do you stare at me so, Miss Merrinan? It is unnerving. And your sister, Eleanor, she is well too, I hope? I imagine she is all grown up, goodness." She peered more closely at Charles. "But why are you *here*, Miss Merrinan, housekeeper to my son? I daresay your father should never have agreed to such a position were he still . . ." She stopped herself.

Charles inhaled, overwhelmed by the onslaught of information she'd just received. "Your Grace, my sister is well, thank you, and my father fares as well as possible. Difficult times, however, necessitated my need for employment, making your son's arrival here in Cumberland fortuitous. I have endeavored to do my best to aid in the revival of Almsdale Abbey, Your Grace, and have made some progress considering how few we are in staff. It pains me that we are not better prepared for guests, but without warning, Your Grace, there was only so much I or anyone else employed here could have done to anticipate your arrival."

The Duchess looked Charles over again, this time more approvingly. "Eloquently said, Miss Merrinan. You've not only your mother's fine looks but her breeding too, though it would upset her, no doubt, to see you relegated to service." Her lips pinched.

Charles took offense. "My mother would be proud to see me gainfully employed, Your Grace; there is no dishonor in honest labor."

The Duchess broke into a grin. "And you've her spirit too. Goodness, what a surprise to encounter you here, my dear. Well, I am glad Roland hired you, if it has helped your dear papa. I shall have to pay him a call," she added. "We will have much to discuss, of times past." Her smile deepened.

"Oh no, Your Grace, you mustn't!" Charles bit her tongue. "That is, my father is no longer well, Your Grace. He is easily confused, forgetting at times even that his wife . . ." She swallowed the rest of her sentence. "I fear he may not recognize you, Your Grace, for he has not been the same since our mother's death."

"Which is why you left London, yes. I know all about Adelaide's atrocious family. There is no excusing the Earl of Denbigh's behavior, none. To leave two young girls with only their unsound . . ." She again stopped herself, frowning. "Tell me you at least had a female companion until you came of age, Miss Merrinan."

Charles felt her gut twist, though she'd not reveal the truth of how desperate their situation had been. "It is all in the past, Your Grace. Please, if you'll excuse me, I must ready your room before nightfall. Might I enquire how long you intend to stay at Almsdale?"

"Oh that depends." Her eyes sparked.

"On what, Your Grace?" Charles dared ask.

"On how long it takes my son to propose to Miss Mowry." Her eyes now positively shimmered. "I'd appreciate it greatly, Miss Merrinan, if you helped facilitate matters some. You know, endeavor to arrange that Miss Mowry and Lord Wellesley be left alone together, as often as is seemly?" She smiled conspiratorially at Charles.

"Your Grace." She looked the Duchess dead on. "That is decidedly outside the purview of my duties here, and as I answer only to his lordship, my employer, I cannot and will not assist you in such matter."

And with that she marched off, leaving the Duchess looking flummoxed. Charles hoped her grace would realize the late Lady Adelaide Merrinan shared more than just a physical resemblance to her eldest daughter. She wanted her mother proud of her just then, for God knew there was much *not* to be proud of. If her mother truly had known this haughty woman, Charles felt sure Mama had stood up to her, Duchess or not. As would she.

🦊

"Charles," a voice hissed. "Fox!" it hissed louder.

Charles put down her pail and mopped her brow, pushing back her kerchief from her sweat-drenched brow. She'd been cleaning like a madwoman for the past two hours, and it showed.

"In here!" the voice hissed once more.

She followed said voice into a darkly shuttered room and beheld his lordship slumped in a chair, drape flung aside. Every other piece of furniture in the room was still covered in dust-laden sheets, not to mention bat shit, which also littered a large portion of the floor.

"My lord," she sighed, "tell me you are not hiding in here from your mother."

"Damn right I am." He motioned her over. "Come, Fox, I am desperate for my mistress."

"I am desperately trying to ready rooms for your guests, sir. I haven't time for—"

"Charles, we can discuss said rooms while you sit on my lap. Now please," he motioned again for her, insisting, "I *need* you."

His eyes pleaded so earnestly that she finally gave in, placing her arms about his neck to quickly kiss him.

"Thank God," he released the words into her lips, then

burrowed his face at her breast, breathing her in. "I am starved for a sensible woman right now."

"Your mother seems quite sensible, sir."

Lord Wells began to hurriedly unhook Charles's dress. "She is anything but, Fox, dragging that lady all the way here just to dangle her before me, like a worm on a line. Only I'll not be the poor fish that takes her bait, oh no." His hand slipped inside Charles's dress; she felt him relax the moment he found her bosom.

"You do realize how inappropriate this is, Lord Wellesley." Charles only half admonished his lordship, her own hand playing with locks of his hair which had grown only more unruly since she'd arrived at Almsdale. She liked his hair long.

"I'll tell you what's inappropriate," he grumbled. "Showing up without warning on my doorstop, that's what, and I intend to throw *Maman* out just as soon as I can."

"Then I must warn you, sir," she whispered in his ear, "the Duchess told me she will leave only once you've proposed to Miss Mowry."

"She what?" He instantly righted himself, nearly knocking her from his lap. "Tell me exactly what she said, Charles, every last word."

Charles sighed, regretting she'd opened her mouth. "Just that, my lord. I asked how long her grace planned to stay and received said answer. She asked me to assist her even, said I was to throw you alone with the lady at every possible turn which"—she laid a finger over his lips to staunch the flow of curses he tried to loose—"I firmly declined to do. I informed the Duchess I take orders from but one master only."

***

Wells loved that she'd just called him master, loved how her eyes shone as she did. He pulled her closer, murmuring into her chest, "Well done, Fox. At least I've you and Cuthbert loyal to me." He began to pet her again, his hands roaming where they pleased.

"Roland," she ventured, "why does she press you so to marry? You are not yet Duke, so I do not—"

"My father is ill, Charles, though how ill I no longer know. I wrote asking him as much but have yet to receive a reply, nor can I rely on *Maman* to ascertain the truth of his condition." He snorted. "She wants me wed and siring an heir before he passes, and since I failed to appease her in this respect when I was last in London"—he rolled his eyes—"it appears she's brought London to me now instead."

"And dare I ask what made you flee London for Cumberland, my lord?"

"I'd betrothed myself to a lady who ran off with another, leaving me at the altar, so to speak, and in the eyes of the *Ton* cuckolded. The ensuing slander to my character, what *I* had done to drive her to another man's arms . . ." He took a breath. "Let's just say I'd had enough of London's rumor-mongering."

"And did you care for her?"

He was surprised she asked. "Enough to be hurt by her, yes, though my pride was wounded more than my heart." He looked straight at her. "I fancied her a good enough duchess, is all."

"I see." Her body tensed upon his lap.

"But I fancy you more, Charles." His lips graced her throat. "Much, much more."

"That is because you've had me, sir." Her tone was terse.

"And who's to say I didn't have her, too?" he jabbed.

She huffed. "One does not bed one's betrothed before taking her to the altar."

"Yet I bedded you, Fox, quite the virgin bride." His kisses deepened at her neck, suckling her tender flesh.

"I was not your bride!" She abruptly got up off his lap, her face flush with anger. "I have work to do, my lord, so you'll excuse me now."

He watched her hastily refasten her dress before she grabbed her bucket and rag, leaving the room in a rush. He pondered why the devil his mistress had just turned on him so, when she'd been all too willing to play but a moment before.

Was it something he'd said?

CHAPTER THIRTY-ONE

Wells was doing his damnedest to avoid Miss Mowry, yet his mother thrust the lady upon him at every conceivable turn. She was the type of ubiquitous brunette the *Ton* wholeheartedly approved, and whom his mother had clearly dressed to impress, accentuating the girl's petite figure. Mowry couldn't hold a candle to Charles, though he was presently mad at his mistress for having ruined the shell room by virtue of serving his guests tea here in his favorite space.

"Why, Lord Wells, it is the most extraordinary room I have ever seen," Miss Mowry gushed.

"Yes, I daresay it is unique." He was barely polite.

She touched his arm with her gloved hand. "Would you be so kind as to tell me its story, sir?" Her eyes fluttered up at him.

Wells despised coyness.

"I am sure my mother will do it greater justice, miss." He threw *Maman* a look.

"Oh no, you tell its history as well as I, Roland." The Duchess wickedly smiled back. "Though I must say your housekeeper outdid herself; the room positively sparkles once more. I am glad she thought to serve us tea in here today, as your parlor's four walls grow old." Her rebuke was as always, pointed.

"Well, when one leaves a residence in utter disrepair for nigh on two decades, Mother, one learns to live with a few minor inconveniences."

The Duchess leveled her gaze at her son but directed her words elsewhere. "The Duke and I used to spend our summers here, Miss Mowry, when Roland was a boy. The shell room was his favorite place to play in the Abbey, wasn't it, dear?"

"It *was*," he emphasized.

"And is it true you captained a ship yourself, Lord Wellesley?" The lady feigned interest; ladies always did. "I can only imagine what exotic treasures you must have brought back from your far-flung travels. How exciting to sail the seas!"

"I brought my men home alive, miss." He watched her face fall. "That was treasure enough."

"Roland is being modest, my dear," his mother interjected, repairing the conversation. "He certainly did have his share of adventure though. Why don't you regale Miss Mowry with your tales of daring, darling?" Her smile by now looked brittle.

"Hmm, let's see . . ." Wells pretended to make nice. "Shall I tell her about the week we spent in the doldrums, eating rats and drinking our own piss till the winds finally lifted? Or would she rather hear tell of the storm that nearly sank us and sent two men overboard clinging to life for three days in shark-infested waters? Till they were burnt black from the sun?" He ruthlessly met his mother's gaze.

Miss Mowry looked faint.

"Roland," the Duchess snapped, "those are hardly appropriate tales for a lady of Miss Mowry's delicate—"

"*Do* forgive me, miss." He rose to take her hand. "My memories tend towards the morose, I'm afraid, for to be so long at sea does things to a man's mind."

The lady looked fainter still, making Wells secretly, inside, grin.

"Excuse me." His lips barely brushed her fingertips in exit. "I'm afraid I must see my steward on an urgent matter yet this morning."

And out he fled, nearly colliding in the hallway with his housekeeper, en route to deliver the ladies their tea.

***

"What were you *thinking* putting them in there?"

Charles was insulted by his lordship's tone, not to mention the fact he'd nearly knocked over her precariously balanced tray. "There aren't enough ready rooms, my lord," she hissed back at him, adding, "I am doing the best I can."

"Well do *better*," he snarled, stomping off with a scowl.

Charles was more than a little peeved at Lord Wells but delivered the tea with aplomb, carefully pouring each lady a cup.

Her grace received Charles warmly. "This, Miss Mowry, is Mrs. Merrinan, my son's housekeeper."

Charles was momentarily confused by the use of Mrs. before she remembered it was *de rigueur* for all housekeepers, married or not. She made to leave, but the Duchess stopped her.

"No, stay a moment if you would, Mrs. Merrinan. I fear my son just abandoned us and there are so few amusements at the Abbey." She sighed rather obviously. "Pray sit with us a while and tell Miss Mowry something of local life here in Cumberland."

Charles found her grace's request more than a little off-putting. She had a multitude of tasks to accomplish, not least of which was filling in as parlor maid while her actual maid currently scrubbed bedclothes. "Of course, Your Grace," she answered like the dutiful servant she'd become.

"Sit, please," the Duchess insisted, "else it shall look as though you are reporting rather than conversing." She took another sip of tea.

Charles grudgingly sat, smoothed her skirts, and turned politely towards Miss Mowry, whose eyes looked awfully wide. She attempted to put the lady at ease.

"If this is indeed your first visit to Cumberland, Miss Mowry, I'm afraid you timed it poorly, for the countryside is least appealing precisely now while the snow slowly melts. In summer and fall our land is at its finest, though even spring-time's May Day is lovely, the village children especially have a grand time of it." Charles watched color begin to revive the lady's cheeks and knew her words were working.

"And the fells and lakes in summer, why, they are simply breathtaking. It is worth the long, harsh winters here to picnic at the foot of a mountain and swim in crystalline blue waters. But I am sure I needn't tell you any of this, miss, as her grace, no doubt, has regaled you herself of all our region has to offer."

Only the Duchess, it seemed, did not share Charles's enthusiasm. "I'll admit most any season is preferable to winter, Mrs. Merrinan, yet I still find the landscape here harsh and oppressive."

Charles found it odd her grace would disparage Cumberland at all, knowing her son intended to reside here with what-ever wife he'd take. She frowned a little at the Duchess.

"I must disagree, Your Grace. The land is not so much harsh as it is wild, free. You can sense it in the air, the fresh breeze on skin, the slap of wind in a storm. And when one lives here year round, one appreciates this power and pulse—how brilliantly nature paints form and color into the sky, how sunrise and sunset are mirrored in the lake water, radiant against the mountainsides. It is, I believe, the most beautiful place on earth."

Both ladies gaped almost at Charles. She blushed. "Forgive me, Your Grace, Miss Mowry. It seems I am out of practice for conversation. If you'll excuse me there is much I must attend to this morning." She curtsied fast and scurried from the room.

From the hall Charles overheard Miss Mowry tell the Duchess, "She speaks not at all like a housekeeper, does she, Your Grace?"

"No, she does not," her grace replied. "Decidedly not."

❦

"Roland, dear, I must say your Cumberland cook is outstanding."

They were dining, and for the hundredth time Wells wanted to throttle his mother's elegant, aristocratic neck.

"Yes, Jenkins is a gem." He was tired of making small talk. He'd done little else for days.

"Wherever did you find her?"

He promptly let loose a string of curse words in his head intended for his mother. "Miss Merrinan," Wells replied tersely, "urged me to sample the cook's rum nicky."

Miss Mowry's face furrowed at the term.

"Ah, Mrs. Merrinan." *Maman* smiled; she knew rum nicky's charms. "A gem in her own right."

"I daresay yes," he expelled under his breath.

Miss Mowry blinked, still confused by rum nicky.

"And how did you find *her*?" His mother needled.

"My housekeeper?" Wells took another bite. "Showed up here looking for work."

"Just like that?" *Maman* arched her brow.

He remained stubbornly silent, not wishing to reveal the truth of Charles's arrival.

"Mrs. Merrinan strikes me as rather well spoken for a servant." Miss Mowry seized upon the lull in conversation. "Why, just today she painted such a vivid, almost poetic picture of the countryside I—"

"Miss Merrinan," Wells interrupted her, "is well educated. As is my steward, Mr. Cuthbert. I find employing competent servants leads to better run households."

"Not to mention loyal," the Duchess muttered.

"Yes, loyal, Mother." His eyes met hers. "More than might be said of others."

The Duchess was not rattled. "Miss Mowry, would you like a proper tour of the Abbey tomorrow? I'm sure Roland would be happy to show you about, for you really ought to see the ducal portrait gallery, and the oriental rotunda of course. You don't mind, do you, son?" she baited.

Wells sighed loud enough it was apparent he did. "I should be delighted, Miss Mowry, though you must prepare yourself for cobwebs, excrement, and perhaps a ghost or two. The Abbey is haunted by quite a few nefarious spirits."

The lady grew pale.

"But fear not, miss, I shall not leave your side." He pasted a smile to his face.

The smile *Maman* beamed back was just as false. "Wonderful, Roland. I'm sure Miss Mowry will be enchanted. After breakfast then, and perhaps a game of cards tonight?"

"Oh yes, I *do* enjoy a game of whist!" The young lady seemed animated by the idea.

"Then we shall need a fourth player," Wells noted. "Suggestions?"

"Perhaps your housekeeper or steward, my lord? Since you say both are educated?" Miss Mowry chimed in.

"Why not?" Wellesley's lips twitched. *Why not indeed.*

ૹ

Yet later, when Wells had located and informed his housekeeper of the evening's plan, she was less than pleased by the idea.

"No," Charles told him, adamant. "I have neither the time nor energy to sit about playing cards while there is so much on my plate."

"Cuthbert doesn't play, Charles, and Miss Mowry specifically requested whist, which requires four. I am sorry but you must."

"I must?" She glared at him. "Since when is whist within my job description, sir?"

"Which job, Charles?" He loved to rile her. "For there are many varied descriptions to your two positions here. Would you prefer I inform Miss Mowry you will be partnering as my mistress tonight, rather than as my housekeeper?"

Wells caught her arm right before she could slap him. "Do not cross me, Fox, not with my mother here. I am in a foul enough temper and do not wish to battle you, too." He softened towards her but did not let go her arm.

He could see her stewing, and with his other hand reached to trace her cheek. "Please, Charles, I barely see you anymore with the two of them constantly underfoot."

"Fine." She relented as he drew her to him, kissing her hard and fast upon the lips, making him ache for her that much more. It had been days since she'd shared his bed, for how could she when his mother now slept in his chamber and he bunked with his men in a hayloft? He sensed the hunger in her kiss, too.

"Thank you, Fox." His lips brushed her ear. "I hope you trounce them both."

"Not before I trounce you, Wells." She smirked.

❧

And trounce him Charles did, for the Duchess had of course paired Mowry with her son, and Charles with herself. The Duchess did not seem at all surprised to discover Almsdale's housekeeper adept.

"And that would be another five." Her grace smiled at their opponents. "One more round then?" She grinned at Miss Mowry.

Only this time the lady begged off. "Why yes, one more round, yet new partners please. I do not think Lord Wellesley is focused much upon his game, whereas your team, Your Grace, is formidable."

"Indeed." The Duchess winked at Charles, who tried hard not to smile back.

"A man is easily outwitted when two smart women team up." Wells caught Charles's eye. "I shall take Miss Merrinan, then, as partner, Miss Mowry, so that you may experience my mother's brilliance firsthand."

"Excellent, Lord Wellesley." The lady rose to trade seats with Charles. "I am impressed by your skill, Mrs. Merrinan. How do you come to play so well?"

Charles hesitated. "My family played, Miss Mowry."

"She plays a sharp game of chess too," Wells chimed in. "Beat me more than once; a better opponent than my steward by far."

"Chess, too?" The lady began to look alarmed as Charles hastened to intervene.

"Miss Mowry, Lord Wellesley fails to explain my father was the village school teacher here and so taught his daughters everything he knew, including chess."

"School teacher?" The Duchess frowned. "But I thought your father was—"

Charles quickly interrupted. "Shall we?" She reached for the deck to begin dealing another round of cards.

And without warning she felt a hand slide to her lap, startling her not a little. For the rest of the game it rested there, teasing and squeezing, till her concentration failed her and their team lost the match, though his lordship did not seem the least bit displeased.

Neither, in truth, was Charles.

CHAPTER THIRTY-TWO

That morning John Cuthbert carried a full basket to deliver his betrothed. He'd asked Eleanor Merrinan just last week to marry him and by God she'd accepted. *Him!* He was happy as a lark, yet feared her sister's wrath. Not to mention Wellesley's wrath. Which is why he'd not told either of them yet.

Nor would he need to, it seemed, for when he'd delivered Eleanor's latest letter to Charles she'd torn into it at once, face dropping precipitously as she began to read. He'd scurried so fast from her he'd nearly tripped hurrying down the hall to the kitchen. He'd packed the basket in a rush, looking a few times over his shoulder as he left the Abbey for fear the blasted housekeeper might tail him, frypan in hand.

Fortunately, she had not.

When Charles sat down between tasks to read anew the letter Cuthbert had handed her, she swore she'd beat the steward bloody and wallop his lordship one too. This could *not* be happening—not so soon. She read it a third time, still disbelieving its contents.

> *Dearest Charles,*
>
> *Your silence is more deafening than you know, sister, for each letter unanswered is like a dagger to my heart. Yet I cannot write what you wish to read, because that same heart demands precisely what you would deny it. John has asked for my hand in marriage and I have accepted. Papa has given me his blessing. At least, he has not rescinded it, though he has surely forgotten, for he is worse, I fear, falling asleep more frequently of late in the middle of sentences. I have noticed a new palsy of the hands too, and this despite how well we now eat. I hope it will pass, but I think you should visit before he has another fit. I do not know if he could withstand one. Come for his sake, Charles, if not mine. Only come soon, I beg.*

Charles's own hands trembled.

> *John and I are happy, and I write you this because you are still my precious sister, whom I love with all my heart. Therefore I must be honest. We are in love and I cannot wait to become John's wife! He intends to speak to Lord Wellesley to see if his lordship will let John live here once we wed. He must obtain a license yet, which will take time, but I do not care how long it takes. I shall wait an eternity for him, if I must. Oh Charles, if only you could share in the joy and fullness of my heart! There is no other feeling in the world, truly, than to love and be loved, to give oneself to another. I understand, at last, why Mother left her family to be with Father, and why he suffered so upon her death. It must have felt, to him, as if he'd lost his very soul the day she passed. No wonder he is now a shell. I should feel the same too, if John ever . . .*

Charles thrust the letter aside, too angry to read more. She nearly threw it onto the fire, stopping herself at the last second and wadding it into a tight ball in her pocket instead, crammed beside Lord Wellesley's timepiece. Her rage was unreasonable. She knew it went beyond mere concern for her sister's future. It bordered on something awful and insidious. If she dared stare deep into her soul, she could see the greenish cast, for in truth she was jealous of Eleanor, that her sister should have the man she desired, the happiness she deserved, and the freedom to express it while she, Charles, would have none of these things, ever, with the man she . . .

Only *that* was too terrible a thought to admit.

Charles threw herself back into her work with brutal denial.

"And it was your great-grandmother who commissioned this turret?"

Miss Mowry asked so many bloody annoying questions Wells could barely keep his answers straight. She kept touching him too—light little touches that made him flinch with distaste. Not for her person; she was a perfectly attractive young woman, good-looking even if viewed objectively. No, it was all the lady represented which made him recoil.

"Yes, I believe so," he mumbled. "A twelfth-century abbey originally, so there may have been a turret here then. Or from when it was a fortified castle. I'm not sure which came first, miss. You shall have to ask my mother for more history."

He moved her along, wishing this charade of a visit would end soon. End yesterday.

"Lord Wellesley." She abruptly stopped in her tracks, looking demurely at her feet. "May I speak frankly with you, sir, now that we are a moment alone?"

His heart sank to hear her say it.

"Of course, Miss Mowry." Wells's smile tightened. "Frankness is ever refreshing."

"I am aware my visit to you, clearly unexpected and at such time when you are renovating the Abbey, is ill-timed, my lord."

She surprised him, as did the genuinely kind tone she used.

"Your mother failed to inform me of your circumstance here, even of your feelings towards marriage." She dared to glance at him. "I am not so naïve as to not see the disagreement between you, and I apologize if my presence here has further complicated your relationship with her grace."

The lady amazed.

"Which is all to say that I apologize, Lord Wellesley, for having descended upon you thus," she rushed her words, "as I would never have imposed upon your hospitality had I known the truth of matters. I feel, to a certain extent, somewhat manipulated by the Duchess, *not*"—she hurried to correct herself—"that she did anything untoward by bringing me with her. Only that, well, she is perhaps attempting to press something clearly undesired by yourself."

Miss Mowry looked anxiously at Wells for a response, in both fear and hope, it seemed. And for the first time this young woman appeared almost human to him, rather than mere object of his mother's machinations. He felt sorry for her, that she'd been dragged here without fair warning, and softened to her a little.

"And you, Miss Mowry, is marriage undesired by you, too?" He searched her face for an indication that she had no interest in him, but found to his dismay the opposite: The lady blushed.

"I am not . . . opposed to the idea, sir," she stammered before she collected herself. "I am of an age to marry and am reliant upon the Duchess now for guidance, given my own mother's recent—"

"I am very sorry for your loss, Miss Mowry," Wells quickly interjected.

"Thank you, Lord Wellesley." She dabbed a corner of her eye. "I am under no illusions, however, as to what marriage entails, my lord."

Her words hit him hard.

"I am aware of your prior betrothal and wish you to know I am not . . ." She struggled. "I have no feelings towards another and no reason to imagine any may develop." She finally looked at him. "Marriage is a contract meant to benefit two parties, my lord, and I would enter into it with no more expectation than that of mutual respect. I am willing to provide a husband heirs in return for the security of his title and income."

He appreciated, for once, that she spoke like an adult and not some simpering chit. And yet her words also left him cold, for she was all duty and no passion. No doubt she'd make a perfectly proper duchess yet remain as invigorating as a sack of potatoes between the sheets.

"And you do not foresee feelings between husband and wife developing over time?" he pressed.

"I would not know, sir," she said determinedly. "I have never been in love."

"I see."

"But I do not find you disagreeable, Lord Wellesley." She blushed again, prettily. "That is, I believe you to be a man of honor, and you are not unattractive in appearance."

He laughed. "Miss Mowry, your honesty astounds me, but I am grateful for it, truly." He searched her face. "And you would not oppose a husband who, in time, might take himself a mistress?"

"Don't all husbands keep mistresses, my lord?"

He searched her face again. "Some wives take lovers too, once heirs are born."

Her eyes widened. "But whyever would a lady . . . ?"

"Because it can be enjoyable, my dear, why else?" Wells's

smirk only made her blush more. Perhaps she was simply inexperienced, he thought, and not frigid.

Yet her answer disappointed. "*I* should never be so bold, sir." She sounded resolute. "For were my husband to engage a mistress I imagine it would simply relieve me of my duties to him."

Wells was again disheartened. "I am glad we had this discussion, Miss Mowry, so we each know where the other stands." He extended her his arm. "Shall we continue our tour?"

"Yes." She smiled up at him, as if grateful to have gotten the matter off her chest.

Inwardly Wells felt anything but grateful imagining this woman his duchess, dictating furnishings and décor, entertaining guests she'd invite from London. For the remainder of their tour, he did his best to hide his thoughts from Miss Mowry.

She did not seem to notice.

"My lord, a word please?"

Charles had traipsed over to the stables that evening—the men's unofficial sleeping quarters—in order to find his lordship. Only upon arriving, his rowdy crew looked up at her as one, and snickered.

"A *word* only," she stressed, "nothing more, you lecherous ingrates."

Pinky was not the least deterred. "*We* don't care no ways, miss." He winked at Charles. "Y' can bed 'im right 'ere, if y' like."

A few smothered guffaws rippled through the hayloft.

"Watch your tongue before I cuff you one, Pinky." His lordship stepped out of the shadows to defend Charles's

honor. "Apologize at once to Miss Merrinan for your impertinence."

"Sorry, lass." Pinky barely looked contrite. "Meant no 'arm
by it. Ain't nothin' wrong with it neither. You an' he make a
better match by far'n that prissy—"

"Enough!" his lordship growled.

Pinky shut his trap as Lord Wells roughly grabbed Charles
by the arm to march her out of the stables, across the courtyard, and up the Abbey's formal staircase down another long
hall and into the shell room.

"What did you wish to discuss, Charles?" He lit a sconce
without bothering to stoke the dying hearth.

"It is my father, sir. My sister writes his health has worsened
and that I ought to go and see him."

"Can it not wait until our guests leave, woman? I do not
think we can spare you right now given—"

"That is the other matter I wish to discuss, my lord. We
require more staff. We haven't enough hands as is to—"

"Yet the moment our guests leave additional staff will be
unnecessary. I'd prefer we simply muddle through until—"

"My lord, we are running ourselves ragged, and any staff
hired now will surely be needed once you . . ." She stopped
herself.

"Once I what?" His face clouded over.

Charles drew herself tall and stuck out her chin. "Once
you marry, sir."

The resounding silence in the room was deafening.

"And *who*, exactly, has informed you I intend to marry, Miss
Merrinan?" Lord Wellesley's face had fallen precipitously, yet
Charles knew there was no going back.

"My lord, I think it is apparent to all here that your mother,
the Duchess, has delivered you a bride." Hurt crept into her
voice.

"I see," he spoke slowly, the calm before a storm. "Which

means I must do her bidding, eh? Must marry whomever my mother chooses for me? Marry Miss Mowry?"

Charles grew impatient. "I do not presume to know what *you* intend to do, my lord. I know only what it is the Duchess rather blatantly hopes will happen. And as it is required that a duke marry and produce heirs, it is reasonable to assume you will someday marry. And seeing as how a perfectly respectable opportunity has been presented to you now I can only assume you are at least considering it. Sir."

***

Her voice sounded pinched, Wells thought. Fierce, even.

"Oh I am considering it, Charles." He pushed back. "I am considering marrying Miss Mowry and keeping you as mistress. In fact, she told me just today she shouldn't mind that arrangement in the least, said she'd even welcome it."

"How *dare* you, sir! How dare you speak of me to her as if I—"

"I did not mention your name, Charles." He'd riled her good this time; he could feel his loins throb in response. "I merely asked her opinion on a mistress, which she wholeheartedly condoned, embracing the fact it would relieve her of wifely duties she seemed none too keen to embark on."

"Wifely duties." Her eyes blazed at him. "No doubt you look forward to despoiling another virgin, sir, as she is pretty enough, I daresay, to turn your ravenous head."

"Oh she is plenty pretty, and yet shockingly leaves me cold. Why do you think that is, Fox? Why is it that ever since Cuthbert dragged you from my coop into my parlor I seem unable to imagine despoiling any other woman but you?" He stepped towards her, predatory.

Charles stepped back. "I am but a convenience to you, sir," she parried, no longer his tamed pet. "You said as much the

day you sentenced me to serve your bed. I am but a convenience and amusement, and as soon as you marry I will leave
this house and never—"

But his lips cut her short in a brutal, bruising kiss, hands
shedding her of her dress with a need days in the making, years
it felt like. She was his, damn it. He did not want the insipid
Mowry, he wanted his Fox, he wanted his mother gone, and he
wanted back the life he'd begun to build here at the Abbey
with his Cumberland mistress, to hell with everything else.

***

Charles relieved Lord Wells of his clothing with the same
blind need his lordship displayed, for she was deuced if she'd
let him go easy into the arms of another woman. He'd marry,
and she'd leave, but right then she would take what she bloody
well wanted and damn well deserved. Her sister was not enti-
tled to all the happiness in this world nor was Miss Mowry enti-
tled to all its comforts. She'd demand her share too, right here
upon the floor of the shell room, under the illusion of stars and
sea. She would grant herself the right to want more from life
than she'd damn well been given.

She would take from *him*.

In the end Charles left Wells naked and asleep upon the floor,
draping his clothes over him to tiptoe back to the musty room
she now shared with Ruby and Ginny. She realized she could
not continue in such a manner with him, not with his mother
and near-betrothed under the same roof. She would not go to
him again save for household matters. Hell, she *had* only
intended to speak to him about such matters tonight. And look
how they'd ended up . . .

She stomped back along the dark corridors. She would have to speak to Wells about Cuthbert and her sister yet too. Everything she'd intended to discuss with him had fallen from her mind the moment he'd kissed her. Why oh why did this man have such power over her? How had she ever allowed him entry to her heart?

She heard her mother's voice, from years past, suddenly echo in her head: *Care for your sister and father, protect them for me, Charles, but protect your own self too, darling girl. Promise me this, for you, dear daughter, are equally precious.*

CHAPTER THIRTY-THREE

Wells watched Miss Mowry across the table break her fast. The lady was indeed not unattractive. He'd have no trouble bedding her for an heir, and she was young enough, at nineteen, to no doubt be fecund. With any luck he'd get her with child within the first month of marriage, meaning he needn't touch her again for another year at least. Then, once a second heir was born he'd be done with her entirely. And so long as he convinced Charles to remain his mistress . . .

"Roland, dear, what are you mulling this morning?" The Duchess broke his reverie.

"Mulling, Mother?" He looked up. "Why, matrimony." He kept his gaze cool. "I have been mulling matrimony, *Maman.*"

Her own eyes widened, as did Miss Mowry's.

"Well, that is indeed a pleasant subject to be mulling, dear." She coolly smiled back. "Might you share your thoughts upon the subject with us?"

Bold as ever, his *Maman.*

"Miss Mowry and I were discussing the topic just yesterday on our tour about the Abbey—what it is we each find most appealing about marriage," he answered.

"Oh?" The Duchess raised a brow. "How intriguing. Do continue, Roland."

"Perhaps Miss Mowry would like to continue instead?" He cast the young lady a look.

She demurred. "Goodness no, Lord Wellesley. Her grace posed *you* the question, sir, not me."

She outmaneuvered nicely; not a bad trait.

"Well I, for one, consider the best part of matrimony to spell the end of *unexpected* visits." He watched the Duchess flinch. "That and of course bedding my virgin bride."

His mother's face contorted. "Roland, I did not raise you to be an ill-mannered boor!"

"You certainly did not, Mother. My apologies, Miss Mowry." He peeked at the young lady, whose cheeks bloomed scarlet.

"Shall I tell her what you told me yesterday, miss?" He forged ahead, not waiting for her answer. "Miss Mowry, rightfully so, looks forward to the protection of a man's title and, of course, his fortune." His mother's face now positively glowered. "She does not mind in the least if her husband takes a mistress and otherwise ignores her entirely," he finished.

"My lord!" the young lady protested.

"Roland, enough!" His mother's fist clenched the tablecloth. "Were you not a grown man I'd—"

"What, *Maman*, have me paddled? Send me to bed without dinner? I need neither your approval nor your affection anymore, and as I am master of my own house and own life, I think it is time you and Miss Mowry took yourselves back to London and let me be. You may report to Father that I am doing my best to restore his beloved Abbey and that I intend to live out the rest of my days here in Cumberland serving its people as their Duke—with or without a duchess."

Miss Mowry looked ready to faint into her plate, yet being

trained rigorously to preserve the peace at all cost, proceeded to defuse the tension as best she could.

She really would make a good duchess.

"Lord Wellesley," she interjected, "would you be so kind as to show me the exterior of Almsdale Abbey today, to complete our tour?" Her eyes begged him to behave. "I should like to see the grounds and do not mind donning boots. The sun appears even to shine a little," she pleaded.

He took pity on the girl. "Of course, Miss Mowry, happy to oblige." He gave her a pinched smile. "Allow me to see to a few matters first, and within the hour I shall be at your disposal."

"Thank you, sir." She wanly smiled back.

Maman opened her mouth as if to speak but must have determined silence more golden in the moment. She shut it just as fast.

Wells, meanwhile, returned to his plate of food and ignored both women for the remainder of breakfast. He had a great many things on his mind more important than marriage.

Later, as they strolled arm in arm outside the Abbey, Miss Mowry felt slight beside Wells; she was half a head shorter than Charles, though her figure was shapely enough. He was pondering his situation again, only half listening to her prattle on about London. Forever bloody London.

". . . and I assume you've been to Gunter's in Mayfair, my lord, at Berkeley Square?"

"I have indeed, Miss Mowry, it is a fine establishment."

"I do so love their tarts, don't you?" She smiled prettily.

"Yes, who doesn't love a good tart?" He smirked but was immediately bored. Conversation with this lady was an arduous pursuit. It did not mean *she* was arduous. That would be unfair. She'd merely been hampered and pampered like every other debutante he knew, making her, well, tedious. Why did women think naïveté an attractive trait?

"Will you visit London again this season, sir?" She sounded hopeful.

"No, Miss Mowry, I've sworn off society for good. I intend to make Cumberland my permanent home now."

"But surely you will keep a townhouse?"

"No, I think not. I intend to settle fully here. The climate and environs suit me."

"I see."

"Do you not like Cumberland, miss?" He could not resist poking.

"Oh no, sir, it is just . . . Well, it is rather remote."

"Yes, remote unto the ends of earth. Precisely why I find it so appealing. Reminds me of my years at sea: endless ocean with nothing in sight but miles upon miles of—"

"Lord Wellesley," she interrupted.

"Hmm?" He was feeling pleased with himself.

"Why do you fight with your mother so, my lord? Has she done something to upset you? That is, other than our visit?"

Her forwardness again surprised, granting him a glimmer of her humanity, and he was warmed by it, though also chastened. He'd behaved poorly at breakfast, though she did not seem to hold it against him now.

"The Duchess and I rarely see eye to eye on matters," he answered honestly. "And as I've no other siblings to distract her, I am the subject of *all* her focus, and so, it seems, the sum of all her disappointment as well."

"Surely she is not disappointed in you, sir."

Wells laughed. "Dear lady, I can assure you she most certainly is!"

"But that is . . . Rather, what could she possibly find disappointing in your person when you are clearly—?"

"Duty, Miss Mowry." He caught her eye. "I disappoint by failing so terrifically to do my *duty* by her."

"But I do not see how you have failed when you—"

"I should prefer we change the subject, miss, as I'd rather not spoil a perfectly fine day discussing my mother. Allow me to show you what will someday be Almsdale's gardens. Once I've finished with the house, that is."

He took her arm to lead her around the back end of a buttress, yet once there Wells surprised himself by asking, "Might I kiss you, Miss Mowry?"

She startled. "I . . . Well I suppose . . . If you should like."

She was so noncommittal he simply took her face in both his hands and stared into her panicked eyes a moment, deciding he might at least *try* to seduce her, see how she'd react.

Yet the moment his lips pressed her own he felt nothing. No spark, no invitation, not even a slight softening. It was like kissing a dry leaf. Hell, even Charles had responded better, drunk on his lap that first night, than this girl did sober by daylight.

He hid his disappointment behind a thin smile. "Thank you, Miss Mowry. I hope I was not too bold just now."

"Not at all, sir," she hurried to reply. "Only I have not been kissed so often as to, well, know how it is one should respond."

Wells was suddenly saddened this woman thought one was taught to respond, when one simply did, or did not, enjoy a kiss. When it truly was that simple.

"You were perfect in your response, miss." He lied to spare her any hurt. "Only it grows chill out here without the sun to warm us. Shall we return to the house for tea?"

"Yes, please." She latched on to his suggestion. "A cup will do wonders, I am sure, to revive me."

Charles chose the worst possible moment to look up from her labors and out the window onto the Abbey's back gardens. For there below her, Lord Wellesley proceeded to declare his intentions more clearly than if he'd spoken the words out loud. She watched him kiss Miss Mowry's dainty lips and felt her heart recoil. It was not just her sister she would lose to Cuthbert now. She'd lose his lordship too, far sooner than expected.

Charles would lose the man she'd somehow, impossibly, come to love.

ACT III

WRATH

Anybody can become angry—that is easy, but to be angry with the right person and to the right degree and at the right time and for the right purpose, and in the right way—that is not within everybody's power and is not easy.

Aristotle (384-322 BCE)

CHAPTER THIRTY-FOUR

"Are you sure she read my letter, John?" Eleanor made his heart twist.

"She did, love." John stroked her hair while she sat snug upon his lap. "Gave it her meself. I've no doubt she did."

"Then why has she not come to see us?" Ellie looked aggrieved. "Or at least written to tell me why? Papa grows worse, and it is not like Charles to ignore him. I know she is angry with me still, but for her to eschew even Father is most unlike her, John. I am worried something is wrong."

"Oi, sweet," he tried to reassure her, "the whole Abbey's a right mess these days, what with the Duchess and Miss Mowry visitin' Lord Wells. He's in a foul mood, and the extra work of guests has yer sister runnin' ragged. I shouldn't even be here meself for all there is t' do."

"And who is this Miss Mowry, John? Is she her grace's companion?"

"Companion?" John laughed. "Lord no, love! She's his lordship's intended." He wrapped his arms about her more tightly. "The Duchess brought 'im a bride, see, so y' can imagine his wrath. And the Abbey's not fit for guests neither, barely enough rooms for us what live there. Wells is sleepin' with his men, if y' can believe it. Forced t' give his mother his own bed."

She was not amused by his news, however; instead, Eleanor looked only more distressed.

"John." She stared straight at him. "Tell me honestly now, does my sister have feelings for Lord Wellesley?"

She nearly knocked him flat with her question—good thing he was sitting down. "Well now," John fumbled, "I can't speak t' her feelings, Ellie. I wouldn't know what yer sister thinks of his lordship."

She would not relent. "I do not ask what *she* has told you, John. I ask *your* opinion, your honest opinion as both her friend and his lordship's, and the fact you reside in that Abbey with the two of them." She repeated her question. "Does she harbor feelings for him?"

And there it was, that same stubborn streak she shared with her sister. John knew that if he married this woman he'd have to be honest with her, or she'd forever hate him for lying to her.

"I believe she does, Ellie, yes."

"And he for her? Does Lord Wellesley care for her too?" she insisted.

"In his own way, I think, mayhap yes."

"I see." She stewed.

"Ellie . . ."

"How long have you known this, John?"

"I don't . . . That is, I weren't at liberty to—"

"And how long have we been courting, John?" Her voice rose.

"Ellie . . ." he tried again.

"Don't you Ellie me, sir." She got up off his lap. "You tell me everything you know, right this instant, or so help me God I'll . . . !"

She was positively glowering at him, making him feel such

love and fear and pain and desire for her all at once he thought he might burst.

"Christ woman, you'll be the death o' me," John finally got out.

"I'll be the death of you all right if you don't tell me this instant what the devil my sister and Lord Wellesley have been up to at the Abbey!"

And John knew he'd no choice anymore but to tell her the whole damn sordid truth. So he did.

Dearest Charles,

John has told me all and spared no detail. I am shocked and furious, but not at you, no, at Wellesley, that villainous, dastardly man whom I defended in my letters. Do not be angry at John. He spoke only grudgingly, loyal to that vainglorious, evil lord, and to you, whom he considers already his sister. I am so sorry, Charles. So deeply, deeply sorry! That Wellesley should have duped me into believing him a gentleman when all the while he'd forced you into ruin, and over two measly chickens! I was so horrified by all John divulged, I nearly ran outside to slaughter the birds. How can we eat their eggs, knowing their cost? It fills me with revulsion and despair and anger so intense I've a mind to storm the Abbey and call his lordship out.

Dear God, Charles thought. Would Eleanor truly be so rash? Her hands shook as she read on.

Sister, I beg your forgiveness. I should have believed <u>you</u> over my encounters with <u>him</u>. I am so aggrieved by how we've quarreled, how you've sacrificed for me and father yet again. If mother were alive she would be beside herself and father would surely shoot him on the spot. And were I a man I'd—well, I would do the same.

Charles, come home. I cannot stand the thought of you remaining

*in that house with that lord, regardless of what John says. He tells
me you are fond of Wellesley now, but how can that be? How could
you possibly have feelings for a man who forced you to such servitude?
Come home to us, come see Papa before it is too late. Live with us
once John and I marry. Charles, if you do not return within the week
I will come for you myself I swear it.*

    Eleanor

Charles put down the letter with trembling hands and met
John Cuthbert's eyes. He did not flinch, having apologized to
her the moment he'd handed her the note. *I'd no choice but to tell
her, miss, y' know how she gets. She demanded the truth and as we're t'
marry I couldn't . . .* But Charles had paid him no heed, tearing
into the letter and reading it with growing horror, her heart in
her throat, Ellie's words searing her insides.

She had to sit down; she felt weak and winded, her heart a
lump of lead.

"Cuthbert, what am I to do?" she beseeched.

"Well, I'd expect . . . That is, y' ought to go and see her,
Charles. Put things right between the two o' you again."

"No, not Ellie, John. What am I to do about . . ." She could
not say his name.

John stepped beside her then, putting his hand warmly on
her shoulder and squeezing just a little. "He'll have t' wed,
miss, much as he won't want to. He's the Duke's only son, he's
no choice. And if not Mowry it'll be some other lady o' the
Ton. He needs an heir and that's all there is to it, Charles. I'm
sorry, gel."

"I know," she whispered. "I have always known, only I did
not expect to feel so much for him." She gulped. "I did not
think I could be so foolish, John, so weak." And she nearly
sobbed then, catching herself just in time, for the last thing she
wanted was pity from Cuthbert, from anyone really. The
steward had seen her low before.

"Miss." His hand squeezed hers again in comfort. "I love him too. He's all the family I have, me best mate. And despite his rough ways he's a good man, regardless o' what yer sister thinks of him now. You and I both know he's flawed but no fiend. Y' see him for what he is, *who* he is, which is why he loves you too, no doubt in me mind. Only he's not like us, Charles. He can't allow himself t' love same as you or me and Ellie can. His duty's to the Dukedom, which by needs must come first. The best y' can hope is t' remain his mistress, gel, and if that's no life for yer then you'll have t' leave, 'cause he'll not give yer up willingly, gel. If I know Wells, he'll keep yer for as long as he can."

Charles hid her face in her hands, knowing Cuthbert was right. She'd seen Lord Wells kiss Miss Mowry just yesterday; their betrothal was imminent. And she knew she couldn't share him with another, she wouldn't. She'd have to leave, and soon, but not to set up house with Ellie and John, no. She couldn't stomach their happiness—not that she begrudged them this—it simply asked of her too much. She'd need to flee much further than her father's house, somewhere Roland Wellesley would not venture to find her. A place he would be loath to look.

Unfortunately, it was a place she loathed just as much.

Wells knew his housekeeper was deliberately avoiding him. Why must every woman under his roof be such a pain in the arse? Bad enough his mother was still gadding about with Miss Mowry, but to have his mistress now ignore him was an affront that cut deep.

Which is why, despite his vow to never again read Charles's correspondence, Wells intercepted another letter, snatching it from Cuthbert's hands.

"Give it here, sir." His steward scowled.

"You'll get it in a minute, John." Wells scowled back, opening the note to quickly glean its contents.

"Yer Grace, y' swore you'd not—"

"I know what I said, John, but I've changed my mind now that she's shut me out, avoiding me at every turn. How the bloody hell else am I supposed to know why she's behaving like a—?"

"Y' could ask her, for God's sake," Cuthbert snarled at him. "Y' could ask her like a man, rather'n the coward you've become."

This felt like a punch to gut, coming from John. But Wells bit his lip and ignored the insult, scanning the letter.

Dearest Ellie,

I am sorry for our fighting too. Forgive me, sister, for not wishing you the very best on your betrothal. It seems there is cause for celebration here, too, as it is only a matter of time, I believe, before Lord Wellesley announces his engagement to the young lady currently visiting.

Wells froze. Did she really assume this?

I promise to be happy on both counts, as best I can, truly, and shall endeavor to visit you and Papa as soon as I am able. Only the work of added guests has me bone tired these days, worn weary. And to worry about Papa now is but another stress.

Only please do not worry about me. Despite all you now think and write of Lord Wells he is not so bad as you believe. Yes, he forced me into the position I find myself in, but I cannot say I have not enjoyed his attentions. It is a slippery slope to allow oneself feelings. I sincerely hope with all my heart that you have found in John Cuthbert a man true and steady. I believe that you have.

I do not hold such hope for myself. I am ruined, after all, and not unwillingly, I admit. I shall leave Lord Wells as soon as he is married and plan otherwise for my future, but I will not impose upon you and John, Ellie. I could not. I am happy for you, truly, but I do not think I could withstand such happiness when my own heart, for better or worse, feels numb. I will recover, sister, do not pity or judge me for my actions, I beg. I love you even when we argue, Ellie, and would steal his lordship's chickens all over again knowing the good it has brought you—not just baskets of food but a husband no less.

Bless you and John and may God keep you both, and Papa, safe.
Charles

So. Eleanor Merrinan knew the truth of him and no doubt despised him utterly. He was surprised the lady had not shown up on his doorstep demanding satisfaction.

And his Fox? She planned to leave him as soon as he wed, *assumed* that he would wed, damn her. Is that what everyone now assumed, including Mowry? He'd not decided himself yet to go through with any marriage, and he certainly wouldn't tie himself to another woman if it meant losing Charles. She was the one bright light in his life, the one female who . . . fit. He'd not lose her. He'd simply need to convince her to stay on as his mistress when he married. She could remain his housekeeper if she liked. Or better yet, he'd find a cottage somewhere on his lands that he could furnish as a sort of 'love nest' for her. Hell, she could open up her own school even if it would make her happy to teach the village children as her father had. In truth, Wells didn't care what she did. He simply couldn't lose her, not over so insignificant a detail as marriage.

"Give it me, sir." Cuthbert's voice cut into his thoughts.

Wells handed over the letter without meeting his man's eyes.

"'Tis the last post I let you read, Wells," John threatened. "Over my dead body."

"Your dead body, is it?" Wells snapped, returning to his

wits. "It's come to this then, already? Marriage to Eleanor Merrinan driving a wedge between us? I told you this would happen, John. I told you falling in love would—"

"Y' don't know a damned thing about love, sir, or you'd not be snatchin' letters from me and instead go talk to the one woman whose poor heart you've broken more times'n—"

Wells was livid. "You speak to me again like that Cuthbert and I'll—!"

The expression on his steward's face stopped him short.

"As yer mate, Wells, I believe I've every right t' say me peace, but as yer steward, no, I s'pose I don't." John's eyes narrowed. "So if y' regard me as servant only, *Yer Grace*, I'll take me leave now." His stare bored into Wells. "Only don't ever call me mate again."

And with that he walked out, leaving Wells crushed by his best friend's words.

CHAPTER THIRTY-FIVE

Charles knew she could no longer avoid the inevitable. She needed to see her sister and father, and she'd need Wellesley's permission to do so. She knocked on the parlor door with trepidation and was told to enter by the Duchess, who was taking tea with Miss Mowry and his lordship.

"Begging your pardon, Your Grace, Miss Mowry." She curtsied to both before she turned to Wells. "My lord, might I impose a moment? I'm afraid it's rather urgent."

The Duchess immediately interjected. "I hope it is nothing serious, Mrs. Merrinan?"

"I hope not either, Your Grace, but my father's health has taken a turn, I'm afraid." Charles's eyes locked on his lordship.

"Then you must go to him at once, Mrs. Merrinan." The Duchess turned to her son. "I am sure Roland can spare you, can't you dear?"

***

Wells wanted to throttle his mother yet again. "*I* make the decisions here concerning staff, *Maman*, not you." He promptly stood and motioned Charles out the door, stomping into the next room over—yet another dust-coated space riddled with grime. It would take an army of servants to fully clean the Abbey, for in truth Charles and her girls had made barely a dent.

Wells launched straight in. "So, your father is sick and you wish to visit. When? And for how long?" He'd let her know he was displeased by her distance of late.

"I should like to leave tomorrow first thing, if I may, my lord. I've asked Ruby to stand in for me and I will return before nightfall, unless my father worsens. I realize the timing is unfortunate, sir, but if anything were to happen to him I should never forgive myself for not—"

"Of course you must go," he interrupted. "If he is that poorly you must go at once, today yet, but I shall expect you by dinner tomorrow, and if you are not back by then I will come fetch you myself."

"My lord, if I should need to stay longer I would—"

"You will return by dinner as that is my order, Charles."

"Your order?" Her voice raised a notch. "As I do not know how ill my father is, I can scarce promise my precise return, sir, surely you understand this."

"Understand?" He inhaled a breath to quell his anger. "I understand very little these days, miss, as you have been avoiding me most blatantly, avoiding even looking at me lately, let alone sharing my bed."

"Avoiding *you*, sir?" she got out, her face clouding over. "It is you who have avoided me these weeks past, fawning over Mowry's fat dowry while you sample all the niceties a well-bred young lady has to offer a man of your ilk."

"My *ilk*?" The mouth on this woman! "I do not care a whit for Mowry, Charles, and you know it." He hauled her to him.

"I care for you, damn it, and I am tired of you avoiding your nightly duty to me simply because she is here."

"Duty?" She struggled in his grasp. "You speak to me, of duty, sir?"

Wells tightened his grip, relishing the feel of her flush against his loins, the smell of her as his teeth grazed her earlobe. "Yes *duty*, Charles," he hissed. "Now do your duty as my mistress and—"

"My duty is clear!" she cried, twisting in his arms. "It matters not whether you care about Miss Mowry, sir." He could feel her heart thudding against his chest. "What matters is that she will be your *wife*, and so it is your duty not to dishonor her by bedding your mistress right beneath her nose."

"Spoken like a true lady," uttered a voice from the door, brittle with fury. "You'd be wise to heed your housekeeper's words, Roland."

Maman.

He was so stunned in that moment that Charles managed to wrench herself free and flee the room, leaving him rooted to the spot, unblinking.

"Is it true, son?" His mother's icy calm continued, her voice cracking with anger. "Have you made your housekeeper your harlot here in Cumberland?"

"Yes." He came back to life. "And I am not ashamed to admit it."

"Of course you aren't." Her rage simmered just beneath her words. "And if you had but chosen any other girl here as mistress, we'd not now find ourselves in this situation, would we?" Her eyes pierced his soul.

"What the devil is that supposed to mean, *Maman*?" Wells defended himself. "Plenty of men have mistresses. Most, in fact. No doubt Father had his share too." He aimed to hurt but saw he did not.

"Why yes, Roland, I was even friends with a few of them."

She pinched back a hollow smile. "This is not about your father, or me, or anyone else right now. It is about you and the woman you dared to defile."

"Defile?" he snorted. "I'll let you know, Mother, that until you showed up, uninvited and unwelcome, with an unwanted lady in tow, Charles Merrinan and I were perfectly happy defiling one another. Ask her yourself, go right ahead. She's been more than willing and eager until now to share my—"

"You've no idea who she is, do you?" She cut in, her tone biting. "Her father, Roland, was your Uncle Carlton's dearest, closest friend during the war, a man who saved not only your own father's life but nearly died trying to save your uncle's life too. The Duke himself petitioned the King for Merrinan's knighting for bravery during the war, then made him his squire here in Cumberland. Sir Benedict even named his firstborn after Uncle Charles."

Wells stared at his mother in disbelief.

"The Duke of Allendale knows Sir Benedict Merrinan to be the very best of men, son, and it is *his daughter* I now discover you have dishonored, shamelessly. Charles Merrinan is a lady, Roland, who should never have been made your housekeeper, let alone your *mistress*." She hissed the word in pure fury. "Miss Merrinan's mother was daughter to the Earl of Denbigh, and though the lady's own family felt she married beneath her to take a mere soldier as husband, not once, I am sure, did Adelaide Enright ever in her worst nightmares imagine her firstborn reduced to such utter ruination as this."

Wells was still shocked. And by now furious. "And just *how*, Mother, should I have known any of this, pray? When Charles's mother is long dead, her father mad as a hatter, and she herself told me nothing of her family's lineage?" He wanted to rip the righteous look off his mother's face and stomp on it.

Instead, he used his words. "Do you know how I met her,

this fine lady you speak of? Cuthbert caught her thieving my chickens, *Maman*, right from out of my henhouse. And when forced to confess, the girl spat in my face—a she-devil, reeking of chicken shit. Should I have presumed from such behavior, *Maman*, that she was a lady? Should I?" he pressed.

The Duchess ground her teeth. "Roland, I do not blame you for not knowing her history, but this does not change the fact you must remedy this situation forthwith. If your father knew the damage you've done Benedict Merrinan's daughter, he would never forgive you or himself. You will marry her at once and make her your Duchess."

"I . . . Marry *her*?" Wells's head hurt. He could barely speak.

"Yes, Roland." Her voice remained clipped. "And I should think you'd be pleased. For if the two of you have enjoyed one another as much as you claim"—she made a face—"then I daresay she will make you a most pleasing bride indeed."

Wells remained stunned.

"I will inform your father of your betrothal to Miss Charles Merrinan and will vacate the premises tomorrow first thing. Though I daresay Miss Mowry will require considerable consolation: a marquess at the very least."

And off she strode, leaving Wells querulous, confused, and in one devil of a quandary as to how to break this news to Charles. For from housekeeper to future Duchess was indeed a momentous change.

He was himself still processing his mother's words. How could he possibly have known who Charles was? And why the hell hadn't she *told* him? Did she not know herself? It would explain much, yet still explained so little.

He dropped heavily into a dust-shrouded chair and stared at the wall before him, imagining his mistress his wife. He'd not thought of her as anything but his lover, yet deep in his gut a spark alit, for he'd wanted her anyway, hadn't he? He'd told her as much when he'd said he cared more for her than Mowry. Hell, he cared more for her than any other woman ever foisted on him in past. What was more, Charles would not balk at living at the Abbey rather than in London. Cumberland was her home. Its people *her* people. They would adore her as their Duchess.

He began to warm to the idea, to slowly even embrace it. *Lady Charles Wellesley, Duchess of Allendale*, he thought to himself. *His* Duchess, and his alone. To have and to hold each night as he'd had her these many nights past. Perhaps this wasn't such a terrible turn of events. Perhaps the perfect wife had been staring him in the face all along, here in his home, in his bed, brought to heel that fateful night covered in chicken shit.

A contented, slow smile began to spread over his face, as his heart whispered *yes, Charles Merrinan, my Duchess*. And a damn fine duchess at that.

※

Charles hid in Ruby's room, shaken to her core. She knew she'd have to leave now—no way out from this. If only she'd kept her mouth shut and not provoked his lordship again! If only she'd remained reserved, her voice lowered so that the Duchess hadn't overheard, hadn't stumbled into that room and discovered her so thoroughly compromised.

She put her face in her hands and wept, because Charles did not want to leave, not when things had been going so well at the Abbey—at least, before Miss Mowry and the Duchess had appeared. She was proud of the household she'd assembled, proud of the shell room she'd restored, even, in truth, proud of the man she'd come to . . .

But she snuffed that thought before it could spread like fire. Roland Wellesley had never been, nor ever could be, hers. He'd said as much himself that no position here was permanent. She had no right to feel anything for the man. She'd been his mistress, was all. And now she'd no longer be his housekeeper, either.

Charles dried her tears, washed her face, and straightened her hair, stilling her racing heart with deep gulps of air. She would face her shame and leave the Abbey with as much dignity as she could muster.

Somehow, she would survive this blow and forge a new path forward. It's what she did, over and over again.

"But . . . !"

On his search to find Charles, Wells overheard his mother deliver Miss Mowry the news. He paused to listen outside the parlor door.

"I know, my dear, I am sorry, but I promised your mother I would find you a match and I am determined to succeed."

He could picture the young lady's displeasure plastered to her face.

His mother further reassured her. "It is simply imperative we now return to London to complete our mission. I can think of two eligible marquises and three perfectly good earls who would more than suffice."

"But . . . !" The lady tried again.

"There, there, Miss Mowry. I daresay you weren't terribly enamored of living out here in Cumberland with my Roland, now were you? We shall find you a London husband instead, and if we leave tomorrow we'll be back by week's end, just in time for all the spring gallery openings."

Wells snuck away, satisfied. *Maman* would leave and take Miss Mowry with her. He was certain the lady would find some titled, London husband more to her liking.

He crept back down the hall, aware he'd dodged a blow by not marrying Mowry. As, no doubt, had she.

❦

"Charles!"

She heard Wells shout, closer this time. His lordship's voice bellowed into the servant's wing, ensuring the entire Abbey heard him.

"Miss Merrinan, you are to see me this instant! I know you are hiding, come out at once!"

Of course she was hiding; she'd not present him her neck. Charles would slip away after dark, visit Ellie and Father overnight, and then make off at dawn. So long as she avoided both his lordship and the Duchess all would be well. It would. It must.

She shut her eyes tight in the cramped broom closet, having shut herself into the nearest hiding space she could find as soon as she'd heard his shouting. Only she was not prepared to have the door wrenched open and Wellesley loom before her, his ability to softly tread floorboards surprising her for the last time, surely.

She blinked in his face before he yanked her out and dragged her down the hall to the next nearest room, slamming the door behind them.

"Why are you hiding from me?" he demanded.

"I should think that obvious, my lord." Charles willed herself to remain calm.

He dismissed her answer with a snort. "Why did you not tell me who you are?"

"I did, sir. I gave you my name and you even met my family." She did not understand his question.

"Why did you not tell me of our families' connection?" he insisted. "The connection to your name?"

329

"What connection, my lord?" She was in truth now confused. "I met your father but once, as a child, and told you as much."

"You are named after my Uncle Charles—Lord Carlton Wellesley—whose very pocket watch I gave you." His eyes searched her face. "Your father was my uncle's dearest friend on earth, my mother tells me, and saved my own father's life in battle more than once. Do you honestly know *none* of this?"

Charles mirrored his lordship's disbelief. "Your *uncle?*" she blurted. "I assumed my parents wished me born a boy, and named me so; there was no talk of Lord Carlton Wellesley or any such stories as these, sir, else I surely should have known."

"And your mother?" Wells pressed. "Why did you not tell me she was the Earl of Denbigh's daughter? Why not seek assistance from her family when your father fell ill? Why come to Cumberland and starve yourselves instead?"

His voice had risen in pitch, even as her own was quick to match.

"Why?" she fumed. "Why indeed, sir. Perhaps because our grandparents planned to have our father committed, that's why, to the most notorious and worst of London's heinous, inhuman asylums. We would neither doom him to that hell, nor remain their wards, pretending he'd died from grief. They gave us only that choice, so of course we fled. How could we not? And why should I tell you about my mother's parents when they chose to disown us, wanting nothing further to do with us once we'd left, pretending we didn't even exist? We are nothing to the Enrights, we are Merrinans only now, for Cumberland, at least, took us in, gave Father the position of headmaster when he could no longer manage as squire. Cumberland, my lord, accepted him as he was while revering him for the soldier and scholar he'd been."

Charles steadied herself. "For ten years, Lord Wellesley, we have lived and breathed an honest life here, far from the stench of London's treachery. You of all men, I should think, might understand this."

***

Her eyes blazed at Wells with such intensity he was overcome with feeling, his body flooding with emotions he could not begin to name.

He took her hand tightly in his own. "Charles, I would have made the same choice myself if I'd been you, I do understand. Only why wait until now to tell me this? Why allow me to treat you as I did that night, humiliating you and your family by assuming you were a common thief, a village bumpkin, when all the while you—"

"*Allow* you?" She shook her head, wrenching back her hand. "Oh that is rich, sir, truly. As if I'd had any choice at all that night, any power whatsoever to sway you. Don't you dare place blame on me now, my lord, for your own despicable actions. I was wrong to steal your chickens, I'll admit, but you forced me into servitude and nothing I said that night or in the days that followed would have made you see me as aught but some impoverished, thieving chit."

Her words struck daggers to his breast.

"And the truth, Lord Wellesley? I *was* that chit! I'd become a lowly thief, just as you'd become a pirate, taking your every pleasure. Using your position as Lord of Almsdale Abbey to slake your base desires."

Wells was at once awestruck and aggrieved, for every word Charles spoke was true. He loathed himself for behavior he was anything but proud of, sickened by the manner in which he'd dishonored and debased her.

"Charles, I'm not asking for forgiveness. I've no right to." He swallowed, nervous. "My actions *were* despicable that night, regardless of crime or family. To treat even a village girl the way I treated you was, I admit, the misdeed of a pirate and not the behavior of a lord. But let me make it up to you now, Fox. Marry me! Be my future Duchess, stand beside me that we may finish the Abbey together. Share my bed, my name, bear my heirs, and remain here with me, far from London's evils. You needn't be my housekeeper any longer, Charles. Not if you are my wife."

Her eyes swelled to round, inscrutable pools of murky green he could not read, could not find answers within.

"Is this what your mother wishes, sir?" Her words came out clipped. "And what of Miss Mowry, my lord? I can offer you no dowry, not like she can."

"I don't give a rat's arse about Mowry's dowry." Wells stepped closer. "And yes, it is what *Maman* wishes. Just now she told me we must marry to preserve your and your father's honor. And after all I have discovered, it is of course the most reasonable solution to—"

"Ah yes." Her voice grew cold. Implacable. "Reasonable, logical Lord Wellesley can now reasonably marry his lusty mistress, knowing her lineage, rather than relegate himself to bedding fresh virginal flesh. How perfect for you, *Your Grace*." She skewered him with the title. "How utterly, perfectly delightful for you. For why shouldn't I now fall further into your lap, giving you all that you desire: a body to lay your seed in and a native who knows her people, who'll no doubt convince them to revere their dashing new Duke. "

She curtsied in such egregious, mocking display he flinched, as if slapped.

"Only I will not, Lord Wellesley." Charles drew herself tall. "I will *not* marry you, not now, and not ever, for you do not get to order me into obedience, nay, into subservience now through marriage, sir!"

Her eyes were so icy he shivered.

"I told you before you'd not claim my soul, and I proclaim

it now loud. You do not own me, Roland Wellesley, nor will you *ever*."

She knocked the wind from his lungs as she hurtled past him, jabbing him hard in the chest as she flew out the door, her legs bearing her away at terrific speed.

For a moment Wells could not breathe. Until he gasped for air, in pain.

CHAPTER THIRTY-SIX

"Ellie." A voice jarred her dreams. "Sister, wake up."

"Charles?" Eleanor pulled herself awake. "Is that you?" She opened her eyes and flung her arms about her sister. "Oh Charles, you came! Thank heavens you came home!" She held on tight and would not let Charles go.

"Ellie, we must speak. Please, it is urgent."

Immediately she rose from her bed to follow her sister into the kitchen, where a candle was already lit.

"Charles, it is the middle of the night! Why have you come to see us so late, sister?"

"Ellie, I leave at daybreak, but I'll not go without seeing you first."

"What has happened? Has he hurt you more? Are you with child? So help me God if that man—"

"No, Ellie, hush," Charles insisted. "It is nothing of the sort. We merely quarreled, and I can no longer stay. It is imperative I leave Cumberland, at least until his lordship marries and forgets me."

"So he will marry the lady his mother brought?" Eleanor willed herself to believe her sister now told her the truth; she knew Charles's feelings for Lord Wellesley were no mere passing fancy.

"Yes. I don't know. If not her, then some other lady. It doesn't matter, Eleanor, what matters is that *I* cannot marry Lord Wellesley. And so I cannot stay, I can't bear to. Surely you understand why I—"

"Then stay with us, Charles. Papa is not long for this world, I fear, and John will not abandon you, I know it. You can live with us, at least until you decide what—"

"No, Ellie, I cannot. I'll not cast a pall over your honeymoon." Her smile looked sad. "And Father won't know if I am here, gone, or all of ten years old still. I shall say goodbye to him now and catch the first coach to London at first light."

"But Charles, whatever will you do in London? You abhor London. We both do. Where will you stay? How will you—?"

"I shall figure that out, Ellie. I am not unskilled. And once I'm settled I will send word, I promise. Only first, sister, you must take this."

Eleanor was promptly handed a small bag of coin.

"Charles." Her stomach flipped. "I cannot accept this, I *will* not. You will need every penny of this in London."

***

She'd known Eleanor would refuse, but Charles would make her see reason.

"I have set funds aside for London, but this, at least, is the dowry I promised you, Ellie. It's not as much as I'd hoped, but Cuthbert has savings too, I'm sure, and you must start your lives somehow—buy livestock and furnishings, a fresh coat of paint for the walls. And when your firstborn comes, Ellie, I shall visit and shower my niece or nephew with kisses." She smiled through her tears, wishing desperately to chase the look of pain off Eleanor's face, for her sister stared back at her so dismally, so unhappily, Charles could not bear to see it.

"Now then." She swallowed. "I promised myself no tears because of course I shall see you soon enough. And you a married woman at that." She forced another smile. "Cuthbert is a good man, Ellie. I should never have doubted him, nor you. Forgive me." She gripped her sister's hands. "He is *more* than good enough for you, dearest, and I regret past words said. I wish you every happiness, truly."

"Oh Charles, I can't!" Eleanor burst into tears. "I cannot let you go again! This feels worse, even, than the night you left to steal those rotten chickens. Please don't leave us. I beg you, reconsider. Cumberland is your home, Charles, not London, not—!"

"Ellie, I must distance myself from Lord Wellesley, for my own sake. He is not so awful as you think him, truly, only I—"

"Do you love him, Charles?" Eleanor could be bold, when she wished.

"Yes," she admitted, "but he does not love me in kind. He is fond of me only, he cannot . . ." *allow himself more*, she wanted to say but did not. "He cannot love like mortals do, he is bound by ducal duty. And I cannot remain his mistress once he marries. I will not share him with another, Ellie, I cannot." Charles held herself in check, having wept enough already.

"Of course you cannot, sister, for you are far too much like Papa, aren't you?" Ellie looked at her with such feeling it made Charles ache. "You give too wholly of your heart. Yet you deserve happiness too, sister. You deserve to *be loved* just as passionately as you yourself love."

"I shall be fine, Ellie. I always am." Charles thrust out her chin. "Let me say goodbye to Papa now, and this you must give Cuthbert, please." She handed her sister a note.

Eleanor looked, at last, resigned. "I'll make you a quick

plate, Charles, to hold you on your journey. It is several days to London. I'll pack you provisions, too."

"Thank you, Ellie."

Charles trod softly to their father's bedroom, to say farewell to Papa. She prayed it would not be forever.

❧

"Cuthbert." Wells pulled him aside. "Have you seen Miss Merrinan?"

John thought his lordship looked oddly aggrieved, considering the circumstance. They'd just seen the Duchess and Miss Mowry off, having loaded trunks and servants back into the ducal carriage. He'd expected Lord Wells to be relieved—not that either lady had looked terribly pleased during their send-off.

"No, sir," John finally answered, still angry at Wells for snatching that last letter.

"If you see her, tell her I wish a word."

"Yes, sir."

"And John." Wells hesitated. "You were right to call me out last night. I should not have spoken as I did."

"I know, sir."

❧

"Ruby." Wells caught the maid's attention. "Have you seen Miss Merrinan? I require her assistance."

"Miss Merrinan's left, milord. Surely you're aware, sir?"

"Surely I am not." The force of his words made the girl pale. "What the devil do you mean she's left?"

"Resigned, sir." She looked nervous. "Said her oal fella were taken ill and needed tendin'. Left a note this morn. Said I were to take over her duties till your lordship found a new housekeeper, like."

"A note? Do you have it? Give it me at once," he demanded.

She reached into her pocket, hands shaking. "'Twere addressed t' me, sir, or I'd've shown it to your lordship sooner. Only I assumed she'd, well, that she'd told you herself she were leavin', milord."

Wells did not reply; he was engrossed in the note, having waved the maid off with a flick of his hand.

Ruby,

I am sorry to leave so rashly now, but my father's health requires that I go to him at once. I do not know how long I will be gone. I trust you'll be a stalwart housekeeper to his lordship in my absence, for you are skilled, efficient, and courteous to all. I am only sorry to leave you so much work, with visitors still about, and beg forgiveness for this burden. Someday I shall make it up to you, I swear. I have told Lord Wellesley he must hire more staff to finish the Abbey. Perhaps you can impress this upon him better than I was able.

Give my regards to all, but most especially to Jenkins and Cuthbert, as they were the best of partners to me and I shall miss both dearly. I shall miss everyone, even his lordship's crew. Only I beg you, Ruby, make sure the girls do not flirt with the men. I should hate for you to lose any staff for obvious reasons.

You do me proud, Ruby Barrows. Hug Ginny, Clarice, and Marta for me. ~ Charles Merrinan

Christ, Wells bitterly swore. She'd actually up and left. Well, he'd see about that. It was an hour's walk to Squire Merrinan's house and he'd have it out with her there, get down on one knee and propose properly if needs must. Was that what this was about? A formal courtship, her father's permission? And then he remembered Sir Benedict's words, how he'd given Wells his blessing over a blasted game of chess. He almost laughed aloud to realize all that nonsense her father had blabbered at him had been true. And given what he now knew, of course the old man had assumed their betrothal. Oh, wait until he told Charles! She'd be tickled.

Eventually.

First she'd need convincing, stubborn woman. He'd go see her this afternoon, just as soon as he had the house in order. He'd tell Jenkins and Cuthbert the news of their betrothal. He felt sure it would be well received.

"Milord." Jenkins's face was bright with anger; he'd never seen her like this. "You can't marry Miss Merrinan, sir, 'tis out of t' question, despite . . ." She put her hands on her hips and glared at him. "Well, I know full well what you've been up to. I daresay everyone in this house does."

Wells was gobsmacked. "What do you mean, everyone?"

"Well, anyone what matters," she ground out. "But that don't mean t' future Duke of Allendale can maff matters by marryin' a common Cumberland lass, 'specially not one who's served your lordship as housekeeper."

"But she is not a commoner, Mrs. Jenkins. That is what I have been trying to tell you." He was duly upset. "Her mother was born a lady, Lady Adelaide Enright, and her father, Sir Benedict Merrinan, was knighted for bravery in battle. He was squire here for years before his wife passed, was he not?"

"Well, sure, afore he lost his nappa, he were a fine squire, milord, but a soldier's still no—"

"Her mother was the daughter of an earl, Mrs. Jenkins, the Earl of Denbigh. I should think that bloodline would suffice."

Wells was growing more frustrated by the minute but could tell Jenkins wasn't ready to let go her grievance. Yet.

"Aye, and you knew this *when*?" she jabbed. "You'd no right t' make that girl your lass, milord, no right at'all, preyin' on her heart like you did, 'specially not if you knew who she were. Installin' her in your house respectable by day and deplorable by night."

He deserved her words; they still appalled.

"If I know Charles Merrinan, she'll want nowt t' do with your lordship now, proposin' only after you've had her, and she a lady like you say. No sir, she'll not have you, Lord Wellesley. 'Tis no wonder she's gang. You're better off takin' Mowry as bride and bringin' on some London mistress once you've made your heir and spare."

Wells stared at his normally kind cook as if she'd grown horns.

Jenkins merely stared back.

"Madam," he began, "I will admit to having acted a cad, but let me assure you that I'd no idea of Miss Merrinan's lineage when first we met, and we met under circumstances which painted her in a most unsavory light, such that I—"

"It matters little t' circumstance what *were*, milord." Her voice remained icy. "What matters now is you leave that poor girl be. And if she's runnin' scared because she's carryin' your—"

"Mrs. Jenkins!" He finally found his voice. "You forget, Madam, with whom you speak!"

She at last looked chagrined. "I beg your pardon, milord. You'll forgive an oal widow her razzie, I hope."

And with that she turned her back on Wells to continue rolling out her dough, wholly unconcerned that Ginny and Marta had been standing there the entire time, mouths agape and eyes wide as saucers.

❧

The entire household was abuzz with the news as one after another of his staff brazenly weighed in on Wellesley's betrothal. He overheard Pinky whisper it was *high time his lordship got 'imself a 'trouble and strife'* and Marta claim she could recall *more'n a few deccs passed betwixt them two.*

Meanwhile, Wells searched the Abbey for Cuthbert, stung by the incriminating looks he got wherever he went—not to mention the tongue lashing he'd received from Jenkins. Her words still rang in his ears, making him feel lower than low. He'd naively thought his staff would be pleased by his proposal.

Apparently not.

"Ruby, where's Cuthbert?" He found her rifling through receipts in his housekeeper's cold bedroom office.

"Makin' a delivery t' Miss Merrinan's family, I 'spect, milord."

"Right, yes. I should have guessed as much." Wells suddenly felt lost.

"Milord, I should like t' congratulate you on your betrothal t' Miss Merrinan. If you should need aught from me I—"

"Thank you, Ruby. I appreciate your stepping in now as housekeeper. I shall increase your wages accordingly."

"Thank you, sir, happy to. Only what I meant were"—she gently met his gaze—"should you need an ear, sir . . ."

Wells was grateful for the girl's kindness, his body sagging almost under the weight of the morning as he slumped against the closet door, swinging it shut.

"I do, Ruby. I need an ear something awful right now, for I've bungled things terribly with Miss Merrinan, making her run off not on account of her father's poor health but because of the manner in which I . . ." He struggled to admit it even to himself. "Well, the way I proposed marriage to her."

Ruby merely took his rough hands into her own two small ones, squeezing tightly. "Lord Wellesley, Miss Merrinan's most fond of you, sir, of this I've no doubt. It may take a bit t' convince her, milord, but we should all like nowt better'n t' see you both wed, eh." Her smile was genuinely warm, making his heart ache more.

"I'm afraid Jenkins does not share your opinion," he muttered.

"Och, Jenkins," she scoffed. "She's *true* housekeeper here, lavishin' praise and punishment on oa' us staff. She'll change her tune soon like." She grinned at him, then looked instantly contrite, dropping her eyes and his hands as she blushed red. "Do forgive me for speakin' so bold, sir. I don't know what came owwer me just now, as I should ne'er presume t' know what your lordship feels or thinks towards Miss Merrinan." She looked a hot mess.

"Ruby." He took her hands in his. "Don't apologize for your kindness, girl. I need it right now." He exhaled. "You've been a friend to Miss Merrinan, and a friend to me. I'll not forget it."

Wells forced a smile and left Ruby to her work, determined to find Cuthbert and Charles and put things right. To put an end to his misery.

CHAPTER THIRTY-SEVEN

John had read the housekeeper's note and now stared at a bag of coin on the table—coin Charles had left Eleanor as dowry. Ellie was in the kitchen fixing him a bite. He took up the letter once more.

John,

Forgive me for leaving in haste, but you know how his lordship will react. I prefer he not know where I've gone. He will no doubt press you, but I beg you, tell him nothing. I know you swore fealty to his family, John, but soon we will be family too. Consider your loyalty to Eleanor in this. I trust you will make her an excellent husband, and I bitterly regret words said to you both, more than you know. You are indeed worthy of my sister, John, and worthy of my admiration and respect. I cannot say the same for Lord Wells, however, not after the words we exchanged. I wish him no harm, but he cannot continue to take what is not freely given. I have left Eleanor the dowry I promised her—a small amount for you to start your lives. You both have my blessing, John, for I know you will make her happy. Bless you also for your kindness towards our father.

With gratitude, Charles

Oi, that twist and twirl's done herself a world of hurt by leavin' now, John thought to himself, for Wells would not give her up so easily. Why the devil those two couldn't find it in their hearts to forgive one another and simply allow for some happiness, he'd never understand. It seemed so simple to him and so damned difficult for them. Thank God Ellie was less stubborn than Charles. A little less, at least.

"John." She put a plate before him, then rested her hand on his shoulder. "What does she write?"

He handed her the note. He'd keep no secrets from his betrothed. "Read it yerself, love."

She briefly scanned the letter before wiping a tear from her eye. "Her blessing, eh?" She kissed his cheek. "I knew she approved of you, John. She was just too proud to say it, I think."

He nodded. "Only she ain't the only one too proud, I fear. Lord Wells won't let her go without a fight, Ellie, not if I know the man. He'll demand t' know where she's gone, if he's not on his way here already, come t' question us both."

"But why did she leave, John?" Eleanor pressed. "She made no mention to me that he'd proposed. She said only that she could not marry him, so I assumed that meant he'd betrothed himself to—"

"Sounds more like it were the *manner* in which he proposed." John snorted. "His lordship ain't the most eloquent o' men, Ellie, and if he insulted yer sister in his askin', it don't surprise me one bit she's run off to teach him a lesson." He paused. "Question is, do we keep our promise t' Charles, or do we tell Wells where she's gone?" He looked Eleanor square in the face. "Y' know her best, Ellie, better'n I ever will."

"I do, John." She seemed lost in thought. "Yet I don't know the answer either. And I don't think I will, at least not until I speak to Lord Wellesley." Her face hardened. "I cannot deny my anger towards him, John. He deserves to be punished; I don't care if he becomes Duke one day. He should not be allowed to take what he likes so absent of all regard. What he did to my sister was unconscionable."

John agreed. "True, love, but for what it's worth, he's not always been granted whate'er he likes. At sea the man saw punishment same as any. Nor is Wells so mollycoddled he can't take a beatin' when deserved, only to stand back up for another round o' knocks."

"All well and good, John"—Eleanor stood to fetch the kettle —"because he'll have no choice now but to take the beating Charles intends to give him." She poured herself a cup. "He must learn to make amends, and if he does, perhaps I might be willing to forgive him past transgressions. Perhaps," she repeated.

John smiled into his mug, which Ellie promptly refilled. He snuck an arm about her waist, pulling her close enough to rest his head upon her bosom. "Damned if I don't love you, woman," he rumbled into her chest.

"Damned if I don't love you back, sir." She kissed the top of his head, but already he'd pulled her to his lap, raining kisses on her lips, kissing her until she sighed with giddy, silly joy once more.

Until the door burst open and his lordship stormed inside.

**

"Hands off her, Cuthbert, not until you're wed." Wells scowled at the two lovebirds. "Where is Charles?" he demanded.

Neither Cuthbert nor Miss Eleanor made the slightest effort to acknowledge him.

"I said . . ." he threatened.

"We heard what you said, my lord." Eleanor broke the silence, her face defiant. "But you'll not command us in our own home."

"*Your* home?" He raised his brow, furious at this woman for resembling her sister so much. "I believe *I* own this house, miss, and the land beneath it, so it is not exactly your home, now is it?"

"Oh no, my lord, it's not, thank you ever so much for the reminder. I am sure my sister was ever so grateful when you reminded her, too, of the terms of her sentence for thieving chickens." Her eyes shot daggers at him.

Wells flinched. "Miss Eleanor, I have apologized to your sister for past behaviors which were reprehensible, to say the least."

"Yet you've not apologized to me, sir, nor to our father, have you?" She got up off Cuthbert's lap to stand before him. "Is it any wonder Charles wishes nothing more to do with you, Lord Wellesley?"

"Miss Eleanor, please," he started, "allow me to—"

"You don't deserve the allowance, sir," she lashed back, and Wells knew he was in for a beating as bad as the one his Fox had meted out.

"I know I deserve your wrath, miss, yet I beg you, let me speak with Charles in private, that she and I might—"

"She is not here, sir, and I will have that apology, straightaway."

Cuthbert looked at Eleanor in awe.

Wells took a slow, deep breath, willing himself to give this woman her due. "Miss Eleanor, you have my deepest and most sincere apology for the manner in which I treated your sister the night my steward caught her thieving my chickens. I abused my position as local magistrate in order to gain person-ally from her sentence. I am not proud of my behavior, but nor, in all honesty, do I entirely regret that night either, for it brought your sister into my life, and I have been the better for it."

"And her, sir?" she cried bitterly. "Is she the better for it too? You paid her coin as your housekeeper, true, and you've kept us warm and fed this winter, none of which I'm ungrateful for, my lord. But what have you otherwise left her? A broken heart, ruined reputation, and a future now doing God only knows what."

Wells was reeling. "Eleanor, where has she gone? Tell me where she is." His heart began to race. "If she's done something foolish now I should never forgive myself. You *must* tell me where she is. Eleanor, tell me where's she's gone!"

She almost told him, he could see it in her eyes.

"No, Lord Wellesley," she said quietly. "I honor my sister's wishes now, not yours." She leveled her gaze. "She no longer wishes to see you."

"Yes, but that is because . . . !" He was so incensed he nearly punched the wall with his fist, stopping himself at the last second. Wells balled his hands at his sides. "Eleanor, I beg you, consider but a moment my intent. I wish to make amends to Charles. I wish to marry her, to make her the next Duchess of Allendale."

"And?" The lady was ruthless.

"And I can think of no better woman to be my Duchess. Cumberland is already her home, she is respected by its citizens, she is accomplished and capable and has assisted in countless ways already to restore the Abbey . . ." He was shocked to see her face remain so impassive, so cold.

"Is that how you proposed marriage, my lord?" Eleanor asked. "To Charles? Is that how you spoke to her?

"Well, along those lines, yes," he mumbled, utterly confused now by the expression on her face.

"Then no wonder she refused you." Eleanor glared at him

before she stormed into the kitchen, leaving him alone with Cuthbert.

Wells turned to his steward. "John, why the devil is no one in all of bloody Cumberland pleased that I'm to make Charles Merrinan my wife?"

"Are you, Yer Grace?" Cuthbert regarded him critically. "Seems t' me yer bride's run off again, not the first that's happened, now is it?"

Wellesley's face burned to be reminded, but Cuthbert would not stop.

"Y' talk as if it's a done deal, Yer Grace, as if you're already betrothed, when y' know full well she turned you down. Y' can't force her t' marry you, not the way y' forced her t' bed you, sir."

"John, I did not—"

"Y' did, sir, and y' know it."

Wells sank his head in his hands, collapsing onto a chair. "What have I done?" he got out, strangled.

"Driven off the one woman able to take yer on, that's what. And damned if you'll get her back now."

"Losing her isn't an option, John, it simply isn't. I *want* her. I've wanted her from the moment I first laid eyes on her, covered in chicken shit. And knowing her as I do now only makes me want her more."

"And did y' try tellin' her that?" Cuthbert shook his head. "Did y' try at'all speakin' from yer heart and not yer bloody duke's voice?" His look needled Wells. "A woman like Charles, sir, has got to know a man wants her, desires her, needs her in his life."

"But she *does* know," he cried. "She must! When all I have done these past months is to show her again and again just how much I—"

"Y' desired her person, sir, but not her true bein'. 'T'ain't the same thing."

"But I love her, damn it. All of her, body and soul! I don't want some other woman as wife, John. I want Charles Merrinan. I can't lose her, I simply cannot." He beat his head upon the table in three hard whacks, nearly splitting open his skin he was so angry at himself.

Silence fell upon the house, stilling the room a good long moment before a voice spoke softly from the kitchen door. "Then go and fetch her, Lord Wellesley." Eleanor's tone surprised. She must have overheard all. "She loves you too."

Wells lifted his head in shock.

"She's fled to London. I've no idea where in London, but she left on the first coach this morning. If you leave now, you may just catch her on the road, my lord."

"Why tell me this now, Eleanor?" he asked, still staring at her, shaking his head almost in puzzlement.

"Because you love her, Lord Wellesley, and if you'd only told her that when you proposed, she'd not have left as she did, I'm sure of it."

Wells got up and gripped Eleanor's hands tightly in his own. "Thank you, miss. Thank you for telling me. I know I don't deserve her, but I swear to you I'll find her and bring her home. And if she'll have me, I will not ever again, so long as I live, dishonor her more."

"You'd best not, sir." Ellie held his gaze. "Or I'll send John here to murder you." She cracked a shy grin at Cuthbert before she put her hands on her hips and ordered, "Out now, both of you. And bring my sister home to me, in time for my wedding *and* hers."

***

John and his lordship left Eleanor in a hurry to return to the Abbey. Along the way, Wells peppered him with tasks he wanted done while he'd be in London, and John took mental note of the growing list, knowing full well he'd never get to it all; his lordship was always overly ambitious.

"Sir, I'll see to as much as I can, as will Ruby. She's a good head on her shoulders and will stand in well for Charles, I'm sure."

"Well, I should hope so, for if I return to find everything in disarray again at the Abbey I've a mind to install all new staff, especially after the dress-downs I received from those ingrates this morning. Jenkins was worst of all. The cheek of that woman, John, the very—"

The steward grinned to himself, secretly pleased the widow had tongue-whipped his lordship. "Well now, Yer Grace, seein' as how you yerself admit the treatment o' yer housekeeper were anythin' but—"

"You needn't keep reminding, John." Wells sulked. "Why the hell does everyone feel the need to remind me when my memory is punishment enough?"

"Is it, sir?" John's grin widened.

"Wipe that smirk off your face, Cuthbert."

"Can't, sir. 'Bout time y' grew a conscience towards yer housekeeper."

"You know damn well I have a conscience."

"I do, sir. We'd not be best mates if y' didn't. Meant only it were time that conscience be applied t' yer mistress."

His lordship's tone turned solemn. "I know I treated her abysmally, John. I couldn't help it somehow. No, I'll not make excuses. Only she got under my skin in ways no other woman has, which made me do devilish things to her, as if she were deliberately testing my limits. And all the while, all along, I kept wishing desperately to do better and *be* better by her."

John fell silent a moment. "Love'll do that to a man, I think. Push him to his limits. You're not alone."

"And do you love Eleanor the same? Have you . . . ?" He

paused. "That is, I imagine unlike myself you've gone about courtship much more admirably."

"I have, sir, and near killin' me, 'tis!" John laughed. "If I could order Ellie t' bed me I'd be sore tempted, Yer Grace."

Wells at last smiled. "You would, eh?" He clapped John on the back. "Well, with any luck, my friend, we'll both be wed in under a fortnight. I'll fetch us both licenses in London."

"Y' would, sir?" John was surprised. "I thought simply t' ask the vicar here to—"

"Cuthbert." His lordship elbowed him. "The Merrinan girls are proper ladies, you know. Their mother was daughter to the Earl of Denbigh."

John's face paled. "Christ."

"So you'll need a proper license to marry Eleanor, and I'm going to get you knighted if I can, good man, to install you here as my squire, just as my own father had Merrinan knighted."

John's eyes nearly popped from his head.

"Don't look so shocked, Cuthbert, it's done often enough and should merely require some groveling on my part, which in this instance I am prepared to do." His lordship's mouth pinched in distaste.

"Yer Grace, I can't let you—"

"You can and will. I don't give a damn where my father found you, or who your parents were, John. You've saved my neck more than once, man, and I'll not lose you to a woman. If the only way to keep *you* is to let you keep Eleanor Merrinan, so be it."

John was still reeling from the news. "An honest t' God earl's granddaughter, Christ," he again muttered. "She could do better'n me, sir. No wonder Charles were so put out."

"My future Duchess put out by her sister marrying my steward?" He arched his brow. "All the more reason to knight you, Cuthbert!" Wells laughed roundly. "Besides, it's about time you learned how it feels to be a person in charge of others. You might not bludgeon me so often with criticism once you're made squire."

"Oh I'll not give *that* up, sir." John grinned back. "'Tis the one thing brings me joy, Yer Grace—to see yer put in yer place."

"You lout, you." Wells gave him a shove, much as they had as boys, and John shoved him back, till they were both in better spirits, hopeful once again.

Along the road, Charles felt sick to her stomach. The swaying and lurching of the coach made her nauseous, as did the sense she was making a mistake. What if she never saw Papa again? What if she ran out of coin before she found work in London? What if she missed not only Ellie's wedding but the birth of her sister's first child? What if, what if, what if . . . Her thoughts took the same twists and turns as her stomach, which tied itself into ever tighter knots.

What if she never saw Roland Wellesley again?

She brutally quashed that thought. She was still bitter over his arrogant proposal. It had hurt more than she wanted to admit, her pride smarting on too many counts. And she couldn't admit *why* it had hurt so much either, at least not to Eleanor.

Partly it was because Cuthbert, blast him, had gone about everything right. He'd been respectful, patient, and loving while courting Ellie, proving time and again how much he cherished her. Wellesley had only ever taken what he wanted, when he wanted it, always considering his own needs above hers. Even in proposing marriage he'd spoken only of how it might benefit him and the Duchy—as if her family's lowered state would make Charles leap at the chance to raise her station through marriage.

As if it would be a bloody privilege to bear his heirs.

He'd not proposed, he had *presumed*, and she was done being his servant.

The carriage lurched left as Charles's head bounced painfully against the coach. She fell deeper into despair, because for all her wounded pride, it was her soul, in truth, that ached. Despite all intentions otherwise, she'd fallen under his lordship's spell these past months—his every act of tenderness and passion making her imagine he wanted her as much as she wanted him. She had secretly hoped he might even grow to need her, too.

But she didn't need him, she berated herself. He was an arrogant lord who would become an arrogant duke. His arrogance could be attractive in the bedroom, was no doubt necessary, even, when captaining a ship, but it was not conducive to a loving marriage. Wellesley was made to lead, as all dukes must, but he could never love like mortals did.

Like her parents had.

Like Cuthbert loved Eleanor.

Charles's eyes filled with tears she angrily brushed aside. She forced herself to stare out the window at the bleak landscape, staving off overwhelming feelings of regret.

Once, when the coach stopped to pick up more travelers and roused her from an uneasy sleep, she thought she saw the ducal carriage hurtle past. At least, it looked like the Allendale coat of arms. She wondered why the Duchess would leave now —unless the Duke's health had suffered a turn. Perhaps, like her own father, he was not long for this world. They were surely of similar age.

Charles's gut twisted again, recalling how she'd said goodbye to Papa while he slept, ignorant of all that had befallen her, of all that was to come.

It was likely for the best.

CHAPTER THIRTY-EIGHT

In her rush to flee Lord Wellesley, Charles had transferred coaches as often as was possible, traveling even overnight. It meant the nearly week-long trip from Cumberland to London was achieved in under four three days, not the five it usually took to travel that distance. She was exhausted; every bone in her body ached. But she'd done it. She'd escaped.

Clutching her small bag of belongings—which consisted of little more than Ruby's stitched frock—she asked the coach driver for the closest, cheapest lodging, yet the man blatantly ignored her. Asking a fellow traveler proved no better, so she looked down both sides of the crowded street she now stood on and decided left was as good a turn as any to take.

She'd forgotten London's charms: the noise, the stench, the very offal that lined its streets. It had been ten years since she'd stepped foot in this city, and when she had, it had been on finer streets than this. She'd need to get her bearings fast.

Rounding a corner, Charles at last spied a sign for a tavern aptly named the Wayward Inn—and looking no less reputable than the rest of this quarter. She enquired after a room, choosing to rent for the night rather than the hour, and within minutes had gratefully sunk into a deep stupor upon a none-too-clean bed.

She awoke after nightfall to the sound of a terrific crash, followed by screams of distress. She ran to lock the door but found no key. She wedged the lone chair in the room against the doorknob and was beginning to think she ought to have brought one of Cook's carving knives with her for defense. But it was too late to ponder that. She crawled back into bed with the room's lone brass candlestick clutched in her fist, praying for morning to come.

Five days later saw Wells in London, staring up at his parents' opulent townhouse in Mayfair. A piece of him shuddered to be back in the city he hated above all others, yet he knew this was but a temporary visit. Besides, he could do worse than see for himself just how poorly his father, the Duke, fared.

As he entered the front hall, trailed by two footmen carrying his trunk, his parents' butler came hurrying towards him, looking as the man always did: perpetually put out.

"My lord." The butler bowed, a frown plastered to his lips.

"Tompkins, inform my parents I am staying but briefly on business. I'd like a bath and a shave. Oh, and a haircut as well."

Tompkins blinked, stating, "My lord," once more.

Wells began the long climb upstairs to his old bedroom when, much to his displeasure, he spotted Miss Mowry rounding the landing and looking none too pleased to see him, either.

"Miss," he addressed her politely as he hastened past.

"Lord Wellesley." She bobbed before scurrying off.

What the devil is she doing here? Wells thought to himself, and then recalled his mother had taken the girl on as her ward.

Damn and blast. He'd have to avoid her as best he could during his stay.

Later, while soaking in a tub to wash the grime of travel from his skin, he contemplated next steps. He'd formulated a plan of sorts on the long journey here, but there were holes. In addition to actually finding Charles, he'd need to speak to his father about knighting Cuthbert, obtain two special licenses for marriage, and pay a call on Lord Enright, The Earl of Denbigh—for which he might actually need his mother. He'd decided that in order to ensure Charles Merrinan be seen by society again as a lady in good standing, he must convince the Enrights to accept her and her sister back into their fold. He did not think the earl would balk if he informed him of his intention to make Charles his future Duchess. Though he would leave out Eleanor's engagement to a former street urchin, for the time being.

Wells sank deeper into the water, allowing the tension of the past week to melt from his body. *Where could she have gone?* he wondered. Or more to the point: If he were Charles, where would he go? For she'd not asked him for a letter of recommendation, and she could hardly apply without one for any positions here in London as housekeeper. What was more, if she'd been educated by her father, rather than sent to any boarding school, she would hardly know a headmaster willing to write her a reference for the position of governess, or even lady's companion for that matter. What the devil would she do for funds? He knew she'd saved her wages, yet he also knew how stubborn she was; she'd likely left half or more to Eleanor.

Wells searched the recesses of his mind for a solution to her quandary. What line of work, with no reference, could Charles hope to find in London? And the more he thought, the more panicked he became, for the one job she'd no doubt earn most at and was now, thanks to him, altogether well qualified for, was the one job he could not stomach her taking: mistress to some debauched London lord.

❦

Charles had not realized her lack of reference would shut so many doors, for every position she found advertised for house-keeper, maid, governess, or companion, any position at all in London required one. Even for laundry, scullery, or char-woman. She felt beat, for she could hardly write Lord Wells *now* to beg him for a letter. No, she should have asked for one before she'd left, only like as not he'd have not given it to her, the cad.

Yet with the very same breath she cursed him, an image of him in bed flooded her mind: thick lashes over sleeping eyes, calloused hands so like a laborer's and so unlike a lord's, the wonders those hands knew how to provoke . . . *Scoundrel!* she reminded herself more vehemently. He'd asked for her hand only once his mother had deemed her fit for marriage, not before. He'd been content, in fact, to marry Miss Mowry and keep her as his sidepiece. And though Charles might have lost much in the way of dignity, she had some pride left. She drew the line at being a married man's mistress. She'd not debase herself utterly.

Yet there remained the matter of her rapidly dwindling funds. Given her lack of reference, she'd visited mills and facto-ries in her quest for employment, but at every one the line of women seeking positions had stretched around the corner. She'd waited patiently like everyone else, but each time they'd closed the gates before she could even cross the threshold to apply.

She'd need to find employment somewhere fast or else find a cheaper room. Already she was skipping meals to save her funds. She'd even asked at the inn if they had need of help in laundry or the kitchen, but no, they did not. *Though if she wanted blunt there were a fellow down the street who'd pay handsomely for a chit with hair her color.*

Charles had quit the innkeeper in outrage.

She scoured the advertisements daily, desperate for any job that might pay, when a heading at last caught her eye: *Madame LeBrecht's.* She scanned the ad, trying not to feel too hopeful, for it had been more than a week of fruitless searching.

Shop girl, attractive, for ladies' garment store. 5 Crawford Ln. French a must. Discerning clientele, service & discretion required. In-person enquiries only.

Well, she'd a better chance at an in-person enquiry for sure. And no mention of a reference, thank God. Though that would surely follow. Perhaps she could simply forge one, though without a seal . . . She shook off the thought. Here, at least, was a lead worth pursuing. And her French, *par Dieu,* was not half bad.

"Enchantée, j'en suis certaine, mademoiselle. Alors voulez-vous entrer, s'il vous plaît?"

Charles heard the voice before she saw the woman at *LeBrecht's* guide a well-dressed young lady into a back room for a fitting, for this was indeed a garment shop—an undergarment shop—and she remembered where she'd heard the name before. Lord Wells had ordered her those stockings and chemise from this same London shop. She blushed to recall the items, now stashed in the bottom of her bag, for when in God's name would she have occasion to don them again? She wouldn't think on it. Not now.

She smoothed Ruby's day dress, checked her hair in the shop window's reflection, pinched her cheeks rosy, and stepped inside. She had one chance to impress.

"May I help you, miss?" an exotic-looking woman asked, her skin a rich bronze, hair so black it was almost blue, and almond-shaped eyes that looked like wells of deepest ink. Charles had never seen anyone so beautiful in all her life.

"I . . ." she stammered before collecting herself. "I came about the advertisement, for the position of shop girl, ma'am." She curtsied low before the woman, willing herself to look a vision of propriety.

"The job is filled, I'm afraid." The lady's voice carried the faintest of accents.

Yet Charles would not give up so easily. "Then perhaps there is another position here, *Madame?*" Her eyes met the woman's with determination. "*Je parle bien français et suis parfaitement capable de servir vos clients.*" Reassuring the woman in French would hopefully do the trick.

"*Et les messieurs?*" The lady raised a brow at her. "Do you know how to serve gentlemen, too, miss?" Her tone suggested service of an altogether different sort than that which Charles had assumed. Yet she would not back out now.

"*Oui.*" She nicked her head.

The lady stared at her a moment and then motioned for her to follow, slipping behind an ornately painted screen into what appeared to be a back office.

"*Asseyez-vous!*" she commanded, and Charles immediately sat down.

"What is your name, miss?" She reverted back to English.

"Charles Merrinan, ma'am."

"That is not a woman's name." The lady pursed her lips, gesturing with her hand. "It must be something more . . . feminine."

"Charlotte?" Charles proposed, wondering why her name should matter at all.

"Charlotte, yes, better." The woman continued to stare. "Let down your hair, Charlotte."

Which Charles did, perplexed.

"Very nice." She nodded to herself. "There are gentlemen who seek this color you have. It is not so common." The lady's stare by now unnerved Charles. "Stand up and turn around. I wish to look at you."

Charles again obeyed, though she was beginning to feel the lady's scrutiny was not without reproof.

"*Bien, bien, parfait.*" *Madame* nodded to herself. "And you say you have experience serving gentlemen?"

"Yes," Charles answered. "I was most recently housekeeper to a duke's son, ma'am."

"A duke?" Her face looked suddenly shrewd. "Which Duke, may I ask?"

"The Duke of Allendale's son, Lord Wellesley, ma'am." Charles decided there could be little harm in saying this, especially if it served as indirect reference.

"Lord Wellesley, eh?" The lady's smile turned cat-like. "He is one of our *clients*, you know." She stressed the word in French, assessing Charles more keenly. "We were very sad to see him leave London."

"I served him in Cumberland, ma'am," Charles clarified.

"Hmm, yes." The lady's eyes bored into her. "No doubt he liked your hair, too."

Charles felt suddenly uncomfortable. "Madam, may I ask what position you are considering me for?"

"Position?" The lady laughed. "What position do you *think* I am considering you for, miss?"

"If it is not that of shop girl then perhaps seamstress? Or maid?" Charles frowned. "I am good at bookkeeping too, ma'am."

"My dear Charlotte." The lady smirked. "I believe we were discussing how you serviced Lord Wells in bed, were we not?"

Charles knew at once she'd made a grievous error coming here. She hastily backed away from Madame LeBrecht, or whoever this woman was. "I am not . . . I can assure you, madam, I am not interested in serving gentlemen in the manner you assume. I believed you to mean I might be of service to them as purchasing clients only, here in your shop."

"Ah but you would, *chérie*," she replied smoothly. "You would work here in the shop, attending to customers, and if you caught the eye of a gentleman and he requested the pleasure of meeting you elsewhere, well, then perhaps you might service him further, for far better pay than the pennies you will earn selling garments here." Her onyx eyes had become two sharp points.

"I see." Charles steeled herself not to react. "And this would remain my choice, madam? I would not be forced into any situation I did not willingly choose to engage in?"

"Of course not." *Madame* gave her a canny look. "It is a matter of honor, my dear, that all *liaisons* begun in my shop should be mutually beneficial and, of course, consensual."

"Then I will take the position, madam, provided what you have told me is indeed true."

"My dear Charlotte, with your looks and a little charm, you will soon find you have no need of a position here at *LeBrecht's*. The gentlemen of the *Ton* will all be falling over themselves to keep you as their mistress." Her laugh tinkled like harsh, bright bells.

"I've no wish to become another man's mistress." Charles scowled.

"Did Wells mistreat you, Charlotte?" *Madame* looked surprised. "I always found him to be a most generous lover, if not always the most gentle." She grinned.

"You mean you were his mistress?" Charles felt her gut lurch.

"It was *very* long ago, miss." *Madame's* smile was almost rueful. "He brought me to this country, you see, when I had nowhere else to go."

Charles was stunned. "On his ship?"

"Yes, years ago now. I do not wish to reminisce." *Madame* returned to business. "Come tomorrow and look your best, flirt with every gentleman who enters, and throw in a little French. Style your hair loose, show something of your shape. Within a day or two, you will have more than enough offers to choose from."

Only Charles had no intention of choosing anything of the sort. She intended to simply work at the shop and save whatever pittance *Madame* paid her. It was a job, after all, and she would have taken any job offered her right then.

Well, almost any.

"*Bien, Madame.*" She bobbed her head, curtsied, and quickly exited the shop, noting how Madame LeBrecht gazed after her through the window.

It gave her chills.

CHAPTER THIRTY-NINE

"Father." Wells took the Duke's hand in his own. "It is good to see you, Your Grace." He looked down at him, more than a little alarmed by his shrunken state. This was not the man he remembered from even six months ago.

"Roland." The Duke smiled, gripping Wells's hand weakly. "You've come home, son." He did not let go the hand.

Wells was surprised by such affection and worried the Duke was indeed not long for this world. "I am in London for a license, father, a marriage license, but I do not intend to stay long."

"Oh?" His interest was piqued. "And who's the lucky lady?" He tried to laugh but it came out a little choked. "Your mother wear you down, did she?" He regained his voice.

Wells found himself smiling. "She did, or rather, the lady in question wore out my heart."

His father searched his eyes. "You're in love with the girl? Who is she?"

"Charles Merrinan, sir." Wells waited for a reaction.

"By God, the eldest Merrinan daughter! Is she as beautiful as her mother was? I would have given my eyeteeth for that strawberry-haired vixen, but she had her heart set on Benedict Merrinan. Never mind I'd a title and wealth and he had neither . . ." His voice faded with his memories.

"And here I thought you married Mother for love, sir."

"Ha!" The Duke struggled for breath. "Respect, boy. I married your mother for respect. One hell of a woman, but I can't say I loved her, no."

It was the most his father had ever said on the topic of marriage.

It was also no surprise.

The Duke continued his questioning. "And Benedict Merrinan? Give you his blessing, did he?"

"In a fashion, yes." Wells chose not to elaborate.

"Good then." The Duke closed his eyes a moment, for rest or from pain it was hard to tell.

"Father . . ."

"Hmm?"

"Did you love again—after marrying *Maman*?"

"Oh, I suppose I loved several," he admitted. "One in particular I kept for close to ten years. She and your mother got along rather well."

"And *Maman* was not jealous of her? Or of others?"

"You thinking already to take a mistress once you marry, son?"

"No." Wells's retort was quick. "I simply fear Charles is currently less than enamored of my suit, sir."

"Vex her much, did you?" His father chuckled. "If she's anything like her mother, the girl's got a temper. A temper and a mouth and a way of bewitching a man that's nigh unholy."

Wells nodded his agreement. "I worry she won't come round, sir, title and wealth be damned."

"Does she love another?"

"I don't believe there is another, no," he answered honestly.

"Then she'll come round. If Benedict Merrinan hadn't

gotten to Adelaide Enright first, I swear I'd have had a chance with her, I would."

Wells smiled to himself, imagining his father head over heels for Charles's mother. "You sly devil you, sir. I can't say I've ever thought of you in such light, old man."

"You're not the only handsome duke in London, boy," his father teased, and then began to cough in earnest.

"Father, should I call for someone?"

"No, no." He hacked bright spots into a handkerchief, then fell back heavily upon the pillows. "Water is all . . . Hell, pour me a whiskey instead."

Wells went to fetch a glass from the sideboard.

His father took the drink with trembling hand. "Now, I want to hear of your progress on the Abbey and of Merrinan's daughter. I assume you met her there, in Cumberland?"

Wells nicked his head.

"It's good she's of the land. Your mother forced me back to London, you know, or I'd have stayed forever. Bloody fine country it is. You're wise to restore Almsdale, son. Lay claim to the Duchy once more. Give up the London townhouse once your mother dies. Waste of upkeep, I say."

"You've read my mind, Father."

"Fine, yes." He appeared lost in thought. "And Roland . . ."

"Sir?"

"You've done me proud, boy, despite the horseshit she lays on you." He was, of course, referring to his Duchess. "Proud of you for captaining a ship, for taking on the Abbey." He closed his eyes. "Marry Charles Merrinan, son. She'll make you a fine duchess."

And Wells decided right then he'd tax his father no more with talk. Instead he sat with him in silence until the Duke fell deep asleep. He promised himself he'd sit with the old man again tomorrow and tell him about the work on the Abbey's south wall.

It was enough to know his father lived and breathed and shockingly, seemed to care.

Though Charles had been in London well over two weeks, she could not grow used to the city. Not only did it stink—worse than Fergus ever had—it was a callous town, its inhabitants surly. The inn was a den of noise at night, with crashing brawls and even louder laughter that rudely kept her awake. And her first day at *LeBrecht's* had been anything but easy. In fact, it had been humiliating.

The shop had two separate entrances, one for the *Mesdames* and one for the *Messieurs*, and she, of course, was relegated to working the *Messieurs* side. She was not alone either, for there was a steady stream of pretty girls who occupied this half of the store and worked alongside her, using the back room to model items for the gentlemen all purporting to be making purchases for their 'sisters' or 'wives.'

Charles had yet to indulge a single gentleman by modeling undergarments for him, and her pay was a clear reflection of this, for *Madame* compensated primarily on commission, which meant Charles earned very little for her time. At this rate she'd either need to find a different job, different lodgings, or come to terms with showing more skin than she'd like.

One gentleman in particular called almost daily on her, intent on purchasing a pair of burgundy stockings and ribbons for his presumed wife and insisting Charles model the ensemble for him. He claimed he could not possibly make such purchase without being assured how the stockings would look on his wife's long legs, legs which were apparently of just her own length and shape, or so he claimed. Charles had held out for days, but by his fourth visit she was worn down. His purchase would mean coin enough for her to eat dinner again, and she was hungry like she used to be, like the day their last two hens had been stolen by that fox.

She gave in.

"*Mademoiselle*, they are exquisite." The impeccably dressed gentleman looked upon her ankles with his own form of hunger.

"*Très bien, monsieur.*" She pasted on a smile. "Shall I box them up for you?" She knew her voice was overeager.

"Not yet, miss." His eyes met hers. "I should like to see the ribbons, too, of course."

Charles nearly wept that it had come to this, as she grudgingly raised her skirt so he might gaze upon the bright, neat bow tied just above her knee, the shape of her calf on full display, a hint of bare thigh just beyond reach. He extended his hand to touch when for sheer instinct she slapped him away.

He recoiled at once, his face amused, while her own, no doubt, seethed.

"You are angry with me, *chérie*," he drawled.

"You have taken liberties, sir," she said through gritted teeth.

"Gentlemen are allowed certain liberties at *LeBrecht's*, dear Charlotte." His lips curled. "If you wish to earn more here you'll need to be a bit more accommodating to *Madame*'s *clients*." He'd said the last word in French while his ice blue eyes, more determined than ever, met hers. "Allow me to touch, *chérie*, and I shall buy two pairs."

With an inward wrenching of her soul Charles turned away, unable to look at him a moment longer, then lifted her skirts once more, subjecting herself to a lengthy and unnerving exploration of her legs by a man whose every finger stroke made her shudder.

❦

Wells asked Li again. "And you are certain it is she?" He no longer cared that the proprietress of *LeBrecht's* saw his desperation.

"I am certain."

"And she's let no man—?"

Li sharply met his gaze. "She is remarkably averse to the many propositions she's received, Wells. I am astounded she's held out so long."

"And she looks otherwise well to you? She is not . . . ?" He held back. He knew he was too eager. Much too eager.

"She grows thinner by the day but appears otherwise in good health."

"Thinner by the day?" He was incensed. "Do you pay her so little, Li, that she does not eat?"

"She earns on commission." His friend appeared wholly unperturbed. "It is not my fault she will not induce more gentlemen to make more purchases."

Wells knew Li was a businesswoman first, but this was too much. He reached for his purse. "For God's sake, woman, if you won't pay her, at least bloody *feed* her."

But she refused his money, gently pushing it away. "My lord." She placed her hand over his. "You must make her suffer some, if you wish to make her yours."

Had he not known Li better he would have backhanded her.

"I know women like your Charlotte." She looked almost wistful. "You must break her a little first, make her realize she needs you. Otherwise she will run from you again."

Wells knew Li spoke from experience. She'd been proud once too—and also nearly broken; he knew what hell she'd suffered. It was why he'd risked life and crew to save her, why his men had threatened mutiny. Perhaps . . .

"My lord?" Li prompted.

"I need another two days." His thoughts raced.

"Very well," she replied. "But Wells—"

"Yes?" His mind was a jumble of emotion.

"I cannot keep her forever. She will soon bolt, if she does not first capitulate."

"Two days, Li, that's all I need." He was firm. "And ensure that she damn well eats."

"As you wish." She bowed, her skirts sweeping her away.

Charles laid the timepiece by her ear upon the threadbare pillow, listening to its steady beat. It soothed her to fall asleep to the rhythmic ticking and helped drown out the obnoxious noises of the inn. She ought to sell this pocket watch, she knew, for it would buy her time to find a different position, one which did not require her to pawn her body to men. She shivered to recall the tall gentleman's hands upon her legs, hands which had felt nothing like his lordship's. There'd been no warmth in 'Redstocking's' icy touch—for that is what she'd dubbed him—no spark of awareness. Instead, she'd felt revulsion.

Yet she could not bear to sell the timepiece either. It was all she had left of Roland Wellesley. Her fingers felt for the indent of the musket ball, there where it had spared his father, the Duke's, life. Wells should never have given her such a gift, but because he had, she felt responsible for it, wishing to return it to his family someday. Perhaps she'd give it to his son or daughter far in the future when all would be forgiven and forgotten. When she might return to Cumberland and make a life for herself on *her* terms, no one else's.

Charles drifted into an uneasy slumber to imagine all she must endure yet here in London before she might escape its awful clutches once again.

CHAPTER FORTY

Eventually the Enrights had, of course, sent an invitation. One did not refuse the Duchess of Allendale and her son. Though Wells suspected they'd delayed their invitation to do some ascertaining of their own, no doubt anxious to determine why, exactly, the Duchess would leave her card.

And it appeared the Countess of Denbigh was still endeavoring to determine this as she sat across from Wells and his mother in the lady's own front parlor, nervously fidgeting over the tray of tea she'd rung for, as if weighing her words.

"Your Grace, my lord." She broke with pleasantries, pinching a smile at Wells and the Duchess. "If I may, to what do we owe this unexpected honor?"

The Duchess smiled charmingly. "Why, to enquire after your granddaughter, Lady Enright. Surely you've heard my son is in search of a bride." *Maman's* smile dazzled as Wells, beside her, stiffened.

Lady Enright's brow furrowed. "We have heard rumors to that effect." She paused. "Though I admit I am confused by your interest, as my granddaughter, at barely sixteen, is not yet come out. Unless, of course, Your Grace wished to secure his lordship an engagement two years hence?"

Wells found the lady's grasping repulsive.

"Ah," his mother answered, coming into her own. "I'm afraid you misunderstand, Countess." The Duchess's smile now menaced. "I was referring to your *eldest* granddaughter, not your youngest."

The lady frowned again. "Forgive me, Your Grace, I have but one granddaughter, my daughter's youngest, Miss Mercy Pendrake."

"You have three," *Maman* informed her sternly, "and it is the eldest we have come to discuss."

Wells was by now actively shooting daggers at the woman seated across from him, daggers which made the lady's lined face appear almost to fold in upon itself.

"I can assure you I do not," Lady Enright stated coldly.

"I assure you, madam, you *do*." Wells's patience broke. "I intend to marry your eldest granddaughter, Miss Charles Merrinan, and have received permission already from her father, Sir Benedict. I have come here out of respect to Miss Merrinan only, to inform you, her mother's family, of my intention. For once it is announced, Countess, you will be forced to recognize your late daughter's children, because if you do not, I can assure you as future Duke I shall no longer recognize *you*."

The woman's countenance paled a shade as she rapidly began to ring the bell, calling for smelling salts and her husband, the Earl of Denbigh, to attend her at once, *at once*!

The Duchess, meanwhile, smoothed her skirts and patted Wells's knee, making him for once grateful for her presence. She would know how to handle the rest of this conversation. He could count on her to make things right now for Charles, and in so doing, make things right for him.

Wells had never been so fond of *Maman* as in that moment.

❧

"Charlotte," Madame LeBrecht intoned, "I can assure you the gentleman in question is a most wealthy, most generous man whose offer, should you prove pleasing, is to keep you in absolute comfort." Her eyes abruptly narrowed. "You *do* know what that means, don't you?"

Charles was stunned but not shocked, imagining the gentleman who'd fondled her legs the other day now had other intentions. "Yes, *Madame*, I am aware what—"

"Then you will surely take him up on his offer, as it is not something a woman in your position dismisses lightly."

"I have no desire to be another man's mistress, madam." Charles was equally firm. "I was Lord Wellesley's mistress long enough to know exactly what the position entails."

Madame LeBrecht hissed at her. "Then you will not be so foolish as to forgo this opportunity, girl, not when I tell you what will happen if you do not."

Charles's ire flared. "If I do not?" she parried. "If I do not, then I shall leave your establishment, madam. I shall find employment elsewhere."

"No, Charlotte." *Madame's* hiss had turned to coo. "You will be forced to continue working for me, only not as shop girl here to my *messieurs*, but as an altogether different sort of girl at my other establishment, a house that sees more frequent and far less sophisticated *clientele*." The lady's eyes burned a hole into Charles's soul as fear began to gnaw in the pit of her gut—fear that she attempted to control.

"You cannot make me work for you here, or elsewhere, madam," she countered, chin up.

"Can't I though?" The lady snapped her fingers and immediately two forbidding strongmen emerged from the shadows of the room, men Charles had not even known were at the shop.

Her fear grew into full-blown panic.

"So what shall it be, Charlotte?"

The two men already flanked her sides, standing terribly close.

"The fine gentleman who wishes to keep you in great comfort, or the *many* gentlemen who will be less gentle when they sample your wares at my other shop." *Madame's* eyes glittered savagely.

Charles's heart sank. She'd no choice but to submit. In an hour or two the chance to flee would perhaps present itself. But not now. She was not so foolish as to tempt fate and be cast into what she could only presume was this woman's cathouse.

"Very well." She savagely stared back at the woman seated so smugly before her. "I shall endeavor to please the gentleman in question." She bit her lip. "But I shall not forget your treatment of me, madam."

"I daresay you won't, *Charles*." A faint smile played at the corner of the lady's mouth. "Nor will the gentleman, no doubt."

Madame rose from her seat and snapped her fingers again, causing both men to grab hold of Charles.

She struggled in their grasp.

"Simply a precaution against your bolting, *chérie*," *Madame* told her. "And to make sure you're delivered to the gentleman's rooms forthwith. Remember, you are to fulfill his every wish, obey his every desire, for if he chooses not to keep you, I shall keep you for myself."

And with that, Charles was dragged from the shop and stuffed into a carriage, to be delivered God only knew where, and to whom. A fate far worse than being caught stealing chickens.

Wells had to admit, his mother had handled the Enrights with aplomb. They'd agreed to welcome both Charles and Eleanor back into the family, even agreeing to outfit Eleanor with a trousseau—provided she returned to London to live with them. Wells was certain Charles's sister would decline the offer; he also chose not to divulge Eleanor's betrothal to his steward. He still needed to speak with Father as to how the hell he should go about knighting John.

On the carriage ride back his mother was remarkably quiet as she stared out the window at the rain-drenched street.

"Thank you, *Maman*." He took her hand and gave it a squeeze. "I am in your debt."

"Nonsense, Roland." She finally looked at him. "You love her, don't you." It was more statement than question.

"I do, *Maman*."

"Then I am happy for you, son, for marriage is not easy."

He was surprised by her candor.

"Promise me you will treat her better than you have, dear." Her eyes focused on him. "She's not had it easy for some time now, nor has her sister, and for all my pushing you to take a bride I . . ." She inhaled a breath. "I do not wish you to imagine all women are like me."

"Whatever do you mean, *Maman*?"

"I mean that I have not been unhappy with your father, Roland, only we were not in love when we married, so it was easier to forgive the other our many failings." She looked out the window again. "Oh, I love the old bugger well enough now, the way one loves an old horse, you know." She grinned a little crookedly. "He's had his mistresses and I my lovers and we get along well enough but *you* . . ." She shook her head. "If the girl truly loves you, you've the capacity to hurt her much more than your father ever could have hurt me, you see."

And he did see, rather suddenly.

"So I would beg you, son, tread carefully now. Ask for her

hand properly, court her a while if necessary. Let her know she is not your second or third choice but your foremost. She must know she is wanted, Roland, desired above all others. I don't care how stubbornly she may refuse you at first."

He patted her hand. "You have given me sound advice, *Maman*, which I aim to take. I do not wish to hurt her more, yet I am still not certain she returns my affection in full. And I must be certain before I—"

"How could she not, dear?" His mother reached out to touch his cheek with her other gloved hand, a rare sign of tenderness for her. "But clearly, you must know this for yourself, I understand." She dropped her hand and withdrew the other to straighten her skirts. "I shall look forward to the announcement of your engagement, son, provided you do nothing so rash as to disappoint me."

And she was back, the mother he adored despising.

"Oh I am sure I will, *Maman*." Wells grinned, shocked at the sudden affection he felt for her.

The grin she returned him mirrored his own. "No doubt you will, Roland. No doubt indeed."

Yet the warmth Wells felt towards his mother was soon eclipsed by remaining, needling doubts. As he gazed out the window of the swaying carriage, insecurity gripped him like a vise. He did not doubt his love for Charles; he doubted the very plan Li had helped him form. Should he trust his old friend's counsel, or trust his mother's words instead?

The carriage hit a rut, further jostling his thoughts as a small voice whispered he was not worthy of love. He was desirable only as future Duke. Despite Eleanor's staunch assurance, Wells feared Charles did not, in truth, return his full affection. She might not love *him*, Roland Rutherford, at all.

As Cuthbert had so bluntly reminded, she was not the first woman to have run from him.

CHAPTER FORTY-ONE

If Charles were to survive this night, she'd need to keep her wits about her and her emotions in check. And she was afraid she'd fail on both counts, so enraged was she by this latest turn of events. The last thing in the world she'd dreamed might happen to her in London was to be coerced, once again, into becoming some man's mistress. Only this time she'd committed no crime deserving of punishment, making her plight feel all the more deeply unjust.

She'd been thrown into a carriage and taken to what she assumed was another of Madame LeBrecht's abodes, yet this house was no shop, but also no true residence. She remained flanked on either side by the two hulking men who'd thwarted with ease her attempt to flee between carriage and doorstep. Their grip on her arms had made it painfully clear escape was futile.

She was now being hauled through the opulent house to some upstairs room, one as yet unoccupied, for the noises heard through doors she passed indicated most rooms were in active use. With a sinking heart she knew *Madame* had not lied.

She would indeed be better off some gentleman's mistress than be kept here serving multiple men.

Her thoughts briefly flew to Miss Griswald, to whom she'd sent Lord Wellesley's crew for just such a purpose. Was this now God's punishment for that? Yet Mamie had been pleased to receive new clients. Mamie ran her own business. As far as Charles knew, the Cumberland madam had chosen her profession, not been forced into it. But then, what did she know of Miss Griswald's past, or even her predilections? What did she really know of anyone?

Before she could blink, Charles was pushed into a dimly lit, ornately furnished room and approached by a stern-looking woman dressed like a housekeeper. The lady snapped fingers over her head to order a bath and within seconds, it seemed, servants carrying buckets of steaming water traipsed into the room. They began to fill a large tub beside a corner dressing screen, which stood to one side of a lavish four-poster bed piled high with decorative silk pillows. The entire room was heavily perfumed with an overly sweet, cloying fragrance that made Charles's nostrils flare in distaste. Oleander, perhaps, or jasmine. Whatever the scent, it was too much. The entire room was garish.

Suddenly the two strongmen were gone and the servants gone and only the stern housekeeper remained, eyeing her from head to toe, frowning.

Charles scowled back.

"In case you get any ideas, miss, the windows are nailed shut and the door locked from outside. Attempts to escape or injure will be thwarted by those keeping watch."

Keeping watch? Charles's thoughts raced. *From where?* Her heart thudded in her chest even as she heard a faint rustle from behind the screen.

"Your gentleman chooses to remain unseen until such time as he will make himself known to you. However, you will obey his orders without question. If you fail to obey, he may choose another mistress instead, leaving Madame LeBrecht to do with you what she will. I have been told this is your opportunity, Charlotte, to prove yourself worthy of this particular gentleman's favor. Do not disappoint him."

And with that, she left the room, leaving Charles terrified.

She felt deeply alone, yet was clearly not alone, because she knew the gentleman in question sat obscured behind the screen. She heard him adjust his seat and felt certain it was the man she called 'Redstocking'—the one who'd fondled her legs. Sure enough, upon scanning the room, she saw a silk banyan laid over a chair and beside it the very same burgundy stockings and ribbons she'd modeled for him just last week.

Charles let out a bitter sigh of resignation. At least she knew with whom she dealt. And yet *how* she should deal with him was another matter entirely.

She steadied her nerves and faced the screen with as much courage as she could muster. She curtsied. "Good evening, sir." She rose slowly to stall the inevitable.

She'd stall forever, if she could.

"Charlotte," came a voice, not quite as she recalled Redstocking's.

She awaited the man's pleasure, swallowing her nerves.

"You may undress and bathe."

With trembling hands, Charles forced herself to pretend she was alone as she undressed—to pretend some stranger was not watching her every move, leering at her body. She gripped Lord Wellesley's timepiece in her pocket for courage, then slipped off her shoes, slowly unrolled her plain cotton stockings, and unhooked even more slowly Ruby's simple print dress. This she folded and laid on the edge of the bed. Painfully slowly she unlaced her stays, her back turned to the man to prevent his viewing her bosom for as long as possible. When her stays dropped to the floor his voice sounded gruff.

"Turn around."

She did, arms covering her thin shift for modesty, a shift which looked all the more threadbare in this overly plush room.

"Step into the bath," he ordered, and without thinking she did, still wearing her shift, for he'd not told her to remove it and damned if she'd give him that chance. She sank into the warm water as the shift billowed up before sinking about her. She felt relief to be now underwater, a moment of respite from Redstocking's probing eyes.

Charles refused to imagine what would come next.

"Wash yourself, I wish to watch," came the voice, again not as she remembered Redstocking spoke, yet it was impossible to tell in a room as cluttered as this, his voice muffled behind the screen. It could easily be one of the many other gentlemen she'd served in the shop; she wouldn't know until the villain showed himself.

She took the soap and cloth from the stool beside the tub and proceeded as slowly as possible to wash. She began with her neck and worked her way down, avoiding looking in the direction of the screen at all cost, focusing solely on her body. She had to admit, it felt good to bathe as opposed to washing from a cold basin at the inn. She tried to enjoy the sensation, yet it was impossible to enjoy anything knowing a man ogled her every move, the end game one she could not stomach. Her hands began to tremble as she soaped each arm, the thin shift clinging like a second skin. She'd been a fool to think it gave her modesty, for it likely had the opposite affect: hinting at things more tantalizingly than if she'd simply stripped bare.

The man behind the screen remained quiet, the room's sole sound that of soft water splashing. She soaped the length of one leg to her thigh, and then the other, her shift hitched high on her hips. She knew this was a view Redstocking would like, so she lingered longer than necessary on her legs, an attempt to please this man enough that he would not send her back to *Madame*. She began to panic inside, thinking she couldn't go through with this, not this time. It had been different with Lord Wells; he'd taken his time with her, coaxed her. He'd given her drink that first night too, easing her anxiety, but this felt . . . Dread rose in her throat. She couldn't do this. She didn't have it in her to—

"Out." His command arrested all thought.

She was filled with fear to leave the comfort of the bath, to step out into the unknown of the rest of this night.

"Now," he insisted.

Charles rose quickly from the bath, her shift clinging to every curve visible through the now transparent, soaked fabric. She heard him suck in his breath. Heart pounding, she reached for the robe to quickly wrap about her, still wearing the wet shift beneath.

Charles stood there in misery, awaiting this man's order. She began to shiver for nerves, feeling desperately cold.

"Close your eyes and let down your hair."

"What?" She was at once alarmed. "I should prefer to keep my eyes open, sir."

"And I prefer you keep them closed," he growled from behind the screen. "And if you cannot keep them shut I shall blindfold you instead."

She quickly shut her eyes tight—a safer choice than to be bound blind—as she hurried to undo her pins. Perhaps if she kept a pin and stabbed him in the eye, blinding *him*, she might escape. Only the door was locked and the windows nailed shut.

Charles nearly wept to think there was no way out.

Yet by the time her hair fell loose, a hand from behind reached to pull the locks from her neck, making her flinch and nearly open her eyes, for she'd not heard him leave the screen. He'd approached so quietly, so stealthily . . . Her breathing increased as she felt the man's breath tickle her neck, the heat of his body behind her filling her with such a rush of terror she leapt from him, keeping her back turned, face hid in her hands.

"Forgive me sir, I cannot do this. I beg you, please let me go!" Her entire body shook.

"Madame LeBrecht assured me you had done this before, Charlotte."

"I did sir, I have. Only I cannot now."

"It is common for a mistress to take a new lover." His voice held an edge.

"I know that, sir, only I did not . . . I did not choose this, sir. I am being—"

"Surely you would rather live a life of comfort than a life of labor?" he insisted.

"I would rather heap dung in a field than bed you, sir!" she burst without thinking and immediately regretted her words, trying in vain to undo the damage. "That is, I did not mean—"

"I heard exactly what you meant," he snarled. "Yet you willingly bedded another. Tell me, did he pay you so well you now eschew my offer? You have yet to even hear what I am willing to give you in exchange for my pleasure. You dismiss me outright, before you have even looked upon me."

"Because you've not permitted me to look at you, sir." She was angered, her fear fast becoming rage. "You hide behind a screen like a coward, ordering me about as if I were already your slave and not a person of free will. Am I to think this bodes well for an agreement, sir? Am I to assume you'd treat a mistress with any decency at all if this is how you treat me now?"

His breath hissed, she could hear it, though she remained with her back to him still, refusing now to look at him, for she doubted very much this was Redstocking. *He* was too controlled to hide behind a screen; he'd have shown his face by now, unabashed. No, this was someone else, which meant she was in uncharted territory . . . and even greater danger.

"I'm a coward, eh?" The man's voice turned ominous. "I rather think *you're* the coward, Charlotte, for not giving me a try." He let his words sink in. "I think we ought to test the waters now and see if we suit. After all, you might enjoy me in bed, as you enjoyed your last keeper."

"He was not my keeper, he was my lover, damn you!" She squeezed her eyes tight and balled her fists to keep from punching him.

"Ah." His voice softened. "You fell in love, I see. It is never wise to let one's heart grow attached, Charlotte. Perhaps you are not mistress material after all."

"No, I am not," she bit back. "So I would beg you, sir, let me go!"

"Only I can't, Fox, not now when I've only just found you, my love."

In a flash he enveloped her body, pressing her face to his chest as she froze. She knew at once it was him—the scent of him, feel of him—and she wanted to scream and cry and laugh all at once. Instead, she pushed him from her, livid.

***

"*You.*" Her eyes flew open, piercing him, and Wells was suddenly unsure.

"Charles, love . . ." He reached for her.

"Don't. You. Dare." She trembled with . . . fury?

"Let me explain," he told her calmly.

"I need no explanation, Wells." She was breathing so heavily she struggled to speak, rage washing like a tidal wave across her face. "It is enough to know you have yet again coerced me into servitude, that you have tracked me down, deceiving and threatening me into believing . . ." She broke off, beginning to visibly shake. "How *could* you?" she shouted as tears began to fill her eyes. "How could you be so beastly? To mock me now, to reduce me to such abject . . . !"

She could not finish the thought, the hurt in her eyes so raw Wells flinched. Yet he'd not give up now.

"Charles, sit with me a moment and let me explain. It is not how it appears, truly. You were never in any danger of—"

"Never in any danger?" Her eyes grew wider still. "You mean you planned this, *knew* the situation I was in?" He watched her thoughts race. "How long have you known where I was, where I worked? How long have you been in London, sir?"

"Charles, if you will allow me to explain everything I can assure you it will all make sense. Please—"

"I don't want your explanation, Wells." She was shouting at him. No, yelling. "I want out. I want out of this room, away from this place, away from *you!*"

He scooped her up in one fluid motion, knowing there was nothing more he could say. He flung her over his shoulder and pounded on the door, which was immediately unlocked, and then he carried her—a wet, struggling heap—down the hall, down the long stairs, and out the front door to his waiting carriage. He deposited her upon the seat, rapped twice upon the roof, and the carriage lurched forward, hurtling off into the night.

He had her. That was all that mattered. For now.

CHAPTER FORTY-TWO

"Are you ready to hear me now?"

Wells was poised at any moment to prevent Charles from flinging herself from the moving carriage. She remained drawn into a ball and curled into a corner of the carriage seat across from him, wrapped in naught but a thin robe over her wet shift, her red-gold locks damp about her shoulders.

"I have no interest in anything you have to say." Her words were terse. "I ask only that you drop me at the Wayward Inn on Rector Street. I also demand the return of my dress tomorrow first thing."

He nearly laughed to hear his Fox remain so practical in the midst of so much chaos. For this was chaos, he knew; it was critical he now court her—woo her—properly.

"I shall fetch your dress, yes, but the Wayward Inn is no place for a respectable young lady."

"Then where, pray, do you intend to bring me?" She glared at him something fierce.

God, did he love this woman.

"To your family, Miss Merrinan, where you rightfully belong." He removed his suit coat, leaning across the divide to drape it over her. She was surely chilled, nor could he deliver her to the Enrights looking quite so disheveled.

"I have no family in London, sir, so unless you mean to transport me in this carriage all the way to Cumberland, I believe you must be lying to me, yet again."

"Charles, I've never lied to you, lass."

"Don't you dare pretend to be honorable, Lord Wells, when you know full well you are *not*."

He sighed deeply, having known she would be difficult, just not this difficult. "Charles, though you do not wish to hear it, I believe an explanation is in order now, before you are further shocked by what awaits you next."

Her eyes, if possible, grew only larger.

"I have been in London nearly as long as you, I believe, having left but a day behind you. Your sister grudgingly informed me you meant to make a life for yourself here, and as I feared for your safety in this godforsaken city, I left immediately to find you."

Wells took another breath; he would speak honestly after all he'd put her through. He must. "I also left in haste for the sole reason that I am desperately, madly in love with you."

She opened her mouth to reply but promptly closed it— and her eyes—as if to shut him out.

He deserved no less.

"It has not been easy—finding you or loving you—but I will leave both those stories for another day. Suffice it to say, I took it upon myself to visit your mother's family, the Earl and Countess of Denbigh, and after some convincing on the part of my own mother, they've agreed to welcome both you and Eleanor back, guaranteeing your well-being while you remain in London."

Charles's eyes flew open as she shook her head, chewing her bottom lip as if she wished to chew off his head. It did not seem humanly possible that he should infuriate her more, yet apparently he just had.

God help him.

Wells rushed to explain before she could voice her protest. "I realize you may not wish to resume contact with your grand-parents, Charles, but given the circumstances, it is your safest option. As an unwed and unchaperoned young lady, you can hardly remain with me while in London, and certainly not while Miss Mowry still resides with *Maman*. Nor can I decently house you with any of my own acquaintances, being as they are admittedly, well, unsavory sorts."

"Like Madame LeBrecht, I presume?" She skewered him with her gaze.

"Yes," he answered. "I will tell you Miss Li's story one day, Charles, and you will better understand her, I am sure."

Her voice was cold. "I will not stay with the Enrights, my lord. I will not set foot in their house."

"I'm sorry Charles, but for the time being you've really no choice."

"I have every choice!" She tried to stand but sat down just as quickly when the wheels hit a rut. "Return me to the Wayward Inn at once, Lord Wells, or I will—"

As she reached for the door handle Wells grabbed her bodily to him and deposited her firmly into his lap, the carriage still chasing London's backstreets towards the Denbigh residence.

In his arms, her body vibrated tension.

"Fox." His lips brushed her ear, relishing the feel of her again as he tightened his grip. He held her damp form close, until she gradually, ever so slightly relaxed. "I am sorry I must return you to the Enrights when I should like nothing better than to take you straight home with me, to my room, and keep you there forever. Because I have missed you so desperately these past weeks, I have worried so about your welfare, it is near killing me to deliver you elsewhere. But Charles, I have vowed to do right by you now, which means restoring your position in society and the freedom and honor that position grants you. I'll not steal you away nor force you to my bed. But nor will I see you do further harm to yourself, love. You cannot remain in London near penniless, staying at some dump of an inn with hooligans and whores and all manner of—"

"Disreputable types like yourself, Roland?" she mumbled into his chest, snuggling closer.

"Yes." He gave her a squeeze. "I'll not see you ruined, Fox."

"You ruined me long ago, sir."

"Charles . . ." His voice caught.

"It doesn't matter." She went limp in his arms, the exhaustion from the past few hours—of weeks past no doubt—seeming to drain her of all sense. "Nothing matters anymore but that you have captured me again, my lord, though surely I do but dream you now."

He could feel her breaths slow, knew well the cadence of her sleep, and hugged her to him, relishing this brief chance to possess her before he must give her up and fight all over again to win her, this time, for good.

Wells had carried a sleeping Miss Merrinan into the Earl of Denbigh's townhouse, his finger pressed to his lips so that no one wake her. Inside, he had deposited her gently upon a bed, allowing a maid to tend her. Then, once downstairs, he was ushered into the parlor and met by the Earl and Countess, both of whom wore expressions of grim disbelief. He asked for a drink, was given a stiff one, and proceeded to seat himself in one of their uncomfortable wingbacks in order to spin them a believable yarn.

"Lord and Lady Enright, my apologies for the late hour and unusual manner in which I have just delivered your granddaughter, but I have only just located and removed her from deplorable living conditions the likes of which I'll forbear divulging for fear you might not withstand the horror."

The Countess grew frightfully pale at this.

"I can assure you Miss Merrinan's honor remains intact, but barely so, for the hands into which she fell would surely have ruined her had I not arrived when I did. Her appearance bears testament to this fact, though I am certain you will do your utmost in the coming days to comfort and outfit her respectably."

He met the Earl's panicked gaze with stern reproof. "I needn't remind you both that it is in no small part your own neglect of your granddaughter which led to her deplorable circumstances. The poor girl had neither the means nor connections anymore in London to ensure her safety, and I find it inconceivable that her own family should have allowed such disregard to continue these ten years past, resulting in the state I found her in tonight. I expect that in the coming days you will do everything within your power to repair the harm done her, and that you will not, I repeat, will not *ever* speak to her about the events leading up to this night. As I declared before, I have every intention of marrying Miss Merrinan and will call upon her daily not only to court her properly, but to ensure she is treated with the respect and deference due a daughter of the Enright line."

He leveled both gaze and words at the Earl and Countess. "For if I find your treatment of her anything but *impeccable,* I will personally see to it that your own reputations, and that of every Enright family member save the Merrinans, be destroyed. Have I made myself clear?" He continued to stare at them both, satisfied by their cowed expressions to conclude his message had been received.

"My lord, I believe we understand you perfectly." The Earl bowed his head in deference. "We are, of course, deeply aggrieved by the hardship our granddaughter has endured."

Wells merely downed his glass and got up. "Miss Merrinan can expect me tomorrow at three." And with that, he showed himself out.

Once back inside the carriage, he expelled a long breath, allowing himself to hope that all he'd set in motion would now pay off. Come morning he would pen several letters, not least of which would be to inform Eleanor Merrinan that her sister had been found and, God willing, would now be kept safe.

Ellie tore into the letter from London.

Miss Eleanor,

It is with great relief that I report your sister safely delivered to your grandparents, the Earl and Countess of Denbigh. By now you should have received word from them, I hope, expressing remorse at having denied you these many years past. I realize you may well have no desire to accept a reconciliation, but would urge you to at least resume contact while Charles remains in their care. I could find no other solution than to restore her to her kin here in London, since my aim is to woo her now with the respect she rightly deserves. Charles will either wed me willingly, or I shall die trying; I can only pray your sister takes mercy on me.

"Father!" Eleanor shouted from the kitchen. "He's found Charles! Lord Wellesley has found Charles and means to marry her! Oh thank God. Thank God he's found her and she's all right."

She hurriedly scanned the rest of his letter.

You may write directly to her at the Enright address, as I am sure she will have a word or two to share regarding how I found her in London. And I would ask you take what she reports with a grain of salt, Eleanor, for the truth shall come out with time, and, I hope, explain my actions. Please know that my intentions towards your sister remain honorable. If only she would believe me in this.

It is my heart's desire to return to Cumberland with Charles my bride, in as short a time as possible, though I cannot predict how long it will take your sister to relent, if ever. I have written to Cuthbert that he join me post haste. He is to be knighted and made my squire, so it is in your interest, Eleanor, to ensure John arrives in London as quickly as possible, wearing one of my spare suits, that beard of his trimmed. I insist on it.

May God keep you and your father in good health.

Your humble servant, Roland Wellesley

Eleanor sat down again to reread the letter, smiling and crying at his lordship's words. She didn't care two shakes about her grandparents, but to know Charles was fed and housed in a decent part of London . . . She shuddered to imagine where Lord Wellesley had found her sister. There would be much to discuss when she saw Charles again. Much indeed.

CHAPTER FORTY-THREE

C harles awoke for the first time in a long time rested. She relaxed into the comfortable bed before wrapping herself into the fresh-smelling sheets, burrowing her head deeper into the soft down pillow. She lay there a moment longer before she stretched luxuriously, then righted herself, heart thudding.

She was suddenly all-too-conscious of her strange environs.

Her body tensed as she scanned the room to ensure she was alone, then slipped from the bed, noting she wore a long cotton night-rail, a most *proper* cotton night-rail buttoned to her neck. She tiptoed to the door and, finding it open, turned the knob to peer down both ends of a dim, empty hall. Just as quickly she returned to the room to look for clothes. Finding none, not even a robe, she grabbed a thick crystal vase from a table and again slipped out the door, gliding down the hall as silently as possible in her bare feet. Wherever she was, she needed to find clothes before she could make her escape. She only prayed no one would see her.

As she clutched the weight of the crystal in her fist, it occurred to her she'd been here before. Not in this hallway but in this very same position: awaking in a strange bed without her clothes. Was she forever destined to—?

Out of nowhere stepped a smart-looking maid in a starched cap and apron. She looked a far cry from the Abbey's staff.

"Why, miss, I were about t' check on yer!" the girl rushed to speak. "Come back at once, please, an' let me assist. Lady Enright's lookin' for a suitable dress for yer, an' Cook's set aside breakfast too." The girl took Charles by the arm to begin marching her back towards the room.

She was so shocked by this, she allowed herself to be led.

"There now." The maid shut the door behind them. "You sit right here an' let me begin on yer hair, miss. An' I beg yer, put down the vase afore y' do something rash. There's no one here as means yer any harm."

She gave Charles a kindly smile, and suddenly the previous night came rushing back.

Charles was in her grandparents' house—*la maison d'grand-père et grand-mère*—where, as a girl, she'd learned to speak French.

She was too appalled by this realization to utter serious protest, so she simply allowed herself to enjoy the fact that someone else now tamed her hair. It had been a long while since Ellie had done the honor, and Charles stared at herself in the mirror—at a wan, thin face which stared back, dark circles beneath her eyes. Events were beginning to return with more clarity now, and she was shocked Lord Wells had bothered to seek her at all. Why had Ellie told him where she'd gone? It felt like a betrayal, yet knowing Eleanor, fear had likely gotten the better of her.

And Charles had to admit, she'd not done well for herself since returning to London.

Yet why the devil had Wells lied to her in the carriage last night? He didn't love her; he simply needed a wife. No doubt he was still trying to appease his mother, and he could try all he liked, because she had no intention of giving him what he wanted. He may very well need her, but *she* did not need him.

"You've ever such lovely hair, miss." The girl began to prattle. "Cook said yer mam had the very same hair, y' look just like her, she says. An' Cook says she remembers yer an' yer sister comin' for Christmas near every year when you was little, though I've not been here long enough t' . . ."

Charles tuned the maid out, closing her eyes. Her conversation with Lord Wellesley still swirled in her mind, while the thought of facing her grandparents filled her with dread. Would she were anywhere but here! Though *here* was a step up from the Wayward Inn, or God forbid, Madame LeBrecht's house of ill repute. How the devil Wells had found her there she'd no idea, nor did she wish to know. She'd demand an explanation from him eventually, but not today. Today she must deal with *grand-père et grand-mère*.

She pushed his lordship from her thoughts.

"Tell me your name again?" she asked the maid. "Forgive me if you already did; I fear I am in shock still." She tried a faint smile on the girl.

"Jeanie, miss. Jeanie Trengove." The girl bobbed a curtsy. "I'm t' be yer lady's maid, miss."

"Well, Jeanie Trengove, you shall have to tell me who's who and what's what in this house so I don't wear out my welcome with the staff. I should hate to——"

"Why, miss!" the girl burst. "Y' couldn't if y' tried! 'Tis *we* who mustn't offend yerself."

Charles remained firm. "Jeanie, I was housekeeper before arriving here, and most recently shop girl. I've been in service long enough to know what work like yours entails."

The maid's eyes grew wide. "Y' can't mean it, miss. Y' can't have been no shop girl nor housekeeper, not as Lady Enright's granddaughter."

"Lord and Lady Enright disowned me and my sister; how else should I expect to make my way if not by gainful work?" Charles decided to plant a seed in the girl's head, in hopes it would grow. Gossip usually did.

"Only whyever would the Countess do such a thing, miss?" The girl looked genuinely confused.

"Because my mother married a commoner, Jeanie, a mere soldier." Old anger rose in her throat. "There's no love lost between myself and my grandparents. 'Tis the reason you found me in the hall with a vase clutched in my hand. I'd not put it past Lady Enright to lock me up and throw away the key now that—"

"Miss!" Jeanie clapped a hand over her mouth.

Charles knew she had the girl on her side. "Now don't tell a soul upstairs what I just told you, Jeanie, but tell every servant below stairs how the Earl and Countess of Denbigh may be blood, but to me they are dead, just as sure as my sister and I were dead to them when they threw us out onto the street."

Jeanie looked fit to explode at this, no doubt bursting to tell all she'd just heard. Charles was satisfied she'd started a rumor that would not only reach her grandparents' ears, but hopefully affect their reputation. They feared scandal more than anything else.

And deserved no less for their actions.

"Jeanie, I'd love some breakfast yet before I leave, and if the same dear cook I once knew is still here, I'll kiss her cheek in gratitude. In fact, I'll dine below stairs with the rest of staff rather than where I'm not wanted. Can you fetch me some clothes first? I'd borrow a dress from you if you think it would fit."

"O' course, miss." She bobbed another curtsy. "Quick as I can I'll return, just you wait here."

"Thank you, Jeanie." Charles smiled gratefully at the girl. There was no better way to know a house than to befriend its servants, and she would need a friend or two to escape her grandparents' house again.

§

Wells sat at his father's bedside, pleased the Duke was in good spirits. He'd informed him of his rescue of Miss Merrinan, quizzed him on how to knight Cuthbert, and then regaled him with the story of the south wall, of his own labors there and how they'd lost a man that fateful day, not to mention several limbs. His father had listened, rapt.

"Son," he told him, "you've done right to restore the Abbey. Always did admire your gumption, your willingness to put in the work."

"I fear *Maman* might disagree, sir."

"Of course she would, it's her job to disagree. You're just like her, after all."

Wells smiled. "Are you saying you regard us both with despair, sir?"

"Yes." His father remained straight-faced. "The bane of my existence, the pair of you." He grinned. "Your young lady will no doubt find you difficult, too, if my life with your mother is any indication."

"She already does, sir." Wells grimaced. "I fear she won't have me."

"She'll have you," his father assured him. "Adelaide Enright fought plenty with Benedict Merrinan, but the two always reconciled."

"And just how would you know this, sir?"

"Visited them plenty. We both lived in Cumberland back then, made him my squire didn't I—just to keep tabs on him and his lady wife, mind. Used to take you along to visit. Don't you recall?"

"No." Wellesley shook his head, early childhood a blur.

"Well, they fought, trust me, but their quarrels only fueled their fire I suspect." The Duke looked distant, as if his thoughts wandered. "You say you saw him again—Merrinan—but that he's no longer of sound mind?"

"Indeed, sir, he flits between times. One minute he's wholly present but the next he speaks as if his wife still lives. It's tragic, really, to see how randomly events play out in his head. Nor has it been easy for his daughters to manage him thus."

"I imagine not." The Duke looked away. "I'd assumed he was well settled when he retired from being squire. Didn't even bother to install a new man there as things seemed to run themselves" His father looked pained. "I should have checked on Merrinan and his daughters. I've not been in good health for some time, Roland. I've let things slide." He sighed. "But for the Earl of Denbigh to abandon them so . . ." He shook his head. "Damned disgrace, the whole matter."

"Enright is an arse, yes," Wells interjected with force.

"Prudish son of a bitch more like it," his father muttered.

Wells could tell his old man was growing tired. "I'll stop in again tomorrow, sir, you ought to get some rest."

But the Duke, unsurprisingly, had already fallen asleep.

§❧

"Lord, Miss Charles, but ain't you the spittin' image o' yer mother. Why, when y' walked in just now I thought I saw a ghost, I did!"

Cook stood by the kitchen's hearth, arms crossed in satisfaction as Charles dug into her plate with gusto. Staff sat about the table watching her eat—with fascination.

Charles smiled up at the portly old woman, recalling well her delicious fare. "Your dishes, Cook, have only gotten better with the years."

"Y' could use some fattenin' up, child." The lady's own

frame generously filled the kitchen. "It's good t' see yer, miss. We all did think on you an' yer sister over the years, y' know."

"We thought of you, too," Charles told her. "Eleanor especially, I admit. Christmas was never the same for her after, and being so young still, but a child really, I fear she missed more than just your fine meals."

"Well, what matters is you're here now, miss," Cook indulged. "An' we're that glad for it, ain't we?" she demanded of the staff, most of whom had no idea who Charles was, but who all nodded in vigorous agreement.

All of which changed the instant the Countess swept in.

"What is the meaning of this?" Lady Enright stopped in her tracks. "Hopkins!" Her tone was sharp, directed at Cook. "Why is my granddaughter not being served breakfast upstairs in the dining room?"

Charles swiftly interjected. "Because I prefer to dine downstairs, *Grand-mère*, as befits my station."

"Charles," her grandmother intoned, "a word, *now*."

"Whatever you wish to say to me can be said here." She continued to blithely eat, ignoring her grandmother.

Lady Enright scowled before she snapped her fingers, dismissing her staff who scurried like so many mice. Then she pulled out a chair across from Charles and stiffly seated herself.

"My dear, I realize you are—"

"You realize *nothing*." Charles lost her temper, insides ablaze. She hadn't known such rage as still harbored in her breast. "I don't know what Lord Wellesley told you to make you take me in, Lady Enright, but I am *not* staying in this house with you, and I refuse to acknowledge you as family."

Her grandmother's lips thinned. "I am not surprised by your anger, Charles, but you really must learn to curb your temper now that Lord Wellesley has offered for you."

"So that is why I am here, is it? How rich." She shook her

head. "How perfectly rich, all of it," she muttered, stabbing a fresh forkful of egg.

"My dear," her grandmother soothed, "it is a great honor indeed that his lordship should court you now, considering how—"

"Oh yes, considering how unsuitable I now am, deplorable even. I am sure the *Ton* do not even recall my existence. No, it is nothing short of remarkable, isn't it, that I should so suddenly suit you and *Grand-père* so well, should be so desirable now as granddaughter, thanks solely to my potential alliance with the future Duke of Allendale."

"Charles Adelaide Merrinan." Her grandmother drew herself tall. "Your mother did not raise you to speak to your elders in such impudent, ill manner. I will not tolerate such disrespect in my own house, young lady, and you will—"

"And I will not tolerate the abject disrespect you showed Father after Mother's death. Nor will I be ordered about as if I were a child, madam, when I am now a grown woman."

Charles stood in a huff, threw down her napkin, and stormed from the kitchen.

CHAPTER FORTY-FOUR

At precisely three o'clock that afternoon Wells knocked upon the door of the Enright residence carrying a profusion of purple hyacinths and a parcel under his arm. He had shaved and dressed smartly, looking, he hoped, every bit a proper suitor. As he was ushered into the drawing room, he debated briefly running screaming in the opposite direction, but he swallowed his pride and steeled himself to receive a certain lady's wrath. That Charles should be angry with him would surely prove to be an understatement.

Seeing her seated primly on the sofa in formal dress, her hair done up in the latest style, was a small shock. She looked nothing like his Fox yet was absolutely stunning.

He swept into a low bow as she curtsied in return, accepting his bouquet with barely murmured thanks before handing it to the footman who placed it in a vase. Then he handed her the parcel.

"I believe this belongs to you, Miss Merrinan, as requested."

"And my other belongings, sir, at the inn?" she reminded tersely.

"I'm afraid those were no longer retrievable, miss. The inn had already let your room to another."

"*Blast*," she swore softly enough only he could hear.

"My lord," Lady Enright entreated, "won't you please join us? Charles and I were about to take tea."

"I had hoped to take a turn about your gardens with Miss Merrinan, Countess." He stared pointedly at the lady. "As the weather is so pleasant today."

"It is, isn't it?" She ignored his plea, making him itch. "Perhaps after tea, Charles, you would like to show his lordship the courtyard garden?"

"Of course, *Grand-mère*, though you shall have to remind me where it is, being, as I am, a stranger to this house." Her eyes locked onto her grandmother with a look Wells appreciated; she was still his cunning Fox beneath her newly coiffed exterior.

"Oh, it has hardly changed since you were last here, dear."

Charles's expression remained unyielding.

The Countess continued unperturbed. "My granddaughters used to love to run about the courtyard when they were children, my lord. It was their favorite pastime when visiting."

***

"That is because Papa preferred the outdoors to anywhere inside this house," Charles reminded her grandmother, inwardly incensed. "We followed him wherever the poor man sought *refuge*."

Her grandmother did indeed wince, shooting Charles a glare.

Charles ignored her. "And what brings you here, today, Lord Wellesley?" She cast him a withering look. "Checking up on me, or simply here to gloat?" She did not like what she saw. His beautiful curls had been trimmed short, ridiculous mutton chops now decorated his cheeks, and a sharp-tailored suit made him look like every other London dandy. This was not the man she knew.

His lips twitched, as if he were amused. "Why, I am here to call formally upon you, Miss Merrinan, as Lord and Lady Enright have granted me permission to court you. I shall visit every day now, to pay you the honor and respect you deserve as my intended."

"And why was I not included in this discussion, sir?" Charles wanted to punch his smug face. "I do not recall giving your lordship the impression I desired your courtship in the least."

"Oh I beg to differ, Miss Merrinan, as you have given *every* impression in past you were most keen to receive my attentions."

The rotten man made her blush, for his eyes perused her body in a manner so brash he clearly imagined other parts of her blushing too.

"My lord, you take bold liberty with your words, for I have given you no reason to—"

Her grandmother cut her short. "Ah, here's our tea now, thank you, Tom." The Countess barely glanced at the footman. "Do you take it black, Lord Wellesley, or in the usual?"

"Black, thank you." He turned again to Charles. "Miss Merrinan, regardless of how you may presently feel towards my person, I assure you my intention remains resolute. I will court you now until such day as you accept my suit."

"You pompous arse, Wells," Charles said before she could even think not to.

The Countess let out a gasp while his lordship laughed heartily. "God, I've missed you, Fox."

"I did not intend my statement to be amusing, sir."

"Oh no." He grinned. "You, my dear, meant it in all honesty, which makes me adore you all the more." He turned to the Countess. "Lady Enright, your granddaughter is so refreshingly direct compared to most other young ladies I find her simply irresistible. I shall not rest until I make her my wife."

But *Grand-mère* appeared not to hear him, frantically ringing for smelling salts as she fanned herself profusely, crying, "Tom, Tom!" for the footman. In despair she implored, "Charles, girl, fetch me some water, please!"

***

Wells watched Charles half-heartedly rise to assist her grandmother. Her hips sashayed nicely in her London dress, encouraging his imagination to roam a tad freely and return to last night.

She placed a glass of water with a small thud upon the table before Lady Enright and then settled herself again upon the settee, pouring herself a cup of tea. She leaned back to stare at him and slowly sip.

"Why did you come to London, Wells?"

"Why, to bring you home, Charles."

"What if I do not wish to go home?"

"Eleanor wishes it, and I wish it too."

"Yet no one is considering *my* wishes," she snapped.

They were speaking as if Lady Enright were not even present.

"For too long no one considered your wishes, Charles. I am as guilty as the next. But I aim to change that now."

"Then I must inform you of continued failure, sir."

"Charles, I am trying. Surely you must see I mean to—"

"What I see, my lord, is a man used to getting what he wants, and when denied his pleasure he resorts to force."

"No one is forcing you to decide anything, Miss Merrinan."

"Aren't you, though?" Her voice rose in pitch. "Did you not

deposit me here, in this house, forcing a reconciliation I do not wish?"

"I told you before I could see no other solution to your predicament than to—"

"You could have simply let me go, damn it."

"What, and allow you to destroy yourself here in London? Leave you compromised, endangered, or worse?" His exasperation grew. "For God's sake, Charles, did you really think I'd let you come to harm?"

"Did you really think I expected your rescue?"

"Damn it, Fox, I will not let the woman I love—"

"You do not love me, sir, you merely lust after me."

He was stunned to realize she truly had no idea of his depth of feeling.

Lady Enright regained consciousness enough to look from one to the other and interject. "Charles," she started meekly, "my dear, perhaps it were best you and Lord Wellesley took that turn about the courtyard now. I shall simply sit here by the window with a clear view to you both. It seems you have some catching up to do." And for a brief moment her eyes met Wellesley's with the faintest hint of sympathy.

He stood at once and presented Miss Merrinan his arm, which she grudgingly took. They left the parlor for the courtyard, to continue a conversation long in coming.

***

Once out of earshot of her grandmother, however, Charles dropped Wellesley's arm and launched her offense. He would answer for his actions. She would demand an explanation.

"Why are you truly here, Wells? How did you know where to find me?"

"You know why I am here, Fox," he answered. "I wish to make you my wife."

"Nonsense." His self-assurance was infuriating.

"It is not nonsense." He looked aggrieved. "I am sincere. If I were not sincere I should have simply flung you over my shoulder and hauled you back to Cumberland with me."

"You did fling me over your shoulder last night and hauled me here, to the last place on earth I wish to be!"

"So you'd rather be at *LeBrecht's* instead, hawking your wares?"

This gave her pause—for but a moment.

"How did you end up in that . . . that house last night?" she demanded.

"As already mentioned, Charles, Miss Li and I are of long-standing acquaintance. When I arrived in London, without a clue to your whereabouts, I realized finding you would be a needle-in-haystack feat, so I met with *Madame* and asked her to place an ad I hoped might lure you to apply."

"*You* placed the ad for shop girl?" She remained as incredulous as he remained insufferable.

"No, Charles, I asked Miss Li to place an ad in hopes that she might ferret you out. It is nigh impossible to find decent employment without a reference in this city, and as I had written you none before you left, I presumed you'd have great difficulty finding another position as housekeeper here in London."

His subterfuge, his scheming . . . Who the hell did he think he was?

"Unfortunately, you were not the only young woman with a head of red-gold hair to respond to the ad, making Miss Li fill the position before you appeared, though she had the where-withal to at least offer you a different job in her shop, one I'd have preferred she *not* give you, but needs must."

He'd muttered that last bit under his breath, looking almost sheepish.

Sheepish was not good enough.

"When she informed me a woman of your name and description was in her employ and being solicited by gentlemen, I had to take matters into my own hands and offer for you myself, as Miss Li remains, above all, a keen businesswoman."

He'd flinched to say the term, but flinching also was not good enough.

"I could not be certain, either, that her 'Charlotte' was my Charles, which is why I needed to take a peek at you first."

"You took your damn time peeking," she shot back.

"Your identity was not the only thing I needed to verify, Charles." Wells's gaze pierced her a moment before he swallowed, seeming nervous. "I also needed to be sure you didn't actually *want* to become some other man's mistress. For all I knew you were enjoying your new position at *LeBrecht's*, encouraging clients in hopes one might offer to keep you in finery and set you up comfortably here in London."

Charles was dumbstruck. "You mean you actually thought me capable of—?"

"How else could I be certain?" He sounded pained. "You took off in a huff after I proposed marriage, when I expected you'd be pleased by the offer, happy even, as I was happy to imagine us together at last, no longer having to skulk about the Abbey like a pair of furtive—"

"Because that's all I ever was to you, *Your Grace*." Charles felt bitter to her core, every explanation he had given ringing false. "A fine fuck, do call it what it was, sir. I've had enough of your false gallantry."

***

Wells was appalled. He took her hands in his and dropped to his knee. "Charles, you are infinitely more to me. I'll admit it was at first perhaps only that—perhaps only that for you, too—

but you cannot deny there isn't more, Fox. I know you feel it too, for if you didn't, why run like you did? If you truly felt nothing for me, why not accept my suit, if only to enjoy my wealth, like every other grasping debutante?"

"Because I don't want your wealth!" she cried. "And you never would have deigned to marry me had your mother not found us as she did or known my bloodline. You would have married Miss Mowry and kept me for sport, when I cannot abide the thought of you in some other woman's arms, fathering children with her while I . . ."

"Fox." He pulled her to him, crushing her skirts to his body, gazing up at her from the floor. "I could not abide it either, love. I would never have gone through with it. I'd have let you go, or let her go. I could never have kept you both."

"Only you *would*." She sniffed, angrily brushing tears from her eyes. "You'd have wanted the best of both. I know you, Roland Wellesley. You are a beast and I am a fool. I am the greatest fool there is for allowing myself ever to fall in love with you."

And out it had slipped: proof, at last! His heart swelled with joy.

***

"Which is why I shall never marry you, Lord Wells." Charles pulled from him roughly. "You cannot take what is not freely given, and I will not marry a man who would just as soon marry another. I will not be molded into a proper duchess to suit you or your mother's whims. Nor will I be kept prisoner here in my grandparents' house." She drew herself up with every shred of dignity she still had left, though inside her soul was crumbling. "So make Mowry your bride and leave me the hell alone."

Charles bolted from the courtyard and ran into the house,

to the comfort of her bedroom, locking the door behind her and throwing herself upon the bed to cry herself silly like some moonstruck girl of fifteen. The last time she'd cried so hard in this house she'd been that very age and just as distraught, only for the sake of a very different love back then: love for her father, her family, her mother freshly lost.

Always and ever, it seemed, Charles wept for love.

Wells eventually returned to the drawing room in a haze of dejection, feeling wrung out to dry. The last thing in the world he wished to do was converse more with Lady Enright, who had surely witnessed their quarrel through the courtyard's glass panes. He dreaded her words as her skirts rustled in impatience, yet he took his seat with resignation.

"Charles Merrinan is worse than her mother, Lord Wellesley."

He looked up, surprised.

"More obstinate, obstreperous, obnoxious even than Adelaide was. And it is entirely my own fault for ignoring the girl." The Countess almost snorted. "I raised Adelaide properly, you know, her sole undoing that rakish soldier Merrinan. But my granddaughter's undoing, I now see, stems from a decade's worth of neglect. I have no one to blame but myself."

Wells suspected the lady was trying to finesse this union before all hope was lost, though if the Countess suspected he had compromised her granddaughter, she might very well attempt to force matters.

And that, he knew, would incense Charles only more.

The lady huffed more loudly, as if the last thing she'd expected or desired at her age was to suffer both character slander *and* her granddaughter. Yet here she was, dealing with both.

Wells did not want to deal with her a moment more.

He rose to excuse himself, and the Countess politely stood too.

"Lord Wellesley, allow me to see you out, sir."

"No need, Lady Enright," he replied. "I shall call again tomorrow, same time."

"You will?" She quickly collected herself. "Good. That is, I am pleased to hear it." Oddly, she patted his arm. "It will take time for Charles to acclimate herself again to life here, my lord. Though no doubt you show great patience with her already."

Wells merely grumbled, "I have not always been so patient with her, Countess, so the least I can do is grant it her now."

Later, after Charles had cried herself dry, her maid, Jeanie, rapped softly at her door. She let the girl in with a fresh tray of tea and the parcel Lord Wellesley had brought, and then she asked her to bring his lordship's flowers to her room too.

Upon returning with the bouquet though, Charles could barely thank the girl for the fresh onslaught of tears that again bathed her face. She held his lordship's silver timepiece gripped in her palm as she stared at Ruby's print frock strewn across the bed.

For the life of her she didn't know why both objects made her weep.

CHAPTER FORTY-FIVE

Lord Wellesley called upon Charles every blasted day now, bearing new blooms each day too, until her bedroom was a veritable hothouse. It had been a sennight since she'd arrived at the Enrights, and in that time she had managed to endear herself to every servant in the house. In the same span of time she'd also managed to infuriate Lord and Lady Enright a hundred times over. That she was punishing them was obvious to all. That she had no intention of desisting was obvious only to herself.

Jeanie proved a tolerable enough substitute for Eleanor whenever Charles felt the need to wax furious over something Lord Wellesley did or said, which was often enough. Charles knew the girl could not comprehend her wrath, nor did she trust her enough to reveal the truth of her relationship with Wells. The maid must have told Charles fifty times his lordship appeared the picture of a gentleman with his oh so fine demeanor and even finer comportment. *Why, she wished some future duke would call daily asking for her hand too!* Charles had bit her tongue at that.

She helped the household whenever she could, clearing her

plate from table to get a rise out of her grandfather, even making her own bed most mornings if the maids didn't get to it in time. The staff all thought her very strange, and the story of her past, of having been cast out by the Earl and Countess, began to take root amongst the servants, spreading even to other households, or so Jeanie said. Word had it the *Ton* itself had begun gossiping about the Enrights again, rekindling the none-too-ancient history of their eldest daughter and a certain brave soldier granted knighthood. It seemed that all of London began to buzz with news that the Duke of Allendale's son was purportedly courting this long lost Enright granddaughter. Would he make her his future duchess? And would she accept his all-too-eager suit? Jeanie regaled Charles daily as to the latest household gossip.

Charles could not have cared less, though it pleased her just a little to know her grandparents were upset by all the talk. *That* she did enjoy.

Wells, meanwhile, was miserable. Not only had he vowed never to return to London, he'd vowed never to put himself through the agony of formal courtship again, yet here he was, doing both. And Charles, it seemed, had no intention of relenting.

She was proving to be a fortress of denial, and he feared she might never crack. His mother, of course, was also needling him about the renewed gossip; he could not deny the stares and titters that now greeted him on London's streets. For every past harm he'd done Charles Merrinan, it seemed the lady would repay him—with a vengeance.

What he needed was for Cuthbert to bloody well arrive so he could be done with his steward's knighting. If John had left the day he'd received Wellesley's letter he might arrive as early as tomorrow, for Wells was beginning to fantasize about simply stealing his mistress back to Cumberland and reinstalling her there as his housekeeper. At the Abbey, at least, he'd have a chance in hell of speaking to her again like they used to, because the Enrights never left them alone. They were forever chaperoned, and Charles had become an insufferably polite version of her former outspoken self. Even her wardrobe began to repel him, the way the Countess outfitted her with flounces, ribbons, and lace. She looked like an overstuffed doll.

Wells missed his chicken-thieving Fox like never before.

❦

"You want me to *what?*" Wells regarded his mother with outrage. They were taking tea in his mother's parlor—at his mother's insistence. He rattled his cup so hard it spilled.

"Yes, I want you to ruin her publicly, Roland. I have secured the Enrights an invitation to the Sedgewicks's garden fête this Sunday at their estate outside of London. There you will ensure a public-enough falling-out with Miss Merrinan so as to compromise her into an immediate and necessary marriage." She looked downright smug. "And I daresay you shouldn't find it difficult, given you've ruined the girl already."

Wells fumed. Apparently, the gossip swirling about town had forced his mother and Lady Enright to form an unholy alliance of sorts with both women now hatching plans to force Charles's hand. The rumor Miss Merrinan was comporting herself like a servant in her grandparents' house had pushed Lady Enright over the edge.

"The difference being, Mother, that I have vowed to court Miss Merrinan *honorably* now, according her the respect and admiration due a lady of her station. As you yourself counseled me to do."

"Roland, now is not the time to turn gentleman on me."

"Do I hear you right, *Maman?* You of all people now tell

me to behave dishonorably, on purpose no less, all to trick the woman I love into marriage?"

"Yes," she snarled, "because your plan is decidedly *not* working."

"This time I am being patient, Mother. Unlike you, it seems."

The Duchess took a deep breath and squared her shoulders. "Roland, love," she began calmly enough, "Miss Merrinan is angry with you, with her grandparents, angry at the world no doubt. And she will remain angry until something occurs to jar her from her anger. What's more, the poor girl is justified in her anger. You did treat her abominably and her grandparents did disown her most reprehensibly, causing her and her sister great hardship. So to prolong her agony by trapping her longer with the Enrights when you could simply carry her back to Cumberland and make her happy, well, what would you wish for her, son, you who claim to love her so?"

He had to admit, there was truth to her argument.

Yet he'd sworn he wouldn't force or coerce Charles ever again. He'd promised her a choice when she'd been denied choice once too oft. He'd not go back now on his word to her, else she'd resent him for the rest of their married life.

If they ever married.

"I am sorry, *Maman*," he told her quietly. "I will attend this garden party but I will not willfully compromise Miss Merrinan into marriage. I cannot do that to her, not after everything I've already done. I simply cannot."

Dearest Charles, Eleanor began, for Charles had snatched the letter delivered on the footman's platter with anxious hands, fearing the worst for Father.

I cannot tell you my relief upon receiving word Lord Wellesley has delivered you into safety. How I have worried about you, sister! Only do not hate me for telling him you fled to London. At first I did not. I scolded him most harshly, John can attest. Yet had you seen him that day, Charles, frantic for you, a man brokenhearted . . .

Brokenhearted her foot. He'd fooled Ellie again, it seemed.

. . . and desperate enough I did not recognize him almost. I knew then that his lordship loves you, Charles, as much as you love him, so I could remain silent no longer. I hope you have forgiven him by now and will come home to us. I hope you will forgive me, too. It was concern for you only which made me break my promise.

Papa is well, though he remains in a weakened state. I am grateful he knows naught of your predicament. He thinks you still at the Abbey and scolds you for not visiting. At least on those days when he does not think you still his little girl, needing scolding for other reasons.

I will end by saying that our grandparents have written to me as well, and that I have responded only out of politeness to you rather than to them. It must surely be a shock to reside again beneath their roof, and I am sorry for it, though I understand his lordship's reasons. Promise me you will not anger them too much, sister; I shall remain by letter distantly polite. Once you are home you need never see them again.

I wish only for your safe return now, for your happiness, and for you to attend my wedding. That and for me to attend your own wedding to Lord Wellesley. Do not frown so, Charles, I can picture you scowling at the very words I write. For once, sister, set aside your stubborn pride. I know you care for his lordship, as he cares for you. As Papa and I care deeply for you too. Write to me soon, I beg, that I may hear from you myself. I love you Charles—be good! Eleanor

Be good? What the devil had made her write that? Charles

angrily set aside the letter, stewing not a little over her sister's words, though she was relieved Father's health was no worse. She would pen Eleanor a response, of course, but would mince no words about his lordship or their grandparents. That her sister could forgive Wells so readily . . . *Hmph.* She didn't know the half of him.

Though she reminded herself it was in Ellie's nature to forgive, while she was of an altogether different nature: more punishing by far.

CHAPTER FORTY-SIX

C harles had been dressed for a party and stuffed into a carriage in a flurry of last-minute activity. No one had informed her she'd be leaving London; even her lady's maid had not known which dress to press.

As she was jostled about on the seat across from *Grand-mère* and *Grand-père*, she revisited the conversation she'd had but a scant hour earlier with Jeanie, wondering anew why she was being bundled off to some garden fête. Did her grandparents mean to show her off? Or did they plan to throw her to the *Ton's* hungry wolves?

"No, miss, ne'er heard o' the Sedgewicks," Jeanie had told her. *"Then again I am right new here."* She'd popped a few stray flowers into Charles's hair from the many bouquets that still littered her room.

"Perhaps Lord Wellesley'll be there, miss." She'd winked at Charles through the mirror. *"An' I see yer blushin', so don't tell me y' wouldn't like it if he were."*

Charles had informed her she wouldn't, though she could recall still the rash bloom on her cheeks. Even now she felt them burn.

Her grandmother's sharp glance across the carriage made Charles force a smile. She'd not give *Grand-mère* a hint of her true feelings. She would never trust her grandparents, no matter how doggedly they now tried to make amends.

Some things were simply unforgivable.

❧

Wells had arrived late enough to the Sedgewick fête for it to be dusk. He'd searched in vain for Charles and the Countess of Denbigh but thus far had found neither—until he stumbled upon an outdoor balcony and observed the masses dancing below him on the estate's grand terrace. Torches flickered along the perimeter, making the scene glow otherworldly. And there, below his vantage point, he spotted his love's flaming, red-gold hair.

She was dressed in white, like all the other débutantes in attendance, and danced with some officer of the Crown resplendent in bright uniform. He wanted to tear her from the other man's arms, but of course he could not. He merely gazed at her in wonder, for Charles looked, remarkably enough, happy. She flashed a grin at the fellow spinning her about, her feet seamlessly following his lead. Wells felt a surge of envy overtake him, to see her so joyous, breathless almost in her twirling.

He could not tear his eyes away.

He remained rooted in agony, watching as she stepped into the next dance with another fashionably dressed gentleman who guided her to the center of the terrace. He could sense the *Ton's* collective curiosity peering at this scandalous young lady so recently, shockingly returned to the bosom of the Earl of Denbigh. He saw her through their eyes: dancing with abandon unlike the other prim misses who kept themselves in check. Charles Merrinan, by contrast, exuded raw sensuality as she swept across the dance floor, and Wells suspected every man there felt it. Gazes young and old shifted almost imperceptibly, unconsciously, to follow the graceful movements of his Fox.

He was gripped with an intense desire to spirit her into his parents' carriage right then and there, but he restrained himself. He would not impose his will upon her, though it killed him to remain a prisoner of propriety. It was her choice with whom she danced. He would not spoil her enjoyment. He dared not.

"You *will* ask her to dance, Roland, won't you?" The Duchess snuck up from behind to look down at the sea of bodies swirling to the strains of a quartet.

"She will decline the offer, Mother, I know it."

"You cannot know unless you try, dear," she nudged. "Go and ask her. I am sorry I suggested so devious a plan to you before."

Had Maman just apologized?

"I have given it more thought, since last we spoke, and you are right not to trick her into marriage."

Wells blinked; *wonders never ceased.* "Why, I do believe the earth just shifted beneath my feet!" he exclaimed.

"Do not grow cocky, boy." She smacked him lightly with her fan, lips twitching. "I merely suggest you may understand Miss Merrinan better than I, having known her more intimately."

"Thank you, *Maman.*" He kissed her cheek. "I shall ask her to dance after this earthquake passes, for who knows, perhaps the entire universe has now shifted in my favor."

He flashed her a smile before he headed downstairs to the dance, but not before he'd seen his mother touch her gloved hand to her face, as if to affirm his kiss were real.

❧

"Miss Merrinan," Lord Wellesley approached between numbers, "may I be so bold as to ask for this next dance?"

Charles was stunned to discover his lordship suddenly standing before her. She'd nervously searched the fête all afternoon for him.

He looked again different, dressed this time in a formal lawn suit, the expression on his face somehow softer, kinder. Who was this handsome stranger? Where was her demanding, imperious master?

"I should be delighted, sir." She ignored the fact that her dance card was full; a duke's heir trumped most.

Wellesley took her hand to lead her to the floor and assume his position across from her. He stared boldly into her eyes, and then, as the music began, circled her, their hands meeting lightly through their gloves, the advance and retreat a delight. Charles's heart skipped a beat when he grasped her waist to lift her in a turn and set her back down. She felt breathless and flustered, though she fast regained her feet.

They turned in crossed handhold next, eyes locked as firmly as their steps, her mind now blank from the sheer pleasure of him as time ceased in the sway of bodies, music, and motion. Weeks of tension dissolved into the flagstone under her feet, her soul suddenly light as air as she floated across the terrace. And when the music slowed, bringing her down to earth—to the moment's inevitable end—his hand at the small of her back burned hot through her dress, searing.

Charles tilted her head, her lips on his own sudden as a summer storm.

***

Wells felt her lips and was lost. He melded his mouth to hers without fear or frenzy. A union of souls.

They kissed in perfect, public silence.

The *Ton's* subsequent gasp barely registered until Charles broke from him and Wells heard titters ripple through the hushed crowd. He opened his eyes to a sea of faces staring with equal parts derision and delight. He was stunned by their interest—until his mind awoke with a curse.

It had come to this, after all.

Wells dragged Charles off the floor, his heart galloping in his chest. When he'd hauled her far enough into the Sedgewicks' shrubbery so as to be hidden from spectacle, he dropped her hand to run his fingers through his newly shorn locks.

"Listen to me, Charles, I did not . . ." He heaved a great sigh. "Regardless of what you think of me, woman, I did not intend to kiss you just now so publicly, damn it." He began to pace, noting how her brow knit with consternation.

"Which is not to say I regret it, mind you. I regret only where it happened, not *that* it happened, because I am so in love with you, Charles—so unbearably in love, Fox—I won't do the bloody honorable thing right now and insist you marry me to avoid a scandal. I'll not do what they all expect, because I know you don't give a whit about the *Ton*, about any of this." His hand swept the estate. "It is but one of many, many reasons why I love you so bloody much." He took another deep, shuddering breath. "I also know you'd rather die penniless in a hovel somewhere than have a man like me dictate what you can and cannot do, but Charles—"

She opened her mouth to speak, but his look beseeched her to let him finish.

"—when you left Cumberland, love, I swore that if I found you I would court you properly, which I have tried but clearly failed to do, failed to sway your opinion of me. And I've no one to blame but myself in this, I know. I cannot force your hand, nor will I entrap you now into marriage. But I want you as my wife, Fox. Every fiber of my being wants you. And if you won't marry me I must insist you remain my housekeeper and return with me to Cumberland. And failing that, I must insist you remain my friend, if not my lover, because somehow, Charles Merrinan, I need you in my life. I cannot imagine life without you."

He dropped to his knees before her, burying his face into the fabric of her skirt and twisting the material as he pressed his very being into her thighs, desperate to make her understand.

***

Charles remained immobile. How was this possible? How did this beastly lord she'd impossibly come to love now debase himself before her, nearly prostrate on the ground? She didn't like what she saw. This was not her haughty jailor. Had she tamed *him* somehow?

Her hand fell to his head, fisting his short curls as she forced him to look up at her. "Roland Rutherford Wellesley, get up, damn you, and stop acting a fool puppy when you are a grown pirate of a man."

His eyes blazed back with a fire that shot straight to her loins.

"I kissed *you*, just now, and we both know it, so the blame falls squarely on me. Nor am I opposed to marriage, sir. I have been opposed to the manner in which you have thrust it at me, presumptuous and demanding. But if you give me your word that you will treat your wife as your equal—that you will grant me my freedom at last—I may consider your suit more . . . seriously."

His eyes sparked with a look that made her legs wobble.

Yet still he did not rise but remained on his knees, hands merely bunching her skirts higher, till he reached her folded stocking tops, his hands slipping further to the bare flesh above, then higher still to the insides of her thighs, grabbing her there until she gasped, "Roland!"

"I take it you prefer pirates to puppies, love?" His eyes burned with as much hunger as her own.

"Lord Wells," Charles only half protested, "I must insist you unhand me."

"Miss Merrinan," he said with a grin, "I'm afraid I can no longer do that, as I intend to abscond with you instead." His hands at her thighs slid slowly further up to roundly cup her bottom, lifting her over his shoulder as he rose, her body suddenly draped across him like thieves' booty.

Charles let out a shriek from upside down across his back, his hands still up her skirts. "You can't seriously—!"

"Oh yes." He laughed. "I think I must." He removed one palm to soundly smack her bum, making her yelp again in protest.

"Roland, put me down!"

"Not now, Fox. Later I promise to lay you flat on your back, darling, but right now I believe the *Ton* demands a scandal and I, for one, have every intention of delivering."

And with that he strode back into the throng of onlookers, Charles slung over his shoulder like the spoils of the sea. He carried her through the crowd of awed and gaping faces to proudly announce, "Ladies and Gentlemen, I present to you the future Duchess of Allendale."

He turned her so her head, and not her derrière, might look out upon the throng, before he swung her around so that he faced the *Ton* himself. "Apologies for our swift exit, Ladies, Gentlemen."

Wells took off without a look back. The future Duke of Allendale had claimed a wife at last.

§

"I've had a license for days, you know," Wells told her the moment they were inside the ducal carriage, wheels rapidly trundling off. He figured his mother could suffer a ride back with the Enrights.

"Have you now?" She smirked.

"Yes, so anytime, really." He stared intently at her. "You've only to say the word, Miss Merrinan."

"And what word would that be, my lord?" Her foot reached out to slide up the inside of his calf, seated as she was across from him.

He groaned. "Merciful God in heaven . . ."

"You wish me to say *those* words, sir?"

"No, you minx, come here." He hauled her into his lap, his hands finding new ways to punish her.

"Lord Wells," she managed to get out between his rough handling and the shower of kisses he rained down on her, "where, pray tell, are you taking me, sir?"

"Home." He buried his face in her hair, its many pins long scattered to the carriage floor.

"Where is home, sir?" she breathed.

"Cumberland." He kissed her neck. He could not stop kissing her. "Only first you are coming to my parents' townhouse, to meet my father. You are not setting foot at the Enrights again." He immediately adjusted his tone. "Forgive me, Charles, but I cannot abide your mother's family."

"Neither can I." She laughed. "Only I rather like my new lady's maid, Roland. Might we steal her from them, do you think?"

"Why not?" He grinned. "I am stealing you, after all."

"*I* am choosing to flee with a pirate," she corrected.

"Charles, did I not just toss you over my shoulder before all of London's *Beau Monde*?" He raised his brow, planting another kiss to her lips until he felt her body give.

"You did, my lord." She softened deliciously in his arms.

Thank God she still liked his rough ways.

And then she shifted in her seat, surprising him more by straddling his lap, her hands falling to his waist to undo his fall as her eyes met his with the most brazen look yet.

He inhaled with a hiss as she mounted him in one swift move.

"I've missed you terribly, you scoundrel," she whispered hot in his ear. Her body fit perfectly over his own. "And I hereby intend, for once and for all, to pay off my fine for thieving. So don't you dare deny me full acquittal after this, *Your Grace*."

"As if I could, Fox." He laughed beneath her. "As if I—" And sucking in his breath, he could not.

CHAPTER FORTY-SEVEN

"Charles Merrinan, by God." The Duke of Allendale held out a trembling hand to her from his sickbed. "If you aren't the spitting image of your mother." He beamed.

"Your Grace." Charles curtsied deep as she instinctively kissed the Duke's ring. He kept hold of her hand.

"Roland, I wish a word with her alone." He waved his son off with his other free hand as Wells met Charles's eye and winked before he exited.

"Sit, my dear," the Duke commanded.

Charles sat on the edge of the bed, the old man now stroking her hand almost familiarly. She felt an odd rush of tenderness towards him, as if she sat beside her own father.

"You love him then," he stated.

"I do, Your Grace."

"But can you live with him, miss?" He watched her keenly.

"That remains to be seen, Your Grace."

Which caused him to laugh, causing a fresh fit of coughing as Charles hastened to assist. He brushed her attempts aside.

"No, leave be. I am old is all." He refused the glass of water she offered from his bedside. "I have managed to live with Roland's mother all these years, my dear, by giving as good as I got; you'll learn to do the same, I'm sure."

"Your Grace is kind to speak to me so candidly," Charles began.

His voice strained with effort. "You must give my regards to your father when you return to Cumberland, Miss Merrinan, for he was ever a friend to me, and the very best of friends to my brother. Roland tells me you carry Carlton's timepiece with you now. I could not be more pleased, dear." He squeezed her hand.

Charles blushed. "I promise to keep it safe, Your Grace. It is an honor to—"

"The greater honor is that you've agreed to marry my son," he told her firmly. "He could not have done better, Miss Merrinan."

The Duke was beginning to fade; she could tell her visit taxed him.

"Be happy at the Abbey, be good to one another, and Charles . . ." He was almost whispering now, a faint grin about his lips. "He loves you too. I can tell."

"I know, Your Grace." Charles smiled as she let her lips, feather-light, brush the Duke's forehead ere she tiptoed out.

"And what, pray, did he tell you, Fox? That I am an insufferable toad of a son you should never have agreed to marry?"

Charles playfully elbowed her betrothed, seated as she was beside him in the ducal carriage. Cuthbert looked a bit green in the face across from them on the seat. Apparently, he'd arrived just yesterday on the evening coach, exhausted and disheveled from nearly four days locked in a swaying carriage.

All things considered, he'd scrubbed up well.

"Your father, the Duke," she calmly answered Wells, "was the epitome of kindness and grace, my lord. He is *quite* unlike you." Her lips twitched before he pinched her through her dress, making her startle. He kept his arm snaked about her waist.

"Roland," the Duchess disparaged, looking the very picture of a lady en route to a wedding, "I would prefer you refrain from manhandling your bride until *after* the ceremony is complete." She arched her brow at them both, making Charles blush and Wells simply squeeze her tighter.

He leaned in to whisper, "She has no idea what I intend to do to you after the ceremony, love," which made Charles blush only more.

The Duchess of Allendale turned her gaze to the window, an audible sigh escaping the lady's lips, while Cuthbert kept his eyes shut tight against the world.

໒໐

And then it was done. Lord Roland Rutherford Wellesley carried Lady Charles Adelaide Wellesley over the threshold of his parents' London townhouse and straight up to his room, where he locked the door behind them. It had been a simple church ceremony without guests, and he'd eschewed his mother's invitation to throw them a celebratory dinner after, or even a wedding luncheon the following day. In fact, he'd informed her he was done courting London society and hoped the gossipmongers spun at least six months' worth of lurid tales in all the papers regarding his scandalous kiss, dramatic exit, and hasty, post-fête marriage.

His mother had merely scowled her disapproval, though it was clear to Wells she cared less for society's rumors and more for seeing Lady Wellesley provide the Dukedom with an heir. She grudgingly promised not to disturb the newlyweds for the rest of the evening, or the coming days for that matter, which had only thrilled Wells more. He wanted his Fox all to himself; he'd waited bloody long enough.

"Roland . . ."

"Yes, love?" Wells mumbled from her bosom, burying his face there and inhaling her scent as one hand played loosely at her delectable hip, caressing.

"Despite my behavior these past weeks I admit I missed you terribly."

"You mean you weren't the least bit tempted to run off with Redstocking?" he teased, his voice still muffled at her breast.

"How the devil did you . . . ?" She pushed him away even as he grabbed her to him.

"He's a friend, Fox. A newly minted Baron, the Baron Milton. I sent him to spy on you; Li told me your name for him."

"You did *what*?"

"Shh." He kissed her silent. "I'd have murdered him if he'd taken advantage of you, love, and he owed me a favor, see, so you were never in any real danger while at Madame LeBrecht's."

"Well it certainly didn't feel that way!"

"I know, darling, and I am sorry." He could not seem to use enough endearments with her now. "I had to know if you loved me or if you merely meant to use some other man to—"

"Roland." She pulled away from him, frowning.

Ripe orbs, he thought, gazing at her breasts, *twin fruits beneath a waterfall of strawberry silk tresses.*

"How could you ever think I'd be another man's mistress?" She looked appalled.

He tenderly traced her cheek. "Love, how could you ever think I desired *Mowry's dowry*? Moreover, how could any man not laugh at a name like hers?" He chuckled over the assonance of those two words paired, seeing mirth return to Charles's eyes.

It made him fall for her all over again.

"You alone, sweet chicken thief, satisfy my every desire for a wife, for you shall keep me on my toes and challenge my convictions. Demand I be a better man, not to mention exhaust me utterly in bed." He grinned at her softening expression, his hands again roving, unable to keep from touching her.

"Oh I have not begun to exhaust you, Lord Wells." She suddenly rolled atop him, pinning him beneath her to nip at his neck. "And I intend to punish you for wrongs committed." She lapped his collarbone with her tongue. "I demand restitution in seed now, sir. Your seed." She sank her teeth into his flesh. "So you'd best deliver, *Your Grace*, and service well my womb."

And for once, Wellesley dared not argue with his Fox but did exactly as he was told.

When Charles awoke the next morning in her husband's capable, strong arms, she suspected he'd been watching her sleep, for his face bore a strange expression, one she'd not seen before.

"Good morning, Lady Wellesley." He kissed the tip of her nose.

She smiled. "Good morning, my lord."

"There will be no more *my lord*, Charles." He pulled her closer.

"That might prove difficult, sir."

"There'll be no more *sir*, either, woman."

She laughed. "I can't possibly go about the Abbey calling you *Roland* before the staff."

"You do realize as my wife you will no longer be my housekeeper." He crooked his brow. "You will oversee the house, of course, but no more scrubbing and polishing and—"

"Roland," she admonished, "you cannot forbid me to work on the Abbey if you continue to toil at the north wall. What's more"—she placed a finger to his lips—"you cannot order me about anymore, so I may do as I wish, and if I wish to continue cleaning rooms alongside Ruby then I will continue to—"

He covered her body, kissing her silent, then kissing her silly, until she was gasping for air. "And you cannot . . . Roland, you cannot—"

"What love?" His hand teased dangerously. "Tell me what exactly I cannot do to you now that you are my wife and I am legally allowed to do anything I wish to you, darling. You do realize I may do anything at all to you, don't you?" And the look in his eyes was so devilishly wanton, she blushed to her roots.

"Just what do you intend to do to me, *sir*?" Charles whispered, aroused and afraid.

"All sorts of deliciously wicked, despicable things, woman. Things I promise you will like almost as much as I will. Almost, mind you." His hand slipped to her core, causing her to gasp with delight.

"But before we begin a new day of marital wickedness, I have something for you, Lady Wellesley." And just as quickly he leapt from the bed to rifle through the pockets of his waistcoat, which he plucked from the floor, their clothes long scattered about the room.

Charles sucked in her breath. "Roland, I have nothing for you, and I know it is customary for bride and groom to exchange—"

He returned to bed to hush her with his lips. "Nonsense, Fox, *you* are all the gift I need."

"As I need only you, too, love." She stopped to see a bright chain draped over his palm, dangling. "My lord, you should not have—"

"I have every right to give my wife a gift." His face grew stern. "And I will brook no argument otherwise, young lady."

"Back to ordering me about, are you?" She tsked. "I see marriage may prove difficult for Your Grace to learn you cannot—"

"For God's sake, Charles, take the bloody gift and thank me." He glowered at her.

So she did, laughing at his expression until she looked down, overcome with emotion. "Roland . . ." Charles struggled to form words.

***

"Do you like it?" Wells asked, concerned. "It is not meant to offend, Charles, it is meant to remind us both, perhaps, of how we began. To remind me, at least, to be a better man, a better husband to you."

A single tear rolled down her cheek, alarming him only more.

"Christ, love, I did not mean to—"

"Roland, it is perfect." She kissed him through her tears. "I am allowed to cry for joy, am I not?"

Wells marveled at her again as he watched his wife gaze upon the ivory pendant in her palm, a cameo finely wrought in the profile of a rooster. It was not so small as to be lost, nor so large as to be garish. She bade him fix it about her neck, which he did, letting it nestle between her breasts, the gold-encrusted rim reflecting the red-gold of her hair.

"You did not steal my chickens, Fox," he told her softly, "you stole my very soul."

"I believe I stole your cock, sir." She flashed him a devilish grin. "Is that why you have given me a rooster for a charm?"

He laughed. "I did think a cock, perhaps, more apt to hang about your neck."

"No string of pearls then, no gems, just a cock. I see." Her eyes glittered anew as she began to inch her way down his chest with kisses, the cameo swinging loose between her breasts. "I must give proper thanks for so generous a gift, my lord." Her mouth landed on his sex.

"Fox . . ." he groaned.

"I insist, love." She spoke between licks.

"*Woman!*"

"Husband." Her lips teased further. "I do so love the gift."

But those were all the words she uttered, her tongue otherwise engaged as Wells lay back in rapturous delight. He'd snared his Fox at last.

CHAPTER FORTY-EIGHT

The journey back to Cumberland took a full week now that Lord Wells and his lady wife did little to rush their return. The pair spent lazy nights in inns along the way and stopped frequently to stretch their legs or picnic during the day.

Wandering into woods for clandestine tête-à-têtes also slowed their travel, though there was one flight from carriage that Wells would gladly have avoided: The day he'd confessed to reading Charles's correspondence with her sister.

She'd stopped the driver in a rage, then taken off into the forest.

He'd known he must come clean, though it had taken him a good hour to convince his wife to return back to Cumberland with him rather than run straight back to London. He should have told her before they'd married and yet . . . It no longer mattered why he hadn't. What mattered was that she forgave him—with the promise she'd bludgeon him in his sleep should he ever knowingly deceive her again.

In truth, Wells had no desire to keep more secrets from Charles. The entire trip back he found himself revealing more to her than she likely wished to know about her husband. A dam had broken inside him, allowing feelings to tumble out alongside the telling of all his stories. Somehow, after confessing to reading her letters, it felt safe to tell her everything.

Liberating.

Cuthbert they'd left behind in London to await Eleanor's trousseau, for the Enrights had agreed to outfit their other granddaughter for her wedding after no small degree of arm-twisting from Wells's mother. He had also tasked his steward with stealing a certain lady's maid from Charles's grandparents. Given his father's health, Wells knew Charles would be Duchess sooner than later, and the attendant duties—not to mention requisite apparel—would be more than a maid like Ruby was equipped to handle.

When the happy couple did, at last, arrive at Almsdale Abbey, Wells carried Charles over yet another threshold before demanding his staff gather in celebration. Only his wife hushed him imperiously, saying said celebration could wait until the morrow. She would not tax *her* staff so unexpectedly and would need first assess how everything had gone in their absence. Ought her new husband not do the same?

Fergus laughed outright to hear their exchange, and Jenkins merely nodded her approval, leaving Wells to ponder whom his servants would now obey: their future Duke, or the future Duchess of Allendale?

He'd worry about that another day.

§.

"Oh milady, I beg you *please* tell us every bit of how it were his lordship found you in London! And what kind of weddin' you had, and what you wore and . . ."

Ruby was positively breathless with excitement, talking

nonstop at Charles while the other girls and Jenkins all sat about the large kitchen table, staring at the new Lady Wellesley in rapt attention.

Charles couldn't help but grin back. "Why, I wouldn't know where to start, Ruby. Only I must insist you call me Charles and not milady when it's just us maids, chatting over a cup of scordy."

But Jenkins wouldn't have it. "Lady Wellesley," she chided, "I'll tolerate no sech familiarity in *my* kitchen, ma'am. This may not be London, but we've class enough in Cumberland t' know when t'—"

"Mrs. Jenkins, please." Charles met her gaze. "We'll put on a good show when visitors come, of course, but when we are alone here I . . ." She took a breath. "If Lord Wellesley is allowed to roll up his shirtsleeves and work alongside Mr. Adams's men, then I can help the household, working alongside my marras."

A roomful of eyes peered at her in surprise.

"I beg you." She grew desperate. "I never, ever expected to marry his lordship, so to imagine I must now become some wholly different person, why I—"

"Well now, I s'pose we might, initially at least, grant you *some* leeway, milady." Jenkins finally relented, pursing her lips. "Least until you hire more housemaids. 'Cause t' be frank, Lady Wellesley, without your ladyship t' scrub and polish alongside t' rest of us, I don't know how we'll be ready for another visit from t' Duchess. The moment her grace's first grandbabby's born, she'll show up demandin' another audience, eh?" She gave Charles a saucy wink.

Charles blushed as Ruby squeezed her hand. "See now, milady, we'll not lob you out just yet, only now tell us, *please*, of oa' your grand adventures with his lordship."

Charles related her story in full, leaving certain details out, of course, but entertaining them as best she could. Surrounded by these warm Cumberland women, sipping scordy while regaling them with her London stories, she felt at last like she'd come home. *Gang yam.*

Wellesley's welcome was of a very different nature.

"Found 'er where, Capt'n? At Li's?"

"Which one o' madam's houses?" piped another.

"Finally wooed 'er, didya?"

"'Tisn't in the man t' woo a woman proper," elbowed in the fellow beside him.

"Still feisty on 'er weddin' night, was she?" came another's sly retort. "'Bout time y' made an honest woman o' that lass!"

Wells scowled at the unruly lot, shaking his head at their lurid chaff and refusing to divulge the particulars of anything. "Listen, louts," he ordered. "A man does not discuss a wife the way he might discuss a mistress, so you can all sod off." He grumbled to himself, "Asking questions to which I'll give no goddamn answers."

Their disappointment was palpable.

He raised his hand as if on deck. "However, winter is past us, men, and I promised you positions only till spring winds beckoned. If you're of mind to return to port I'll arrange for transport back to London." He paused, falling serious. "Although if you wish to stay on here in Cumberland, at the Abbey, I could use the help." He took a breath. "And I'd be honored if you did."

The men fell silent, looking one to another as if they'd already discussed the matter amongst themselves.

"Remain with you, in bloody Croakumshire?" Pinky hollered from the back.

Fergus stepped forward. "Yer Grace, we'll all stay on, as one."

"All of you?" Wells was taken aback. "I figured some might, but—"

"We're a crew, sir," Fergus told him plain. "Loyal t' our Capt'n, so if you'll have us, you'll have t' keep us—to a man."

Wells grinned, clapping Fergus on the back. "Damn right you're a crew. Finest bloody crew to ever sail the oceans, lads." His grin broadened. "I am humbled you'd choose to stay with me on land and promise you each a respectable position in this house, although it might"—he turned a sharp look on some—"require a change in grooming and uniforms, eventually," he amended. He could hear the start of mutterings and knew they'd balk at this. "But first, crew, we've a celebration to plan in honor of my marriage, yes?"

To which shouts of *Here, Here!* were heard, amidst less exemplary exclamations.

"We'll feast and drink and dance and—"

"Yer Grace," Fergus interrupted, "the lads an' I've been discussin' certain work conditions in yer absence, Capt'n, an' we think it's time y' hired more staff, if y' ken me drift."

Wells arched his brow. "Would you be referring to more *female* staff, Fergus?"

"I would, sir."

"Then I'm afraid you must take the matter up with Lady Wellesley, good sir, because I am no longer in charge of household decisions."

Disjointed groans filtered through their crowd.

"But she'll hire only ugly ones!" shouted one man.

"That woman'll thwart us at every turn," claimed another.

"She keeps 'er girls so penned in tight they'll not even—!"

"Now you yobs listen good." Wells fixed them with a stare. "Charles Merrinan gave you Mistress Mamie, did she not? So don't you dare insult my wife by saying she . . ." Only he thought better and instead deepened his scowl. "I've no doubt

Lady Wellesley will hire the goddamn prettiest girls in Cumberland just to torture you brutes further."

His crew groaned to imagine such a fate: forever tempted yet never allowed to touch.

"You play your cards right, boys, staying on, and you may just meet and court a proper village lass one day, settle down and marry even."

"Marry?" someone said. "Only fools marry."

"Damn right." Wells laughed. "Lucky fools at that."

Although he wished for nothing more than to spend more time alone with his lovely new wife, that same afternoon Wells accompanied Lady Wellesley to her father's house, to deliver Charles to her sister, as promised.

Eleanor greeted them at the door by throwing her arms about her sister in a hug that would not end, until Wells had to interrupt them, coughing a little to indicate he should like to be welcomed also.

Eleanor peered sharply at him over Charles's shoulder, but then motioned him inside, where he greeted Benedict Merrinan with the utmost respect.

"The Duke of Allendale sends his regards, Sir Benedict, and wishes you well, sir."

The fellow's watery eyes looked up. "Make an honest woman of my daughter, did you?" he demanded.

"Yes, sir," Wells answered. "She is now Lady Wellesley, sir, and will one day be Duchess of Allendale."

"Good, good." Merrinan nodded. "And your father, boy? Still standing, I presume?"

"Barely, sir," Wells reported. "I fear he lies abed most days."

"Damn shame, damn shame," Merrinan muttered. "Terrible to grow old, I tell you. God-awful business."

"My mother sends her regards as well, Sir Benedict."

"Fine woman, yes. Fierce, but very fine. Always did like your mother, boy. Gumption . . ." he trailed off.

Charles put her hand on her father's arm. "Papa, would you like to lie down a bit and rest?"

"That you, Addy? Where is Charles? She run off again? Tell her his grace is here to visit. He's brought his boy, let them play."

"I will, Papa." She helped him rise and gently guided him towards his bed.

Eleanor fixed her gaze on Wells. "I should like a word alone with you, my lord."

Wells knew he was in for it but gave her his arm anyway. "Shall we take a stroll about your garden, miss?"

She accepted his offer, but once outside, she tightened her grip and her words. "My lord, as your sister now, I am at liberty to speak freely, am I not?"

"Eleanor, I believe you are at liberty to call me Roland, and I recall you did not hesitate even before I married your sister to speak freely to me."

She pursed her lips. "Be that as it may, *Roland*"—she tried on the name—"not only are you now my brother, but John too, by marriage, will soon be brother to you also."

Wells was pleased by the thought. "Why, so he shall, Eleanor. It seems I will be doubly blessed."

"And doubly cursed, sir." Her eyes locked on his. "For if you ever again mistreat my sister in so shameless and baseless a manner as you did before, so help me God both John and I will—"

He stilled his steps to take both her hands in his. "Eleanor, I believe this conversation were better had with Charles, for *I* am a reformed man and shall endeavor the rest of my days to please my wife. She, on the other hand, shall likely punish me for the rest of our married life." He did his damnedest to look contrite. "So I would beg you remind your sister not to abuse her husband too terribly in future, though he may rightly deserve it."

Eleanor took one look at his face and threw her head back in merry laughter. She slipped her arm in his, reminding him very much of his wife in that moment. "I look forward to deepening our acquaintance, brother, for I've a feeling we shall both be turning to one another in future when it comes to Charles."

$\clubsuit$

"I'm scared, Fox," Wells quietly told her as they lay spent upon the shell room's floor, having snuck away from the evening's revelry—their own wedding celebration no less. They'd fled the festivities just as they'd fled them at Christmas, finding refuge here amongst the sea and stars.

She pursed her lips. "Dread Pirate Wells, what in heavens has you scared? You, who are without doubt the most brash, cocksure, vainglorious, conceited—"

"You, Charles," he told her truthfully. "I am scared you will regret marrying me now and run off again, taking a new lover and leaving me here to—"

"What nonsense is this?" She leaned up on one elbow to stare him down, looking every bit a haughty, naked duchess.

"You *can* be rather frightening." He was unwilling to meet her eyes.

"Roland, look at me."

He did, grudgingly.

"You are not only foolish to think such things, you are a coward even to speak them." He tried interrupting but she would not let him. "No, it is true—and exactly what I feared would happen." She let out a snort. "Now that you have gotten what you wished, you no longer want it." Her mouth hardened into a line. "Husband, have you tired of me already?"

He was pained to think she thought so little of him so soon. "No, you misunderstand entirely, Charles. I am in earnest, for I fear that despite marriage now I still don't . . . That is, I won't ever *have* you in the truest sense." He met her eyes at last.

She stared at him a moment in shock. "You wish to own me."

"God no!" he cried. "As if I ever could, woman. As if I'd even want to break the very spirit that endears you to me so."

"Then I do not understand you, sir, that you should question so utterly the vows we spoke in marriage. Do they mean so little to you?" She seemed suddenly rather bitter, and he was at once desperate to fix matters.

"No, Fox. Only my own father kept mistresses, my own mother took men to her bed, and they, like us, spoke the very same vows before God."

"Yet they are not us, Roland, and we are not them. My parents took no other lovers; you see how my father suffered the loss of his wife. So do not tell me love is fickle. Do not tell me vows are made in jest, for I meant every word I spoke the day we wed. Every word."

"You did not mean the vow of obedience to your husband, Charles," he wagered.

She sniffed, her lips at last softening. "Well, that is a ridiculous vow no woman ever spoke in earnest."

Hope alit in his breast.

"And I certainly don't expect you to be like my father, mad from grief the day I die. Not when I know you'll quickly find another to warm your bed."

"Well I should hope I don't go mad." He huffed. "I intend to poison myself upon your death, like Romeo beside Juliet."

She poked him in his middle, hard enough that he grabbed her wrists.

"You think I jest, woman?" Wells stared fiercely into her eyes. "I do not, Charles." He grew grave. "Do not even speak to me of death, love. I could not bear it. I cannot bear the thought of losing you. *That* is what I fear. I'll not deny I've not enjoyed the chase, have not relished taming you these many months past, but life is fickle, Fox, its tempest never fair, so I will never have you in the purest sense of having."

"Roland Rutherford Wellesley." She raised her chin, possessed of some secret, feminine knowledge, he thought. "You will kiss me now and cease such nonsense, here in the ocean of this room. You will make love to me again and forget all your fears and worries, all that consumes you by day. Each night you will come to me so that together we may make things right, even though we shall argue and disappoint and yet again fight. For so long as love be true, husband, all other fears shall be put to bed, to rest. I promise you this."

And in that instant he believed her, wholly and completely. Wells took her lips in a kiss leagues deep, knowing in his soul his Fox would anchor him forever, even when everything would inevitably go wrong again.

Perhaps that was *having* after all—having faith in love to steer life right.

The End

EPILOGUE

LONDON, 1839, FOUR YEARS LATER

(Teaser to *The Bastard in her Boudoir*,
book two in *The Dubious Mates* series)

Li poured Wellesley's tea in characteristic fluid motion, the hot green liquid arcing through the air. He watched, hypnotized. No matter how often he'd seen her perform this ceremony in the backroom of *LeBrecht's* or in the hold of his ship, he remained entranced. Flashbacks from his past flooded his mind as he stared at her slender wrist.

"Remind me again why you have interrupted my day, Wells?" Li did not look up from pouring. She was business-woman first, friend and erstwhile lover second.

He returned to the present, to the reason he'd come. "Banks wants to run *The Painted Lady* to the Americas."

She appeared not to register his words.

"He also wants to rename her."

Li finished pouring and bowed deeply before the tea. Wells

knew he'd have to wait a good minute for her response while she finished, so he filled that minute with more talk.

"I don't like either idea."

She remained prostrate.

"Li . . ." He was impatient.

"Do you not have a child at home and a wife soon expecting another, Your Grace?" Her eyes finally met his.

Wells harrumphed. "How does that have anything to do with Banks?"

"Precisely." Li's lips made a moue as she shifted her position and raised the dish to sip delicately, wisps of steam licking her perfect, oval face. She carefully placed the bowl back upon the low table. "You gave Banks your ship, Wells. You are now the Duke of Allendale, no longer *The Painted Lady's* captain. Your Duchess has given you a strapping male heir and is about to birth you another. Why are you even here?"

He felt like he did every time he dealt with Li: wishing to wring her elegant neck.

"I am in London on account of Charles's family and, as you well know, for Milton's wedding. My wife's cousin will be presented at court in a matter of days and we must attend the girl's ensuing coming out ball. Otherwise I'd not even—"

"No, Wellesley, why are you *here*, in my shop." She stared him down. Li could be annoyingly prescient.

He swallowed. "Banks is making a mistake, so I'd hoped you might . . ."

Her expression turned. "You hoped *I* might talk sense into him?" She arched one painted eyebrow so high it looked ready to topple.

"Yes."

Li's lips formed a line. "It does not cease to amaze me, Wells, how both you and Jasper, our new Baron Milton, show up in my shop at such similar times. He was just here himself, demanding I outfit his betrothed while dropping none too subtle hints about Banks." She exhaled a slow sigh. "And as I am beholden to both you ingrates"—she threw him a look rife with meaning—"I will speak with Banks."

His shoulders sagged in relief.

"However, I guarantee you nothing, Wells. He is his own man, captain of his own ship. Your *former* ship. He will make his own mistakes, just as you made yours."

She was right, of course. Li was frequently right. He simply wanted to spare Banks more trouble. Hell, he wanted to spare the man his life if he was going to risk trading goods where slavery was still legal.

"Thank you, Li." He met her gaze. "I know I can't change his path, but a word from you, having yourself . . ." He didn't need to finish. She understood what he meant.

Li raised the bowl again in fluid motion to her lips. Wells knew he had a duchy to run, a son to raise, and a hot-headed, pregnant wife awaiting his return. He was a very lucky man. Yet the past would never leave him. He would always worry about his friends—Milton and Banks—as well as Li. Cuthbert he could keep close. As Allendale's official new squire, John, at least, was going nowhere. Nor would Eleanor let him, not with Cuthbert a father now himself. Even his former crew remained under his close watch at the Abbey, up to no good, as always. But here in London . . . This city did things to a man.

He knew what it had done to Milton.

Wells picked up his bowl and downed the tea, earning a glare from Li. He was supposed to drink slowly, to savor the brew, stare at its residue.

Instead, he was suddenly eager to return home to Charles.

"Leaving so soon, Your Grace?" Li quirked her lips.

"Duty calls, *Madame*." He flashed her a rogue's grin, only no blush suffused her flawless face. His charms had long ceased to work on Li—the attempt sheer reflex anymore.

"Give my regards to *Charlotte*, Wells." She smirked. "Bring her with you, next time you call. We have much to catch up on again."

❧

Charles was playing with her husband's thick locks upon her lap, sprawled as he was across the large chaise in his mother's London townhouse. He had his head and hand pressed to her belly to feel the babe therein kick. He liked to drape himself across her lap this way, like he had the first time she'd been with child.

"Roland, was Lord Redstocking very angry that his wife came to visit me today?"

The poor girl had arrived in a sorry state that afternoon, and this barely a week since being married. Charles was concerned for the lady, yet also eager to return to Cumberland. She did not want to give birth in this city. She wanted her dependable Cumberland marras by her side—and her capable midwife.

"Milton, you mean?" Her husband lazily rubbed circles atop her midriff.

"Of course, Milton, you oaf." She lightly smacked his head. It was their running jest, to refer to Baron Milton as 'Redstocking.' It was also Charles's way of reminding her husband of less-than-stellar past behaviors.

Poor Milton, to be the butt of their jokes.

"So?" she pressed. "Was Redstocking angry? It is common enough for a married woman to make social calls unaccompanied. Was it because she drove his phaeton here by herself?"

"Hell if I know, Charles." Wells shifted nearer to her swollen belly. "Whatever's between Milton and his new wife is their business, not ours." He pressed his lips to her middle.

She pulled his hair to gain his attention.

"*Ow*, woman! What the devil was that for?"

"I happen to like Redstocking's Baroness, Roland. I do not wish to see her hurt."

"Charles, Milton would never hurt his wife. I can assure you he'd not—"

"Not physically hurt, you nimwit," she chastised. "Emotionally hurt. The girl knows very little of him but already must adhere to what sounds like an incredibly strict litany of rules he's imposed. It cannot be easy for her, marrying a near stranger who—"

"Nimwit, eh?" His hand suddenly slid under her skirts and directly up her leg.

"*Nimwit,*" she repeated, a little breathless.

"And would Her Grace like her nimwit to be of service to her?" He dropped from chaise to floor, beginning to bunch up her dress.

"My nimwit may"—her breaths increased—"consider it, yes." Charles lay back and opened her legs to her husband. The man had a way with his tongue which was sinfully wicked.

The Duke now knelt before her, having pushed her skirts to her waist and braced his hands at her thighs. Ever so lightly, his breath tickled her sex.

"Nimwits have their uses, do they not, Duchess?" His voice sounded muffled coming from under her dress.

Charles let her hand drop once more to his head, to urge him on. "Why yes, husband," she breathed, "they most certainly do."

AFTERWORD

HISTORICAL NOTES

The Duke of Allendale is a fictional title, as is Almsdale Abbey. An actual Duke of Cumberland existed in 1835 when this story takes place, but the peer who held that title became the King of Hanover, Germany in 1837. In fact, the region known as Cumberland in the 1830s was abolished in 1974 and is today called Cumbria. However, when Sir Benedict Merrinan refers to campaigns he fought alongside Lord Wellesley's father and uncle, those were real battles waged during Britain's war with Napoleon in the early 1800s.

Squire was originally a medieval term for a knight's apprentice, later for a village leader, and later still applied to landed gentry. Squires were often related to peers and lived as gentlemen in the village manor house. They sometimes performed important local duties like Justice of the Peace or selecting the parish rector. In this story I use the term to underscore how Charles's father had been a person of significance in his community before his health deteriorated. His bravery in battle would have earned him the knighthood, though it's a stretch for John Cuthbert to earn this title. Cuthbert's bravery at sea may be revealed in future books.

As to culinary dishes, *rum nicky* is a traditional Cumberland short crust pastry tart from the late 18th century containing dates, ginger, rum, and brown sugar. The ingredients reflect the region's trading roots; it was a hub for importing goods from England's Caribbean colonies. The *wassail bowl* was prepared from spiced and sweetened mulled wine or brandy and garnished with apples. Coffee was indeed drunk in Regency England and coffee houses were all the rage for a time. Discussions of politics, philosophy, and the natural sciences often took place in these establishments. By 1853 England's coffee trend had reversed as plantations in India churned out ever more tea.

Rousseau, Locke, and Hume were philosophers from the 1700s, contemporaries of Voltaire who espoused ideas of equality. When Wells cobs Charles for spitting in his face, he's inflicting a form of (undemocratic!) punishment used by seamen in the 1800s which consisted of blows to the buttocks using a strap or wood paddle called a cob or cobbing-board. When Charles recalls her mother's admonishment that 'pride goes before a fall,' she is referencing proverb 16:18 from the Bible: "Pride goeth before destruction, and a haughty spirit before a fall." In fact, the book's three acts each reflect one of the seven deadly sins in Roman Catholic tautology: Pride, Greed, Lust, Envy, Gluttony, Wrath, Sloth. I am pretty certain each sin makes an appearance in this novel, except perhaps sloth. Pride perhaps most frequently of all.

Cuthbert calls Charles *gel* instead of girl in a rather tongue and cheek way, having likely picked up the term from Wellesley. It's actually mid-1800s British upper class slang, *gel* being simply girl with an affected pronunciation. The OED defines *gel* as "an upper-class or aristocratic young Englishwoman," and Cuthbert, as we know, senses Charles is a lady long before Wells gets a clue.

I did some research into the cost of bread for when Charles negotiates what she'll earn for each loaf she bakes his lordship.

The highest price according to a July 1835 edition of *The Sun* newspaper was listed as costing 7d (or 7 pence) for a 4 lb loaf. I adjusted this to 5d since the story takes place in Cumberland rather than London. Charles correctly does the math when Wells asks her to multiply this by the 3 loaves she baked, arriving at 15 pence total. Since a shilling was worth 12 pence, she gives her answer as 1 shilling and 3 penny. To put this into perspective, one pound was worth 20 shillings and her fine for thieving was 30 pounds. She'd have to earn 600 shillings to pay off the fine, or bake close to 600 loaves of bread.

The dialects used by characters in this story are a bit of a mash up consisting of Cockney (Wellesley's crew from London) and Cumbrian (Charles's townsfolk), though some (like Fergus) speak with a more Scottish flavor. *Croakumshire* was Cockney slang for Northumberland, a region neighboring Cumberland. The term makes fun of the 'croaking' pronunciation of the people of this region, said to be born with a 'burr in their throats' (From Francis Grose's 1811 *Dictionary of The Vulgar Tongue*). *Twist and twirl* is Cockney rhyming slang for girl, *trouble and strife* for wife, while *yob* is reverse Cockney spelling for boy. See the glossary that follows for more Cumbrian words and Miss Li's French.

If you enjoyed Charles and Roland's story, I hope you'll consider reviewing the novel on Amazon and goodreads—reader feedback means the world. Stay abreast of future releases by signing up for my newsletter or following me on social media.

Yours in romance both steamy and polite,

~Constance
constanceremillard@gmail.com
https://remillardromance.com

A GLOSSARY

OF FOREIGN WORDS AND PHRASES

French *(in the order it appears in the novel)*

- *par Dieu* by God
- *Enchantée, mademoiselle, c'est sûr! Alors, voulez-vous entrer, s'il vous plaît?* Charmed, I am sure, miss. So, won't you please come in?
- *Je parle bien français et suis parfaitement capable de servir vos clients.* I speak French well and am perfectly suited to serving your clients.
- *Et les messieurs?* And the gentlemen?
- *Asseyez-vous!* Sit!
- *Bien, bien parfait.* Good, excellent.

Cumbrian *(in alphabetical order)*
Note: the is often shortened to t' and all shortened to oa'. Filler words like and eh *are often added at the ends of phrases. In some regions speakers drop the 'h' at the start of words making 'he' sound like 'ee' but in other regions they don't. I left the 'h' to make the text easier to read. For more old Cumbrian expressions I recommend:* A Glossary of the Words and Phrases of Cumberland *by William Dickinson.*

- **babby** baby
- to **bag yourself** to be frightened (I was baggin' myself)
- **bewer** slang for a common woman
- **cleppets** or clemmies mean testicles (or stones=clemmies)
- **decc** a look (take a decc at that)
- **donnat** idiot or fool, pronounced 'donnert'
- to **doss** is to sleep, laze about, do nothing; **dosser** (person who dosses)
- **flaiten** frightened
- **fratch** argument or squabble
- **gadgies** men or blokes
- **gan** going; 'gan yam' means going home (gang=went/gone)
- **hoor** whore (pronounced hoo-a)
- **sporney** lucky
- **laal** little
- **ledgeful** embarrassing or unfashionable
- to **maff matters** to make a mess/mess things up
- **marra** friend or mate
- **nappa** head
- **nowt** nothing, like naught
- **oal** old
- **oa'** all
- **owwer** over
- **razzie** a fit of anger, 'to have a razzie'
- **scordy and scran** tea and food
- **smart** (also means a pretty, good-looking woman)
- **sommit** something
- **styan** stone
- **tapped** crazy or mad
- **whisht** shush, meaning be quiet or 'shut up'
- **yam** home

THE WORDS OF OALD CUMMERLAN'.

Ya neet aa was takkan a rist an' a smeukk,
An' snoozlan an' beekan my shins at t' grate neukk,
When aa thowt aa wad knock up a bit ov a beukk
 Aboot t' words 'at we use in oald Cummerlan'.

Aa boddert my brains thinkan some o' them ower,
An' than set to wark an' wreatt doon three or fower
O' t' kaymtest an' t' creuktest, like "garrak" an' "dyke stower,"
 Sek like as we use in oald Cummerlan.'

It turnt oot three-cornert, cantankeras wark,
An' keep't yan at thinkan fray dayleet till dark;
An' at times a queer word would lowp up wid a yark,
 'At was reet ebm doon like oald Cummerlan'.

John Dixon, o' Whitt'en, poo't oot ov his kist,
Ov words 'at he thowt to hev prentit, a list;
An' rayder ner enny reet word sud be mist
 Yan wad ratch ivry neukk ov oald Cummerlan'.

Than Deavvy fray Steappleton hitcht in a lock,
An' Jwony ov Ruffom gev some to my stock;
Than, fray Cassel Graystick a list com, fray Jock;
 They o' eekt a share for oald Cummerlan'.

Friend Rannelson offert his beukks, an' o' t' rest
(O man! bit he's full ov oald stories—the best);
Aa teukk am at word, an' aa harry't his nest
 Ov oald-farrant words ov oald Cummerlan'.

Than naybers an' friends browt words in sa fast,
An' chattert an' laft till they varra nar brast,
To think what a beukk wad come oot on't at last—
 Full o' nowt bit oald words ov oald Cummerlan'.

Than, who can e'er read it—can enny yan tell?
Nay, nivver a body bit t' writer his sel!
An' what can be t' use, if it o' be to spell
 Afoor yan can read its oald Cummerlan'?

WORKINGTON,
  July 15th, 1859.

From the 1859 Dictionary by William Dickinson.

455

ABOUT THE AUTHOR

Constance Rémillard has been a romantic for as long as she can remember, devouring books when young and now penning them with a vengeance in middle age. She's lived part of her life abroad, immersed in other languages and cultures, and another part outdoors, immersed in the botanical. She now resides with her family of humans, chickens, cat, and plants in the United States. She hopes you enjoy her stories as much as she enjoys writing them.

facebook.com/Remillard.Romance

instagram.com/remillard.romance

amazon.com/stores/Constance-Remillard/author/B0C-S1TJ5V8

bookbub.com/profile/constance-remillard

goodreads.com/Constance_Remillard

threads.net/@remillard.romance

pinterest.com/remillardauthor

ALSO BY CONSTANCE REMILLARD

The Worthy Peers series:

The Earl's Debt

To Woo a Maid: a novella

The Dubious Mates series:

The Fox in his Henhouse

Coming soon: *The Bastard in her Boudoir*

www.ingramcontent.com/pod-product-compliance
Lightning Source LLC
Chambersburg PA
CBHW071340020726
47502CB00001B/189